Amber Laura

After She Fell

Publisher: LitLiber

COPYRIGHT

AMBER LAURA
AFTER SHE FELL

ISBN: 978-0-9986608-6-8

Copyright © 2019 by Amber Laura

Cover art by LitLiber

Book cover model
Amanda Dornhecker
Used with permission.

This is a work of fiction. Characters, names, places, descriptions, and events are either the product of the author's imagination or are used fictitiously in nature. As such, nothing within it should be read as real or actual, in fact or likeness; any resemblance otherwise, to person, place, or thing is entirely coincidental.

Amber Laura's biography, also known as "Five Fun Facts about the Author":

1.   As a writer, Amber Laura does her best daydreaming as a window-gazing passenger on long car rides.

2.   If there's creamer, she's drinking coffee. When she edits, there's always creamer.

3.   A blogger, she also writes web fiction—(free stories updated chapter-by-chapter, week-by-week). Check it out at www.litliber.com.

4.   Psst! Her debut novel, *Topaz and Lace*, a contemporary romance set in a fictitious Texas town, got its start on that same blog.

5.   While she may physically reside in the beautiful country of Northern Minnesota, in her imagination, Amber Laura lives all over the world. She considers it one of the best perks to being a writer: easy, cheap travel. That and the oddball characters she meets along the way….

To my beloved cat, Deppy. My mascot. I love you eternally. Thanks for all the times you sat on my lap, peering curiously (sometimes jealously) between the keyboard and the computer screen, only to meow anew when you realized— wait, if she needs both hands to type… Well, that left you singularly unpetted, didn't it? And still, you loved me. Ditto, babe.

Forever.

TABLE OF CONTENTS

Chapter One

As the shadows of her fingers grew long against the darkening office walls, Christina bit back a yawn. Rolling her shoulders, she glanced up from the glow of her computer screen. Blinking past the glass paneling that separated her desk from those of the rest of the employees, she canvassed the main floor; the private secretary to the owner of the company, Christina was stationed at the forefront of his outer office, giving her an overarching view of the workplace. The building was all but empty by now—it was going on for six in the evening and business hours had ended at five o'clock. The weekend loomed enticingly.

Beside her desk, she felt, rather than heard, the door to the inner office glide open. She hardly bothered to glance in that direction though, her fingers scattering rhythmically across the keyboard once more. She just had one more document to import and then her Friday night awaited.

Now, she did yawn.

"You still here?" her boss, Mr. Gordman, asked as he came fully into view, a briefcase held loosely in one hand. Giving her a frank look, he reached back to shut the door to his private office. The sound reverberated with reproach.

"Almost finished."

"Good." He eyed her knowingly. "Don't stay too late."

Christina nodded absently. "I wouldn't dare."

"I mean it."

She sighed theatrically, flicking her eyes up to his. Her fingers hovered impatiently above her desk. "I know."

One large hand lifted to wag a finger at her. "Don't make me nag you."

"It's not very often that bosses reprimand employees for working too hard." Christina's drawl was deliberate.

"All right, all right." He chuckled quietly. "I'll see you Sunday?" But it wasn't really a question.

Christina hunched her shoulders. "About that—I'm not sure…" she stalled. The soft incitement, the knowledge of what it would bring with it, was enough to make her drop her gaze.

He sighed. It had a weary sound. "Don't make me sic Mary on you."

Despite it all, Christina felt her lips pull up in an unwilling smile. "Don't even."

Mr. Gordman whistled in a predatory fashion. "I'll take that as a yes, then. Remember, lunch is at one o'clock. Don't be late."

She gave her computer a hard stare, but her stomach was doing that weird thing again. It happened every time he threw out invitations like that. Her fingers hit the wrong keys. "You know, I'm not even religious," she grumbled.

"Not that old argument again."

Still, she didn't look at him. "It's kind of a crucial component—"

"We don't plan to baptize you."

Christina's eyes narrowed.

"It's just lunch."

"On Easter."

Mr. Gordman pursed his lips. "I can only assume you're fighting me on this because you'll be heading home for the holiday this year?"

Christina made a scoffing sound in her throat, but her eyes flinched just slightly at the not-so-subtle nudge.

Determinedly avoiding his gaze, she missed the pointed look tautening his features. "I thought not."

"I don't want to impose." That wasn't quite true....

"I don't have time for this," Mr. Gordman assured her. "I'll tell Mary to give you a call this evening. You can convince her that you're an imposition. My sympathies when she hears you say that."

At the second mention of this threat, Christina chuckled. "Okay, okay," she relented, as she'd known she would all along. She raised her hands, her eyes following the motion. "I give! Lunch at one o'clock."

"A sensible choice."

Christina arched one telling eyebrow. "I didn't know when I applied for this job that it'd come equipped with a built-in family."

Mr. Gordman only laughed, the sound a low rumble in the otherwise quiet building as he began walking toward the exit. "What can I say?" he called over his shoulder, shooting her a mischievous smile. "I'm a generous employer."

Christina didn't respond. Instead, she watched him leave, her fingers unmoving, frozen as she laid them down on the keyboard. Her thoughts spun furiously as she accepted her fate—twirling frenziedly, they centered on that most pivotal of considerations. The question of her wardrobe. Closing her eyes, Christina mentally unpacked every scrap of clothing attire in her closet. Within seconds, her bed was loaded with rubbish and not a scrap of fabric remained on her hangers. Groaning, she shook her head, her eyes opening with the motion. It was stupid to worry about it. It wouldn't matter if she showed up in joggers sporting a tutu and wearing a window curtain for a shirt!

Which was exactly how she wanted it, wasn't it? Still, just the thought of spending the afternoon at his home sent her heart skidding in her chest, her breath turning light and sluggish. Balling her hands into fists, she waited them out—the sensations flooding her person. She'd had plenty of practice at it. Especially when it came to him.

"Hell! Calm down, Christina," she scolded herself forcibly bending her mind back to the work waiting on her computer screen. "Don't be a spaz." Punching in updates for the company's profit and loss statement, her fingers pounded against the keys with unnecessary vigor. "It's one day. One afternoon. It'll be fine."

She frowned as she tallied up the records. She'd missed a comma on the third cell.

"It's not like he's ever bothered to notice you before. Not in that way," she hissed to herself and without quite realizing it, her eyes lifted, traveling down the path her boss had just taken. "And it's not like you care. It would be a terrible idea."

And she knew all about terrible ideas.

Christina spent the rest of Friday and all of Saturday in dogged denial of the approaching holiday; still, even if she wouldn't admit it, she never lost track of the countdown to Easter. And, despite the innumerable reasons she used to explain the purchase, she bought a new outfit—a lovely navy-blue skirt with a flowing, short-sleeved flutter shirt in a soft floral beige. She wore it on Sunday.

And so, all too quickly and yet precisely on time, she found herself stuffed inside her car as all around her churchgoers flooded the streets in heavy mid-afternoon traffic. Carefully navigating the crowds, she was soon winding down the familiar road which led to the Gordmans' house. Those dogged denials now laying shattered at her feet, her hands tightened reflexively on the steering wheel as their home came in sight. Sweeping her car up the long, semicircular driveway before their stately address, she reluctantly put the car in park. According to the radio clock, she was twenty minutes early. For the Gordmans', that was almost late.

For a moment she remained in her car, unmoved. Absently, her eyes glanced over the magnificent opulence of the greystone estate before her. No matter how many times Christina saw it,

the beauty of the home always stole her breath—the large,
double-doored entrance, settled halfway down its immense
expanse, the latticed bay window overlooking the family living
room, and, at the opposite end of the house, the white-framed
floor-to-ceiling windows taking up an entire wall of the ever-
spotless kitchen. Topped with black, scalloped roof tiles, the
elegance of the architecture simply radiated aesthetical charm.

She took a deep breath. Idiotically, she leaned forward, her
gaze stretching to follow the remaining curve of the drive. Then
her eyes flicked up to look out her rearview mirror. Hers was
the only vehicle parked in front of the house. The knowledge
did little to settle the zip of expectation biting at the sides of her
stomach. But it did offer her time.

With it, she flipped down the visor to re-check her reflection
in the small mirror attached there. Patting down her perfectly
coiffed blonde hair, Christina nodded. Her lips were dusted a
pale pink, and her eyes held just the slightest of smoky accents.
Flawless. That's how she looked.

There was little conceit in her silent admittance to this. She
was a beautiful woman. It wasn't something she denied, nor was
it something she put much stock in. After all, her looks hadn't
always worked to her advantage, despite the misconceptions of
tall, leggy blondes and their easy acceptance in society.

"Cool and composed," she assured herself, flipping her visor
back up. "Now act like it." Alighting gracefully from her
vehicle, she reached into the back seat, grabbing for the covered
pie-pan resting on the floorboard. "And for God's sake, smile."

But each step she took toward the impossibly tall double-
doors marking the home's entrance, proved a challenge. Her
stomach clenched, her knees shook, and she was breathing far
too quickly. These sensations were far from unfamiliar. They
assaulted her every time she advanced toward those remarkable
doors. She should have been used to it by now. It had been over
four years since the first time she'd knocked on this door. Four
years of family gatherings, picnics, and holiday festivities. Four

years and she still felt breathless, her hands gripping the pie-pan with a noticeable tremor.

Yet no matter how many times she told herself it was due to a feeling of dread, she knew it for a lie—these feelings were pure, unadulterated anticipation.

On that thought, her gaze skittered back toward the driveway. Her car remained the sole occupant on the cobbled pavement.

Good.

Great.

Her stomach knotted, compressing.

Gaining the front at last, she wasn't even allowed to so much as ring the bell before the door was flung open by Mr. Gordman, standing apparently at the ready, waving her inside. "Ah. Right on time," he announced warmly.

Christina pursed her lips and, refusing to give ground to the knots only intensifying in her stomach, said coolly: "When have I ever been anything but, Mr. Gordman?" Still, her eyes wouldn't quite meet his. Instead, she smiled vaguely somewhere near the vicinity of his head, her eyes catching the sweeping staircase standing against the back wall of the wide entrance hall.

Out of her peripheral vision, she saw him frown. "Knock it off with the 'mister'," he scolded gently. "How many times have I told you? Around here, it's Matthew."

She nodded, her lips pulling into a tight grin. "Right."

"House rules. Only first names are allowed."

Shrugging at the words, Christina shifted the covered dish in her hands. "Mary's in there?" she asked nodding in the general direction of the kitchen.

He made an exaggerated face. "Where else?"

"I'll go see if she needs anything." And with that, Christina turned smartly to the left, her feet taking her through the large, rarely-used dining room and into the kitchen. The sun shone brightly into the large room, bringing a warmth and earthy quality in through the wall of paneled glass. And there, standing at the double wall ovens, her peppered hair slightly askew, an apron tied anyhow around her waist, stood Mary.

"You're here!" the older woman exclaimed, turning at the sound of Christina's entrance. Rounding the island, she rushed toward the younger woman. In one seamless move, Mary snatched the pie out of Christina's hands, setting it down blindly on the countertop before grabbing her for a hug.

Laughing softly, Christina let herself be embraced.

"My God, I think you're even thinner than last time," Mary insisted, breaking her hold. Her hands squeezed just slightly around Christina's slim waist.

"Measuring me again?"

"You're taking all the leftovers home. I can't have you wasting away on me," Mary tut-tutted.

"Hardly."

"Matthew would be lost without you," Mary teased, winking conspiratorially.

Christina smirked. "On that point, I'll agree with you." As they were talking, Mary reached for the pie pan. Opening the lid, her nose crinkled as a lemony fragrance wafted into the room. "Delicious," she murmured as she placed it back down on the island.

Christina only shook her head. "And you're worried about my weight? That's got enough calories to last us for days."

"Good, that's settled then."

"What is?"

"You'll take the biggest piece."

"Oh, Mary." But Christina only laughed.

With nimble steps, Mary shuffled to the stove, her gaze taking in the simmering pots before her. "All I can say is, I hope you brought your appetite. I've gone all out today, and I expect heaping platefuls. Naturally, Matthew bought the wrong style of gravy for my famous…"

But Christina was hardly listening. Her ears pinned for any outside sounds, she tried to calm her nerves. If her stomach bound itself any tighter, she wouldn't be able to eat. And then Mary would probably start force-feeding her.

But there was no crunch of tires reverberating against the paved driveway. There was no accompanying shrill of the doorbell. *You idiot*, she scolded herself on the thought, *of course, the doorbell wouldn't go off. He isn't a damned guest....* Smoothing damp palms down the side of her skirt, she fought for composure. Her mouth felt dry. Her palms sticky. And her breath shallow.

God, would this never end? How many dinners had she shared with this family? Far too many. And still, she acted like it was the first time.

"…but I think I can make do—hey!" The sound of a hand slapping against the counter brought Christina's eyes up. Mary had twisted back around to look at her, one starch eyebrow raised in suspicion. "Are you even listening to me?"

"Huh?"

"You're just as bad as the boys," Mary grumbled, shaking her head. "Here I am, having a great conversation, only to realize that I'm having it with myself."

"Sorry, Mary," Christina confessed with a lopsided grin.

"Well, at least I keep myself entertained," Mary huffed, but the smile she shot at Christina let the younger woman know she wasn't upset.

"Can I help with anything?" Christina asked belatedly, taking in the copious bowls and spoons, crocks and whatnot scattered across every inch of workspace. It might prove a good distraction. Clearly, she needed one.

"Now, as to that…" Mary canvassed the kitchen as well. Her eyes lit up when they landed on a glass dish. "Would you set up the relish tray, my dear?"

Christina laughed. It had a rich sound. "You know, Mar," she insisted, opening the fridge to pull out the pickles and olives, "I *can* actually cook."

"And who said you couldn't?"

"In all these years, this is the only thing you've ever let me touch."

Mary grimaced. "I'm not very good at relinquishing control of my kitchen."

"Right."

"I'm not."

"Admit it, you don't think I can boil water," Christina teased with a mock show of sorrow. "I get it."

Mary banged the side of her wooden spatula against the saucepan in front of her. "That's not true."

Christina wailed mockingly, "Don't bother denying it." She wagged a finger at Mary. "I'll bet you're terrified to try some of my pie."

Shifting in Christina's direction, Mary hefted up her chin. "Am not."

"No?" Christina looked over at the dessert in question. Picking it up, she held it out to Mary. "Are you sure?"

In response, that woman smiled devilishly. "Oh, I'm sure." She turned back toward the stove. "I love Carmen's bakery."

Christina's smile fell. "Carmen's? How did you know?" Her eyes flicked to the pie. She'd even taken the time to transfer it to the metal pan she'd bought at a rummage sale a few years back—just to give it a look of authenticity.

Mary winked. "The nose knows."

"But let's get serious. Were sensory glands even necessary? I've seen this girl try to make a PB&J sandwich before…the bread looked like it'd been ravaged!"

Christina stilled, her hands gripping the pickle jar too tightly as soft male laughter followed the low-timbred statement.

"Jason!" Twisting around sharply, Mary eyed her son, who was standing just inside the kitchen.

Christina felt him step into the room. She just barely managed to suppress a shudder. With her back to him, she was glad for the moment's reprieve.

"Hey, Mom," he said warmly, his arms already opening as Mary shot forward. He coughed as she caught him up close, her own arms squeezing in welcome. "A little tighter," he teased, "I can still breathe."

"Oh." She took a step back, letting her arms fall at her sides. A large smile melted her features. "Sorry."

"Couple of cracked ribs," he assured her dryly. "Don't worry about it."

Christina could hardly hold the thread of conversation. Letting her eyes quickly roam over the white veins intersected throughout the quartz countertop of the kitchen island, she tried to focus her breathing, to clear her thoughts.

She could feel a muscle in her jaw spasm.

Jason.

He was there.

Well, of course, he was. She knew he would be. It was why...

Her face felt hot. Uncomfortably hot. Her fingers itched to press against her cheeks, to cool them. Oh, God—was she turning red? Taking a half-step backward, Christina was overcome with the need to check her reflection in the mirror.

Mary swatted at Jason's wrist. "And don't go teasing Christina."

At the mention of her name, Christina knew his eyes were on her. Turning slowly—because what else could she do?—Christina leveled him an even glance.

"Hi, Chrissy," Jason offered easily. His right arm he kept slung over his mother's shoulder. "Kill any slices of bread lately?"

"Jason," she acknowledged. Her voice fell flat. Tucking an imaginary strand of hair back in place, she frowned. "And it's Christina," she reminded him darkly.

He smiled, showing even white teeth. "Right. Sorry." He didn't look in the least repentant.

"And the jelly was cold. It wasn't my fault it pulled the bread apart."

"Of course not," he soothed.

"Oh, shut up," she threw at him.

"Bickering all ready?" Matthew Gordman, coming into the kitchen, sent his wife a knowing look. "Is that a record?"

Mary grinned wickedly. "It's got to be."

"I'm not bickering," Christina muttered. "He is."

"Your face is getting a bit red there, Chrissy."

"It's Christina," she told him forcibly. "And if it's red"—dammit, why did it have to be red?—"it's only because you're so infuriating."

"Easy, Christina," he enunciated carefully. "Or I might think you're being serious."

"That'll be the day." Pushing herself off the island, Christina turned pointedly toward Mary. "If you'll excuse me?" Nodding in the general direction of the swing door that separated the kitchen from the rest of the house, Christina didn't wait for a response, she simply sailed through it.

Her heels clicked softly against the polished floor as she entered the dining room; crossing that distance in no time, her eyes concentrated forward, she kept moving, her feet headed straight for the small powder room tucked underneath the sweeping staircase in the foyer. She needed a moment. Just a moment.

"Pull yourself together, you raving idiot," she grumbled to herself once she was safely locked inside the narrow bathroom. She took a peek at her face. Damn him. It *was* red. Patting her hands against the flushed skin, she frowned at her complexion. "Just be cool," she hissed. "Act nonchalant."

That, unfortunately, was easier said than done.

Because she didn't like Jason Gordman.

No, stupid fool that she was, Christina was in love with him.

Chapter Two

Staring at her reflection in the oval mirror hanging above the sink, Christina twisted on the faucet. Patting her cheeks with the cold water, she tried to count her breathing. Instead, her mind spun, splicing through that most fateful of memories...

She'd been new at work. It had happened on a Thursday evening—she remembered that well. Despite her best intentions, she'd never lost that day. Thursday evening, a little over four years ago. It had been a frantic week, which Christina had spent obtaining and organizing presentation packets and travel arrangements for an important business meeting Mr. Gordman had scheduled for the following morning. Christina had been on the verge of shutting down her computer and heading home when she'd seen them...

See, it hadn't been just any business meeting. It had been *the* meeting. The one that, if successful, would change the entire trajectory of his business.

Held halfway across the country, Mr. Gordman's flight had been scheduled to take-off early Friday. But as Christina stood up to grab her coat off the back of her chair, she saw them. All those hours spent designing, proofing, formatting. Wasted.

Because sitting on the edge of her desk were the presentation packets. In his rush to get home and get packed and ready to go, he'd forgotten them.

Groaning at the sight, Christina remembered holding them out to him as he'd prepared to leave that evening. He'd placed them on her desk as he'd shucked into his suit coat, simultaneously reminding her she didn't need to come into the office the next day.

"You've more than made up the time," he'd assured her nicely. "And I really appreciate all the hard work you've put into this thing."

She'd mumbled some sort of thank you, her face flushing darkly. Compliments had become hard to hear.

He'd patted his pockets, making sure his car keys were available. Then he'd sent her a wink. "Wish me luck," he'd said, bending down to grab the briefcase he'd set by his feet. "We really need this client."

Now, staring wearily at the packets, she moved on instinct. Turning to the employee list, she thumbed through the contacts until she located Mr. Gordman's personal cell phone. Dialing quickly, she waited for three rings.

"Matthew."

"Mat—Mr. Gordman," she stammered. "It's Christina. Christina DeLuca, from the office? The packets, sir. You left them here."

"I did?" She heard the sound of frantic scrambling, no doubt as he looked through his briefcase. "Dammit."

That one word sent her eyebrows up to her hairline. She'd worked at the office for all of six weeks at that point, but never once had she heard him offer up so much as the mildest of cuss words.

Then, almost before she knew what she was saying, Christina suggested: "I'm just about to leave. Would you like…I mean, I can bring them to you."

There was a long silence and then a heavy sigh. "No, Christina. I can't ask you to do that."

"You didn't ask."

"Still." But already his resolve started to weaken. She heard it in his voice. Turning around would have set him back almost an hour. It was time he didn't have.

"Well then, I insist," she told him. Besides, it wasn't like she had a lot going on that evening. Or any evening, for that matter. And she really needed the job. "Look, it's no trouble and it hardly makes sense for you to come back here when I have to leave anyway…"

He sighed and then, finally, relented. "I, yes, okay. Thank you, Christina. That would be—are you sure you wouldn't mind? I don't want to keep you…"

"Not hardly." Grabbing a sheet of paper, she asked for his address, jotting it down quickly.

Less than half an hour later, she pulled up at his house. Parking her car in the curved sweep of the driveway, her eyes grew wide as she spied the impressive stone structure, replete with white trimming and a massively framed doorway.

Getting out of the vehicle, the folders clutched nervously in her arms, Christina marched up to the front of the house and rang the doorbell without delay. Pulling her shoulders back, she shook her hair gently behind her. Her eyebrows furrowed as she waited, her heart skidding suddenly in her chest. Now that she was there, she only hoped she hadn't made a mistake. She didn't want to give out the wrong impression.

She wasn't given a chance to change her mind before one of the two doors before her swung open.

But it hadn't been Mr. Gordman standing on the other side of the threshold. Nor had it been Mary—though, at that time, she hadn't actually met Matthew's wife. Instead, it had been a man, a man she'd never seen before, though he looked faintly familiar—tall and lean, with blond-streaked brown hair and large hazel eyes, the latter heavily fringed with long lashes. Early thirties she surmised in that instant analysis, fit and with a masculine grace. Instinctively, she frowned.

In response, he smiled at her. There had been something so magnetizing about him. Something that made her want to drop the papers in her hands and step into him.

Her frown deepened.

"Hello?" The greeting held just as much welcome as blatant amusement.

Christina's whole face seemed to blink. Strangling the folders tighter to her person, she braced herself against that ridiculous sensation. Defensively, she brought her chin up a notch. "Excuse me," she offered politely, "I'm looking for a Mr. Gordman."

His grin lengthened. It was slightly crooked. She resented him that. "You found him."

She narrowed her eyes. "I'm afraid not."

He laughed then, a real, genuine chuckle, which for some reason only further put Christina on edge. She wasn't used to being on the wrong side of confident. Through stiff features, she watched while he turned his head slightly, raising his voice to say: "Dad? Dad, there's someone here to see you."

Christina caught her breath. He was Mr. Gordman's son? His *son*? Granted, she'd heard Mr. Gordman make mention of his only child before, she just hadn't pictured him to be so, so…

Shifting back to Christina, one edge of his mouth quirked up just slightly. "And she's not messing around, either."

Now she knew he was laughing at her expense. Feeling her lips pucker in annoyance, Christina was spared making a regrettable remark by the sound of approaching footsteps. Peering pointedly over the man's shoulder, she saw Mr. Gordman come into view with something akin to relief.

"Ah, Christina!" Matthew exclaimed, his arms raising in welcome as he rushed forward. "Please, come in, come in."

At the urging, Christina felt her feet step carefully over the threshold, watched as both men shuffled to one side, granting her further entrance. Absently, she saw a tanned hand reach out to grab the door, the long-tapered fingers pushing it firmly shut behind her, but she was working hard not to look directly at him.

Instead, she held the folders up for Mr. Gordman's inspection, her gaze determinedly steady on his countenance. "Got 'em."

"You're my savior."

A smile broke out across her mouth, her lightly painted lips pulling up into a gracious curve. Ignoring a pair of hazel eyes, which watched this exchange with that damnable amusement, she muttered, "It was nothing."

"It was everything," Mr. Gordman insisted, taking the papers from her. "And you know it."

"Who's at the door, Matthew?" But the caller to this question didn't wait for a response. Within seconds, Christina found herself looking into a pair of warm brown eyes. She knew, from the picture that sat on the edge of Mr. Gordman's desk, who the woman was. His beloved wife.

"Oh. Hello," Christina rushed to say, smiling nervously. She held out a small, perfectly manicured hand. "I'm Christina. I don't believe we've met…."

"No, but I've heard a lot about you," that lady offered kindly, taking Christina's hand. "I'm Mary. And you must be the efficient Ms. DeLuca." She smiled, her eyes crinkling at the corners. "Matthew absolutely raves about you, and I quote, 'the best hire he's ever made.'"

Christina felt her blush, which had finally started to recede, rise again. Out of the corner of her eye, she caught the youngest Gordman watching her again. His lips were pulled up sardonically and there was a look in his eyes—

"What brings you…?" Mary's words trailed off, her shrewd eyes zipping from Christina over to her husband, her expression mirroring the thoughts tunneling through her head. When her swift glance caught sight of the newfound folders clutched in his grip, a new look came over her face. "Matthew?" She nodded toward them accusingly. "What are those?"

There was a certain quality to her question. It was not to be dismissed.

He sighed. "Ah, paperwork for tomorrow's meeting?" he asked her, as though he were testing out this excuse.

Mary made a sound in her throat. Her foot tapped rhythmically against the flooring. "Let me guess, you forgot them at work?" Her head swiveled from the folders to Christina and back again.

Mr. Gordman looked sheepish.

"And then you made her bring them out to you?"

Mr. Gordman squirmed. He actually squirmed. Christina had to bite her lip to keep from smiling "Not exactly. Christina offered—"

Ever the faithful employee, Christina nodded quickly. "That's true. I suggested it."

"Matthew!" Mary swatted at his arm. "Don't you have any consideration, at all? Do you even know what time it is?"

"Ah…" His eyes flickered toward the large hall clock hanging overhead.

"I suppose your supper is ruined now, thanks to my thoughtless husband?" Mary asked, turning to look at Christina.

"Oh, no. No, no," Christina assured her. "I hadn't had anything planned anyway, so it didn't matter…" Which, in retrospect, had been exactly what Mary had been hoping she'd say.

"Well then, that settles it," Mary informed her. "You'll stay and have dinner with us."

Christina blanched. One foot took a step backward almost before she knew it. Her gaze went shyly toward Mr. Gordman's less-than-surprised countenance. "Thank you. But, ah, no. That-that's not necessary."

Mr. Gordman only shrugged, as though it were a lost cause to fight.

"It most certainly is," Mary told her staunchly. "In fact, it's the very least we can do." She shot her husband a dark look. "I mean, *really,* Matthew? Asking her to come all this way?"

"She insisted!"

"I really did."

"Then you'll appreciate that I insist now. You'll stay for dinner. I won't take no for an answer. We have more than enough food."

"You'll be helping us out, I assure you." This tidbit of teasing had come from the only person who'd yet to be introduced. Groaning at the soft elbowing Mary sent him, the man smirked, rubbing his side. "Mother has a tendency to overfeed."

"Besides," Mary argued, her voice riding roughshod over Christina's instincts. "I would feel terribly guilty if you missed a proper meal because of my louse of a husband."

"Easy, Mar."

"You hush."

"Yes, ma'am."

Christina could have almost been amused at this small, rather intimidating woman. Except she was too unnerved to do anything but stand there.

"I don't want to impose."

"Impose?" Mary smiled. Over the years, Christina would learn never to trust that particular smile. "What do you call asking an employee to run business errands after work? If anyone here has been imposed upon, it's you, my dear."

"No. No-not at all." Christina had shaken her head so hard that her teeth clenched together. She could not afford to alienate her boss. She needed this job. She needed it for more than the money.

"Look, you can fight her on this all night," Matthew interrupted finally—and if Christina had hoped to find an ally in him, she was quickly found mistaken. He sent his wife a loving, if somewhat long-suffering, glance before bringing his eyes back to Christina. "But in the end, you'll eat dinner here. The question is, do you want it now while it's still hot, or in an hour when it's cooled considerably?"

"Jason, take her coat."

With a slight lift of one eyebrow, the youngest Gordman looked at Christina, waiting. And so, with three pairs of eyes on her, she did exactly as expected. With a glance to beat defeat, she brought her nerveless fingers up to her coat, popping the large buttons free, one by one.

"Really, though," she continued as the jacket fell open. "It's not necessary—" but then she felt Jason's hands skim across the tops of her shoulders. She hadn't seen him move behind her, only felt that strange sensation spread across her chest again as his fingers caught hold of the thick material of her coat, stealing her breath.

But then, it wasn't such a strange sensation, was it? She'd felt it before—with Bill. She knew the pitfalls of this type of awareness, the pain and betrayal inherent in this kind of responsiveness. Gritting her teeth, she held herself stiff as the silky inner-lining of her coat fell from her arms. She hardly dared to move.

And then, at last, and really far too soon, Jason's hands were gone.

Afraid they'd noticed her sudden stillness, Christina threw out a hasty smile. "Well," she admitted shyly, anything to cover her unease, "I guess I *am* hungry."

"Good girl," Mary encouraged.

With that one small acquiescence, Christina's relationship with the Gordmans had changed forever. She'd felt the warmth of Mary's gentle mothering, the ease of Matthew's welcome, and—as for Jason, the spark of enduring warfare.

They'd just sat down at the table when Jason had looked across the expanse separating them and remarked: "So, Chrissy—"

"It's Christina."

He tilted his head. "Are you sure? Chrissy seems to suit you."

Her smile tightened. "It's Christina."

He shrugged. "If you insist." Still, the gesture was pointed—clearly meant to infer that he found this fussy, uptight. In the years following, his continued insistence to call her by that name only proved to solidify this opinion.

Her eyes turned to slits. "Oh, I do."

"Christina," Mary said, cutting in ruthlessly. "Matthew says you're not from around here originally?"

"No. I was raised in Illinois."

Jason whistled. "Long way from home."

"Depends on how you look at it."

Firmly taking back the reins of conversation, Mary smiled politely. "So," she asked casually, "what brought you to Minnesota?"

Christina took a drink from her glass of water. "I saw a picture of the city on the back of a postcard—"

Jason snorted. "Really?"

Christina sent him a lowering glance. "No, not really."

"I'm sorry, Christina," Mary said, coming between them again. "That was none of my business."

"No, no," Christina insisted, her hands splaying out wide as her gaze switched from Jason to his clearly upset mother. "It was a bad joke on my part. I apologize." Still, no one asked her a second time. And she never elaborated beyond saying: "I just…sort of ended up here."

"Very mysterious, Ms. DeLuca." Jason's eyes twinkled mockingly across the table, the only family member unwilling to let the comment pass. She'd later learn to always expect that from him.

"Ignore him," Mr. Gordman said then, sending his son a speaking glance.

Christina smiled sarcastically. "Only since I got here." She'd been trying to, at least.

Jason grinned all the harder, as though reading her thoughts. "Not with much actual success, I see."

She'd felt those words all the way to the base of her spine. They'd made her stomach muscles contract, the nerves tingle. He had been right, of course, but she'd have been damned if she'd ever let on.

Instead, her eyes had slipped helplessly toward his gaze. She'd had no recourse left but to glare. She'd only ever hoped it was enough.

Chapter Three

The soft knock on the other side of the bathroom door snapped Christina out of her reverie. Spinning around, her eyes flickered toward the locked door, her mind flashing back to the present as her fingers gripped the edge of the vanity for support.

"Christina?" At the sound of Mary's soft voice, Christina stiffened. "Honey, is everything all right?"

With a start, Christina realized she'd been in the bathroom for a while—for too long. Probably over ten minutes. Flushing hotly, she pushed herself off the sink. Slapping a quick smile on her face, she reached forward, her fingers curling around the brass doorknob.

Swinging the door open, her eyes met the quiet worry, mixed with equal parts curiosity, mingling in the older woman's gaze. "Hey—"

Mary's forehead creased. "Is everything okay?" she asked again, her voice gentle as she took in Christina's less than usually composed self. Her hair hung a little flatly in her chignon, her makeup was smudged, and her cheeks, thanks to the blush still darkening her countenance, shone brightly under the bathroom lights. Mary wasn't sure she'd ever seen Christina look anything but utterly poised. It was startling. It was more than a little concerning. Especially after the way she'd run out of the kitchen.

"Yeah. Sorry about that," Christina mumbled, fanning a hand in front of her face emphatically. "I just, ah, got really hot in there for a minute. I needed to cool down."

"Oh," Mary said weakly, trying to disguise her disbelief. "Yes, well, it does get so awfully warm in that kitchen when I'm cooking that much food," she offered anyway, kind soul that she was. The truth of the matter, Mary and Matthew's kitchen was far too large to be bogged down by the heat of a few pots on the stove and a bird in the oven.

Christina loved her for that generosity of spirit. "Yeah."

"You're feeling better now, though?" Mary asked anxiously.

"Much." *Not unless Jason had pulled a disappearing act...* "Just, give me a second to fix my face, huh?" Patting her hands futilely against her hips, her fingers connecting with the thin material of her skirt, she frowned. Her eyes zeroed in on the pedestal sink, the lack of cosmetics housed on the sparse space, the lone bar of soap at her disposal.

Mary, watching the telling expressions play out on Christina's face, smiled. "Not much for reinforcements in here. I'll go grab your purse, okay?"

Christina glanced wearily at her unkempt reflection in the mirror. "Please. Thank you."

Reaching forward, Mary squeezed her shoulder. "Of course." By the time she returned, Christina had managed to wipe away the traces of smeared mascara from underneath her eyes and rub smooth the streaks in her foundation; her cheeks, mercifully, had dampened down to a becoming shade of pink.

Wordlessly, Mary handed over the small clutch handbag. Instead of leaving though, she edged herself fully into the bathroom, her short body coming to lean against the doorjamb. "How's the office been?"

"Oh, the usual," Christina replied absently as she reapplied her lipstick. Snapping the lid back on, she bent her attention to her hair, her fingers expert as they rearranged the loosened strands.

"That's what Matthew always says, too," Mary grumbled. "Let me guess, he's ordered you to say those words to me."

Glancing over her shoulder, Christina smiled. "Now Mary, you wouldn't be asking me to tattle on the boss, would you?"

"God forbid," Mary exclaimed, throwing up her hands as they exited the bathroom. She shot Christina a sidelong glance as they crossed the foyer, the younger woman tossing her purse on top of the small table near the entrance as they passed. "It wouldn't be worth the effort, anyway. You'd never turn."

Christina only chuckled as they reached the dining room. Their steps were quick as they walked the length of the hardwood floor to the doorway at its other end.

"Ah, there they are!" Matthew smiled as Christina and Mary reemerged into the kitchen. He and Jason (who had clearly not disappeared, after all) were already seated at the family table— the one regularly used for meals—which was situated before the wall of paneled glass overlooking the front lawn. "We were worried you got lost there for a minute."

Jason made a choking sound that he valiantly attempted to turn into a cough.

Christina's face reddened.

"Matthew, sometimes I swear you are completely hopeless!" Mary cried, bringing her hands up in exasperation. With sure footsteps, she strode to her chair. Pulling it out, she sat down.

Christina, on the other hand, faltered, her eyes narrowing— Matthew was sitting in the spot she usually occupied. Before she could question his sudden change of place, her boss glanced up at her with a sanguine smile.

"Separating the enemy camps," he said meaningfully, nodding across the table at his son. "I figure it'll be better for my digestion."

Christina clamped her jaw tight, battling a second wave of humiliation in as many seconds, her fingers gripping the back of her newly-appointed seat. "Don't complain to me," she said as she plunked herself down.

Matthew raised an innocent eyebrow. "I don't see anyone else who argues with him," he said pointing a fork at his son.

"I don't argue. I defend myself," she informed the table haughtily, crisply laying a napkin on her lap. "And besides," she mumbled under her breath, "who invited who here?"

Matthew only laughed. In that way, he was so like his son. It was impossible to properly fight with someone when they just kept on joking about it.

Jason leered at her good-naturedly. "What do you say, *Christina*? Think the change in seating arrangements will make any difference?"

She smiled tightly. "It's doing wonders for my appetite already."

"All right, all right," Mary said forcefully, holding up a hand to stem whatever retort would surely follow. "New topic."

Matthew looked from his son to his receptionist. His eyebrows arched. "Yeah. Good idea."

Mary turned to ask Jason something then. Christina wasn't sure what though; she'd stopped listening, her eyes carefully lowered. As the family's voices floated gently over her head, she considered that she'd lied earlier. She most certainly *did* argue with Jason. Deliberately.

She provoked him. Prodded. Picked and picked...

It was the safest recourse, after all. Because, sometimes, and there had been instances, brief but true, when she and Jason hadn't found themselves sparring against one another. Times when they'd been almost friendly. Which had been far, far worse. Friends had a way of getting too comfortable with one another, too familiar. They were allowed to look at one another and smile, to grin at each other's jokes, perhaps even touch one another. It was too easy for friends to slip...

Like the time her car had broken down on the side of the interstate. Unusually frightened and stressed by the breakneck pace of the other cars racing past her, she'd nonetheless managed to maneuver her car onto the shoulder. Then she'd called Matthew. In retrospect, it would have made more sense to call for a tow truck, but the thought hadn't even occurred to her rattled wits. Matthew would take care of her. Only, when he'd answered the phone it was to casually inform Christina that no, he wasn't at home. In fact, he and Mary were on their way to the theater, and what was it she needed?

Christina had balked at the words. She hadn't been about to ruin their evening…

With deliberation, not a hint of dread entered her voice when she replied airily: "Oh, it's nothing." Her fingers clenched around the edges of her phone, but her voice betrayed no signs of stress.

Despite her efforts, Matthew wasn't deceived. "Out with it," he coaxed her gently.

"Really—"

"Christina."

She sighed, her head hanging low. "Well, actually, I'm sort of stuck."

"Stuck?"

"My car broke down—"

Before she knew what was happening, Mary, sitting beside Matthew and shamelessly eavesdropping, interrupted Christina's explanation of what had happened and where. "Christina? Don't worry. Jason is coming."

"What?" The breathlessness of her surprise whispered out before she could catch herself.

"I just called him."

Christina's mouth pulled taut, a frown etching lines between her eyebrows. "I really wish you hadn't done that."

"Nonsense," Mary chided her voice ringing despite her distance from the mouthpiece. "He was nearby. He should be there any minute."

"I see."

"We'll wait on the phone with you until he shows up," Mary insisted. It wasn't a long wait. Within minutes, Christina's turbulent eyes watched as his black SUV drove up behind her on the side of the road.

"He's here," she said dully, her voice disrupting Mary's excited chatter about the musical she and Matthew were on their way to see.

"He is? Oh, good," Mary said, easily diverted. "That was fast."

Christina sighed silently, her fingers curling convulsively as she watched one jean-clad leg come into view, followed shortly by the other as he exited his vehicle.

"All right," Matthew said, cutting in. "We'll leave you both to it then."

Surprisingly, Jason was good with cars. Despite his designer loafers and leather jacket, he'd quickly acquired the necessary equipment to jack her car up and, while simultaneously asking her to open her trunk for the spare, started on the business of changing out the tire.

"Stupid thing," Christina cussed inanely a few minutes later, standing beside him as he quickly finished the task, tightening the last bolt.

Jason grunted. "You ran over a nail."

"Ah," she sneered unjustly, her hands coming to rest against her hips. "Only to be expected in the faulty driving of the female sex, I suppose?"

Squinting up at her, his hair lifting slightly in the breeze, Jason frowned. "I wasn't insulting you, Chrissy."

"I'm so sure."

Standing up, he shook his head. "Believe it or not, I'm well aware that nails don't discriminate."

Against her will, she laughed, her mouth breaking into a smile of mingled truce.

"Wow—so that's what it sounds like."

She raised a quizzical eyebrow, but the heat was gone from her gaze. "Hardy har."

Jason grinned. "Give me a hand with these?" he asked, nodding towards the jack and lug wrench laying at his feet.

"Sure." Reaching down to grab them while he picked up the punctured tire, Christina followed Jason to the back of her car.

"Hey," she said while he hefted the tire inside her trunk. She shifted on her feet. "Thanks. For helping me."

Jason didn't bother to lift his head, his hands urging the tire to lay flat. "Of course."

"I-I didn't know that Mary was going to ask you. If I'd known—"

"Then I wouldn't be here. I know." Ducking clear of the trunk, Jason smiled at Christina. There was nothing of accusation in the look, but the words were pointed.

"I didn't mean it that way."

He grinned. "Uh huh."

"I'm just saying, I'm sure you had better plans for your Friday evening," she insisted, unable to help herself. "I hate that I spoiled your night."

Jason didn't immediately respond. Instead, taking the tools still held in Christina's grip, he walked to the back of his truck and tossed them easily into a toolbox stationed there. "Who said you had?"

Christina arched an expressive eyebrow. "This was what you'd penciled in—help someone on the side of the road?"

Jason winked at her. "It's the perk of living in the cities. There's always someone."

"God."

Rounding his vehicle, Jason shook his head. "Chrissy, couldn't you just leave it at thanks and shut up?"

Pursing her lips, Christina couldn't quite fight the smile that broke across her face. With a slight bow of her head, she obliged him. "Thank you, Jason."

"It was my pleasure."

"I'm sure—"

"Uh-uh," Jason uttered, wagging a finger at her. "No ad-libbing."

"My apologies."

"And hey, for what it's worth," Jason said, pulling his keys out of his pocket. "I'm glad you weren't able to dissuade Mom's intentions."

There was something different, something soft, in his tone of voice suddenly. The usual teasing glint was missing from Jason's eyes. Staring across the small space separating them, Christina couldn't quite break away from that hazel gaze, that quiet admission. His cheeks were ruddy from the wind and his shirt, underneath the leather jacket, was being flattened against his chest.

"I—uh," Christina's mouth formed the treacherous words, "I'm glad too."

Jason's lips slowly pulled upward. In response, Christina's dipped down slightly. She shouldn't have said that. It was a dangerous thing to admit. It was an inviting thing to voice. And yet, she never found the fight to truly regret the statement.

"Christina."

At the sound of her name, at the intensity and hunger behind it, she started, her eyes widening as she waited....

But whatever he'd been about to say next was quickly checked out by the sudden rumble of a semi-truck barreling past. Blinking at the upsurge of dust as the eighteen-wheeler flew by, Christina dropped her gaze. The disturbance was enough. Regaining her bearings, remembering her promise, she took a step backward. Just in time.

Tucking her hair behind her ear, she smiled stiffly. "Well, I shouldn't keep you." To punctuate the statement, she made a production of looking down at her watch. "It's still early. You never know, you might just have time to save another distressed driver."

Jason tipped his head. "Have a good night, Chrissy."

"Yeah. You too," she lobbed over her shoulder, already turning back to her car.

"And get a new tire!"

In reaction to that piece of cheekiness, she'd done little more than lift her hand in salute. Cowardice taking control, she'd wrenched open her car door, landing with a plop in the driver's seat. Her stomach had coiled as she'd sat there, catching her breath.

But if something had slipped at the side of the road that day, the sparring giving way to whatever it masked, it was nothing to what had almost, *almost* happened at her work Christmas party only last December. Matthew had, as usual, thrown a spectacular event for his employees. Held at his home, he'd hired a string quartet, arranged for white-gloved waiters, and offered up an open bar. The latter had been Christina's downfall.

After spending the first part of the evening quietly but firmly rejecting the advances of colleagues who always seemed to figure that employee parties were gimmes for drunken mistakes, a more-or-less "what happens at the holiday party, stays at the holiday party" kind of mentality that she'd always found repulsive (especially considering how many of her female colleagues fell for it only to be found bawling their eyes out that next Monday morning in the women's restroom, puking up their regrets), Christina had planted herself staunchly beside the makeshift bar and ordered one too many whiskys—after all, she figured that, if she had to sit through this mockery of decorum, she was going to need a salve…

An hour later, she realized her mistake. Ducking her head to keep others from seeing the vulnerability in her too-bright cheeks, she kept her back carefully braced against the bar counter, her fingers now gripped tightly around a glass of water. But it wasn't until Jason strolled up to her that she realized she had reason to fully panic.

Seeing him, she blinked as her stomach thrummed with excitement and then dread. What was he even doing there? She squinted. His outline was just the slightest bit blurry.

"Not dancing?" Jason asked casually, sidling up beside her to order himself a beer. A few couples were moving softly to the strains of music spilling onto what had become the dance floor. She tilted her head. Was that Bart Cooper whose arms were wrapped so tightly around the junior intern, Jessica?

She made a face. Married with young children, Bart's hand was far too low on Jessica's back…

Christina would have made a disparaging remark but her tongue felt too thick in her mouth. Instead, she shook her head, her eyebrows arching with pointed meaning.

"Yeah. Okay, I hear you," Jason conceded, following her gaze. He smirked. "What's the front receptionist's name, again?"

Christina stared up at him groggily. Then she answered slowly, "Grace."

He nodded. "I swear the woman doesn't know the meaning of the word harassment."

"But you, you don't work for the company." Some of Christina's words ran together, but she pretended not to hear it.

Jason grinned. "Good on you for noticing that." He tipped the glass of beer to his mouth.

"So…" She cleared her throat. "Why are you here then?" Not much of a filter but hey, at least the sentence was clearly enunciated.

He cocked an eyebrow. "With a welcome like that, it's probably a good thing you're not the first line of defense for clients at the office."

She snorted. "I'm meant to play bulldog for your father."

He grinned. "I see." He was absolutely devastating when he looked at her like that. Christina didn't have the energy or the wits about her to fight the thought. She smiled back at him sloppily.

He looked nonplussed.

"What?"

He shook his head, smiling gently. "Nothing."

She tilted her head. Then she giggled.

His eyes widened just slightly in reaction.

At his look, Christina stilled. She'd regret this moment in the morning; she read that in his facial expression. Inking through her dulled mind, sanity reared, reminded her that she needed—

"Excuse me," she mumbled. With a slightly shaking hand, Christina put her glass down on the countertop before pushing blindly forward. She'd rarely been so conscious of her movements. Which was probably why she shifted too quickly, making it hardly unpredictable when Christina stumbled in misstep, tripping slightly.

Jason's hand grabbed for her elbow instinctively, steadying her. "Whoa. Hey there."

Her mortification was complete. She knew it with a sudden flash of clarity. "Jason. Please." Her eyes were wounded in her downcast face. "I-I, please don't."

"Don't what?" His voice held genuine confusion. "Are you okay?"

Christina blinked rapidly. "I, no..." She shook her head. "No, I have to go."

"Go where?"

She lifted pleading eyes. "I think it's altogether possible I've had too much to drink." Her lips felt foreign as they tried to twist out the words.

Jason's mouth parted slightly.

She held up a hand. "And before you start, please spare me your lectures."

"No lecture here."

"I have to go," she reiterated, making to move away. Jason's hand tightened around her arm.

"Wait. Just wait," he said. "Or do you want to make a spectacle of yourself?"

"No, I—"

"You're weaving."

She smashed her lips together. "I know," she confessed hatefully. "I have to go."

"Okay, it's okay." There was a hint of amusement in the words. "Just hold on—"

"I can't let them see me like this," she whispered harshly.

"Who?" Jason laughed, his eyes taking in the people milling around. "I doubt anyone would notice. Most everyone here is drunk."

She closed her eyes. "Oh, God."

"Chrissy, it's no big deal."

"Maybe not to you."

"Can't let them see you lose that precious control?"

"Don't tease."

"Sorry." And, for once, he sounded it. His hand was still on hers. "But really, what are you so afraid of?"

Him. Falling apart. Losing that hard-won composure.

"Please, your father. I couldn't stand to embarrass him." Even in her muddled brain that sounded plausible. Certainly, it wasn't untrue. It just wasn't exactly honest, either.

Jason nodded. "Okay. Let me help you."

She lifted her eyes. "How?"

"Follow my lead" was all he said. With that, he brought his hand down to the small of her back and with a terse nod, led her into the thick of the crowd. The doors leading into the foyer, leading to her escape, were on the other end of the room. When they reached the dance floor, set in the middle of the open space, he turned her firmly into his arms.

"Don't fight me," he said in her ear when Christina was about to do just that. His right hand, pressing against her back, guided her fully into his embrace. "Dance with me?"

"What?"

He looked down at her misty expression. "Trust me."

"I guess I'll have to." Bringing her arms up and around his neck, feeling the weight of his left hand joining his right one low on her back, Christina allowed herself to be swung slowly onto the dance floor.

He laughed softly in her ear. "That's as close to an endorsement as I wager I'll get."

She felt his breath whisper across her cheek and the muscles of her stomach clenched, the nerves whirling, trembling across the band of her waist. Closing her eyes, Christina let her body sway, her legs quivering when they brushed up against the length of his thighs, her skin tingling where his hands curved around her waist.

He had beautiful hands. Musician's hands, though she'd never seen him so much as pick up an instrument.

Jason glided her expertly across the floor, his steps masking her fumbling footfalls. It wasn't until the song ended that Christina realized what he'd done. Seamlessly twirling her across the room, as the last strain of the music died, Jason deposited Christina right to where her exit awaited.

Leading her gently off the dance floor, his right hand falling once more to the small of her back, his arm unobtrusive as it guided her movements, Jason only stopped walking once they reached the foyer, clear of any unwanted attention.

"Thank you," Christina said demurely, her eyes lifting no higher than his chin. "But I think I'll be fine now." She nodded toward the sound of music spilling out of the living room. "Please, go back inside. I'll just call myself a cab."

"And blow my perfectly executed cover?"

"Pfft."

Jason only shook his head. "I don't think so. I'll take you home."

Panic invaded her person. Half an hour stuck alone in a car with him, her senses dulled by alcohol? Holy terror wasn't the phrase. "You don't need to do that."

But he wasn't listening. "It's no big deal."

"But the party?" Christina waved vaguely behind her. "By the time you get back, everyone will be gone."

He shrugged. "As you said, it's not like I'm an employee anyway."

"But—"

"Chrissy," Jason told her, taking her arm and steering her toward the massive double-doors at the estate's entrance, "it's me or my dad, which would you prefer?"

"Why does it have to be either?"

"Because I want to make sure you get home safely."

When Christina opened her mouth to argue, Jason effectively stopped the rush of words by placing one finger over her lips. Stunned by the action, she only managed to stare up at him, her eyes unusually large and imploring in her oval face. "It's not a negotiation," he assured her. "And the more you fight me on this, the bigger the crowd."

So, he'd brought her home. And that was when things had really taken a turn. That was when her carefully constructed façade had shifted, when she'd forgotten her lines, gone off-script, when things had almost, *almost*—

No. Forcibly, Christina blocked the memory of what happened next.

Perhaps in respect to her or in mutual agreement as to the cruelty in doing anything other, the next time they'd met, Jason had joined her in pretending that nothing had transpired after that fateful car ride. He'd gone back to teasing her and she'd continued to bristle at him. It was safer that way.

One thing she'd always wondered though, which had niggled unanswered at the back of her mind: why he'd been at that party in the first place? Still, for all the resulting turmoil, she lived on the short memory of being in his arms, however briefly, on that dance floor.

And she set great sights on never reliving anything like it with him again.

"...what do you say, Christina?"

Blinking at the question, she once again found herself hurled back into the present moment at the sound of Mary's voice. Lifting her face at the question, Christina saw three pairs of eyes staring back at her. She blinked. "I'm sorry. What was that?"

Mary laughed. "Well, you say I don't have any faith in your baking abilities. Here's your chance to prove me wrong. Are you in?"

Christina nodded quickly, desperate not to be found out unawares. Her fork played absently with the turkey on her plate. "Oh. Yeah. Sure, okay."

Jason grinned at her knowingly.

"What?" she asked him against her better judgment, setting her fork down sharply. She hated that grin.

"You have no idea what you've just agreed to, do you?"

Christina sputtered. "I'm sure I don't—"

"Don't tell me we caught you daydreaming again?" Mary asked.

"Again?"

Mary nodded, buttering her bun. "She was doing it earlier too. When she first got here."

Jason leaned back in his chair. "Wonder what about?"

Christina's face froze. Her hands fell to her lap, her fingers clenching against her napkin at his patently amused stare and Mary's curious gaze. Honestly though, she couldn't blame them their countenances. Clearly, her defenses were down. She was normally much better at keeping these dangerous thoughts checked, hidden. She was just tired, that's all. That's why his presence was frazzling her more than usual. The walls of her staid existence had started to close in on her just lately, the loneliness biting at her, the work for Mr. Gordman no longer enough to quiet her restlessness. And dammit, she was tired of the pretense, of pretending to hate him, when in reality…

With a weary sigh that didn't quite make it past her lips, she realized that she'd been right all along. It had been a mistake coming here.

"All right," Matthew said then, coming to her rescue. "Leave poor Christina alone."

"Oh, dear!" Mary cried softly, her gaze looking out the window behind where Matthew and Christina sat. A better-timed red-herring couldn't have been presented. She frowned. "It's snowing."

"It was forecasted," Jason reminded her.

"But it's April," she wailed. "They were supposed to be wrong."

"Damn Minnesota weather," Matthew murmured turning to look over his shoulder at the fat flakes falling heavily from the sky…and just like that, much to Christina's relief, the conversation shifted.

Chapter Four

Christina took care not to let her mind wander again. As conversation ebbed throughout dinner, she made haste to take an active interest.

Like when Mary continued to peer outside, her eyes growing anxious in her face. "It's really coming down now," she said worriedly, her gaze following the driving snow. "I don't like the idea of you and Jason out on the roads if this continues."

"Don't worry," Christina had comforted her, without so much as bothering to peek outside. "We're all seasoned drivers in this stuff."

Or when Matthew and Jason started arguing the merits of foreign policy. Christina had glanced around the table, her lips pursed when she announced, "Honestly, I subscribe to the notion of survival by wealth and power" which had set the entire family off.

She even stooped to ask the Gordmans' how the Easter service at their church went, which was hardly common for her.

"Oh, you know," Matthew grumbled good-naturedly, giving his wife a teasing wink. "The usual. A lot of singing and praising."

"A lot of Alleluias," Jason added dryly.

Christina smiled vacantly. She hadn't been raised in much of a Christian household.

"You know, if you came with us, you wouldn't have to ask," Mary offered in her not-so-subtle way.

Christina shrugged uncomfortably. She should have seen that coming. The family had never missed an opportunity to invite Christina to...well, hell, to anything. It had started that very first Christmas after she'd moved to Minneapolis. Coming out of his office the last day before the holiday break, Matthew had innocently asked Christina about her plans. When she'd stuttered out a badly-concocted lie, he'd done something so unexpected it'd stolen her breath. He'd asked if she'd join him and his family over the festive weekend. Though she'd declined attending church...staring up into his gentle, compassionate eyes, she'd swallowed past the pride stuck in her throat. No one wanted to be alone during the holidays.

Shucking the thought aside and clamping down on the irritating swell of sentimentality which kept nicking her attention, Christina gave Mary a long-suffering look. "Yeah, well..."

Mary raised her eyebrows. "Yeah well, what?"

"Maybe some time," Christina grumbled at last, shifting her gaze demurely down to her plate.

"Yeah. I've heard that one before."

In hindsight, Christina wondered if being caught daydreaming hadn't been such a bad situation, after all.

"What does your family do on Easter Sunday?"

Christina looked up sharply at the question. Out of the corner of her eye, she saw Mary swat at her Jason's arm.

"What?" Jason asked his mother. "She always comes here. I just thought—"

Matthew cleared his throat loudly. "Christina, was that dessert I saw you bringing into the house earlier?"

She sent him a grateful glance. "Yes. Would you like some?"

"Please."

Rising eagerly from her seat, Christina lost no time retrieving the pie pan. "Anyone else?" she asked, turning back to glance at the table, though her gaze barely skimmed over Jason's head.

It was then that she really took notice of the snow. Shoot. Mary hadn't been kidding earlier. It *was* accumulating out there. The roof of Christina's car held at least two inches, and it'd only been a little over an hour since the first fat, heavy flakes had fallen from the sky. From the looks of the frenzied, whipping flurries scattering crazily about, it didn't appear to be stopping any time soon.

Following Christina's frowning gaze, Mary nodded pertly. "I told you," she accused mildly. "I bet we're in for a storm watch."

Matthew patted her hand. "It's spring. You know how it goes, the snow comes quick, it goes quick. Don't worry."

"Yeah," Jason said, but Christina could tell by the tone of his voice that he, much like his father, was simply placating Mary. "Once it stops snowing, it'll melt within an hour or so."

"Humph." Mary crossed her arms over her chest. "I'll believe it when I see it."

And, as so often turned out to be the case, Mary was right. By four o'clock, there was fast approaching five inches of snow on the ground. Opening the weather app on her phone, Mary informed the table—perhaps a bit smugly, but that was to be expected—that they were, indeed, in the midst of a winter storm watch. According to the forecast, the cities were in for another five to eight inches before all was said and done.

Christina wore her best poker face. While her car was front-wheel drive, the tires weren't great and she lived almost half an hour from the Gordmans' house. But to give way to her nerves would only set Mary over the edge. Instead she laughed in that way Minnesotan's have, as though driving through blizzardous conditions were a badge of honor to be worn on prominent display.

She waved away Mary's deep scowl. "I'm sure the plows will be out. It's just a matter of taking it slow, you know?"

But even Matthew looked concerned now, his gaze scowling over the oppressive whitewash gaining headway in the front yard. "You're not thinking of driving home in this?" he asked but it clearly wasn't a question so much as a statement of fact. Her car was barricaded on either side by drifting snow. The driveway was awash in rolling waves of the fresh powder. Christina cringed inwardly.

But to the family, she played it cool. "I certainly wasn't planning on walking in it."

Matthew narrowed his eyes. "You know what I mean."

Christina had a sinking feeling she knew where this was headed. "Now Matthew…"

"Don't you *'Now Matthew'* me."

"Yeah, that's my job," Mary informed her, crossing her arms cozily over her chest.

"I think, all things considered, it would be best if you stayed the night," Matthew informed her. He glanced outside. "I just wouldn't be comfortable with you out in this. It's not easing up even a bit."

Yup. Closing her eyes briefly as a hot wave of resentment rolled through her person, Christina recognized that she'd been right. She *had* known where this was going. "It's not my first snow," she informed him haughtily. She was an independent, grown woman. She jutted her chin toward Jason, who'd remained strangely silent up to now. "Besides, I don't hear you telling him he can't drive."

Jason made a face. "Grow up, Chrissy."

She could've choked. Her fingers curling into fists, her teeth snapping together, Christina was on the verge of responding to that high-handed dismissal when Matthew's voice overtook the conversation.

"Of course, I didn't," he said, answering her accusation calmly enough.

Jason smirked.

"*He* doesn't have to be told to know that he's staying the night."

"Wait. What?"

Now it was Christina's turn to grin. "Didn't see that one coming, huh?"

"Shut up."

That set her teeth on edge.

"Jason, it's a blizzard outside."

"That's putting it strongly."

"No, that's starting to look pretty accurate in description," Matthew argued.

"I can't stay," Jason said in that infuriating way he had of sounding like the only rational person in the room. "I have school in the morning."

Mary snorted. "Doubtful at that."

Jason smiled tightly. "My house isn't that far away," he returned.

"It's not that close, either."

"Mom." It was the way he said her name; just like a son.

"Jason Harlan Gordman—" But whatever Mary had been about to say was interrupted by a sudden incessant beeping on her phone. Looking down, she read the alert which flashed across her screen.

Glancing up then, she waved her phone at Christina and Jason gleefully. "Well, that settles it," she decreed. "According to the local police department, they've announced an official travel advisory and are asking that only essential personnel be out on the roads." She grinned with supreme satisfaction. "It looks like you're staying. The both of you."

"What, let me see that." Snatching the phone out of his mother's hands, Jason bent his head down to read the text message.

"What does it say?"

"Whiteout conditions and slippery roadways and…" With a muttered curse, he handed the cellphone back to Mary, glowering with the action.

"And you'll be staying here for the night," Mary finished for him.

Christina couldn't help the flutter of nervous anticipation that radiated throughout her body as she saw Jason's resigned submission and Mary's delighted expression. She knew then that her own surrender was merely a matter of time. She'd be spending the night at the Gordmans'. She'd be spending the night under the same roof as Jason. *Jason.*

Her stomach clenched. He'd be just down the hall from her. She'd see him in the morning, across this same table, all disheveled and scruffy with sleep. It felt very intimate. Cozy. Her hands shook at the thought, at the delicious image.

"Dammit," Jason muttered.

"Double damn," Christina concurred, clasping her hands together tightly on top of the table.

"Hey now," Matthew said. "Talk like that is bound to hurt me and Mary's feelings."

"Yeah, yeah," Christina scoffed, but she did so lightly. "Mr. Sensitivity over here."

"I happen to think we're pretty fun people," Matthew said with a look at his wife.

She clapped her hands. "It'll be like a slumber party."

"Mar," Matthew grumbled, "you're making us look uncool."

Jason nodded.

"Oh, shove it, Jas," Mary told her son, batting him on the shoulder with the back of her hand. "That's no way to behave towards your mother, who only wants what's best for you."

"Sorry." But he didn't sound very repentant.

Christina sighed, her eyes traveling wearily once again toward the blinding snow, the whipping wind slithering against the windows.

"Couple of mopes, these two," Matthew teased his wife.

Mary laughed. Jason frowned, a line of irritation forming between his eyebrows.

"I know what'll change those sour expressions," Matthew continued with a sideline glance to his amused wife. Then, clearing his throat, he asked: "Who wants a scotch?"

Jason's lips only turned down farther. "Me."

"God, yes." Christina nodded vehemently.

Rising to his feet, Matthew nodded. "Mary?"

"I'll take a glass of wine, please."

Matthew smiled. "I'll pour. I've got a heavy-hand tonight, too," he assured the table at large with a wink. "I mean, hey, if we're going to be snowbound, we might as well take advantage of the right to get a little lousy."

"I'll just get these dishes soaking," Mary murmured, reaching for the dessert plates still scattered across the table. "Be with you all in a moment."

"I'll help," Christina insisted. Rising quickly from her chair, she reached forward, grabbing up the remaining coffee cups. The clatter of tableware overrode Matthew's footsteps as he left the kitchen, his body steering him in the direction of the living room where the wet bar was located.

Trailing after his father, he was halfway to the kitchen swing door when Jason suddenly stopped. Tossing a look over his shoulder, his eyes sought out Christina, who was fast wiping down the table. "Look on the bright side, Chrissy"—he smiled mischievously, pursing his lips when her head turned in his direction—"if Dad's making doubles, at least this time you'll have a short commute. You've just got to make it up the stairs and down the hall."

Christina shot a quick glance at Mary, who was standing at the sink now, busily filling one of the basins with dish soap. Humming softly to herself, the older woman's concentration seemed to be solely fixed on getting the kitchen cleaned.

In two short steps, Jason closed the distance between them. Bending down, his voice a low murmur of sound, he added: "And I happen to know you love a good whisky..."

Christina glared. Unfortunately, some of the effect was lost since she couldn't quite seem to meet his eyes. "It's a delightful kind of person who makes fun at someone else's expense."

"Oh, come off it," Jason scoffed.

"One time. I had too much to drink one time and—"

"And it's okay to laugh about it."

"You are such a child," Christina grumbled.

Jason's eyebrows arched. Tilting his head, he gave her a cursory glance, his eyes traveling markedly across the breadth of her rigidly set shoulders, shifting to take in the sight of her curled fists down at her sides, sweeping passed the length of her locked knees.... His winged eyebrows rose just slightly, his green-brown eyes flicking at first indifferently over her stiffened stance. And then he saw it. The almost imperceptible throb at the base of her throat, the subtle tremor in the fingers strangling the towel in her hand. Narrowing his gaze, Jason stilled, slowed his appraisal.

Christina felt that look all the way through her body. Her breath caught as his gaze climbed back up to her face, his cheekbones taut as they caught the glimmer shining in her own eyes. It was like a livewire of electric shock.

And then it was gone, replaced with something easy. Jason's lips twitched and suddenly, just like that, the tension vanished from his face, almost as though it'd never been. "Maybe so," he agreed, smiling with boyish charm. Then his voice lowered. "But you could use a little playfulness. A little fun." Those words floating in the air between them, Jason straightened and, turning on his heel, exited the kitchen.

Staring after him, Christina swallowed. Dropping the towel on the table, she clasped her hands together, their pale-pink polish glowing in the soft evening light. Frowning, she chipped at one fingernail with another.

Jason was wrong. The very last thing she needed was a little fun. She knew from experience that a little fun carried a whole lot of consequences.

A little fun was a dangerous thing.

Especially with a man like Jason.

If only she could convince herself that she wasn't tempted all the same.

Chapter Five

Following at a more leisurely pace, Christina and Mary entered the living room a few minutes behind the men. Crossing her legs carefully as she took a seat on the cream-colored leather couch, Christina accepted her glass of scotch from a waiting Matthew. Beside her, Mary swirled a glass of wine daintily in her hands. Directly across from the large bay window, the women had an all-encompassing view of the falling snow.

This was always Christina's favorite part of her visits with the Gordmans—the post-dinner drink in the living area. They'd scatter across the furniture, lounging back after eating too much and sink into a lazy afternoon peace. Now and then, Mary and Matthew would reminisce about people and events before Christina's time; at other moments, Jason would tell them anecdotes about the trends and stories of his students; sometimes Christina took part in the conversation but usually, she just settled back against the plush cushions, her fingers wrapped around her cocktail glass as she let their words float easily over her.

This evening, however, talk eddied into a slow lull as every eye flickered out the window, as if assuring the viewer that it was, indeed, still snowing. Though she wouldn't likely admit it out loud, Christina found the scene out the window oddly romantic. This was partly due to the fire that Matthew had just brought to life in the large brick fireplace, the spicy warmth of the alcohol playing against her tongue, and the knowledge that she didn't have to brave the dangerous driving conditions. Of course, this opinion was certainly enhanced, did she but refuse to admit it, by the weight of another presence in the room. Without meaning to, Christina felt her gaze twitch, jerk toward Jason.

The idea of a sleepover wasn't helping her conflicting emotions, either.

What would he wear to bed?

God.

Sinking a little farther onto the massive couch, she banished the thought. "Well, dammit anyhow," she said, her voice a distraction as she nodded toward the snow glittering against the windowpane, "at least it's a hell of a view."

"Oh, don't I know it," Mary agreed, taking a sip of her merlot. Winking at Christina, she laughed. "I frequently find snowstorms to be more entertaining than the television."

"Snug as a bug…"

Mary nodded. "With no place to go."

"Or no way to get there," Christina countered dryly.

Mary snorted. "Well, yes, I suppose in your case."

Sauntering over to the lounge chair on one side of the window, Jason smirked. His hair was a little unruly in the front, as though he'd only just run his fingers through it. "I'd say it's reminiscent to being grounded."

"I bet that happened to you a lot as a child," Christina couldn't resist saying with a pointed raise of her eyebrows.

He made a disparaging sound. "Let me guess, you were the apple of your parents' eye?"

At the words, innocent though they were, Christina's smile faltered just the slightest bit. In reaction, she lowered her gaze down to her lap. Yes. She supposed she had been the apple of their eye. Once upon a time. An old hat to the residual pain that crept up her throat at the thought, Christina forced out a laugh. It had a husky quality to it, but otherwise, it sounded perfectly at ease.

Lifting her glass in a calculated salute, she agreed. "Let's just say, my parents never had cause to ground me." No, they'd only had cause to kick her out of their house entirely. And they had. In the most damning way possible. Then again, that was another story. For another audience.

And by another audience, she meant absolutely no one.

Jason didn't bother to hide his disdain. "Color me surprised."

She bristled, her body pitching forward. "No, I'd rather color you—"

"How about we play a game?" At Matthew's brisk, loud redirection, Christina swallowed her comeback. Letting her back recede into the couch cushions once more, she turned her head slightly, to where her boss was leaning beside the fireplace. Reaching for the poker, he prodded at the waning fire before shutting the glass screen with a firm hand.

Mary narrowed her eyes. Leaning just slightly forward, she placed her wine glass carefully on top of the coffee table. "What kind of game?" There was suspicion in her voice.

With a sly look at Jason, Matthew shrugged.

Christina didn't like that look.

"Oh, I don't know." Matthew shrugged one shoulder, the gesture delivered just a touch too casually. "Canasta?"

As if on cue, Mary and Christina groaned.

"No."

"We always play that game!"

"Can't we play something else?"

Mary nodded eagerly. "Yeah. Something fun."

"That everyone's good at?"

"Or, just nothing at all?"

Christina smiled in agreement. Before meeting the Gordmans', she'd only been vaguely aware of the card game, and that it was usually played by women past the age of retirement, flaunting shoulder-padded blouses, lipstick-stained dentures, and poodle-curled hair. Then she'd met the Gordmans'.

Matthew waved their instantaneous grumblings aside with a flick of his wrist. "Come on, ladies. You only say that because you two always lose."

Jason choked with mirth. The sound echoed into his glass.

"Well, yeah," Mary agreed, her eyes sparkling with mild temper. "You wouldn't like it so much either if the roles were reversed."

Matthew pursed his lips. Rubbing his hands together, he glanced from his son to Christina and Mary, and then back again. A slow smile formed on his mouth. "What do you say, Jas? Up for a little challenge?"

"Switch up the teams, you mean?" Jason narrowed his eyes as he momentarily assessed the women perched on the couch. The silence stretched on as he weighed the options before him. It was more than a little insulting.

With a plop, Christina set her glass down. "Really, are we such a pathetic pair?" She was pleasantly pleased with the coolness of her tone, the steadiness of her hand, the vague laughter in the question. Composed and collected.

Jason made a face. "Well…"

"Be very careful, Jas."

He winked. "I love you, Mom."

Mary laughed. "Oh, get out of here."

The boys finally conceded, perhaps the girls weren't completely hopeless. Talking as though Mary and Christina weren't even in the room, they grinned at each other conspiratorially—perhaps all they needed was a little mentoring. At this bit of conceit, the women were left with little more choice than to sit and glare at the boys.

So, the teams were switched, much to Christina's chagrin. Somehow, she'd known that she'd end up on Jason's team. It had been Matthew's idea. For, as he'd assured the room at large, if they were put on a team together, forced to work together, perhaps they'd be too distracted to snipe at one another.

Smiling demurely, Mary had promptly agreed. The turncoat.

Back in the kitchen again, the game about to begin, Christina shifted uneasily in her chair. Sitting directly across the table from Jason, with Mary on her right and Matthew seated at a diagonal to her, Christina discreetly fanned the cards out in front of her face.

She felt nervous. Jittery. And not just because Jason was competitive.

"Ready?" Jason asked, smiling at her. He winked. "And don't worry, you lucked out with the right partner. The better partner."

"Yeah right," Matthew scoffed from behind his cards, but neither Jason nor Christina were listening. Mary, however, patted his forearm in quiet agreement.

"My hero," Christina breathed at the youngest Gordman, batting her eyelashes outrageously.

"Stop flirting with me," Jason said, bringing Christina up short. With a wink, he settled back in his chair. "I need to concentrate now."

"Don't flatter yourself," she muttered darkly, her eyes staring fixedly, blankly at the cards in her hands. The colors and numbers swam dizzily before her eyes. Her stomach churned as the power of that accusation hung in the air, undoubtedly gaining the attention of the other pairs of ears in the room. *Flirting.* She felt naked, exposed as she sat there, sure that everyone in the family was watching her knowingly...

But when she finally chanced a glance up she saw, to her relief, that no one was paying her the least bit of attention. They were reading their cards, shuffling them into a semblance of order—something she should have been doing.

Silence thrummed for a moment as the players readied themselves. And then Mary, glancing over her cards, addressed the table. "Whose turn?"

Matthew looked at his wife. "Since Jason dealt, why don't you draw first."

Jason nodded. Christina inclined her head in silent agreement.

"All right." Smiling eagerly, Mary reached forward to pick a card off the top of the deck which was set in the middle of the table. "Hah!" With a start of excitement, she laid down a red three. She grinned at her husband as she drew another card off the stock. "Now, how was that?"

"Beautifully done, darling," he said dryly. "I never doubted you for a second."

"Mm-hmm," she said, with a knowing glance at Christina.

Conversation flowed in stops and jerks during the next few hours as the pairs bent their attention to the game at hand. The teams raced forward, neck and neck, as they advanced in points. It was a little after nine in the evening when they found themselves in the final round of the last match. Both teams were within range of reaching the five-thousand points it took to win the game. It all boiled down to who went out first.

Biting her lip, Christina surveyed the cards in her hands, her gaze flicking from them to the board she and Jason had accrued, then to the point sheet, and then back to the cards in her hands again. Her eyes were watchful, careful as she checked and double-checked for a possible meld, her head quickly tallying up the numbers to make quite certain…

Mary yawned.

"Yeah, any day now," Jason drawled, his foot tap-tapping against the floor. Christina narrowed her eyes, not paying him any mind.

This is where she always got hung up. In the clutch, when the pressure was on. But finally, clicking her tongue to the time of her math, Christina nodded her head. With a deliberate snap, she laid out each and every last card in her hand—and with it, produced a win for her team.

Jason's eyes grew wide at the unexpected sight. "Wha—?"

Matthew whistled. "I didn't see that coming." He smiled at Mary. "Sorry, sweetheart."

"Well, I mean she deliberated so long," Mary murmured absently.

Christina turned her eyes to Jason. There was a challenge in their depths. "Worth the wait, I hope?"

He shook his head, grinning widely. "What the hell kept you?"

"I just wanted to make sure I had it all correct," she mumbled.

Leaning back in his chair, his eyes drawn to the cards on the table, a new gleam entered his eyes at the words, at the evidence before him. "That's a win all right." He sent his father a mischievous look. "Which reminds me, what was that we wagered, Dad? Oh, yeah." He snapped his fingers together. "That's right…"

"You wagered on us?" Mary asked Matthew.

He shrugged. "Just a friendly bet."

Rubbing his hands together, Jason laughed. "If that's what you want to call a bottle of your reserve whisky."

Mary groaned. "Matthew, you idiot."

He looked grumpily across the table at his wife. "Thanks for the input."

"That stuff was expensive," she reminded him.

"I'm well aware of that."

"It's what makes it all the sweeter," Jason assured his mother. With that same infectious chuckle, he turned back to a silently amused Christina. His grin lengthened. "Thanks, partner."

"Now who's the slouch?" she couldn't resist asking with one haughtily raised eyebrow.

"Not you, darling." His lips twitched. "I'd be drinking cheap beer but for you."

She nodded pertly. "Don't forget it."

"…lost in a revolving vortex of bottom-shelf drinks…"

Christina shot him a quick look.

"Doomed for defeat—"

"Oh, all right," she muttered. "Enough."

"Here we go again," Matthew said to Mary.

She shrugged. "Well, it was nice while it lasted."

Jason's eyes never wavered from Christina. "No, no. The accolades are all yours." He wagged his eyebrows outrageously. "And I could kiss you right now for the effort!"

At the unexpected response, Christina stilled, her eyes widening. In the back of her mind, she vaguely heard Jason's voice prattling on: "…no idea how good his stock is…"

Before she could help herself, she felt her body reacting to the words, a sort of tension filling her person. Feeling her face flush, she quickly looked away. *I could kiss you right now.* Battling back a strange wantonness, she swallowed with difficulty.

Grappling for composure, her neck throbbing as she tried to fight a sense of casualness to her expression, Christina reached for her scotch. Too late, she realized as she pressed it up against her lips, the glass was empty. Breathing in the heady scent, she quietly dropped the tumbler back down to the table. Only, she hadn't been quick enough to have escaped the notice of the people sitting around her, their eyebrows raising questioningly, tellingly. Too late, she realized that Jason was done speaking, that the family was waiting, watching.

For her response.

Speak. Say something, for Christ's sake. "God," she muttered, finding her voice at last. "You are such a Neanderthal."

The comeback may have passed muster but for the flustered, breathless quality of her voice.

And she was only too aware that everyone heard it.

Especially Jason. She'd watched his lips shift uncertainly in those beats of time, his eyes growing cloudy as they observed her flushed reaction from across the table. She'd witnessed the expressions playing out across his face: puzzlement and confusion, something like amusement and then a quiet sort of questioning.

Oh, God.

Years of careful bantering, of a perfectly crafted arms-length sort of friendliness, were quickly circling the proverbial drain. She didn't know what the hell was wrong with her. She'd always been able to hold her poise around Jason before. She'd always been able to shrug off his playfulness as though he were an annoyance to be endured.

Clearing her throat, Christina tried to hide beneath the cover of comedy. "Really Matthew—" she agonized artfully, turning toward her boss. Only, whatever she'd been about to say next died on her lips at the look she surprised on his face. He disguised it quickly enough, but not before she saw it: dawning curiosity.

Mixed with a certain amount of trepidation and, what was that, pity?

Fucking Christ.

"Knock it off already," Jason said with mock hauteur, and for once, she was glad of his incessant teasing, his impeccable timing. "It was just an expression. It's not like I'm going to attack you."

She tossed her hair over one shoulder, her eyes slithering back to his. Well, not quite. Her gaze hovered somewhere near his brow line, though. "As if."

"Correct." His voice practically oozed with honeyed assurance.

"Spare me your ego," Christina returned, rolling her eyes. Her shoulders relaxed a little on the words.

He chuckled. "I don't think *my* ego is the problem here."

She grinned in an infuriating fashion, but her cheeks lost some of their color all the same. "Then quit requesting kisses."

He leaned back in his chair. "Get over yourself."

She leaned forward. "You first."

"I wish I had a whistle," Mary complained to her husband.

"All right, kids," Matthew said then, placing both palms flat out on the table. "Let's call it, huh? It's getting late, I'm tired, and I don't want to hear the two of you bickering all night."

At the words, Mary turned to Christina. "Speaking of that," she said, pushing back her chair. "Why don't you come upstairs with me and let's see if we can't rustle up a spare set of pajamas for you."

Christina hesitated. She hadn't thought about that. Her eyes skipped over her beautifully styled blouse and designer skirt. Though she desperately did not want to borrow sleepwear from her boss's wife (that felt like way too many shades of inappropriate), she realized the impracticality of anything else.

And so, she brought herself both gracefully and reluctantly to her feet. Without bothering to spare Jason a backward glance, she followed Mary out of the room and up the massive staircase at the front entrance.

Chapter Six

Standing on the thick, plush carpet in her softly-lit bedroom, Mary leaned inside the impressively tall double-door wardrobe, her eyes narrowing at the articles of clothes on display—then she looked down at her generous curves and over at Christina's much taller, slimmer frame. Then back to the wardrobe. She grimaced, her hands quick as they shuffled through the hangers. Finally, snapping the doors shut, she shook her head. "Well, shoot. I don't have anything that will fit you," she admitted, wrinkling her nose with distaste. "I kind of hate you for that."

Christina laughed softly, but her arms, wrapped tightly around her stomach, spoke of her self-consciousness and discomfort.

Mary, seemingly oblivious to this, brought a finger up to her chin. "Now, let me think."

"It's fine, Mar," Christina insisted for the umpteenth time. "Really. I don't mind…" She'd sleep in her skirt. In fact, the more she thought about it, the more she liked the idea.

Having Easter dinner with your boss and his family was one thing, but standing inside his *bedroom*, even in the company of his wife, rifling through their closets was, well, it was weird. Worse, she was absolutely terrified that Mary's next suggestion would be to unearth the contents inside her husband's dresser drawers.

Taking a quick, firm step backward, Christina shook her head. "Honestly, it's not a big deal. I can sleep in this." With a flippancy she was far from feeling, Christina's hand waved to take in her appearance, though her eyes refused to follow the gesture, refused to risk cringing at the fitted, thin material that contradicted the option. So maybe it wasn't quite ideal, but neither was this.

Mary, on the other hand, obviously didn't seem to find anything out of the ordinary about having her husband's secretary in her bedroom. The irony of the situation was almost too rich. Nor, for that matter, did she consider her next proposal just as scandalous. "Oh. I've got it," she said, snapping her fingers together. "Jason."

Christina's eyebrows rammed together. "Ja-Jason?" Her stomach jerked. How the hell was Jason supposed to help Christina with sleepwear? It was a dangerous thought, one she regretted immediately as her mind flashed, wondering just what it was *he* would be wearing for bedtime.

She'd only seen him without a shirt once, but it had been enough. Matthew and Jason had been playing basketball out in the front courtyard on a particularly hot summer evening. Christina had been invited out for dinner but when, afterward, the boys had gone outside, she'd made the mistake of bringing them cold beers at Mary's suggestion.

Not an overly tall man, Jason had been all wiry, chiseled masculinity—with a light sprinkling of hair covering his flat stomach, which had only managed to enhance the rugged, glistening view she'd gotten as she'd stepped outside. The muscles in his arms had bunched, all sinewy strength, as he'd lifted the basketball for a fadeaway shot. Just before she'd jerked her gaze away, her eyes had watched him with soft, unselfconscious pleasure.

"Follow me," Mary said, her voice jerking Christina out of her reverie. Grateful, Christina found herself being led out of the bedroom and into the hallway. Her relief was short-lived, however, when she watched Mary's hand turn the knob on the door at the end of the long passage.

"Wait…?"

"Jason will have something you can wear," Mary said, looking back at Christina as though this had already been explained, and hadn't she been paying attention?

Which was how Christina found herself in Jason's childhood bedroom—and five minutes later, emerging out of the adjoining bathroom tucked against the back wall—wearing one of his old high school T-shirts along with a faded pair of shorts from when he ran track in college. Pulling at the blue mesh material of the shorts, which were far too loose around her legs, Christina felt a blush rising on her cheeks. Much as she'd done in Mary's bedroom, she kept her eyes safely lowered. Her body stiffening, her muscles seized at the energy she could practically feel radiating out of the room.

Of course, it wasn't his bedroom anymore, and the blue-and-white plaid flannel blanket over the bed no longer felt the weight of his body every evening, the alarm clock on his bedside table no longer set to greet him in the mornings. The air didn't carry his particular fragrance, and the trophies and miscellaneous posters on the walls no longer denoted his tastes (and yes, okay, so her eyes *had* wandered a bit…); still, it was *his*—it would be his again that night.

It had undoubtedly been years since he'd worn the clothes Christina currently modeled on her body, and yet her skin seemed to break out with every brush of the cotton and polyester against the swell of her breasts, her thighs. It was so intimate. So familiar. So…her stomach tingled deliciously at the thought.

"Okay, perhaps it's not exactly stylish," Mary said, misunderstanding Christina's hesitation.

At the prompting, Christina laughed as she was supposed to do. "No? But I thought this was so cutting edge." Smiling impishly, she struck a pose. "Chic meets sporty."

"Very trendy," Mary said dryly. With a wave of her hand, she beckoned to Christina. "All right, all right. Come on," she urged teasingly, her eyes twinkling as she unlocked and opened the closed bedroom door. "Let's get out of here before Jason notices."

Christina chewed on her lip, her eyes skimming over the room one last time. "Yeah, it does feel kind of wrong to be in here without him," she confessed. She blanched at the words, heady with an unintentional intimacy. "What I mean to say is—"

"Oh, don't I know it," Mary responded lightly. "He used to have a no trespassing sign posted outside the doorway."

Christina rolled her eyes as the women stepped out into the hallway. "I'll just bet he did."

"I wasn't even allowed to vacuum the floor without his go-ahead," Mary continued with a tsk-tsk, leading Christina halfway down the wide gallery hall before coming to a stop before one of the doors. "But anyway, enough about his room," she insisted, reaching for the brass doorknob. "Tell me, what do you think of yours?" With a flourish, she thrust the door open wide. Flicking on the light switch, a warm glow, courtesy of a bedside lamp, illuminated the small space.

Christina blinked. She wasn't sure, but she thought her mouth dropped open for a second. The room was something all right. Pink carpeting and maple furniture, replete with a lacy canopy bed and a sash window overlooking the backyard, with tall, imposing flowered curtains flanking either side. She blinked again. Her eyes took in a small vanity stashed in a narrow nook beside the wardrobe, and that impossibly frilly lamp sitting beside a bowl of flowers on the nightstand.

"Wow," Christina said. Because what else was there to say? She looked at Mary's expectant face. "This is...wow!"

"I know," Mary crowed, her hands clutched against her chest. She sighed in a dreamy manner. "I guess it's because I never had a daughter."

Christina giggled. "You think?"

"You don't think it's too much?"

Christina would never have admitted such a thing. She loved Mary. To hurt her feelings didn't bear contemplation. "What? No way. I think it's every little girl's dream."

"Good. Well," clasping her hands together, Mary nodded. "Is there anything else I can get you?"

"No."

Mary took a half step backward, receding once more into the hall. "You'll be comfortable for the evening?"

"More so than at my own home," Christina assured her. Walking into the room, she smiled at Mary over her shoulder. "But then, I usually am when I'm here."

Mary pursed her lips in a pleased sort of way. "What can I say, I love spoiling you."

"And you do it well."

"All right," Mary said, patting the side of the door with her hand for effect. "I should probably be getting to bed myself. Sleep well."

"Goodnight, Mar."

"See you in the morning." With a decisive nod, Mary turned and walked back down the hallway toward her room. Sighing, Christina pushed the door shut behind her weary body. Leaning back, she let her head fall against the ornately carved structure.

The fingers of her left hand played with the hem of Jason's shirt. "God, get a grip," she reprimanded herself. But she could feel the soft possession of his shirt like a brand. She felt…woefully juvenile. Like she'd never give the shirt back. Never wash it. Never take it off.

"Get a grip," she repeated, her voice stronger, harsher now. "Let it go." Shaking her head, she grimaced as she considered how far her command had fallen that day, how loose her hold suddenly seemed to be when it came to Jason. The daydreaming, the wanting, the blushes.

"It's official, you've been alone for too long," she berated herself, pulling her body off the door. With a whelp of frustration, she flopped face-first onto the bed, groaning into the heavy pink coverlet. "You've lost your damn mind."

He was going to be sleeping two doors down from her.

All night.

So close.

Like anything could happen.

Like something was bound to happen.

"Oh, no," she whispered, bracing herself up on her elbows. "No. Definitely not. Not happening." With unnecessary force, she brought herself to her feet. Pulling the covers and sheet back with a vengeance, her movements were almost violent as she climbed into the bed. Tucking the quilt over herself with determination, she laid her head on the pillow. "Absolutely not. No good will come from that kind of thinking. Nope. You're going to bed. Right now." With an exaggerated gesture, she flicked off the bedside lamp and closed her eyes.

Five minutes later, she wondered what time it was.

With a peek, she opened one eyelid, her gaze zeroing in on the discreet alarm clock snuggled up tight to the lamp.

10:02 p.m.

She squeezed her eyes closed again, readjusted her neck on the pillow, and took a deep breath. Okay, bedtime. Yup.

By 10:54 p.m., she gave up the pretense. She'd tried counting. She'd tried blinking really fast. She'd thought about some boring reports she needed to import at work…nothing. She was wide awake. Opening her eyes, she stared up at the bluish shadows dancing above the canopy overhead. The house was silent. Too silent.

That was probably it. She was used to a tiny apartment where she could hear the constant humming of the fridge, the crack of tree branches scraping against her bedroom window, the soft footfall of the upstairs neighbor who worked overnights.

She just needed a little distraction.

Scrambling out from underneath the warmth of the comforter, Christina brought herself up and out of the bed. Tiptoeing carefully to the door, lest she should wake someone, and by someone she meant Mary, who'd fret and worry that she'd somehow failed to produce a perfectly sound asleep guest in her home, Christina held her breath as she clicked open her door, her feet slipping silently out into the hallway.

Vigilant, she led herself to the giant staircase at the center of the sweeping hall. Her bare feet were stealthy on the carpeted stairs as she slowly descended to the main floor. She'd barely stepped off the last tread when she heard it. Quiet, muffled laughter. Shocked, Christina spun on the balls of her feet, her stomach muscles coiling at the sound, at the low timbre of the voice. Because there, emerging from the depths of the living room, the low-lighting offset only by the glow of a single reading lamp, an amber-colored drink in one hand, was Jason.

With a deliberate kind of calm, though her body vibrated with shocked surprise and a surge of…of excitement, Christina forced herself not to react. Other than a slight lift of one pointed eyebrow, she remained silent. By this time, hastily setting his drink down on the nearby coffee table, Jason was practically bent over double, his eyes dancing with mirth.

"All right, all right," she grumbled. "What already?" With a practiced move, she placed both hands on her hips.

He only shook his head in amusement.

She narrowed her eyes.

"It's you," he finally managed to say, his breath ragged. He waved toward her general person. "In that get-up." He chuckled again. "Are those my old running shorts?"

Christina felt her face flame. She'd almost forgotten she'd been wearing them. Crossing her arms over her chest, she gave him a lowering look. "That's enough. You've had your fun."

"No, it's just…I don't think I've ever seen you so"—he shrugged, seemingly at a loss for words— "casual."

She rolled her eyes.

"You've got nice legs."

Christina stilled, her expression searching, seeking…. Pulling her shoulders back, she scrambled for a response.

Jason, however, didn't seem to have the least bit of squeamishness about his comment. "Really nice." With a flick, he brought his eyes back up to her face.

Christina couldn't quite make herself meet that look. "Always quick with a joke, huh?"

But for once he didn't respond to her baiting. Instead, he motioned toward the staircase behind her. "What are you doing down here, anyway? Couldn't sleep?"

At his change of topic, Christina felt her shoulder blades loosen. She shrugged half-defensively. "Not really." She glanced up at the clock. It was only a little past eleven. "Honestly, I'm not usually in bed yet."

He grinned. "Yeah. Me neither."

She nodded unsurely. She'd worked hard all these years to never be left alone with him. And yet, even knowing this, her feet made no move toward retreat.

Again, Jason was there to fill the gaps of silence. Glancing pointedly toward the liquor cabinet behind him he sent her a questioning look. "Want something?"

Christina hesitated, but only for a second. "Yeah. Okay, sure."

"Scotch?"

"Whatever."

Turning nimbly toward the wet bar, he paused only long enough to ask over one shoulder: "You going to stand there all night or come inside?"

Christina frowned darkly from the staircase. "Of course, I'm not going to stand here…" she muttered, stomping quietly into the living room. Why was it, he could always make her feel like an overgrown child? Clumsy, off-pitch…. Which was particularly offensive because, to the rest of the world, she practically radiated sophistication and finesse. With anyone else, she wouldn't have had to be reminded to enter a room, she'd have already been lounging in one of the chairs, her body sinking gracefully against the cushions.

Christina watched him surreptitiously, his hands deft as he reached for a particular bottle, unscrewed its cap, and poured her drink. She'd only just sat down on the couch when he finished. Coming up to her, he held out a scotch, neat.

Warily, she glanced at his outstretched hand. There was absolutely no way she could take it without touching his fingers. Bracing herself for the feeling that always followed—it was only the rush of the forbidden, she firmly reminded herself— Christina let her hand reach forward. Her fingers shook slightly as she curled them around the cocktail glass, but she consoled herself with the knowledge that it was only the finest of tremors.

"Nervous, Christina?" Jason asked quietly, expectantly, his body leaning just slightly toward hers, his left hand coming to brace itself against the armrest. His eyes stared daringly into her face.

Apparently it hadn't been that fine of a tremor after all. Cupping the glass with both hands then, Christina tried to play it cool. He was far too close. In response, she sank farther into the cushions. It was a telling move, but for once, she didn't care. "Of what?"

He nodded at the stranglehold she had on the alcohol. He filled her vision, closing in around her as he bent nearer yet, his other hand finding support against the back of the couch cushion. "You tell me." His words were soft, but still, they fell against her consciousness with a blow. His eyes narrowed on her fingers, the unusual whiteness of her knuckles. "You're trembling," he informed her needlessly. His breath singed across her senses, the sound of his voice caressing against her half-open mouth.

A last-ditch defense, she raised her glass jerkily to her lips, anything to barricade herself from his proximity, the liquid sloshing violently against the sides of the tumbler with the motion. Only, at the last second, she changed her mind, lowering the untasted drink down to her lap. She doubted she could've swallowed just then anyway. Clearing her throat, her eyes falling to a warm droplet of scotch which had landed on her knee, Christina felt her control slipping, cracking.

"You know what," she said, the words coming out adamant, hard. Moving blindly, Christina set her glass down on the end table. "I think maybe I'm tired after all." With a sudden move, she scrambled wildly to her feet, swatting at one of the arms enclosing either side of her. The motion forced Jason upright, forced him to take a step backward. Still though, he had her pinned, the backs of her legs pressed against the couch, his chest only inches away from her own.

With a wild snarl, she made to push fully past his crowding body.

"Chrissy…" Jason's hand shot out, forestalling her rushed getaway. Standing at full height now, he stared down into her averted features. Their bodies were so close now that they were almost, but not quite, touching. Except, of course, for his hold on her captured wrist.

"Let me go, Jason," she commanded, tugging futilely against his hold. Her eyes flicked up and then away from his knowing gaze.

"Not before I get an answer," he returned.

Exasperated, she felt her chin tugging up, her eyes clashing with his. "To what?"

"A theory," he said, half under his breath. Before Christina had time to process this cryptic statement, his mouth swooped down, covering hers.

Chapter Seven

Jason's lips were cool as they pressed against her mouth. Christina barely knew what was happening before she felt her body responding to the gentle pressure of his tongue as it glided along the tight line of her lips. Gasping in reaction, her eyes fell helplessly closed at the soft, questioning invasion. That gasp was all the more invitation he required. Sweeping across the inside of her mouth, his tongue darted past her teeth and into the darkness, where it tangled with her own. Her stomach plummeted at the sensations, her head tilted, granting him further access.

Seemingly of their own accord, her hands rose, her fingers splaying out across the expanse of his chest. Her legs trembled as she sank into the feeling of his mouth molding to the contours of her lips. His left hand was propped under her elbow as he slowly leveraged her body closer to his; his right hand was cupped against the underside of her jaw, his thumb stroking against the edges of her bottom lip. The silence of the room was broken only by the rasp of Christina's fingers against his sweater, the rush in each other's breathing…

When his tongue slid under the silky moisture of her upper lip an instinctive groan escaped from Christina's throat. Reacting without thought, she retaliated in kind. Her teeth catching at his lower lip, she tugged gently. Then it was his turn to growl. And still he penetrated her mouth, his movements precise as his tongue slipped in and out, swirled around and around.

Christina's heart beat hard against her chest, her skin pulsing and clenching at the growing contact, her senses dizzy as she tasted him.

When she felt his lips slowly break contact from hers, at first Christina's body followed blindly after him. Opening her eyes, she breathed up at him from underneath a fringe of wet lashes. "Jason?" Her voice came from far away, dazed with the suddenness of what was happening between them.

He half-smiled down at her in the stillness of the dimly lit room. "And here I always thought you hated me."

Christina blanched. Reality crashing against her consciousness, she had just enough time to remember what he'd said seconds before his lips had captured hers—that he was testing out a theory. Swallowing back a whispered scream, for the second time in as many seconds, Christina's body moved on impulse. Clambering frantically away from the couch, she bolted. Jason only barely avoided being bulldozed in her mad dash.

Bringing a hand up to her mouth, Christina bit down on the approaching sob itching its way up her throat. What the hell had she done? What had she allowed him to do? History was repeating itself. The memory of minutes ago now lay cold in her stomach. Scurrying for the entryway to the room, her eyes pinned themselves to the foyer beyond, her body hurling for the staircase.

She only knew she had to escape. To breathe. To…oh, God!

Her legs shook with the force of her feelings, but she refused to slow down. The hard, humiliating edge of regret pressed against her chest. Something had happened. Something…!

"Wait. Hey, hey!" Jason said, one reaching out to brush against her upper arm—she hadn't realized he'd followed after her.

With a wrench, she pulled herself free. "Don't."

"Whoa, okay. I'm sorry." His voice lowered, changed in those moments. Gone was the conceit, the deliberation. In its place, she heard newfound concern and confusion. She heard tenderness. She heard the continued sound of his footsteps following behind her. "Christina, would you just stop for a minute? Talk to me."

Helplessly, Christina felt her movements slow. Pausing mid-step, her shoulders stiffened as she half-turned in his direction. Her eyes, glancing at him over her left shoulder, were wary, guarded. "What?"

He raised his arms in the air at her expression. "Jesus. Will you stop acting like I'm some kind of lecher?" He swore softly. "I wasn't the only one doing the kissing."

One side of her lip snarled. "Not a lecher. A louse, perhaps."

His eyes narrowed. "In that case, let's not forget what happened after the employee Christmas party last year."

At the words, dark and ominous, Christina's body jerked. Her eyelids flinched, flicking away from the mockery on his face, in his voice. Reeling, her gaze snapping forward once more, Christina looked straight ahead, though she hardly took notice of the large arched entryway standing before her, the foyer just beyond—she only knew the flat, cruel statement swirling boldly around them. He didn't need to elaborate. They both knew what he meant. Unbidden, pictures of that night materialized in her mind. Losing the fight, Christina's eyes drifted tightly shut at the onslaught of the wracking memories, the damning reminder.

She saw herself outside her apartment door, large brown eyes staring invitingly up into his hazel ones, full lower lip pulling down under the weight of her slightly bared teeth. And then—

No. She shook her head, trying to rid it of the thought. She'd promised herself she wouldn't rehash what had happened. And until now, she hadn't. At least, not so she'd admit, even to herself.

Throwing her shoulders back, she fought for some likeness of pride. Lifting her chin, though she didn't dare to look back at him again, Christina spoke. Her voice rose like an eerie fog: "I had too much to drink that night."

"Yeah, maybe," Jason conceded from too close behind her. And then she felt his hands on her waist, slowly, deliberately turning her back around. "But not tonight," he reminded her. "You didn't even touch that glass of scotch."

And there it was.

"Aha," she murmured harshly. "So that was the reason behind your little science experiment then?" His fingers were still pressed against either side of her waist. She could feel the imprint like a live thing, but she refused to give him the satisfaction of shucking out of his grip.

His eyes widened momentarily at her words.

She laughed, nodding toward the couch. "And this was what, a controlled environment for testing out your *theory*?" The question was sharp and hard as she threw his words back at him.

But if she'd wanted a reaction, he didn't give her the kind she desired. Instead, Jason smiled in an off-kilter sort of way. He even shrugged. "I wouldn't call what just happened controlled."

She felt her stomach pinch. "No?"

He grinned wider. "But timing is everything."

"And you were bored and needed someone to amuse you?"

He cocked his head to one side, as though in serious thought. "I would hardly say I was amused back there."

She lifted one eyebrow. "Flattered then?"

He shrugged. His very casualness set her teeth on edge. "By a woman as beautiful as you? Who wouldn't be?"

Christina rolled her eyes, but a half-chuckle escaped out of her mouth all the same. It was just like Jason to do that, to make her laugh when it was the last thing she expected to do.

"So flattered that you felt the need to shame me?"

His face shuttered. A dangerous glint entered his eyes. "Shame you?"

She gestured with her chin. "The Christmas party?"

To his credit, Jason winced. His jaw clenched as his fingers tightened their hold on her waist. "I shouldn't have said that. I'm sorry."

"So you keep saying."

"Well, I was feeling pretty shamed myself."

With a sigh, Christina felt her features soften. "I didn't mean—that's not...." Stuttering, she bit back a sigh of frustration. "Still, it was a mistake."

He pulled a face. "Maybe. Though it doesn't explain..."

When he didn't finish, she felt her eyes narrow. "Explain what?"

"Why you've pretended to hate me all these years."

She jutted out her chin. For some reason, though she shouldn't have been, she found herself *almost* enjoying the conversation. "Who said I was pretending?"

Jason sighed. "Not that old ruse again." With a charm she really could hate sometimes, he took an entreating step nearer. "Don't make a liar of yourself twice in one night." A quick thread of excitement she couldn't contain leaped into Christina's body at the words. Too late, her eyes traveled to his lips.

He stilled. "Unless?" The word was suggestive, meaningful as Jason shifted his body closer to hers. When Christina didn't immediately side-step out of his way, he smiled slowly. She was already breathing too quickly, her legs trembling against his when Jason's mouth slowly started its descent.

His lips were so close she could almost taste his whisky-scented breath. With a strength she wasn't aware she possessed, Christina moved. Ducking out of his reach, she brought a hand up between them, pushing at his chest half-heartedly. "No."

"Christina?"

"No." Her voice was firmer now. "This is a bad idea. I meant what I said. It was a mistake."

"What?" Frustration lined every letter of that word.

"This," Christina insisted, gesturing between them. Slipping fully free of his proximity, she forced her feet to walk into the hallway, her body pedaling carefully as she navigated backward toward the staircase. "It's a bad idea."

"Why?"

She scowled, her eyes drifting expressively up the stairs. "You know why."

He followed her gaze. "Because of my father?"

Her hand cut aggressively through the air. "Yes, because of your father!" Christina returned hotly. "He's my boss."

"I'm aware."

"Don't joke."

"Then don't say stupid things."

Christina made a sound low in her throat. "You wanted to test out your hypothesis?"

"Theory," he corrected quietly.

"Well, there you go. You figured it out. I'm a fraud," she informed him. Twin spots of color dotted her cheeks but she refused to break eye contact. There was something vindictive in the action, the knowledge that she'd hurt him more than herself with the admission.

She was right. He grimaced. "Hey. That's not—"

"In fact, I was attracted to you from the very first moment I met you," she continued hotly, tossing the shreds of her pride at his feet mercilessly. The slash of color highlighting his cheekbones was almost worth the cost. She pointed toward the front door. "Right there. I saw you and everything went…" She shrugged, laughing in a whispered bark. "Everything went black."

He had the grace to look away, his eyes clouding over uncomfortably. "Christina."

"But your father is my boss."

"And you think he wouldn't, what, approve?" Jason asked. "He's not a snob, Chrissy."

"Don't call me that!" she cried, curling her fingers into impotent fists.

He held up his hands. "Christina."

She shook her head. "And anyway, it's not really about your father."

He scowled. "But you just said—"

"It's me. I have this thing. Oh, you know," she said, flicking her wrist artlessly, "for forbidden men. Simply because I shouldn't have them, I want them. It's always the same, but it's not real. You know? It's just a fun fantasy, something to alleviate the boredom because-because it's not based on anything of merit," she rambled. "And really, dating the boss's son? That couldn't be more cliché." She managed one cruel laugh. "So I've kept myself to myself. Or, at least, I've tried to."

"Jesus."

Christina shrugged, one of her hands reaching back the grab tight to the stair rail. She gave him a pointed look. "There. Now you know the truth. I am attracted to you. Kind of. In a totally dysfunctional way. Does that answer all of your questions?" She yawned protractedly. "Because I'm tired and I'd rather like to go to bed now if you don't mind."

His face contorted. "Don't let me keep you then."

With a curt nod, Christina turned on her heel, her knees buckling as she carefully traveled the stairs. Halfway up, however, she stopped and turned to look back at him. He hadn't moved, his eyes watching her progression speculatively, as though she were a fascinating specimen under his microscope.

"Do me one favor?"

Jason inclined his head.

She forced the words out of stiff lips. "Forget about tonight."

His response was slow in coming. "Oh, I very much doubt I can oblige you on that."

Her thinly plucked eyebrows rose to meet over the bridge of her nose. "Jason." His name was a warning.

He shrugged. "The best I can do is promise not to bring it up."

Christina stared at him for a moment. Then she nodded again.

"And I'll probably break that promise anyway," Jason added when she would have continued her incline.

Her hand tightened on the balustrade. "Don't."

He held up his hands. "Forewarned is forearmed."

Chapter Eight

Christina woke to a bluish morning light wafting through the curtains of the bedroom window. But before she even opened her eyes, the events of the night before flooded her consciousness. She knew immediately that she was in the guest bedroom of Matthew and Mary Gordman's house. And she remembered explicitly what she'd done, what she'd said to Jason.

That she was attracted to him.

Had been since the moment she'd first seen him.

And how she'd almost let him kiss her again.

Groaning painfully, she flung her forearm over her tightly closed eyes.

"Oh, God," she whimpered, sinking disgustedly into the soft mattress underneath her. "What the hell did I say?!" She could feel heat infusing her body, her limbs growing stiff as the image of Jason's face—utter shock and revelation—passed across her mind. She moaned as the words she'd slung at him so heatedly returned to her in the stark coolness of day.

Well fuck.

How the hell would she ever face him again? The urge to vomit, to physically be ill, crawled up her throat. It had felt only too natural at the time. She hadn't known a twinge of regret as she'd assaulted him with the words of her great secret. In fact, she'd felt oddly powerful, hurtling the reality of her feelings at him, calling him out for playing on her vulnerabilities.

No, she hadn't felt regret. Not then. But she did now. A terrible, lowering regret. The kind that usually follows an evening of over-indulgence with alcohol. The kind that comes after the sort of knock-down drag-out fight when terrible, untrue things are said, used to punish….

What was it about the seductive cover of night that makes nothing of pretense and protection?

"Shit," she whispered, as tears squeezed out of the corners of her eyes. Her chest felt tight, and her breathing came in sharp gasps. "You idiot. You stupid, stupid idiot!" Turning on her side, she curled her legs up to her stomach, huddling into a ball under the covers of her blanket.

How was she ever going to face him again?

With a muted cry of despair, Christina threw the covers up over her head. It was the discreet knock on the other side of the door, however, that reminded her she couldn't stay in hiding forever.

"Christina? Are you awake?" Mary's voice softly inquired.

Christina swallowed thickly. "Um…yeah. Yes, I'm awake," she called out, ignoring the slight quiver in her voice and praying it hadn't traveled through the thick door separating them. The last thing she needed was questions from Mary.

"Breakfast is ready."

Christina blanched. "Oh. Uh, thanks, but I'm, ah, I'm not hungry…"

"Nonsense. It's important to start the day with a hearty meal," Mary returned just as Christina knew she would. No one said no to Mary—not when it came to food.

Still, she had to try. To sit across the table from Jason, after everything that had transpired the night before, would be interminable. "I, uh, I can't. I have to get home. T-to change clothes and you know, get ready…"

"Oh, posh!" Mary hollered, still speaking through the door. If she found this to be unusual behavior (and she most certainly did!), she didn't let on. "Matthew will understand if you need to come in a little late this morning. It was at our insistence that you spent the night, after all."

And that's how Christina found herself, uncomfortably dressed in the clothes from the day before— her shirt a little wrinkled and limp, and her skirt a bit rumpled—crossing the massive foyer and into the Gordmans' kitchen, twenty minutes later. There was nothing she could do about her clothes, but her hair, swept artfully off her freshly scrubbed face, with carefully plucked tendrils cascading down her high cheekbones, looked model-ready. Thanks to the small array of cosmetics she always kept in her purse, her lips were coated with a nice amber-hue and her eyes sparkled alongside the iridescent pale pink she'd painted over the arch of her lids.

Christina had learned long ago that her best defense against a cruel world was to hide inside the armor of a beautifully turned-out exterior. With determined steps, she took herself in for breakfast. The last to arrive, she kept her eyes focused on her plate, which Mary had already piled high with toast, bacon, and eggs.

"I knew it was a good idea, the two of you spending the night," Matthew said, his eyes twinkling up at her and Jason before his fork dipped into the flaky food on his plate. "I had a feeling this would happen. Usually, it's just plain oatme—whoa there!"

Moving in an instant, Jason caught Christina's glass of orange juice, righting it just as it'd been on the verge of emptying its contents all over the table.

"You okay?"

"Yeah, sorry," Christina mumbled, one hand rubbing her wrist where she'd knocked it against the side of the glass at Matthew's words. Her stomach coiled at the innocent remark.

Carefully steadying it, Jason's eyes were focused intently upon the un-spilled juice. "No worries, Christina."

Matthew's eyebrows rose at the words, the quiet inflection in his son's usually jovial voice, his face shifting quickly toward his wife.

"I guess I'm a bit of a klutz without my morning coffee," Christina said, smiling brittlely down at her lap. Embarrassment flooded her system; she knew the table was watching her, dissecting her. "Th-thanks, Mary. For the breakfast," she emphasized, flicking a glance up at her hostess. She gestured to the plate with her fork. Her voice floundered a little. "This looks…really amazing."

Even Mary's eyebrows went up at that. Christina had long since stopped acting like a timid guest at their dining table and yet, here she was, practically squirming with shyness in her seat.

"Of course, sweets," Mary said, waving the words away. Then her eyes moved to her son, sitting quietly in his seat. Too quietly. He hadn't offered up so much as a chastising joke about Christina's fumbled orange juice. Indeed, he'd seemed almost protective in response to her chagrin. And had he called her *Christina*? Studying him closer, she caught the telling lines of strain creasing his forehead. Mary frowned. "You look tired, Jas."

As if on cue, he yawned. Stretching his back, Jason nodded. "Yeah. I had a hard time sleeping last night."

Christina choked on a mouthful of egg.

"You okay?"

"Christina?"

In response, she held up a hand. Swallowing hard, she muttered: "I'm fine." Her round eyes slithered up to Jason's hazel gaze and then skittered away again, just as quickly.

He stared back at her blankly.

"Yeah," Mary said, but her eyes were watching Christina a bit worriedly. "I thought I heard you prowling around last night."

"Christina?"

"What's wrong now—?"

With a frenetic movement, Christina tossed her napkin down on her half-eaten plate of food. "Actually, I just remembered…" Pushing her chair back, she didn't even bother trying to make eye contact with the faces turned to her as she brought herself to her feet.

She couldn't do it anymore.

"I have to go."

"Honey?"

Christina made a frantic gesture when she heard the note in Mary's voice, the one that hinted that an argument would ensue shortly. "No, I do. I-I, thanks again for…well, everything."

"Are you okay?" Christina hadn't realized that Jason had gotten to his feet too. Stunned, her eyes jerked up at the feel of his hand curling against her upper arm, gentling her movements.

"Yes. I just—I have…" She laughed with a husky sound. It was a mess.

Mary and Matthew exchanged more glances with one another.

"Goodness, at this rate, I'm not going to get to the office until almost ten o'clock."

"Make it eleven," Matthew countered.

"No. No, there's too much to do. I, ah, I'll see you later," Christina returned and the growl in her voice was not to be ignored. Then, with a twist, she broke free of Jason's hold. Smiling stiffly, she lifted her hand in a half-wave, but she didn't wait long enough to see if anyone responded. The kitchen, silent in the wake of her flustered exit, was alive with the echo of her scurrying feet clipping smartly toward the entryway.

Chewing on a thick slab of bacon, Matthew's frown deepened and the lines on his forehead wrinkled in consternation.

~ ✯✯✯ ~

Christina had been right. It was almost ten o'clock by the time she showed up to work. She breezed through the main lobby in a startling contrast to the woman who'd been at the Gordmans' breakfast table. Gone were the wrinkles, the limp clothes, the stale acknowledgment of a recycled outfit.

Underneath a long, coral-colored trench coat, beautifully turned out in a tailored suit with a glass-green button-down shirt, her feet tucked into black pumps, and her face and hair refreshed, Christina marched to her desk. She should have felt better. This was her power outfit, after all. It was the suit she wore when the company was meeting an important client. It showed off all her best assets in a demure and understated, though still unmistakable, way hinting at the feminine curves underneath the fitted jacket and blouse, the pants hugging the long, lean lines of her legs. She'd only ever felt confident, coolly in control when she put it on. Except for today. Today, she only felt like the fraud she'd confessed to being the night before. Entering the outer office to Matthew's suite, she popped her purse determinedly in the filing drawer she reserved for herself before chucking her coat over the back of her chair and moving resolutely to her computer.

She knew without bothering to knock on his door that Mr. Gordman was already in his office; she could see the faint line of light shining from under his door. Still, she was hesitant to knock and ask if there was anything he needed. And that was the whole problem, wasn't it? It was their standard operating procedure. She was his personal assistant, after all.

Making a face, Christina pulled up a necessary document on her computer screen.

Everything felt different. She felt different. She hadn't been so blinded that morning that she hadn't seen Matthew's searching look, his tense silence. Not much went unnoticed by Matthew Gordman. When he'd gone to bed the night before, everything had been as usual. Jason and she had been bickering as always, Christina had been warm and generous with Mary, but then this morning…well, try as she might, Christina had never been much of an actress.

Clearly.

She'd felt the friction in her shoulders, heard the mechanical tone of her voice.

She looked longingly at her boss's door. Every morning since she'd started, she'd greeted him with a cup of coffee and a notepad, ready to get a jump start on whatever project he had lined up that day. And now, here she sat, like a coward, unwilling to so much as announce her presence. It was supposed to be Jason she was uncomfortable being around. Not her boss. Not Mr. Gordman.

And yet….

It had spread. As she'd known it would. It had spread, just like last time.

"Ironic, isn't it?" she whispered to herself, the spreadsheet blurring before her unfocused vision. She'd stopped Jason last night because she'd wanted to avoid this scenario. Because she'd refused to ruin the great job she'd carved out for herself here. She'd refused to wreck the closest thing to a family she'd found in Matthew and Mary.

With her degree in business management, Christina was drastically overqualified to be a receptionist. Yet, every time a potential promotion had presented itself, she'd declined submitting her resume. And yes, she'd seen the slightly confused expression play out over Mr. Gordman's face each time he'd reflected on the applicants. It wasn't that she wasn't ambitious. She was. Truly. There were things she wanted to do, but…

Against her will, her eyes returned to his closed door.

But they would have taken her away. And she knew first-hand what happened when the ease of proximity was shattered by distance.

She stared blindly at her computer screen. Her fingers lay numb across the keyboard. She probably should be checking the company emails right now. It had been a long weekend. There was bound to be quite a queue in her inbox. If she did that, though, she'd eventually reach one that would need to be directed to Mr. Gordman for confirmation and—

"…Christina? I'm not sure if she's in yet. I'll go and check." The muffled words, coming from behind Mr. Gordman's sturdy door, jolted Christina out of her reverie. The statement was shortly followed by the muted sound of his shoes against the flooring.

With a half-strangled sob, Christina pushed her body roughly away from her desk. Bringing herself out of her chair, she was halfway across the cluttered office bullpen before she knew where she was going. Her heels clicked sharply against the concrete floor as she raced for the staircase on the other side of the building. Within minutes, she found herself on the basement level, her body propelling her furiously toward the only office down there.

Knocking sharply on the side of the already opened-door, Christina hardly waited for an answering response before stepping inside. A large architect table stood in the center of the room. Multi-colored posters of every shape and size were taped haphazardly to the walls. And sitting in the midst of this mess was a slim, dark-haired woman.

"Please tell me that after two months of dating, you've decided that Max's charms were greatly overrated?"

Without so much as a flicker of surprise, the brunette shifted from the mock-up laying across her desk to glance at Christina. She grinned dryly. "Hey, girl."

Christina nodded at her friend sharply. "Well?" She waited impatiently for the other woman to speak. A coworker in the graphic arts department, Jackie was probably the closest thing to a friend that Christina had—and that only because, with her faultlessly turned-out couture style, she'd been instrumental in helping Jackie attract the attention of her now-fiancé, Max Thompson. If Christina hadn't been in the building's bathroom when she had, if she hadn't intervened when she'd seen Jackie leaning over the mirror, desperately trying to pair her dark, petite looks with that garish red lipstick, well, Jackie would probably still be single, and Christina would be talking to herself right now. As it was, the girls had bonded over Jackie's ensuing infatuation with the gorgeous man and Christina's cunning at romantic machinations.

Leaning back in her chair, Jackie tapped a finger against her chin contemplatively. "You know, I'm kind of getting used to your particular way of beginning conversations."

Christina only raised an eyebrow.

Jackie smirked. "You know, without preamble or backstory?"

"One of my more attractive qualities, I'm sure," Christina replied, grinning a little herself. Then she straightened. "You still haven't answered my question."

"No, I haven't." Jackie pursed her lips. "Is this the part where I'm supposed to ask his name?" It was altogether too obvious that Jackie was enjoying this role-reversal.

Christina not so much. "I wouldn't if I were you."

"I see."

"Wipe that grin off your face."

"No can do, buddy."

"You suck."

In answer, Jackie reached across her desk for a large bag of candy sitting to one side of a stack of papers. She held it up for Christina's inspection. "Want some chocolate?"

Begrudgingly, Christina found herself being lured forward, her hand already reaching for the bag. "Shot of whiskey would be better."

Jackie gasped. "What would Mr. Gordman say?" she asked mockingly.

Christina bit her lip, her eyes closing painfully on the unintentional words. The hand holding the candy fell limply down to her sides.

Jackie pulled herself upright at that look. "Whoa. Hey. What's going on?"

Christina smiled thinly. "I've done something rather stupid, I'm afraid."

"I doubt that."

Christina shook her head.

Jackie's eyes narrowed. "Tell me." She pushed her work to one side of her desk. "Now."

Chapter Nine

Christina frowned. Taking out an individual bar of chocolate, she tossed the remaining bag of sweets back onto Jackie's desk. Turning, she paced, her hands repeatedly twisting and untwisting the candy wrapper in her hands, mangling the foil packaging hopelessly.

"Mr. Gordman asked me over for Easter dinner," she said quietly. She didn't see Jackie's eyebrows rise incredulously when she added quietly: "And things got a little, uh…"

"Oh, my God," Jackie whispered, her hands coming up to either side of her mouth. Her eyes widened nervously. "Oh, my God," she repeated, stunned. "Tell me you didn't?"

"Huh?" At her pleading tone of voice, Christina turned to look at her friend.

Jackie gulped, forcing the words past stunned lips. "Jesus. He's married, Christina—"

"Whoa. Wait." Christina held up a hand impatiently, cutting Jackie off midstream. She laughed. It held a decisive edge. "Do you think…me and *Mr. Gordman*?" Christina's face tautened self-righteously. "As if!" She threw her head back and laughed again, but she was clearly not the least bit amused by Jackie's assumption.

Jackie squirmed at the look on Christina's face. Shrugging defensively, she mumbled, "Well, you two have always been close."

"We're friends," Christina spat, her face flaming. "He's my immediate supervisor. And just so we're clear, I'm also quite close to his wife." Curling the piece of chocolate inside her fisted hand, she glared across the large architect table at her friend. "And I don't appreciate the insinuation that I, that I would…" The skin across her cheekbones turned blotchy, but Christina couldn't make herself finish that sentence.

Jackie had the grace to blush. Tucking her chin up to her chest, she mumbled, "Sorry."

"I'm not that kind of person," Christina continued fiercely, forcefully.

"No," Jackie agreed, smiling apologetically. "Of course, you aren't." She made a comforting gesture. "I shouldn't have said that. Only, it's the way you said it…"

"I wasn't talking about Mr. Gordman."

"Okay," Jackie agreed softly. "Then who?"

Christina made a great huffing sound. "His son!"

And the smile was instantly back on Jackie's face. "I see."

Christina's glare only darkened, but this time Jackie wasn't the least put off by it. "No. I seriously doubt that."

"Jason Gordman's hot," Jackie said with a slick grin.

"I thought you were supposed to be too besotted with Max to notice things like that?"

Jackie laughed. "True. But I'd met Jason long before setting eyes on Max."

"Whatever."

Jackie wiggled her eyebrows. "So, something's going on with you and the boss's son?"

Christina's left eye twitched slightly. "What? No. No."

"No?" Now Jackie looked thoroughly perplexed. "But you just said—"

Christina sighed. "Right."

"I'm confused."

Pressing her lips tightly together, Christina nodded her head once, sharply. "Me too." Her voice held a faraway sound as her eyes glanced absently at the shelves and filing cabinets lining one wall of Jackie's office.

"Well, whatever it was must've been a real doozy to get the usually so unflappable Christina, well, flapped."

Pushing the now rather mauled piece of candy into her pants pocket, Christina folded her arms tightly across her chest. Her eyes wouldn't look directly at Jackie, instead, they focused somewhere above her forehead. "He kissed me."

Jackie's eyebrows shot up. "I thought you said it was nothing."

"It was. I, it—he was just teasing."

"Oo-kay," Jackie sounded out slowly. "You two kid this way often?"

"Knock it off already," Christina pleaded, lobbing an irritated glance at Jackie. "Of course, we don't."

"That's why you're so flustered," Jackie said, smiling gamely. "You like him."

"Oh, don't be childish," Christina snapped, her high-heeled shoes marching pointedly from Jackie's desk to the door and then back again. This had clearly been a bad idea. "No—that's not…. You know me better than that."

Jackie tilted her head to one side in concentration. "Okay. And he made the first move?"

Christina gave her a dry look. "Yes!"

"Then what do you have to feel stupid about?"

Christina sputtered, her hands flitting around her person again, smoothing down her jacket, gesturing emptily. "I just, I told him I didn't find it funny…"

"Being kissed?"

"Jackie…"

The brunette held up her hands. "I'm just checking in."

"Yes."

"Because he offends you?"

Christina's eyes narrowed. "I'm not sure you're—"

"He's repulsive to you?"

Christina glared harder. "You know that's not—"

"Because you've secretly been dating someone else on the sly?" Jackie smacked the tips of her fingers against the edge of her desk. "You minx."

"No! I'm not dating anyone." Christina's voice was a mastery of frustration.

Jackie nodded. "Then you do like him."

Christina growled low in her throat.

"Just admit it." Jackie gave her a level look. "Because you're not hiding it very well anyway."

And just like that, Christina's shoulders sagged, her bravado petering out. "You can't tell anyone."

"Who would I tell?"

"I mean it, Jackie."

Jackie lost her wry amusement immediately, her face taking on a more somber expression. "Okay. I won't say anything."

"Nothing can come of it."

"Okay."

"It would be inappropriate."

Jackie cocked her head to the side. "Would it, though?"

"I'm Mr. Gordman's personal assistant."

"Yeah?"

"How would it look, me chasing after his son?"

"Sounds like he was the one doing most of the chasing."

"Dammit." Pinching the bridge of her nose between her fingers, Christina inhaled deeply. "You're not helping me here."

"What do you want me to say?"

"I don't know!" Throwing her hands up in the air, Christina's face flashed in a mesmerizing display of outrage, despair, and desperation.

Jackie whistled. Leaning back in her chair, she crossed her legs, smiling wolfishly. "You *really* like him."

"You suck."

"Yeah, I believe we've already covered that."

"Never mind," Christina muttered and with a last, disgusted look at her friend, marched toward Jackie's office door, her back stiff as she made to leave. "Thanks for nothing." With a huff, she walked out, her clipping footfalls hardly disguising the other woman's trailing: "Come on, you'd say the same thing to me. Christina!"

But Christina didn't respond, nor did she slow down. Instead, she took herself quickly and sharply back up the stairs and across the crowded cubicles littering the main floor. Her legs shook by the time she reached her desk. Jackie was right. In her shoes, Christina would have said the same things. Cut out the bullshit and get straight to the point.

The knowledge of this didn't make Jackie's words feel any less obnoxious, though.

The problem was, she did like Jason.

"But that's just too damn bad," she muttered darkly to herself as she plopped back down in her chair. She was done hiding. Nodding aggressively at the newfound strength in this declaration, she took a deep breath. Things didn't have to change. She could make sure of that. If it killed her, she could make sure of that. With a concentration she was far from feeling, she scanned Mr. Gordman's appointment book for the day, and though her finger shook slightly when she pressed the phone's intercom button, her voice rang out professionally enough.

"Morning, Mr. Gordman. Don't forget your one o'clock lunch appointment with…"

And just like that, everything went back to normal. Or, at least, normal enough. Mr. Gordman's voice answered her easily and when he asked for a brief conference with her in his private office minutes later, it was solely to discuss an interoffice memo he wanted her to draft up for him that afternoon.

It was only as she'd stood up to leave that he said: "How were the roads heading home this morning?"

"Not bad," Christina assured him, feeling her body react strongly to the concern in his voice—it never failed to shock her, how much she loved hearing it. She forced a chuckle. "Parking was a bit tricky from the plows."

Leaning back, he grinned. "Let me guess, snow piled high on either side of the street?"

"To my chin."

"I remember those days."

She grinned, slapping her notepad softly against the palm of her open hand. "Well, a certain worrywart I know gave me a shovel for just such instances."

Mr. Gordman smiled. "You're lucky to have him."

She rolled her eyes. "Oh, the luckiest. Sir."

He laughed that booming laugh that always made her feel at home. "All right, brat. Get out of here."

Back at her desk once more, Christina took a deep, calming breath. "It wasn't real," she whispered to herself, her fingers pecking faultlessly on the keyboard. Her chest released, and the next breath felt full, deep. "You imagined the tension, the weirdness. You're fine. *He's* fine."

And she could almost believe it.

The rest of the week seemed to only confirm this impression. She and Mr. Gordman's relationship resumed it's normal, everyday routine. Certainly, whatever awkwardness she'd felt with him early Monday morning seemed to have melted into nothingness—the workings of an overanxious mind. The misguided fears of a woman once scorned.

And okay, if her hands shook every time the phone rang, if her fingers hovered over the receiver as she tried to catch her breath, wondering if Jason was on the other end, and if she felt her heart kick hard against her chest every time she spotted a tall, slim shadow reaching the threshold of her door, her hands clattering nervelessly over the keyboard and eyes flying with breathtaking alarm toward the doorway, well, she tried not to notice that.

Certainly, she didn't let on.

She refused to let it interfere with her ability to do her job, desperately ignoring the slight itch of curiosity as to what he was up to, if he was thinking about her? She refused to let it stiffen her smile when Mr. Gordman teased her or inquired after her day; she pretended not to feel guilty when she lied to both him and herself. What had she done last night? She'd fallen asleep thinking about his son. No. Scratch that. She'd made dinner and read a book. Nothing too exciting. She wouldn't become a fumbling, bumbling mess of a personal assistant. She would remain the cool, collected Ms. DeLuca.

She wouldn't be distracted.

She wouldn't be tempted.

Not when she had so much to lose.

She'd been there, done that. Kisses led to empty promises, which led to broken homes and broken hearts.

Only. By Friday, Christina found that, with every client on the other end of the insistently ringing phone, with every unexceptional employee who entered her office, their earnest faces intent on seeing Mr. Gordman, her irritation rose. Her embarrassment swelled.

Really, Jason hadn't needed to pretend the kiss was so shattering just to spare her feelings. He hadn't needed to make such a show of wanting to kiss her again if, if...

Not a word. Not a drop-in. Nothing.

If this train of thinking failed to make logical, rational sense, Christina also chose to ignore that.

Christina frowned at the expense sheet pulled up on her computer screen. Stifling a sigh, she swiveled her chair around, her eyes darting to the tall windows covering the top half of the wall directly behind her desk. Spring in Minnesota could be absolutely beautiful. The smell of hot, wet pavement after a rain shower, the glow of yellow and orange flowers popping up all over the city.... Unfortunately, it could also be a washout of bluish gray overcast days. That morning was of the latter variety. Across the street, towering buildings stood glumly in the foggy haze of a downcast April morning.

Not a word. Not a drop-in. Nothing.

Unbidden, an image struck behind the back of her eyes, transporting itself from her memories—a thin, lean face smiling across a rose garden at a young, freckle-faced Christina. Holding out her hand, her palm thick with the rich dirt of the earth, the woman beckoned the child closer. Letting her head fall against the padded back of the chair, Christina felt tears swell under her tightly closed eyes. Her breathing quickened, tightened. Christina hadn't thought of her mother in years. An ache exploded in her chest as she allowed herself, in that silent, stolen moment to miss her. Terribly. Opening her eyes once more, Christina stared unseeingly out the block of windows, her gaze absently watching the busy sidewalk, the bicyclists and drivers bustling about in the fine mist below.

Up in her fifth-story suite, Christina felt alone, removed.

It would have been nice to talk to her mother about everything.

About Jason.

They used to have the best conversations.

"Come here, baby girl," she'd say when Christina would enter the house with a petulant expression on her face. Those long, elegant arms would open, those thin, tapered fingers coming to rest on Christina's young shoulders. "Tell me what's put that stink on your face."

Chuckling now, Christina felt her lips tug dangerously downward. She'd taken it for granted how special those moments were and how limited they would turn out to be.

Feeling her chest constrict a little on the thought, Christina twisted away from the window. That's when she saw him. She hadn't heard anyone enter the office. She'd been so lost in her thoughts, she hadn't realized someone was watching her.

With a yelp of surprise, her chair clattering wildly on the hard floor, Christina reached forward, her fingers gripping madly for the edge of the desk as she steadied herself.

"Jason." Her voice sounded breathless.

Smiling wryly at her ruffled expression, Jason nodded in greeting. "Hard at work, I see?"

She tossed him a dry glance, still struggling to regain her composure. "Oh, spare me."

He laughed.

"Wh-what are you doing here?" she asked. At his slow smile, Christina felt her cheeks tauten instinctively. Flipping her gaze downward, she took in the large desk calendar beside her computer. "I mean, I presume you're here to see your father?" Her finger was already moving blindly toward the intercom button.

He gave her a funny look. "Who else would I be here to see?"

Offering him an irritated glance, Christina seethed. "I'm sure I don't care one way or another."

"No?"

She smiled tightly. "You aren't on his schedule, that's all."

"Ah," Reaching inside his coat, Jason produced a pen. Grabbing for the desk calendar, he quickly swung it in his direction, blatantly ignoring her huff of indignation. With a scrawled, flourished scratch of his ballpoint, he wrote his name down. "We can't have that, can we? All fixed."

In response, Christina pressed her finger down on the intercom, her nail almost splitting from the force of the pressure. "Mr. Gordman," she called out, her voice unnaturally high. "Your son's here to see y—" she wasn't even given the chance to finish her sentence when Mr. Gordman's door opened, that man himself scuttling quickly out of it. As though he'd been only standing at the ready, his jacket was slung over the crook of one arm. His gaze zeroed instantly on Jason.

"Jas!" he cried, for all the world as though it'd been ages since he'd last seen him. Stepping forward, Mr. Gordman patted him rather avuncularly on the back.

"Ready for lunch?" Jason asked, flicking a look down at the watch on his wrist. He glanced over at Christina then, who, for her part, was trying to look both desperately busy with the single sheet of paper on her desk and totally disinterested with the display going on before her. "Hungry, Chrissy?"

Startled by the question, Christina didn't have time to school her features. Abandoning the paper in her hands (for really it was a lost cause; no one believed her anyway), Christina's eyes flew up to catch Jason's gaze.

"I, uh…"

"We're getting Thai," Jason continued, his eyes crinkling amusedly at the corners. "I believe that's one of your favorites."

But before she could fathom another thought, much less a word, Mr. Gordman was speaking. "Come on, Jason," he said gruffly, shucking into his jacket. "Let's get going. I've got a meeting at two o'clock." There was a barely perceptible pause. "Christina, you'll need to have the Benson file completed and on my desk by the time I return." He didn't so much as glance her way when he said this.

Blinking, Christina tried to catch her breath at the thinly veiled snub. "Of course, sir."

He nodded impatiently. "I'll be back in an hour." And then, as though he couldn't help himself: "Would you like me to bring something back for you?"

"Uh, no. I'm fine, thanks." The words were stilted, uncertain. Not that it mattered. He'd hardly waited for her response. Ushering Jason out into the bullpen, Mr. Gordman's long stride took them quickly through the building—his steps easy, relaxed...almost as though Jason hadn't just offered her an invitation to join them, as though Mr. Gordman hadn't just as obviously rejected it, just as though Christina hadn't been witness to it all.

Sitting at her desk, mouth slightly agape, Christina could do little more than watch furtively as they exited from her sight. She tried to swallow normally, but her body seemed to have stopped producing saliva. Her tongue felt thick in her mouth, her breathing coming too fast, almost choking her with the force. Humiliation, in all its myriad shapes, settled over her person. She could feel the infusion of heat coating her cheeks.

Mr. Gordman had excluded her. At this stage of preparation, the Bensen file wouldn't take more than a couple of minutes to organize and he knew that as well as she did. He'd rebuffed her presence, declined the pleasure of her company. Right to her face.

Because of Jason.

"Shit," she whispered to herself, turning forcibly back to her computer screen. The report on the screen blurred before her eyes. Rows upon rows upon columns of financial projections swarmed nonsensically…. There went her hope that Mr. Gordman hadn't noticed anything amiss between her and Jason.

There went her hope that nothing would change.

There went everything.

"Shit," she whispered again, for no other reason than the sound of her voice, no matter how small and fragile, filled the looming ache rising up her throat.

The imprint of Mr. Gordman's slighting hung like a heavy cloak over her shoulders. He'd never done that before. Ignored her. Left her out. Treated her as though…treated her as though she were merely his secretary.

Chapter Ten

For the second time in as many minutes, Christina felt that pinch in her stomach, a scratchy texture ripping at the backs of her eyes…and once again, she knew an almost overwhelming urge to see her mother, to talk to her, to call her up on the phone. Just to hear her voice. Staring harder at the computer screen, her eyes blinked that woman's face to life, transposing her image over the data on display there.

Dark blonde curls hanging just past her shoulders, paper-thin lines crinkling out from the corners of her eyes—this most noticeable on Sunday mornings when she used a little too much ivory-tinted powder as she preened in preparation for church services—startlingly green eyes, and a thin, hard mouth more prone to frowning than anything else. Yet, when she chose to smile, the result was masterful, always worth the effort; nothing else mattered but the upward curl of a burgeoning grin on her face. Natalie DeLuca was, had always been, a stunner. A tall woman, she'd never known weight problems, and hadn't easily suffered what she considered fools of this epidemic, nor had she ever truly faced the anguish of high-heeled shoes. Broad-shouldered, she'd have been masculine if not for the width of her hips, the shapeliness of her legs.

A fiercely proud homemaker, who'd wielded a sponge as determinedly as a judge with their gavel, she'd always been there when Christina got home from school, and always with a batch of hot cookies just out of the oven.

Though, if cookies and an apron slung over her hips sounded homey and sentimental, that was as close to that image as Natalie DeLuca truly got. She was a tough woman. Born on a farm with more brothers and sisters than there was food on the table, she'd learned how to fight. That's pretty much how she'd caught hold of Edward DeLuca—pure determination to never live that kind of life again. And lawyers' wives, after all, didn't have to worry about something as frivolous as a grocery bill. Yet, if you were lucky enough to be loved by her—Christina sniffed, the corner of her hand coming up to wipe at her nose discreetly—well, then you knew how comforting that fierce, fighting protectiveness was when it was defending you. How safe.

Almost without knowing it, Christina found her lips jerking up a little at the sides. If her mother could see her now, moping over a man! "Lift that chin up when you talk about yourself," Christina could almost hear Natalie say in that husky rasp she'd perfected over the years. "No man will make my baby feel less of herself. Especially when you've done nothing wrong."

Christina frowned.

Of course, that would rather be the tricky point, wouldn't it? Proving to her mother that, indeed, Christina hadn't provoked this undue attention on herself. That she hadn't chased after Jason in the first place. That she'd actually put her respect for Matthew and Mary Gordman above her feelings for a man.

No. Natalie wouldn't believe Christina.

After all, she'd been fooled by her daughter once before.

Shuttering, the memories transforming, turning nightmarish now, Christina could still hear her mother's voice screaming on that long-ago day, her face almost puce with rage when she'd found out, her thin cheeks pulled taut over a clenched jaw. Flinching, Christina tried to block the memory, but it shouted between her ears.

"What the hell were you thinking?" Shaking, Natalie's eyes had snapped fire. "You're, you're exactly what women are terrified of. Did you hear me, we're terrified of girls like you! Sneaky snakes in the grass who steal and lie, covet and cheat!"

Disgust had radiated off the pucker of her mother's lips, her hands, clutched into fists, shaking with fury and the purest form of disgust. Christina could still feel the curved design of the door panel pressing against her back as she'd slinked away from her mother's wrath, as she'd faced the reality of her actions, the consequence of what she'd allowed herself to do, to become.

What she'd become.

"I raised you better than that," Natalie had spat, her lips grimacing as they took in the shrinking form of her daughter. "I know I did. I know it! I sure didn't raise this," she insisted, her hand flicking over Christina's shaking person.

For her worth, Christina had tried to explain. "Mama, please!"

Flushing, Christina could almost still feel the crack of her mother's hand as it slapped across her cheek, the sting of the air as it pressed up against her raw, bruised flesh.

"Get the hell out." Natalie's voice had been strangely even then. "Get out. I don't ever want to see you again!"

Pressing her lips close together, Christina could all but rememb—

"Hey, Christina. Christina? Are you okay?"

Jerking up at the question, Christina half-turned to see Ashley Brightly, another in a long line of twentysomething office interns, standing beside her desk, a deep frown etched across her overly-tanned face. A couple pieces of paper were held tightly in her left hand, but then Ashley seemed to have forgotten them in her anxious scrutiny of Christina's pale countenance.

At the look, Christina felt the wet stain of tears pressing against her cheeks. She hadn't realized she'd been crying. Brushing them back with the cuff of her sleeve, she sniffed.

"Yes. No." With a sudden, desperate shake of her head, Christina rolled her chair back. "No. I'm not."

Ashley's eyes widened.

But Christina hardly noticed. She only knew she had to get the hell out of there. Now. Before she made an even bigger fool of herself. Gaining her feet abruptly, she tried to smile at Ashley. The result was an ugly twitch of lips and eyes.

"I have to leave," she insisted, grabbing her coat off the back of her chair. "Please tell Mr. Gordman..." She paused, shrugging into her coat. Honestly, she didn't care what Ashley told Mr. Gordman. "Tell him I'm not feeling well."

"Yeah. Sure thing," Ashley assured her, her head nodding along with this nonsense all too eagerly.

"Probably just allergies," Christina murmured, one hand chopping aggressively through the air in accompaniment. Prowling relentlessly toward the door, her eyes avoided Ashley's probing stare. "But I-I need a day."

"Sure..." but Ashley might as well have saved her breath. Christina was already gone, her steps, a little uncoordinated in her rush, taking her tersely through the bullpen and out the front door.

Wiping her fingertips impatiently under her eyes, Christina fumbled her key into the car's ignition switch. Cranking it over with more force than necessary, she nonetheless heard the gentle hum of the vehicle as it came to life. But even as it sat idling, offering an escape from the humiliation of her exit, Christina didn't back out of her parking spot.

Her neck seemed to collapse. Falling forward, her chin tucked into her chest as the sobs she'd held in check far too long—years too long—wracked her body. Her shoulders heaved violently, her stomach convulsing with the weight of her shuddering misery. It was stupid really, letting herself get so upset. She knew that, but all the same, heartbreak fell from her mouth in broken, gasping breaths.

It shouldn't have had the power to affect her this much. Not anymore. It'd been over four years since she'd felt the imprint of her mother's hand on her cheek, since she'd turned on her heels in the aftermath of that moment, marching up to her bedroom only long enough to pack one suitcase of belongings, the last of a lifetime of possessions.

It had been over four years since she'd last seen her mother. Natalie DeLuca had stood outside on the back steps, her arms folded tightly across her slim waist, expressionless as her daughter had walked away. The wind of a chilly autumn had lifted the edges of her blue paisley-patterned dress as she'd watched Christina clamor unsteadily into her car.

Pressing the palm of her hand tightly to her mouth, Christina meant to push it all back inside—the sobs, the wildness spreading through her body, the screams itching up her throat. Choking, she drove her hand all the harder against her lips, shoving back the urge for release, until she felt her teeth clench with the pressure.

But it achieved the desired effect. The distraction of pain stemmed her tears, the last rolling unheeded down her cheeks as she slowly dropped her hand down to the shifter. Her fingers curled against the plastic lever.

"Get a fucking grip," she whispered. With a jerk, she put the car into reverse and with a quick, hard stomp of her foot, she swung out of her parking spot.

Late model brick buildings with their banks of windows winked down at her as she pulled out onto the busy street. Concrete parking ramps, billboards half-hidden behind an overlay of business fronts and traffic signs, and a few faded canopies assaulted her senses, crowding her in. For the first time since she'd moved to Minneapolis, Christina wished to be far outside the city limits. The compulsion to leave was almost breathtaking as she braked to a stop, waiting at the first set of stoplights.

A sense of claustrophobia she'd never experienced before invaded her body. Her foot fidgeted nervously against the brake pedal in her desperation for flight. She just needed to get out of there.

No, she amended. She needed to go somewhere safe, quiet, someplace where she could lock the rest of the world away. She needed to go home. Before the rest of the memories from that day could force their way in…

Her lips twisted with self-depreciation. Because the loss and torment hadn't ended with her mother. Christina hadn't driven away from her family home in a cloud of dust like the ending to some Hollywood movie. No, it had been far more humiliating in its reality. The stubborn anger riding high in her stomach as she'd sped halfway across town, the mascara smearing black against her complexion, had only been the beginning…

She'd hardly been aware of the houses twinkling by as she'd driven that inauspicious evening, her flip-flop pressed firmly down on the pedal.

Chestnut Ave, Green Light Cir, County B—

Roads had whirled past in a distant blur she'd hardly had the presence of mind to notice. Her heart had been beating too hard in her chest, her breathing ragged as she'd anxiously sped forward, waiting for one particular street sign to come into view.

There.

Her lips had pulled into a hopeful smile as she'd thrown her left blinker on, the car slowing as she'd turned up an all-too-familiar road.…

"No." The sound of her own voice shook Christina from her reverie. With a shock, she saw her hands working on the steering wheel, watched as the quiet, sparsely tree-lined neighborhood sprang into view as she pulled up outside her apartment.

"Shit," she whispered as she navigated her car into a spot on the street outside the duplex she'd considered home for the past two years. She had no memory of her drive, no recollection whatsoever of exiting the business district. The ride had been totally eclipsed by images of the past.

Forcing away the feeling of anxiety that always clawed at her whenever she did something so completely on auto-pilot that she had no actual remembrance of it, Christina unfolded herself from the driver's seat.

Her heels clipped against the cracked sidewalk as she made her way toward her apartment's overly large, and badly chipped, blue porch. Its garish color was a stark contrast to the modest shade of her shoes as she mounted the first step. How different the ground under her feet had looked that terrible night, some four years ago. How utterly disconnected, the porch of her present from the professionally-stained wraparound deck of her past.

336 Harbor Lane.

She'd never forget it. Couldn't forget it.

A little over four years ago, a pair of worn flip-flops strapped to her feet, Christina had skittered up the crushed rock driveway of a home she thought she'd known well, the muscles in her neck pulsating visibly as the front door came into view. Twilight had descended, casting a thin veil of gathering night. The windows in the house had stared back at her darkly. Her car had sat untidily under the streetlight at the curb where she'd hastily parked it.

"God, you must've looked so pathetic," she spat to herself now, one hand clutching the railing as she climbed to the top of the slightly sagging porch. Her fingers were gripping her house keys too hard as her feet plunged forward, her mind reeling, spinning backward...

Christina hadn't gotten halfway up the short rocky drive when the front door had thrust itself open, a thin shadow emerging from within. In a flash, the dark shape was hurtling toward her, loafer-clad feet almost tripping in their haste, blocking her path.

Her lips pulled up tremulously when he came into full view. She opened her mouth to speak—

"What the hell are you doing here?" he hissed, one hand shooting out to grab hold of her upper arm and yank her out of sight, into the shadows. His fingers squeezed against the tender flesh. He glanced over his shoulder toward his still quiet house.

"My mom…" Christina's lips trembled. "You know what she—you know why I'm here."

That brought his head back around to her. "No! Absolutely not." His fingers cut into her skin at the words. "Are you out of your damn mind?"

"Stop!" she cried reflexively, pulling her arm back.

Vacantly, he dropped his hand down to his side. Then, just as quickly, he was running it through his hair, his eyes once again swiveling back to the house. The threshold remained empty, the front door firmly closed. His head slowly rotated back around. "What the fuck do you expect me to do?"

His eyes were accusing, defensive. Nothing like the way they'd looked before.

She lifted her hands weakly, let them drop. "Expect?"

He seemed to sag. "Fuck."

Christina reached out for him. "Look, it doesn't matter that she found out."

He swore under his breath.

"It doesn't! It's what we wanted—"

With an explosive gesture, he shook off her advances. "What we wanted?" He laughed. It had a hard, hollow sound. "No, it most certainly is not what *we* wanted."

Blinking stupidly, absolutely unwilling to process what he was saying, what was happening, Christina only continued to shake her head. "I don't understand."

He growled as he loomed over her.

She tried again. "You said—"

"Oh, hell!" With a curse, he was running his hand through his hair again, making the soft brown strands stand up in uneven clumps. "I said a lot of things. Most of them I regret now."

If she'd thought her mother's hand had left an impression…. Snapping her head back so hard it hurt her teeth, Christina's next breath came out in the shape of a hiccup. "Stop it. Bill, stop it!" she whimpered. "Why are you saying that? Why are you talking to me like that?" And on and on, she pleaded, her wide eyes running hopefully, fearfully over his strained expression.

He smiled thinly. "Because I want you to leave my property. Right now."

She remembered staggering backward, the heel of her left foot falling out of the flip-flop and stabbing against the powdery rocks. "Wh-what?"

"And I don't want you to ever return."

Though she'd hate herself for it the rest of her life, Christina had felt large, terrified tears sprint to her eyes. Her lips trembled so badly the words she spoke next were barely comprehensible as she stared at him. "But I don't—Bill, my parents kicked me out. I'm…I don't have anywhere to go."

"My wife is inside, Christina," he hissed, taking one intimidating step forward before bringing himself to a controlled stop. "What would you like me to do, hmm?"

Her lips quivered all the harder, and now it was her eyes that skipped across the immaculate lawn toward the curtained living room window. "Your wife?" The words echoed dully, flatly.

He lifted one stiff shoulder. "Don't, Christina. Don't say it."

"What about me?" she whispered petulantly, her eyes imploring, her mouth trembling.

He took a deep, stabilizing breath. "Christina…look, I'm sorry if you misunderstood the situation but this"—he gestured between them—"this was never supposed to be anything more than…than what it was." With what she supposed was diplomacy, he didn't actually say the words. Instead, he let the unsaid things hang meaningfully in the air between them.

"Why, of course," Christina insisted, sniffing back tears. She may have lost everything else, but she wasn't about to give up the last shreds of pride that remained. Her voice was watery. "How silly of me to believe all that bullshit you sprouted."

"Shh!"

"Yes, wouldn't want to upset her, now would we?" Her sneer was complete.

"Christina." He sighed, but there was a lack of real compassion in the sound. And she'd known. After all, he'd sighed with genuine longing for her at one time. And she'd fallen for it. "Look, I'm sorry, but—"

"I'll just bet you are," she said, her body ripping backward. "I'll just bet you are." With what dignity she had left, and admittedly it was almost none, she forced her feet to turn, to walk back the way she'd come, her ravaged face held high.

"Christina..." At the reluctance in Bill's voice, silly girl that she was, Christina stopped and turned back to him.

He made a gesture. "Just don't...don't do anything stupid."

She laughed. It had a wild edge. "I'm afraid it's a bit late in the day for the advice, isn't it?"

"Dammit, Christina!"

But that time she hadn't stopped. Her feet dragging, fumbling, half-slipping against the crushed rocks, she'd somehow managed to get herself back to her small, compact car. She'd somehow managed to drive away...

Her mind distracted by the chaotic onslaught of memories she'd vowed to forget, her hands shaking with the intensity of her shrieking past, Christina only barely succeeded in unlocking her apartment door. And not a moment too soon. Her feet only just passed over the threshold, shoes flung haphazardly in her wake, one arm swinging violently as she shut the door behind her, when she broke.

It started with one wrenched sob, as tears she'd thought long since shed and forgotten bubbled up to the surface, rising in her throat and frothing out of her lips in terrible half-strangled sounds.

Horribly unattractive.

And just as unstoppable.

Collapsing against one side of the narrow hall of her small entryway, Christina thrust a fist into her mouth, trying to curb the shocking sounds erupting from there, but to no real avail. Her blonde hair, mushrooming beside her face where it was smashed up against the wall, vibrated with the force of her crying.

The vaguely dirty edge of her thin flip-flop pressing down on the accelerator.

Her last view of Bill, shrugging with irritation as he turned back for his front door, dismissing her just that easily from his thoughts.

The image of her mother, standing stoically and unmoved as her daughter packed up her small car.

Trying to catch her breath now, her body slumping toward the hard tile of her floor, Christina felt her diaphragm marching to the beat of her rapid breaths. She'd gotten into her car that night, totally alone in the world. Totally lost. Scared. Forgotten.

Shucked aside like so much garbage.

Something oddly reminiscent of a laugh, if somewhat hysterical in nature, broke its way past Christina's lips at the thought. In the space of fifteen minutes on that long-ago night, she'd lost her home, her family, the supposed love of her life.

And it would only get worse from there, if that were possible. Because then she lost her friends. It was so low-brow, so beneath their class status, the shame and embarrassment of her particular situation. *That's what happens when you decide to, well, become like someone from the slums of society. I warned you but you wouldn't listen, would you?* her oldest friend, Miranda Crabtree, had informed her before turning and literally shutting her door on Christina's desperately pleading face.

Carolyn had been much the same, though less brutal. *I'm sorry, Christina. It's just...what would people say? I mean, Bill plays golf with my dad...it would just be too weird.*

Tanya had simply stopped taking Christina's calls.

"Hell," she said to herself now, her voice a croak of sound. Mortification swamped her all over again, as fresh as it had been all those years ago, making her body curl into itself. "Fucking love? Yeah right." And there was that laughter again only this time it was threading itself around her very words, shaking through the lines of her teeth.

It was with a sense of feverish relief that she felt the gurgle of amusement growing, driving out the last of her sobs, bitterness overtaking the sweeping grief. Wiping her face free of tears, Christina forced her feet back underneath her. Pushing one hand against the wall, she brought herself erect once more. Her stomach felt empty, quivering in the aftermath of a violent quake.

Chuckling now as she'd been crying moments before, Christina ran her fingers through her hair, settling the mussed curls as she moved forward, her bare feet chilled against the ceramic tiles. She left her purse on the floor by the door; she wouldn't need anything in there tonight. Carrying herself to the living room, the tips of her fingers trailed along the wall as she went.

Chapter Eleven

She'd done exactly as Bill had requested that night. She'd left his property and she'd never returned. Not even when he'd called her unexpectedly (or was it really so unexpected?) a few weeks later, the timbre of his voice flooded with apologies and promises anew. He was leaving his wife! For real this time. For her. He loved her! Couldn't she understand and forgive him? He'd been stupid, a fool to push her away. He hadn't meant it. It had just been the shock and surprise of it all. Couldn't they just forget that night on his lawn and yada, yada, yada.

She'd hung up the phone on him mid-excuse.

She'd learned too much by then to believe him. No, that wasn't quite it. She'd learned too much to want him anymore.

Christina could live with herself—barely—for what she'd allowed to happen with Bill. But she'd be damned if she'd let him ruin her life twice.

Twice!

With a little less than two hundred dollars in her banking account, after all, she'd been only twenty-three years old at the time, freshly out of college, and more-or-less living off her parents', Christina had walked away from Bill, she'd walked away from her mother and her father, she'd walked away from her friends and everything once familiar and safe.

She'd left town. Left Kerrington, Illinois.

Hell, she'd left Illinois.

And she'd never once returned.

"Not that anyone cared," Christina reminded herself with a scoff. Even Bill, she was sure, had suffered nothing more than hurt pride at her lack of response to his belated overtures of affection.

Without conscious thought, Christina's footsteps brought her to the smallish steamer trunk that doubled as her living room coffee table. Settled neatly before her couch, she'd found it at an antique store a couple of years ago, the right corner of which was slightly marred from what the owner figured had probably been a fire at some point in time. It had the old look of history, with its intricate buckles and straps, but Christina had never been fooled.

It was nothing more than a replica. Even the scorched fire marks she'd always considered looked a little too staged.

"Whatever," she muttered to herself as her fingers deftly worked the lock. With a creaking sound, she popped the lid open. The damp smell of must and old hay, which clung to the lining of the chest, invaded her nostrils as Christina slipped her hand inside; seconds later, she produced a bottle of cheap American whiskey.

She'd thought her friends would come to her defense eventually. She'd thought they'd miss her quirk and wit. She'd thought, given some time, they'd realize their mistake.

Turned out, she was the one mistaken.

And her mother...

Well, that was the worst of it.

Those first days, sitting in that ungodly motel, the only accommodation her meager savings would afford, her legs crossed anxiously over the edge of the bed, her eyes burning down at the terracotta-colored carpet, she'd waited, prayed for a phone call that never came.

She'd stayed in that low-rent scumbox for three days waiting for something.

Remorse.

Guilt.

The smallest act of love.

But her phone had remained silent.

She'd been abandoned. Forgotten.

On the fifth day of her exile, thoroughly fed-up with it all and refusing to remain in the squalor she'd found herself in, Christina had paid the motel manager, thrown her scanty belongings in the passenger seat of her Honda, and she'd driven north along the interstate—taking her car on its last trip down the freeway until she'd entered the city lights of Minneapolis, Minnesota.

A classmate from college, Toni, had moved there on the promise of a copywriting job at a small publishing house. When she'd heard that Christina had left home, though Christina had never told her the exact circumstances leading up to that abrupt exit—she hadn't been about to lose the last semblance of a friend she had—Toni had been quick and genuine in her offer to let out her spare bedroom.

Christina had waited four months before she'd shut off her phone and changed her number. It had been an act of rebellion, of devastating pain. In all that time, they'd never reached out to her.

Not once.

"My own mother," she whispered, unscrewing the cap on the bottle of whiskey. She didn't bother to hunt for a glass, instead tipping the bottle back against her lips. She took a long pull.

Natalie DeLuca had never once tried to contact her daughter. Not in all these years. For all that Christina knew, Natalie had been too busy all this time convincing anyone willing to listen that she'd never had a daughter—Christina who?

Then again, she'd never heard from her father, either. Though, to be fair, that hadn't really surprised Christina. After all, her mother had always called the shots in their family, and the first person she would have converted to the theory that Christina was nothing more than a figment of everyone's imagination would have been Edward DeLuca.

And for his Natalie, he'd have believed it.

But for all that, Christina had silently begged and entreated, waiting for her parents to forgive her, to tell her they still loved her. Assure her she wasn't a terrible person. And she'd needed to hear those things. Especially then, when she hadn't believed the truth in those words herself.

After those four months, when her phone had only rung with the few infrequent dialings of Bill, who'd refused to believe she'd be able to hold out on his charms for long—ha! Christina had given up.

She'd chucked her phone.

Literally.

After throwing it as hard as she possibly could against her bedroom wall, and watching the casing and battery fall out of the back, hearing the oddly satisfying sound of the screen cracking as it smacked against the hard surface, she'd felt something broken inside herself start to heal.

Staring past the cracked plaster of the walls, the overhead lights shining blindly down on the mess lying at her feet, she'd felt somehow vindicated. And just like that, she'd walked across the faded carpet of her room and into the kitchen where she'd grabbed the broom and dustpan and, with little more than an indifferent sweep of her hand, she'd caught up the remnants of her cell phone.

And the last tangible hold she'd had on her old life.

The next day she'd gone to get a new phone.

And that had been that.

Shortly after arriving in Minnesota, Christina had landed her job with Mr. Gordman. Two months after that, she'd moved into a studio apartment. About a year later, she'd moved here.

And not one other fucking thing had changed.

Sitting crouched on the floor, wedged between her couch and the steamer trunk, knees drawn up tightly to her chest, Christina stared numbly at the bottle in her hands. Across the room from her sat the television, but she hadn't bothered to turn it on. Hell, she hadn't even bothered to scoot up the foot and a half it would have taken to bring her seated onto her couch.

Her finger absently traced the paper label on the side of her whiskey bottle as she forced her mind to a quiet place. She'd somehow managed to thrust thoughts of Bill and her mother, those bastards she'd once called friends, those terrible moments before her life had changed irrevocably, to a hidden place. And all these years, they'd stayed safely tucked away.

But now that she'd opened that room, she couldn't seem to get the door closed shut again. Bringing the bottle back up to her lips, Christina took another long swallow.

At a sudden sound, a kind of rap-tap coming from outside, Christina stilled, lowering the whiskey as she tried to identify the noise. It came again.

And then it occurred to her. Someone was knocking on her front door.

"What the—?" Setting the bottle down on her carpeted floor, her fingers working the cap distractedly, she scrambled to her feet.

But she actually had a pretty good idea who it might be knocking at her door in the middle of the workday. Bracing herself for the look on his face, Christina took herself quickly back to her small entryway. Sucking in a boozy gulp, her fingers were already reaching for the doorknob as she spied a tall silhouette shadowed through the linen curtain pulled across the half-pane window of her door.

But when she swung the door open, Christina found she'd been wrong. It wasn't Mr. Gordman standing on the other side of the threshold, coming to check in on her with that knowing, concerned look on his face that clearly said he hadn't bought her flimsy sick leave excuse.

At least, it wasn't *that* Mr. Gordman.

"Jason?" Christina's forehead wrinkled in confusion. She looked somewhat desperately over his shoulder, but he appeared to have come alone. "What the hell are you doing here?"

His lips made a grim line. "You left work."

"Ever the observant one." Gripping one hand to the side of the doorway, Christina stared him down.

"Heard you went home sick."

She raised an eloquent eyebrow. "Yeah?"

"Drinking, Christina?"

She gasped.

He nodded. "Judging by the smell of liquor on your breath, if you're not actually sick now, you will be shortly."

"Quite the deductionist, huh?"

"Hardly a prophetic gamble," he quipped.

"Hardly your business."

Jason shrugged. "Bound and determined to end up with your head in the toilet?" he mused, but without much humor.

Her fingers tightened their hold on the doorknob. She sighed. "Jason, just go home. Or better yet, go back to work."

He grinned unrepentantly. "It's spring break. School's out for the week."

She nodded slowly. "And?"

With a quick, uncharacteristically conscious movement, Jason rammed one hand through his hair. "Look—"

"Why are you here, Jason?" Christina asked. "Just so damned worried when you heard I wasn't feeling well that you had to rush down and make sure I was still breathing, that my head was above the toilet water?"

The mockery in her voice hit hard. Jason frowned. "No."

"Then what?"

"I need to talk to you. When I got back to the office and you were gone…." His fingers splayed through the short hair at the crown of his head. He sighed. "I didn't think it should wait."

"What the hell are you talking about?"

"He knows."

Christina stilled at the words, her body buzzing, nerveless fingers letting go of their hold on the doorjamb. "What?"

Jason's face was somber as he repeated himself: "Dad knows. About us."

Her teeth snapped together at the words, her body springing stiffly erect despite the low fizz of appeal those words fostered in her chest. "There is no us," she hissed.

"Well, hell," he replied, throwing his fingers through his hair yet again. "You know what I mean." And for once, he didn't sound amused.

"What? How?"

He held up a hand. "I didn't tell him, if that's what you're thinking."

She stared at him dumbly.

With a meaningful look over his shoulder, taking in the empty porch and side street behind him, Jason turned back to Christina. "Listen, can I come in?"

It took her a little too long to respond, but finally, Christina nodded. With a slightly less than gracious move, she took a step back, waving him inside. "Why not?" she tossed out, turning on her heel as he crossed inside. "The damage has already been done, right?"

Without waiting for him, Christina returned to her living room, only this time she took a seat on her couch. Sitting primly on the edge of the farthest cushion, she watched him enter.

With a barely perceptible glance at the bottle of whiskey hugged up beside the steamer trunk, Jason followed Christina's lead, nabbing the small accent chair just to her right. Leaning forward, each arm braced across the tops of his thighs, Jason gave her a direct look. "If it's any consolation, I'm the one he's mad at."

Christina picked at a loose nail. She wasn't sure that it was, actually. Finally, she screwed up the courage to face him. "What happened?"

He shrugged. "Hell if I know. One minute we were ordering Pad Thai and the next he was asking me—" Pausing, Jason shook his head. "He figured it out on his own. I mean, he didn't know the details or anything, but he knew something was up. Apparently, we, neither of us, are any good at acting."

She nodded once, distracted. She supposed it explained one thing: why Mr. Gordman had deliberately excluded Christina from their lunch.

Jason pursed his lips amusedly. "And if he hadn't known already, your abrupt departure this afternoon would have *probably* tipped him off."

Though she wanted to defend herself, Christina swallowed the instinct. Instead, throwing her hair back over her shoulder, she pinned him with an expectant stare. It was ironic, all the times she'd found herself picturing him inside her apartment…and now that he was there, she wished him anywhere else. "What did you tell him? I mean, about that night." She tried to force her breathing to a quiet rate. Oddly, she felt calmer than she would have expected. A familiar sort of feeling settled over her shoulders. Her body went still, a defense mechanism she'd learned four years ago, steadying her nerves, bleeding, blotting out the emotion. She'd survived this kind of thing once before. The fallout. The repercussions. She braced herself. She could do it again.

Jason shrugged. "What could I tell him? The truth."

Closing her eyes painfully, Christina felt herself sinking into the leather upholstery. Dammit. Okay, maybe she wasn't quite as emotionless as she'd thought.

"I told him I made a pass at you, and that you politely but firmly rejected me," Jason continued softly. At the words, Christina's eyes popped back open.

Her brown gaze clashed with his hazel one. Again, she saw a gentleness in his expression. It was almost her undoing. "You what?"

Jason's hands were steepled together, his chin resting on top of them as though he were deep in thought. "I told him you were quite clear that nothing could happen, that you weren't interested in pursuing something that could potentially affect your working relationship with my dad."

Christina's eyes widened. "What else did you say?" The words came out as mere whispers of disbelief, her fingers clenching together tightly as she waited for the ball to drop.

He half-grinned. "Nothing. What else was there to say? That was that, and I told him so."

She felt her eyes narrow in consideration, her chin tilting a little to one side. "You know as well as I do that that's not exactly—"

Christina wasn't allowed to finish her thought. Jason cut her a sideways glance, a devilish gleam entering those hazel eyes. "Do I look like a stupid man to you?"

Christina gave him a quietly pensive look. No, at that moment he looked more attractive than any man she'd ever seen. Protective. Strong. Kind. "That's all you said?"

"That's all I said."

She let out a loose breath. "And that was the end of it?"

"Yes."

Holding her body stiff, Christina just managed to suppress the shudders that threatened to topple her with relief.

"And Matthew? What did he say?"

"Nothing," Jason said, shrugging. "He went back to ordering lunch."

"And that's it? He knows that nothing happened? Subject closed? No more questions?"

Jason nodded. "No more questions, no more anything," he restated patiently.

Christina's eyes closed momentarily as she savored the words. A deluge of feelings swept over her senses. The intoxication she'd been keeping so carefully at bay up to then swarmed in dizzying spray, beating against her head. A small, forbidden rebellion crept to the surface; *Matthew knew just enough now to be dangerously unaware.*

Blinking, Christina balked at her unguarded thoughts. Still, her eyes shifted restlessly toward Jason, his trim, fit body leaning forward earnestly in the chair, a few errant strands of hair falling boyishly over his forehead. And she ached. She ached for his mouth. His arms. For everything she'd been forced to deny herself. "Thank you," she said softly, "for not telling him…well, you know, everything."

He hadn't betrayed her. Hell, he'd taken the blame for her.

Jason sighed. "Of course. I'm not vindictive, you know. What you said," he shrugged nonchalantly, as though this were a normal, everyday conversation, "that was private, just between us."

Just between us. Subject closed. Private. The words swirled attractively, chaotically, woozily. A minor infraction. Just between them. *No more questions.*

Mistaking her silence for disbelief, Jason growled. "Jesus, Christina, I know I may tease you from time to time but—"

She pursed her lips. Relaxed now as she'd been taut moments before, her body felt suddenly fluid, flushed with reaction—her head whirling with the residual, leftover remnants of unexpressed anxiety and the numbing, loosening agent of whiskey. Leaning forward, she felt her hair spill over one shoulder. She watched, amusedly, as his eyes instinctively followed the movement. "But you're a man of honor?"

He stared across the small space separating them. His eyes held an intensity she wasn't often allowed to view. "Yeah. I like to think so." Then he smiled.

She laughed. It had a husky note to it. In the maelstrom of sensations assaulting her, of impulses she couldn't begin to sort out and untangle, she welcomed the recklessness stealing over her, blinding her to reality, distracting her. "Yeah? What happened to forewarned is forearmed?"

His face flushed, his eyes narrowing speculatively, gauging her expression. "I thought you wanted me to forget about that night."

She shrugged artlessly. "And I thought you were going to convince me otherwise."

Jason's mouth moved, but for a moment no words came out. The conversation had changed tacks so drastically, so quickly. "What is this, Christina?" He sounded wary, uncertain. Still, something darkened in his gaze.

She took her time answering, as if in consideration. In truth, she knew exactly what it was. Self-punishment mixed with just a little bit of carnal lust—an almost uncontrollable need to forget the knot of fear still crawling at her throat, for a weakness to hate herself for later. "*This*," she stressed, leaning forward, "is something private, as you so eloquently put it. Just between us."

She curved her lips upward in a practiced move of seduction. She'd learned a lot from Bill.

"Nothing happened, right? Subject closed? No one's asking any more questions?" Christina's smile lengthened as she saw Jason connect her meaning. "Might as well use the advantage while we've got it. That is, if you have any more theories to test out?"

Chapter Twelve

A beat of shocked silence rang through the small apartment. Perched on the edge of her seat, Christina waited—but when another long second passed, followed by yet one more, she felt the beginnings of rejection settle over her skin.

Sitting on the chair beside her, his body leaning forward, Jason still hadn't uttered a sound. Indeed, his lips seemed to be stuck, silently formed around the beginning of a question. Only his eyes, which had grown steadily wider, showed any form of reaction to her words.

Briskly, with the weight of humiliation hanging over her shoulders, Christina slapped her hands against her knees and with that, got to her feet.

"Or maybe not," she muttered, but she couldn't make herself look at Jason when she said this. The best she could do was an empty gesture in his general direction. "Try not to overthink it okay, Jas? It was only an idea. Clearly, a stupid one." Letting out a weak laugh, she walked toward her kitchen.

She didn't need anything in there, didn't, in fact, know what she'd do once she made it inside the small space. All she knew was it was the only room in which she wouldn't have to stare into his knowing eyes. It was little more than a stall tactic, a way to expedite his no doubted hasty exit.

Her stride never wavered, not even when she flapped a dismissive hand back toward the bottle of whiskey still on the floor. "Hell, let's blame it on the alcoh—ah!"

With a gasp of surprise, Christina felt two hands grip the backs of her arms, and then she was being spun around, and before she had time to get in a proper breath, she felt her body being pushed backward, forced up against the wall separating her living room from the kitchen. Her chest heaved at the abruptness of it all, her frantic eyes clashing with Jason's stormy glare.

His body was pressed up tight to hers. She could feel his quick breaths. She could feel the muscled proximity of his thighs crowding against hers. That, for some reason, calmed her a little.

"Shut up, Christina," he said, his voice gruff with the words, erratic. His eyes traveled over her face, his gaze stopping curiously over her parted lips. "Give me a damn minute to catch my bearings."

In control again, Christina laughed up at him coquettishly. "You need a minute to decide if you want to kiss a woman?"

His eyes narrowed. "You have a way of confusing me."

She licked her lips, her body tingling at the intensity in his eyes, at the feel of his weight enveloping her. "Then, by all means, tell me what you want."

"Hell—" With little more than that rough word hanging in the air between them, Jason's head dipped, his lips crashing into hers. It wasn't a light kiss. It didn't linger over her lips, playing teasingly there.

No, it was almost desperate in its heatedness. No sooner had his mouth touched hers than Christina felt his tongue skimming against the seam of her lips. With little more urging than that, she obliged him. Moaning at the insistent pressure, at the feeling of his lips twisting, biting, sucking against hers, his tongue plunging into the recesses of her mouth, Christina sank against the wall behind her.

His hands were at her waist now, guiding her hips more firmly into the curve of his lower body. Christina's legs trembled at the contact, her tongue pushing against his in response, tangling with it as her fingers slowly trailed up and down his chest, searching, desperate, unwilling to stop until she'd touched everything in reach.

Breaking her lips just slightly from his, her breath falling hotly against the side of his neck, she whispered into his ear, "Is this what you want?" Her hands were already feeling for the top button of her blouse. With a flick, she popped the first one free, then the second, her body arching under his heady appraisal.

The sound of mingled breathing filled the room as she let her fingers slide down the front of her shirt. "No strings, no expectations," she promised him, peeking up through the fringe of her eyelashes. She snapped the third button free. "Just a little fun."

Jason's mouth was on hers again before she finished speaking, only now his hands were thrusting themselves through her hair at the base of her neck. His teeth nibbled against her lower lip as Christina's hands dipped steadily lower down her shirt, until the last button was loosened, the blouse hanging open at her sides.

Rocking her hips, her back bowing with the movement, she wordlessly urged him to touch her. In response, his left hand lowered, his fingers trailing across her shoulders, following the motion of her body, answering her silent plea until they captured the lacy cup of her exposed bra. When the heat of his palm enveloped the sensitive skin, she felt her neck droop back bonelessly against the hard plaster of her wall; the guttural sound of her whimper echoed across the room, swarming them, surrounding them. When his thumb ran across the silky material there, her legs buckled.

"God, you're beautiful," he breathed, his lips trailing the lines of her exposed neck, nuzzling softly.

She pressed her body fully into the weight of his hand. "Convenient too," she reminded him breathlessly.

"What?" Lifting his head, Jason gazed down at her. Nonplussed, his hand lifted just slightly from its contact with her body.

But Christina only shook her head, her arms drawing him close again. Her lips licked against the lobe of his right ear. She laughed throatily. "You don't even need to tell me you love me." She bit down softly on his cartilage.

"Wait. What?" Straightening slightly, her lips falling out of reach, he shook his head. Blinking, his eyes cleared at the cynical twist of her features. "What the hell are you talking about?" Casting off her advances, Jason took a short step backward. His eyes were alert suddenly. Guarded.

Christina smiled playfully. "No talking. No feelings. Just sex." Twirling a finger over a button on his shirt, she smiled. "You use me. And I use you right back. No one gets hurt."

"Jesus." Jason's head reared back. Then he took another step away from her.

Christina felt the rush of cool air hitting her bare skin in his absence.

"No." He shook his head once. "What the hell, Christina?"

"Well, there's no reason to look scandalized," she drawled, but all the same, she felt the shift in the air, the tension filtering between them. Still, she waited, her back still slightly arched, inviting.

His eyes, however, didn't waiver from her face. He winced at the expression he saw there. "No reason to make it sound cheap, either."

"It is cheap," she returned easily. But there was something in the way he was looking at her that caused Christina to catch the folds of her shirt and wrap them back around her body. She laughed. "You're going to tell me I'm wrong?"

"I don't even know—" He took a deep breath, his hands gesturing wildly, his eyes flickering stonily. "Is that what you think of me? Of yourself?"

Christina's eyes widened, the muscles in her neck flexing at the chastising tone of his voice, the distaste laced so intricately within those words. Sobering, her fingers tightened their hold instinctively on the edges of the shirt draped scantily across her upper body.

Jason sighed, one hand scraping through his hair. "I don't underst—"

"Get out." Stung to the point of excruciating shame, Christina's voice was a rough squawk. When Jason didn't immediately move, she felt her lungs expanding painfully. "Get out. Get fucking out!"

Jason stilled. "Christina?"

"Now, Jason. Right now."

He held up his hands. She watched as belated remorse entered his eyes. "Whoa. Wait. I'm sorry. Christina, I didn't mean to—"

"Leave!" she shrieked, her voice cutting him off midsentence. Blotchy tears filled her vision. Clutching the sides of her blouse with one hand, she pointed toward the door with the other. Her eyes blazed across at him. "Go. Jason. Please, just go."

It was that last pleading command that made up his mind. With one last futile look, Jason turned and did as she requested.

It was only at the small catch of the door shutting behind Jason that Christina felt the first spasm of reaction slither across her skin. Face flinching with disdain, shoulders heaving with the force of her confusion, soon her entire body was shaking, trembling. For the second time that day, she found herself sliding in a freefall down her wall. Bending her legs up tight to her chest, she bit down brutally on her bottom lip. Shame and misery vied for attention as tears she refused to shed misted in her eyes.

"Shit," she moaned, her arms wrapping themselves around her body as she let her forehead fall onto her knees, her throat gulping down the wash of quaking wails shimmering in her stomach, the regrets desperate to retch themselves out her mouth. "Get it fucking together."

"It's not worth it," she muttered, rocking slightly forward and then back, her words a soft command. Hiccupping hoarsely, she felt the jarring pace of her breathing as she fought for enough air to breathe. Slowly, she swayed to a stop, exhaustion falling over her.

"What is wrong with me?" she mumbled as she curled up, lying down on her side, the soft fuzz of the carpet tickling her neck. "What the hell is so wrong with me?"

What had she been thinking? Jason had come to tell her that everything was okay—if slightly awkward—on the Gordman front. She should have left it at that. Certainly, that's what he'd expected her to do. It's what she would have predicted she'd do. Instead, she'd thrown herself at him. Worse, she had absolutely no idea why she'd done it. And then…God, he'd denied the invitation.

At the last thought, Christina's eyes winced closed. Pressing them tightly shut, she welcomed the blackness which seemed to swirl behind her eyelids, blotting out the look on Jason's face, the shock and suspicion in his eyes when he'd jerked away from her, the muscles of her eyes squeezing harder and harder until a kaleidoscope of colors exploded against the inner-veil of her lids. Focusing on the pop and ricochet of the bombastic sprays of gold and blue and green splashing behind her closed eyes, she felt her body start to loosen, her breathing slow. It was a technique she'd learned to master a long time ago—a painful but effective way to escape, to bolt down and block out the threats pressing against her consciousness.

"You don't even have the right to be pitied," she guzzled, sniffling almost lazily now as the sweet weight of fatigue began to settle over her fraught nerves. "You're the asshole here."

With a concentration she'd carefully procured, Christina fixated on the whirling light show still billowing across the canvas of her eyelids, the soothing hum emanating from the insides of her ears as she plugged her nose, anything to stifle, to drive out the painful reminder brimming just beyond the distraction.

Sinking into the floor, her limbs growing heavy, her chest relaxing, Christina allowed her mind to slowly drift as she fell into a shattered sleep—but not before one lone, solitary tear wedged itself past those tightly closed eyes, tracking a cold trail down the side of her nose to settle in a pool at the edge of her lips….

She woke up the next morning in that same position.

It was the ringing of her phone which roused Christina from her slumber. Groggy and stiff from the hard, scratchy surface, she blinked slowly awake. Her eyes were dry and itchy, and the worst kind of headache beat at her temples.

Just another reason that crying was the absolute fucking worst.

"Oh, for Christ's sake, shut up," she mumbled at the insistent chirping of her phone. After crawling semi-drunkenly toward her purse, which was sitting in a heap by the front door, she ruffled frenetically through the designer bag, snatching hold of her cell phone on the fourth, shrill ring.

Automatically, her eyes lowered, checking the caller ID.

Shit.

Christina froze at the sight of the name flashing across the screen, her thumb hovering over the answer button uncertainly. Images of the previous evening flooded her awareness, reminding her all over again of what she'd said, what she'd done—hell, what she'd practically begged *him* to do. For the first time in memory, she considered ignoring the call.

She couldn't handle this.

The phone rang again.

Well, it wasn't like he would've told them what had happened last night.

"Dammit." With a jerk, she felt her thumb swipe right. Bringing the phone up to her mouth, Christina cringed. "Hello?"

"Thank God! I've been trying to call you—"

Christina's throat tightened. "Oh. Uh. Sorry, I, um, I overslept."

"It's fine, it's fine," Mary said, sounding distracted but to Christina's overly sensitive ears, not particularly upset. "Listen, now that I've got you, can I ask a favor?"

Christina frowned even as relief swarmed her stomach. Nodding dumbly, she tempered her voice. "What? Sure—"

But Mary was already talking, her voice rising sharply. "Is there any chance you'll have time to stop by the bank this morning?"

Christina's eyebrows furrowed. What? "The bank?" she queried. "Why?"

"Well," Mary sighed dramatically, "I was supposed to break down some change for the cash box, but I completely ran out of time. I'll reimburse you for the money when you get here."

"Oh." Christina squinted past the dried clumps of mascara clinging to her eyelashes. Her wits felt slow, addled. She wasn't sure what to say to that. Fact was, she didn't have a damn clue what Mary was rambling on about. "Um, actually…"

"Do not tell me you're canceling on me." There was no mistaking the threat in Mary's tone.

Christina felt her nose crinkle. "Canceling?"

"Listen, Shelley already texted me yesterday with some lame excuse as to why she couldn't come, and Sharon's mother isn't well, so she had to back out too."

Christina fought hard to make some semblance of sense out of this.

"If you don't show up, there won't be anyone to run concessions," Mary continued.

"Concessions?"

"For the baseball tournament!" Mary said exasperated. "Please tell me you didn't forget."

And suddenly, Christina heard the soft strains of a half-remembered conversation float through her mind. Closing her eyes, she nodded. Dammit. It had been at Easter dinner—

"Well, you say I don't have any faith in your baking abilities. Here's your chance to prove me wrong. Are you in?"

Christina nodded quickly, desperate not to be found out unawares. Her fork played absently with the turkey on her plate. "Oh. Yeah. Sure, okay."

Jason grinned at her knowingly.

"What?" she asked him against her better judgment, setting her fork down sharply. She hated that grin.

"You have no idea what you've just agreed to, do you?"

Christina sputtered. "I'm sure I don't—"

"Don't tell me we caught you daydreaming again?" Mary asked.

And they had. Only she'd refused to admit it. She'd refused to admit she hadn't been paying a lick of attention to Mary. And once again, Jason had been right—she'd had only the haziest idea of what she'd agreed to.

But it was coming back to her now. Mary had needed volunteers to help run the admissions and concessions booths for the Caldwell High School baseball team's Midwest Best Tournament. Caldwell High School, where Jason worked not only as a political science teacher, but also served as the head coach of the boy's baseball team.

Shit.

Shit, shit, shit!

"No. No, I didn't forget," she said, speaking quickly. "But, ah, but I actually I don't think I *can* go…"

"What?!"

"I'm sorry—"

"Christina, I need you there today." Mary sounded frantic and more than a little overwhelmed. "I can't do it all alone!"

Her lips compressing in a tight line, Christina swallowed twice. Either way she sliced it, Mary sounded upset. Clearly, the woman was desperate. Hell, she was practically crying. And all because of Christina.

"It's just," Christina licked her lips nervously. Her fingers tightened around her thin black phone. "Jason and I sort of had words yesterday…" That was putting it mildly.

Mary made an amused sound. "Oh, is that all?" She laughed. "Shoot. You two are always having words."

Christina blew out a hard, long breath. "Yeah, not like this."

"Why? What happened?" Immediately, her tone shifted—carrying that particular mixture of suspicion, expectation, and concern that mothers seem to come by naturally.

Christina felt her stomach clench. There was absolutely, one-hundred-percent no way she could tell Mary. Her face flamed at the mere thought. It had been a mistake, saying even that much. Mary was like a bloodhound when she smelled a story.

"No-nothing. I mean…." Christina felt her lips twitching, her body tingling at the realization of what she had to do—her only means of escaping this particular conversation. "What, ah, what time do I need to be at the ball field?"

"Really?" Mary's voice was carefully hopeful. "Ten-thirty. And Christina, thank you."

"Of course."

"Don't worry," Marry assured her, "I'll make sure Jason doesn't bother you one bit."

Christina's finger picked absently against a scuff on the heel of one of her shoes. "Yeah." She sighed. "That'll be the day."

Chapter Thirteen

Twenty minutes later, Christina reluctantly locked the door to her apartment building, her eyes staring pleadingly up at her bedroom windows as though the inanimate objects could somehow throw her a lifeline, give her some reason to run back inside…

No such help came.

Defeated, she walked to her car. Pulling the zipper of her thin coat up a notch higher, she shivered. It was a blustery April morning, and she spared a thought to the poor kids that were going to have to play out in this weather. Shoving her hands deeper into the silk lining of her jacket, she only hoped the concessions booth would be kept suitably warm. Well, whatever. She'd brought along a pair of mittens, just in case.

Tugging her hair, wet thanks to a frantic shower, through the back of the ball cap she'd unearthed in her closet, she sighed. Her look was hardly glamorous but then, she didn't feel beautiful. She felt ragged and worn. Dried out and shriveled.

Scrambling inside her car, Christina made a mental note of the errands she had to run yet.

She needed to go to the bank.

The grocery store for hotdog buns and hot chocolate packets.

And then Carmen's Bakery.

This particular tournament was being hosted by one of the myriad organizations Mary belonged to—and so, among the regular hamburgers and potato chips, the concessions was also hosting a bake sale, with cookies, pies, brownies, and whatnot. All to which Christina had agreed on Easter to help produce. All of which meant, well, that she was calling in reinforcements. In the name of the local bakery.

Pulling out of her parking spot, Christina chanced a quick glance at the radio clock. It was only a little after nine in the morning. It was going to be an impossibly long day.

At least the acid churning, eating away at her stomach, which had seen her repeatedly sprinting for the bathroom ever since waking up, had diminished to a dull ache. Still, breakfast had been out of the question. Hell, she still wasn't sure she could even swallow a cup of coffee. Her head thrummed in the aftermath of the night before…and okay, maybe a little bit due to the whiskey. Torturously, her mind kept replaying the things she'd said, the things she'd done.

The way he'd reacted.

And no amount of "Well, what's done is done, you can't change the past" helped. Every time she thought about Jason, and it was almost ridiculous to think that more than five minutes spanned between bouts of that pastime, her face felt hot all over, her hands shook, and this weird sort of hollowness erupted inside her body.

She felt like dry-heaving.

And yet, in a weird way, she wanted to see him. To get it over with, the meeting after, to put the whole sorry business behind her, relegate it to a best-forgotten memory and move on—to quiet the regrets swirling around inside of her, threatening to engulf her….

But hey, at least her stomach felt better.

~ ☆☆☆ ~

If Christina had hoped her conflicting emotions would eventually settle to a noxious, if idle and avoidable awareness, she was doomed for disappointment. Parked in the school lot, sitting half-hunched in her car, she felt full-blown panic flood her system. She'd no sooner arrived than she'd spotted Jason's SUV, sitting snugly beside any number of buses. Just the sight of it had sent her senses spiraling, knocking around inside her. After a quick, surreptitious glance around the ball field, her eyes located him in one of the dugouts with what looked to be the team manager, a sloppily attired man wielding a clipboard.

The team was busy practicing on the field.

Jason's back was turned to her, had been, in fact, ever since she'd pulled onto the school grounds. He couldn't have known she was there. Even if he turned around, he was probably too far away to see her. Yet, she felt the magnetic pull between them, was sure that he felt it too.

And, of course, there was Mary. Buzzing around, her hair flapping in the breeze, she was hard at it, setting up a sign in front of the food stand, informing passersby about the fundraiser going on.

Peering out over her steering wheel, Christina huddled down even farther into her seat. In a minute, she'd get out of her car. Maybe two minutes. Mortified by her cowardice, still she didn't move. Imagine, Christina DeLuca crouched low in her seat, sweat pooling coldly against her deodorant, eyelids flinching as she hid half-seen in her very conspicuous vehicle.

With a dozen desserts stacked up behind her.

The last thought brought a begrudging smile to her face. She couldn't let Mary down, could she? Then again, she had no idea how she was going to handle being around Jason. She wasn't sure she *could* be around him. But Mary was counting on her. What if Jason ignored her?

God. What if he didn't?

"Christina! You're here, oh, thank you!" At the squeal of sound coming right outside her door, accompanied by the wrap of a knuckle against the window, Christina's gaze jumped, following the noise. She'd been so lost in her thoughts she hadn't seen the small woman approach.

Before Christina could so much as respond, Mary pounced. With an impatient tug of her wrist, Mary swung the door open unceremoniously, the action effectively ending Christina's reign of concealment.

Desperately trying to look like she hadn't just been slinking slowly to the floorboards, Christina pretended to be looking for something. "Uh, yeah. Yup. I'm here."

"Well?" Mary furrowed her eyebrows and with an eager wave of her hand asked: "What are you waiting for? We've got set up to do, darling!"

Christina threw her a hasty glance. "Yeah. Sorry, I just dropped, um, something," she mumbled, straightening up once more. Then, with a sense of finality, she reached for the deposit bag, lying on the passenger seat beside her. Nodding her head, she motioned Mary toward the back of the car. "Baked goods are in there." Keeping her eyes lowered, she begrudgingly alit from the safety of her vehicle.

"You're an angel," Mary cried, throwing the back left-side door open with gusto. Ducking her body inside the low-slung car, she emerged seconds later, her arms piled high with desserts. "Follow me."

The only good part about setting up the concession booth, Christina soon learned, was that with only her and Mary to do it all, she quickly warmed up. Shucking off her jacket in the small wooden structure, the inside of which was nothing more than rough plywood, Christina double-checked that all the appliances were plugged in and turned on before she started setting up the condiments and, when that was finished, organizing the cash register.

At some point, Mary left her to take over at admissions, which she was currently piling with the tournament schedule and team programs, and of course, a little something explaining the fundraiser taking place—something which Christina was still woefully ignorant about. Unfortunately for Mary, due to the stiff wind, all the papers had to be held down by the weight of large rocks; Christina doubted the perilous sight would encourage people to inquire further about…well, about whatever the fundraiser was about.

Wiping her hands together, Christina focused her thoughts back to the task at hand. There was still about fifteen minutes before the start of the tournament, but already cars were pulling into the parking lot. Reaching for a dry-erase marker, she turned toward the whiteboard running along the back of the booth. Her last undertaking before opening the large order window was to write out the menu.

She was just finishing the list of the beverages on sale when she heard the door open beside her. "Almost finished, Mar," she mumbled around the cap of the marker, which she'd stuck between her teeth.

"I didn't think you'd come."

At the sound of Jason's voice, Christina froze, her writing marring the last couple of letters in "Hot Chocolate."

She was still trying to absorb the shock of his entrance when she heard the door shut behind him as he stepped fully inside. Her fingers squeezed the sides of the marker too hard.

"Christina?"

Her eyes stared fixedly straight ahead. "What?"

She heard his quiet sigh. "Will you look at me?"

With calculated movements, borrowing time, she slowly lowered her hand and, taking the cap out of her mouth, popped it back on the marker. Then she slowly pivoted in his direction.

His hair was windblown, his cheeks showing the ruddiness of a biting cold. He wore a coach's uniform tucked into a pair of pressed khaki pants. He should have looked ridiculous. Should have.

Raising her eyes up to his, Christina only just kept herself from flinching. She knew her face was a mess—blotchy from lack of sleep, swollen and slightly pink around the edges. "Well?"

"What the hell happened last night, Christina?" But Jason didn't hurl the demand at her. It was said softly, curiously even. If he was angry, he hid it well. No, he just looked concerned.

She wasn't sure she actually preferred that, but then again…

Shrugging with an indifference that cost a great deal, she let her eyes skip away from his. "Nothing," she managed. "We had a misunderstanding, that's all."

He whistled. "You think?"

But when he didn't say anything else, when his eyes remained steady on her averted face, Christina felt herself bristling. "What do you want me to say here, Jason?"

With a quick movement, before she was fully aware of what was happening, he shot forward, his hands reaching out to grab her upper arms and pull her toward him. Surprise flashing across her face, Christina was left momentarily breathless, her wits scattered by the unexpected touch of his fingers. His eyes were stormy as they searched hers in the close confines of the booth.

"I want you to tell me the truth. There was no misunderstanding. Something happened last night. You changed the rules halfway through—"

"Does it spare your ego to think that?" she baited him, pushing against his chest. He didn't budge.

His teeth snapped together. "Dammit, Christina. Don't be an ass."

"God, Jason. Get over yourself. And while you're at it, get the hell out."

With a quick tug, he drew her body closer to his. "Maybe I should refresh your memory?" His head dipped lower, his lips hovering just above hers. "Perhaps I'll get some answers this way," he threatened in a whisper.

Christina's eyes widened, her head shifting frantically toward the door and back again. "Jason," she warned nervously, "someone could walk in here." But she wasn't fighting him very hard, her hands only half-heartedly pushing against his hold.

He smiled. "You mean, my mom or dad could walk in, right?" There was nothing but hard mockery in the accusation. "Those are the only people that you care about seeing us together, am I right?

She felt her eyes harden. "Yes," she hissed. "You got me. Okay? I don't want your parents to see me with you." Shaking free from his grasp, her eyes condemned him where he stood. They condemned the knowing, snarky smile biting its way across his lips. "Nice trick, by the way. Using my attraction for you against me." She curled her lips. "That's low, even for you."

He narrowed his eyes, but all he said was, "Do my parents have anything to do with what you said last night?"

"God!" Throwing her hands up in the air, Christina stalked to the other end of the booth. "Stop. Just stop already."

"I want answers."

"And I want you to leave."

Jason shook his head. "That might have worked last night—"

"It's going to work right now as well," Christina assured him. With a pointed look at the clock, she took in the time. It was less than ten minutes to the start of the game.

Jason growled, following her gaze. His eyes moved back to her. "This isn't over."

"Oh, but it is."

"Christina."

She held up a hand. "You didn't want me last night, Jason."

"That's not tr—"

"Well, I don't want you now."

The first deep breath Christina took that morning came at the sight of Jason's turned back exiting the small concession stand, the door swinging determinedly, angrily shut behind him. Slumping against the service counter, she tried to gain some perspective. The games were set to start in a matter of minutes and, judging by the sounds coming from outside, people were already lining up to get food before finding a seat.

With as much enthusiasm as she could muster, which admittedly wasn't a whole lot, Christina opened the customer window. Throwing a smile on her off-white pallor, she pretended a casualness she was far from feeling when the first in line came up to her.

"I'll have a box of popcorn, nachos, and two cups of hot apple cider…"

And with that, the orders came pouring in. Soon enough, Christina found herself wishing for a tank-top and running shorts. It went without saying, by the sweat beading down her forehead and the unfortunate flush donning her cheeks, that concessions was not meant to be a one-man operation.

Christina did not personally know Shelley—the woman with the incredibly lame excuse for backing out of her volunteer shift today—but she knew she hated her. Absolutely loathed her. Then again, maybe that wasn't quite the truth. The harried pace was actually okay. At least it gave her no opportunity to think about Jason, to remember, to fantasize about the feel of his lips pressed up against hers, or hear the confidence in his voice when he promised her their conversation wasn't over….

Of course, the rush died down eventually. The pace couldn't last forever, when the fans would find themselves huddling over to their seats, ready for the first pitch. Using that time to quickly re-organize the room, ready some more hotdogs, open extra bags of pre-popped popcorn, and refill the hot apple cider, Christina was kept in mind that these reprieves were short-lived. There were ten more games set to be played between the four baseball fields on the school grounds, with teams rolling in and out at different intervals, bringing with them new customers and more orders.

So that, other than those brief spells of silence, which were so packed with cleaning and replenishing and nothing much else, Christina found herself unable to think beyond the necessity of the moment. And for once, just once, she got her way with Jason. He, too, was kept busy all day. Whether he wanted to or not, he stayed away.

Idiotically, she was oddly disappointed about this. (Not that she was willing to admit it to herself, though.)

"I should probably thank Mary for this," she muttered to herself hours later, when she had a chance. Evening was finally beginning to fall, and with it, her fingers scrubbed the customer counter clean for the last time. It was nearing five o'clock and the tournament was winding itself to a close. First place stood between Jason's team and one from Hastings. Wiping a weary forearm over her brow, Christina dropped her sponge. Moving methodically around the small space, she began unplugging the copious food and beverage machines.

Concessions was officially closed for the day. And Christina was officially past the point of exhaustion.

Her shoulders ached, her back was sore, and her fingertips had long since gone numb from the sizzle of melting hot cocoa. Still, it was worth it. All day she'd managed to keep the fiery cavity of anxiety to a controllable simmer. She'd even managed a couple bites of a hamburger. "Without her, I'd probably be two cartons of ice-cream into it by now." Expertly, she deconstructed the hotdog roller. She wasn't in a rush to clean the parts. The only thing waiting for her was an empty home. And those ice-cream treats. With a twist of her wrist, she turned on the tap water at the small sink settled halfway down the long countertop.

"Knock, knock!" At the sound of Mary's voice, the door to the concession stand opened.

"Hey, Mar," Christina tossed out in greeting.

Mary took a quick look around the booth. She whistled. The condiments were still out, the popcorn boxes stacked haphazardly on the floor, a smell of slightly burnt apple cider permeating the air. "At this rate, you'll be here all night."

Christina shrugged. "I didn't have time to put things away during business hours."

Mary rolled up her sleeves. "Well then, it's a good thing I did."

"What?"

"Throw me a wet rag?"

Blinking, Christina gaped at her, but still, she reached blindly for the hand towel. "What about admissions?"

"What on Earth do you think I brought Matthew along for? The conversation? Please." With a laugh, Mary started scrubbing down the prep area.

For a few moments, the women worked in silence. It was only after Christina placed the cleaned hot dog roller back on the rack, and Mary finished taping up a storage box holding paper plates and cups, that the questions started.

"So," Mary said carefully, setting the cardboard box down on the floor. "I take it you and Jason didn't have a good talk then?"

Christina stilled, her hands holding the large crock pot of apple cider. "Um...excuse me?"

"Just before the games," Mary explained, her hands moving to tackle the napkins, her eyes avoiding Christina's penetrating look. "He came in here. And by the look on his face when he came back out—"

"You knew about that?" Christina's voice was somewhere between amusement and incredulity.

Mary shrugged.

"Well, thanks!" Christina dropped the pot in the sink with a hard, clanking sound. "What was all that nonsense earlier about keeping him from bothering me? You were supposed to intervene, not spectate!"

"Oh. That." Mary cleared her throat. "As you know, I'll say just about anything to get my own way."

"Mary!"

The older woman took a quick peek at Christina's face. There was a knowing look in the older woman's eyes. "And honestly, if I'd truly thought it would bother you—"

"Oh? And what's that supposed to mean?" Christina placed her hands on her hips, her fingers leaving wet trails where they touched her clothes. In all the years she'd known the Gordmans, she wasn't aware of ever raising her voice to Mary before. At the knowledge, she took a deep, even breath.

Mary made a gesture, her eyes skipping back to the napkins again. "I was young once too."

Christina narrowed her eyes.

Mary sighed, her eyes shifting up to meet Christina's accusing glare. "Okay. Matthew told me," she confessed. She flicked a hand absently toward the younger woman. "About what happened between you and Jason. On Easter."

Christina sucked in a mouthful of air. The sound was answer enough. "I see."

Not backing away anymore, Mary leveled Christina with a motherly look. "I was surprised, to tell the truth."

In a frenzied movement, Christina abandoned the apple cider in the sink. Prowling restlessly, she took herself to the condiment stand, her hands doing little more than shifting bottles around absently on the counter. Standing to one side of Mary, she could more easily refuse to meet that probing stare. "No more than I was, I assure you—"

If she'd thought that tactic of prevarication would work, she was wrong. The next words out of Mary's mouth stopped Christina's defense dead: "You really turned him down?"

Christina froze, her eyes rounding. The last thing she'd ever want to do was insult Mary. And there she was, throwing that woman's son over. "No! No, Mary, it wasn't like that—"

"But you've been in love with him all these years."

Chapter Fourteen

The red plastic bottle of ketchup catapulted out of Christina's hands at the words. She was too startled not to face Mary head-on. "You know?" It must also be said, she was too surprised to lie.

Mary shrugged one shoulder, her eyes soft and gentle on Christina's broken gaze. "If it's any consolation, I'm the only one who does."

Christina nodded. Slowly. Thoughtfully. "Yeah. Actually, it is." She righted the ketchup bottle.

Mary touched her arm. "And, if that's the way you want it, I'm the only one who ever will."

Christina inhaled. One finger picked at the cap of the ketchup bottle. "Thank you."

"But," Mary paused. "Look, I know it's none of my business, but can I ask why?"

Christina didn't pretend to misunderstand. Her eyes roamed over the counter, her gaze searching for an answer. "Statistically, it's a bad move."

"Huh?"

"The odds are against any relationship actually making it." She pursed her lips. "Most end with a break-up."

Mary's forehead creased, her amazement landing like a slap against Christina's downcast eyes. "The better option is just not to try?"

"In this case."

"What does that mean?"

Christina didn't respond for a moment, her throat swallowing past the instinctive desire toward flippancy or ignorance.

"Christina, if you love him…"

"I also love you."

Mary blinked. "Well honey, I love yo—"

"And Matthew."

Mary's mouth opened in confusion. "Okay?

Christina laughed. By now, she found little point in subterfuge. "Come *on*, Mary."

Mary's arms swept open in exasperation. "We don't have anything to do with you and Jason."

"Maybe not directly."

Mary sighed, her arms dropping back to her sides. "These are a lot of riddles you're throwing at me."

"Because you're deliberately not putting the pieces together."

Mary lifted a telling eyebrow at the charge.

Christina gave in at that look. "The risk is too high." Her voice was little more than a slip of sound.

"Because you think it's inevitable that you and Jason wouldn't make it, as you say?"

Christina's lips twitched from the barrage of words she was desperately holding back. "And when that happened, I wouldn't just lose him. I would lose all of you."

Mary's eyes widened. "You think you would lose me?"

"I know I would."

"Oh, honey—"

Again, Mary wasn't allowed to finish her sentiment. "And," sniffing inelegantly, Christina could barely force the next words out of her mouth. It was difficult. Speaking in this manner. She hadn't been raised to it. Feelings were a potential weakness to be exploited to the highest bidder. Yet, she couldn't quite stop herself from talking, either. "I don't mean to sound, whatever or

anything, but you're all the family I've got left. My parents—
we aren't close."

There was a beat of silence and then Mary nodded. "Yeah."

Christina almost laughed. "You knew that, too, huh?"

Mary pursed her lips. All pretense of packing away the
concession stand was over as she leaned against the counter. "I
sort of put two and two together."

Christina blew out a tough breath. It was getting cold inside
the booth again. "Yeah."

"So that's what this is really about," Mary said on a sigh, her
voice barely carrying to the other woman.

"No!" Christina swore vehemently. "No, it's not about
them."

"Them?" Mary frowned, her forehead crinkling. "Y-your
parents? That's not what I meant—"

"It's about lessons learned."

But Mary wasn't easily deceived or diverted. Her eyes were
quiet, but unwilling to be put off. "Look, I don't know what
happened between you and your family…"

Christina shrugged. The move was stiff, short. "It's a long
and terrible story, I assure you."

"And not all that different from whatever's happening
between you and Jason?" Mary hazarded.

"Bingo."

"Except," Mary said, her voice sharp, "for one rather large
distinction."

Christina laughed in surprised amusement at Mary's gruff
insistence. "Yeah, and what's that?"

"No matter what happens, you and I, we will always have
each other. Nothing will change that."

Christina snorted. That was her only response. With deft
decision, she reached for the ketchup and mustard again, her
quiet snub as obvious as it was expected. With a decided clank,
she dropped the bottles noisily in their allotted container.

"Well, I'm here you know," Mary said. As close as the two
women had become, they'd never spoken like this before. It was

unknown territory for each of them. "If you ever want to talk about it."

Christina turned her head. The look she leveled at Mary wasn't pretty. "You don't want to hear it."

Mary sucked in her lower lip. "I'm sure that's not—"

"Trust me. I'm more villain than victim."

Mary pulled herself up to her far inferior height. Her eyes were unwavering. "I won't believe that."

"You should."

"Then let me prove it."

Christina's hands tightened reflexively, skimming past the condiments to grab a roll of ticket tape beside them. She shook her head. "And lose you anyway?" She laughed hollowly, but she kept her eyes averted again. Because she *would* lose her. If Mary knew—good, strong Catholic woman that she was—she'd never look at Christina the same way again.

Against her better judgment, Mary reached forward, one hand settling over Christina's tense shoulders. "You could never do that. Never."

With a twist, Christina broke Mary's hold. "You may want to wait before making rash statements."

"You won't scare me off."

"No?" Christina said, her voice a rasp of anger. A sob lodged itself in her throat as memories swarmed against her battered consciousness: Jason's hand pressing against her back, his breath cool against her ear, *"Dance with me?"* It was the first time she'd ever found herself in his arms. Her whole body had trembled. And then last night, his lips trailing along her neck, nibbling, tasting. She'd never wanted him to let her go as he'd breathed against her skin, *"God, you're beautiful."*

What had she done in return? Ruined everything. This morning, slipping out of his embrace for the last time…. *"Get over yourself. And while you're at it, get the hell out…. I don't want you now."*

She'd pushed him away to keep Mary. And now. It had all been for naught. Staring blazingly into that woman's brown eyes, Christina swallowed back a cry of regret, a plea to turn back the clock. It was her own damn fault. If she'd just left well enough alone on Easter, if only she'd stayed tucked in her bed that night, instead of traipsing down to the living room. But she hadn't done any of those things. And there was no going back.

She'd managed to fool them for so long. And now it was all over. Because Mary just wouldn't fucking let it go.

In that instant, Christina raised her gaze, almost challengingly. Fine. Mary wanted to prove herself? Great. Who was Christina to stop her? Lips curling, she spat: "I had an affair with a married man." The bald statement fell with a hard, flat effect.

It was oddly satisfying, the pain that seared into Christina's side when she spied the power of those words on Mary's gentle features. Later, she knew, she'd drown in regret, but just then, she felt almost vindicated. It wasn't the first confession of late that had been born of an impetuous tongue and an out spring of resentment. Perhaps it was the aftermath of everything that had gone on recently, the injustice of wanting against her will, the shame of lying to herself, and the fear that if she didn't talk soon the memories would slowly consume her. Or maybe not. Maybe she was just tired of fighting her demons alone. Weary with pretending to be somebody she wasn't. And maybe she *almost* wanted Mary to hate her. Because she was hurting, and she wanted to hurt. After all, she deserved it.

Christina watched Mary start with reaction, her mouth dropping open in surprised shock. She made no sound, though. No movement in retreat. No flicker of emotion otherwise. Instead, she just stood there, waiting.

Christina raised her eyebrows. "And before you ask, yes, I knew he was married. I knew it and I did it anyway."

There was no going back.

There was no more hiding.

Mary looked nonplussed. Swallowing, she was clearly trying to find the right words to ask the untold questions brimming in her wide, searching gaze. But Christina didn't give her the chance.

Perhaps because it was already out there—her sordid little secret—or perhaps because it was the first time she'd told anyone about it, and it felt somehow relieving to say the words out loud, to realize the monster didn't change shape in the transition from silent disdain to audible shame, Christina kept talking. Turning away from Mary, because her bravado from earlier had worn itself out, Christina looked toward the service wall.

"He was my father's partner at their law firm," she confessed, her features wincing with the words. That had been the worst part of it all. Her mother could have probably seen past her daughter's transgression if it hadn't been for that.

Strangling the raffle tickets still in her hands, Christina heard her voice come as if from far away. "It had started out as a mild flirtation…"

As most things of this nature probably started out, she'd always supposed. She'd known Bill in an offhand sort of way for years before he and her father had decided to start up their own law office. But she'd been only a child then, hardly interested in a colleague of her father's.

"They started the company when I was nineteen," she heard herself say, one finger pressing at the edges of the blue paper in her hands. She shrugged. "The summer after I graduated college, my father thought it'd do me good to intern at their practice. Learn the ropes, so to speak, before making any final decisions about my career."

And that's when it had started in earnest. She'd bring him coffee and he'd smile just a little too slowly as she'd cross over to his desk, making sure their fingers grazed as he took the cup from her grip. She'd find excuses to seek him out, dropping off a piece of paper she'd magically forgotten to give him earlier with his mail or asking him questions she could have found out from any of a number of paralegals working there.

His eyes would skim over her outfit as he'd walk past her cubicle each morning—a lightning glance that he couldn't seem to help as he offered her a "Morning, Ms. DeLuca," but it spoke volumes. For her part, she'd make sure to wear shirts that were demure yet which showed off the cleavage of her breasts, or skirts that, while perfectly appropriate for the office, were perhaps a little tight, hugging the rounded curve of her backside.

And then one day it all came to a head. She'd been helping Bill sort through some documents for an upcoming court appearance. It had been nearing the end of the workday when he'd asked if she'd mind staying a little later that night to help him finish up. Her breath had almost choked her at the thought. A few hours alone with Bill? It wasn't a big case, so there was no reason for anyone else to remain behind with them.

Of course, she'd said yes. Huddled up in his office, with lamps lit to beat back the night throwing shade into the large windows facing out behind his desk, they'd sat there, pouring over the books. It had all been relatively innocent until her highlighter had run dry. They'd been sitting on either side of the couch, their bodies angled toward one another. Getting up, she'd intended to go grab another marker from her desk. Making room for her to pass by, he'd also gained his feet.

Finding themselves suddenly face to face, almost nose to nose in the space between the coffee table and the couch, there'd been hardly a breath of air separating them. A sort of static had gone off in Christina's head at the proximity. She'd felt his breath on her forehead as she'd paused, her gaze lifting searchingly…

"Excuse me," she whispered nervously, her body shifting instinctively in retreat. Then his hand lifted, lightly grabbing her elbow when she would have moved away. There was something dangerous in the glint of his gaze as he stared down at her, his nostrils flaring with the force of his breathing. His hand tightened its hold. She didn't try to back away, and he did absolutely nothing to aid her progress.

They stood like that for too long. They both knew it. Her lips opened just the slightest bit under his direct gaze. His thumb, against the soft lining of her suit jacket, became unconsciously caressing.

"Christina?" he finally whispered, his voice rough and seductive in the dim lighting. "We shouldn't do this."

She nodded mutely.

"We both know this is a bad idea," he said again, but his fingers pulled her closer, not farther away. At the slight pressure, her hands went up to either side of his chest, pressing against him.

He'd been right. She had known it was a bad idea. Then again, it'd also felt wildly romantic. For months, she'd watched him, taunted by the forbidden fruit of her father's partner, a married man, someone years too old for her.

And suddenly, there he was, staring down at her as though he'd die to have her lips. She'd made a tiny whimper of sound in her throat, and that was all it'd taken. In the next second, his head had swooped down, his lips colliding urgently, almost violently, with hers.

What had once been a memory she'd sworn to cherish now left her almost nauseous in the remembering.

"The affair lasted for almost three months," she said, her voice hard in the retelling, cold and distant. Her fingers continued to pick at the roll of raffle tickets in her hands. The thin paper crinkled and curled under her ministrations.

"I don't know when he started telling me he'd leave his wife, but after a while, he swore it," she admitted. She lifted one shoulder. "But I think I knew, even then, that it was all talk. I think I knew he was lying."

By now, Mary's hands were curled defensively down at her sides, the knuckles shaking with the pressure of her straight, unmoving stance. Christina had spared her the more intimate details of their affair, but still, the news alone was enough to draw lines of concern and distress across the older woman's face—and it was clear that the telling was having a similar effect on Christina, who couldn't help but remember every minute, terrible scene.

"Who knows how long it would have continued," Christina said, her voice so filled with self-loathing it was almost hard to make understood. Dropping the roll of raffle tickets, she shook her head in finality. "But my mother caught us."

Bill had been over at the DeLuca's house going over some tax information with her father. Christina had watched him covetously from across the room, her skin tingling. It had been intoxicating, the quiet anticipation of being with him right under her parents' noses, without their having any clue.

It was the thrill of the forbidden all over again.

She'd bided her time, her eyes tracing his features lovingly as she'd waited for him and her father to take a break. And when, at last, that moment had come, she'd made a big production of getting up to leave the room, chiding her father teasingly that all his tax talk had bored her stiff!

She'd made her exit then, but not before silently mouthing to Bill over the backs of her parents' heads. Ten minutes later, excusing himself on the plea of a private call he needed to make (apparently, he'd told her father he'd be out in his car so as not to be disturbed), he'd met her in the upstairs laundry room, just as she'd instructed him to do…. Her bedroom would have been too risky and the bathroom too heavily trafficked.

That was where her mother had found them—entwined in a deep embrace, his mouth ravishing hers where they stood backed up against the washing machine.

Natalie DeLuca hadn't even seemed embarrassed when she'd calmly announced her presence and watched Bill jump back, his hands frantically righting his hair and re-tucking his shirt into place, his mouth mumbling incoherently.

Dumping the empty laundry basket on the floor by her feet, she'd only nodded. Almost as though she'd expected to stumble upon this scene. "Bill, I think it's time you went home now. To your wife," she'd enunciated quite clearly. She'd sounded almost pleasant when she'd said it, her hand even reaching out to pat his shoulder as he'd shuffled out of the room.

No, it wasn't until he'd walked out that Natalie's face had morphed into something harder, something darker as she'd looked at her daughter's face.

"What did you *do*?"

Shivering a little at that last memory, Christina took a deep, halting breath. "And that was that. They told me to get out." Actually, that wasn't quite true. In an effort to shield her husband, Natalie had waited until she'd heralded Edward out of the house on some made-up errand before she'd spoken. Still, there had been no doubt that she'd spoken for the two of them.

"Your parents?" Mary whispered incredulously. They were the first words she'd spoken since Christina had started her tale.

At the horror in Mary's voice, Christina found the courage to lift her eyes to the older woman again. What she saw in those dark brown depths was staggering. "I shamed them, Mary," Christina tried to explain.

But Mary couldn't, or maybe wouldn't, believe that. Her face echoed her dismay. "Oh, sweetheart, no! Of course, no—"

"Yes, I did!" Christina insisted, her voice coming out harshly. "My mother told me—I still remember the words exactly. She said I was no child of hers."

"Christina." Without thought, Mary reached for her hand. "I'm so sorry."

At the contact, Christina started. Her eyes were wild, shining with unshed tears. She swallowed back a sob. "Don't be. I have only myself to blame." She even managed a mangled sort of laugh. "I did this. I ruined everything—"

Christina hadn't intended to say so much. She'd meant to keep the story flat, cold, one-dimensional. Unfortunately, she got lost along the way. Ripping open the memories that she'd secured tightly behind a door of slippery locks, she was now so thoroughly engulfed in them it was almost as though she were physically reliving them. And, in a way, she was.

"And you've been punished enough," Mary finished, her voice firm.

Christina pursed her lips. "Do you know what she told me? She said I was the kind of girl that other women are afraid of," she admitted, brushing at errant tears with the back of her wrist. Christina gave a watery laugh. "And she was right. Do you know what that's like, Mary? To be the kind of person that others are warned about? To be someone you hate?"

Mary's lips trembled. "Stop. Please, stop," she pleaded, raising a hand between them.

At the look on her face, Christina seemed to snap. The words she meant to say died on her lips. Wincing, she dropped her gaze. And then she was moving, her motions frantic, frenzied as she reached blindly across the countertop, her hands grabbing for anything they came into contact with.

"I'm sorry," she muttered, her eyes blurring everything in sight. Her hands furiously shoveled random objects into an empty box, the items scattering anyhow. "I shouldn't have burdened you with this." Her hands were stretching to grab the next object. "I-I tried to tell you—"

It was only as her fingers gripped the roll of raffle tickets again that Mary reached for her arm, pulling her up short. "Christina. Stop. Yes, you made a mistake."

Christina's eyelids flinched at the damning words. What else had she expected?

"But, oh, honey, so did they."

"No." Christina shook her head so hard her teeth clenched.

"Yes," Mary insisted, and this time her hand actually shook Christina. "Mothers don't turn their backs on their babies. Not ever."

At the words, a weird, terrible sound erupted from Christina's voice.

"And what of Bill? Was that his name?" Mary asked harshly. "What was his punishment in all this?"

Christina tilted her head as though the thought had never occurred to her. In fact, it hadn't. "Nothing."

"Nothing?"

Christina shrugged. "And *publicly* announce the scandal to the entire town? That would have hardly done. No, Bill wasn't the problem."

"The hell he wasn't. He was older than you, Christina. In a position of authority. He took advantage of you—"

"No," Christina argued, "he didn't. I knew what I was doing. I had just as much power, just as much leverage as he did. I could have said no. I could have done the right thing. But instead I—"

"You were young."

"I was twenty-three."

"As I said, you were young. And impressionable."

Christina scoffed. "Those are excuses, Mary."

"Fine," she conceded. "Though I still don't agree."

Christina's lips twitched with weary amusement.

"But either way, people make mistakes," Mary claimed. "And, if they're good, they learn from them." Her eyes were steady on Christina's averted face. "And while they're picking themselves up from their fall, they still deserve to be loved. That's grace."

Christina's shoulders shook. Closing her eyes, her lashes stemming back the tears threatening to spill down her cheeks—because really, there had been enough crying by now—she tried to breathe. It came in jerky gasps.

"Some things are unforgivable."

"Perhaps," Mary consented, "but not between a mother and her child. And certainly not that."

"You don't understand," Christina persisted. "My mother, she grew up poor, with barely enough food to eat. She was so ashamed of her family, of her history. And she swore—"

"I don't care what she swore," Mary said. "You may have let her down, but she let you down, too."

It was too much suddenly. It was all too much. With a wrenching sound from deep in her throat, Christina jerked out of Mary's reach. Half-stumbling in her haste, she turned and, deaf to the sound of her name on that woman's lips, flew for the door. Her fingers scratched at the handle but finally, she felt her feet clambering out of the stand, felt the bite of the wind against her cheeks as she staggered for the parking lot.

Gaining the outside of her car, Christina half-collapsed against the driver's side door. Her fingers splaying against the glass, she sucked in a forceful breath of air. And then another, until she slowly felt her sobs subside. Swallowing for control, it was only as she unlocked her door that Christina became aware of a set of eyes on her down-bent head.

Hesitantly, with infinite care, she lifted her gaze out across the ballfield separating her from Jason. He was standing there, on the first base line, a hat slung low over his forehead. But she could still see his eyes, watch them scrutinizing her. At his look, Christina felt what little strength she had left drain from her body.

His eyes narrowed as they settled on her face, and even from that distance, she could feel the questions etching themselves across his features, catch the slight marring on his brow line as concern flashed there briefly. She supposed she looked a fright, her hair tucked anyhow underneath her ballcap, her eyes wide and her skin red.

And for an instant, she didn't want to fight anymore. She didn't want to turn her back on him, to pretend she didn't feel the effects of his gaze. Her legs ached to stretch across the distance between them. She wanted to feel the weight of his arms pulling her close, the strength of his body wrapping around hers, taking the burden of her into his capable hands.

She wanted the damn moon.

Which was nothing new, was it? Only now, the subterfuge had dropped, deserted her.

Something flickered in Jason's eyes when she held his searching look. He made a seemingly unconscious move toward her. Swaying just slightly at the sight, Christina held her breath, but in the next second the unmistakable sound of a baseball bat connecting with a ball exploded in the evening air, followed almost immediately by the mad cheering of Jason's team.

And then he was turning away from her, his arms up in the air, hooting just as loudly as the kids in the dugout as one of the boys rounded home plate.

Christina shook her head as she felt her fingers pull the door open. "Well, what else did you expect? It's kind of your thing, isn't it?" she asked herself as she hauled her body into the seat. It was only then that she realized she was still holding that roll of raffle tickets. With a defeated sigh, she tossed it wearily onto the passenger seat.

She didn't have it in her to bring it back to Mary. Not after all that.

With tired eyes, she let her gaze roam over the baseball field one last time as she turned the key in the ignition. From the looks of the kids scattering across the field, Jason's team had won. She couldn't help a sad smile as she watched them all try to tackle him to the ground.

Her fingers brushed over her lips absently.

"The wrong time, wrong place," she muttered as she put the car into reverse. "And always the wrong guy."

Chapter Fifteen

Christina had no sooner driven away from the ballfield then she turned off her phone. She wouldn't turn it back on until Monday morning. Resolute, she kept her doors locked, her curtains drawn, and her social media presence quiet for the duration of the weekend. Snuggled deep under the warmth of her favorite paisley throw blanket, she did little more than lounge on her couch, watching one romantic comedy after another. The irony of the situation hadn't been lost on her, either.

If that weren't enough, she'd absolutely forbidden herself to think about it. About Jason. Mary. Her job. Her family. Her heartbreak.

Which was probably why Monday brought with it a pounding headache underneath her shiny blonde hair, and dark splotches beneath her perfectly applied makeup. But if she'd harbored any worries about her reception that morning, they'd been for naught. When Mr. Gordman arrived, pausing beside her desk on the way to his office with a free, easy smile, he'd offered little more than a pleasant good-morning, the quiet delight that she was back, and the fervent hope that she was quite recovered from her sick leave, "You're certainly looking better than you did on Saturday. I'd meant to pop over and see how you were, make sure you weren't overdoing it but, between admissions and Mary, I never had a minute! And when I finally got the chance, you'd already left."

Fumbling for an answer to the quiet curiosity in those last words, Christina achieved little more than a mumbled, feeble response. Only two things had managed to penetrate her numbed mind at that moment: the first, for all his ease of conversation, Matthew clearly didn't know what had transpired in the concession booth on Saturday; and second, he was just as obviously determined to pretend he didn't know about Easter, either.

Fine by her.

But if Mr. Gordman's attitude had lulled Christina into a false sense of calm, she was doomed for future upset. It was two hours later, with both eyes glued to her computer screen, one hand reaching blindly for her third cup of coffee, when Christina heard the soft ringing of her cellphone. Placed snugly beside her keyboard, the mobile device was equal parts inconspicuous and inescapable. Pausing with the mug halfway to her mouth, Christina glanced down at it distractedly.

She almost upturned her coffee when she saw Mary's name flash across the screen. Bringing the cup back to her desk with a plop, Christina's right hand dropped limply to her lap—this was closely followed by the left one. Swearing softly under her breath, Christina froze, her eyes watching the mad vibrating of her phone. But she didn't reach forward to answer the call. Instead, her fingers clenched together, interlocking, grasping each other. Holding her breath, she just watched it, waiting.

Her heart shook her with the force of its beating. Her eyes couldn't seem to blink, staring with bloodshot intentness at the slithering phone. The swig of coffee she'd last swallowed seemed about ready to recoil up her throat. Thankfully, her phone couldn't ring forever and soon enough, the possessed thing went still and silent.

Christina slowly loosened the aching grip of her hands. Okay. It was fine. Dragging her eyes determinedly back up to her computer screen, Christina nodded. Shaking out her fingers, she placed them stubbornly over the keyboard. She had work to do. Straightening her back, she prayed for muscle memory to take over.

Mary filled her vision—accompanied by that sad, almost lost look on her face Saturday evening.

Dammit.

Christina took a deep, calming breath. It was fine. Everything was fine. She'd known what she was doing last Saturday when she'd told-all. She'd known this would happen.

And there was no going back.

Everything…the darkest secret. The one that, hidden away, gave Christina the ability to be someone else. At least, to appear to be someone else. The secret was out.

Her phone vibrated again. Just once more. Jolting at the sound, Christina cursed under her breath when her knee knocked against a side drawer. She didn't need to look at her phone to know what had happened. Mary had left her a voicemail.

Christina's hands left the keyboard, her body sagging with the weight of that realization. All that nonsense of being *fine* forgotten, she closed her eyes painfully, anything to avoid the now darkened screen on her phone. All thought of working gone, her fingers splaying flat against her desk, seeking the reassurance of its bulky, steadfast strength, she blinked her eyes back open. Good Christ, she'd just screened a call from Mary. She'd never done that before, would have never thought to do that before.

Not to Mary.

If that thought stuck in her throat with imploding consequences, it was nothing to the thought that followed next. Even knowing that, she didn't want to call her back.

Without thought, her fingers grabbed her phone, hovering over the notification. She wasn't sure if she intended to listen to it or delete its existence—whichever it was, however, would remain a mystery because, at that moment, she became aware of the sound of approaching footsteps nearing her outer office. Automatically, her lips pulled into a polite, if slightly stilted, smile. Then she saw who was rounding the corner. Her smile faltered just the slightest bit.

"Jackie?" Christina asked, her eyebrows crinkling pointedly. With an effort, she tried to smooth out her features. "What are you doing up here?"

The other woman made a face. "You know, I am allowed to see the daylight sometimes," she drawled.

Christina hitched up one corner of her mouth. Still, the effect fell flat. "Be careful you don't burn."

"Ha, ha."

"All right, all right," Christina conceded. "What's up?" The question was fair since Jackie had no business with Mr. Gordman scheduled in the books. As the head of graphic design, she didn't usually make trips upstairs without a portfolio in hand and a client in the meeting room.

For a moment, Jackie looked almost uncomfortable, taken aback by the direct question. Then her lips pursed, her shoulders pulling back visibly as she cleared her throat: "I, ah, I heard you went home sick last Friday?"

Christina waited for her to say more, but when Jackie didn't expand on this, she nodded. "Yeah?"

Jackie tilted her head a little to one side. "You're never sick."

"Okay." Christina tried to sound disinterested. Her stomach hurt and her throat throbbed. Life had become one long series of bad timings as of late.

Jackie's eyes narrowed as she canvassed Christina across the desk. "In four years of work, you've never once gone home in the middle of the day."

Christina made a dismissive gesture. "Yeah, I'm not sure what you want me to say…?"

Jackie seemed to have regained her confidence. She took a step closer to Christina's desk, her voice lowering. "You don't look like you."

"What?" Christina couldn't keep the frustration out of her voice. "That doesn't even make sense. What does that mean?" The harried quality of these questions was probably overdone.

It was probably testimony to Jackie's allegation. Christina chose to ignore that.

"And you weren't sick on Friday."

Christina made a big production of sighing. "No? What, is Dr. Max teaching you medicine on the side now?"

But if Jackie was offended by the crack at her fiancé, she didn't look it. In fact, she smiled. "Even your insults are off-key."

Christina surrendered. She was too exhausted to fight anyway. "Yeah. I guess they are." She sighed in agreement. "I'm sorry."

Jackie waved the words away. Instead, she plowed forward guardedly. "I, um, I also heard that Jason came to take Mr. Gordman out to lunch on Friday?" Though the tone may have implied it, there was nothing conversational in the question.

Christina's back stiffened. "What of it?"

"That wouldn't have had anything to do with your sudden defection, now would it?"

Pinching her lips together, Christina only stared her down. But Jackie was braver than she looked. Jutting one hip against the side of Christina's desk, she nodded. "Yeah. I thought so."

"Take your thoughts somewhere else, if you please." With a wave of her hands, Christina motioned for Jackie to get off her desk. "I'm busy."

Jackie didn't budge. "Want to talk about it?" All pretense of teasing was gone, replaced with something quieter, something kinder. Leaning down, she waited.

Christina rolled her eyes. "What is it with everyone and wanting to talk about every damn feeling they come across?"

Jackie cringed. "Look," she said, her eyes shifting, her face flushing, "a few months ago, you said this thing to me, that you'd spent the last few years sitting at home, alone, in your pajamas with a glass of wine and a romance novel." Spitting the words out forcibly, Jackie stopped then to take a stabilizing breath.

Christina bit down on the inside of her mouth. Though she wanted to deny any memory of it, she remembered very well the afternoon she'd said those words to Jackie. It had been in the early days of Jackie and Max's relationship—hell, it had been in the early days of Jackie and Christina's friendship.

Slipping into the bathroom at the close of the business day, Christina had offered her services as both a makeup artist and emotional counselor when she'd spotted Jackie leaning over the bathroom sink, overwhelmed and entirely ill-prepared for her approaching first date with the handsome pediatrician…

Jackie stared at her across the bathroom mirror, her eyebrows pulling together unsurely. "Thank you but…don't you have work to do? I don't want to—"

"Are you kidding me?" Christina cried. "Girl, when I'm done with you, he'll be eating out of your hands." She made a face at the lipstick Jackie was wearing. She clicked her tongue. "But if I leave you alone…. I mean, hon, what is that color? No, I don't have work to do." She flipped her hair over one shoulder. "Besides, you look like you're about to chicken out."

Jackie scratched the side of her neck. "That bad?"

"I'm digging for my bronzer, aren't I? You're as white as a ghost."

"God."

Christina wiggled her eyebrows. "Chin up, Jackie. Dating is supposed to be fun!"

"Not for me. I've had some pretty awful dates in my life."

"Do tell?"

"You really want to hear all about my humiliations?"

Christina grinned. "A little. Yes." She laughed playfully. "Does that make me a bad person?"

"Terrible."

"I can live with that."

Jackie couldn't help herself. She laughed.

"See? I'm making you feel better already. Just think how much good it'll do, dishing all. Think of it as therapy. At least Dr. Max won't be as bad as…?" Christina paused deliberately as she began to wind Jackie's hair into a neat chignon. "Well? Go on. Give me the worst of the lot of 'em."

"You're tireless."

Christina rolled her eyes eloquently at the words, words which ultimately forged the beginning of their friendship. "Listen, no matter what, at least you won't spend tonight—or the last four years of nights—sitting at home, alone, in your pajamas with a glass of wine and a romance novel. So, you're already less pathetic than me."

She'd spoken rashly, stupidly that day. Now, it appeared those words had come back to taunt her.

Reliving that moment all over again, Christina felt her lips curl. This. This was exactly why she didn't talk about her private life. It gave people power. She'd been reckless lately with her secrets, with her emotions. With a flick, she threw Jackie a hard stare. "Okay?" The edge in her voice was not to be ignored.

"You called yourself pathetic." Jackie's face blushed a little over the words.

Christina wanted to throw something. Preferably Jackie out of her office. "I see."

"Look, I'm just saying, maybe you aren't pathetic, maybe you're just hiding out." She gave Christina a perceptive look. "If you could have seen your face the day after Jason kissed you."

"Shh!" With a frenzied look, Christina's eyes zeroed in on Mr. Gordman's firmly closed door. "Shut up!"

Another secret she should have kept to herself.

Jackie held up her hands. "Sorry."

Christina cleared her throat, her eyes moving from Mr. Gordman's door back to Jackie's earnest expression and then down to her desk. Her hands fiddled with a stack of papers beside her computer. "Well, that's rather the point, isn't it?" she muttered. "At home, alone with my books, I get to fall in love from the safety of my own couch."

"To a man who isn't real."

"Even better."

"Oh, come on!" Jackie exclaimed. "Do you really believe that?"

"Yes. No." Christina closed her eyes. When she opened them again, her voice went down an octave. "It's just, it's easier that way. There's no chance of getting hurt. Nothing has to change."

"Christina—"

"I really have to get back to work, Jackie," she said, cutting her off in a too-bright voice. Raising up a hand pointedly, she looked forceful. "Thanks for checking in on me, but I'm feeling much better."

"I doubt that."

"Don't trip heading back downstairs," Christina said cheerfully with a half-wave.

Jackie snorted. "Coward."

That night, lying curled up under the soft weight of her comforter, her fingers clenching the edges in a childish wish to hide away, craving the security of a blanket to buffer her from the naked vulnerability of her actions, Christina waited patiently for the quiet hum of sound, the slight whirl preceding the recording—the only noise allowed to break through the sanctuary of quiet surrounding her, its soft resonance reverberating on repeat across the walls and ceiling, tucking around her.

Christina, it's Mary—

Christina couldn't quite deny the slight reflex of pain those words, their very timid quality, produced. She wondered when she'd stop flinching at the slight inflection of change.

I've been trying and trying to get ahold of you but you're still not answering—though I'm glad the phone actually rang this time. That's progress, I suppose. Look, I didn't want to leave a message but, but who knows, maybe it's for the best that you just listen to what I have to say. I...Christina, I love you. I need you to hear that if you hear nothing else. What you told me Saturday hasn't changed that fact. Nothing will change that. And I'm sorry. I'm so sorry. That you lost so much at such a young age, that you can't seem to forgive yourself....

There was a long pause and then:

Listen, I don't think I have any right to say this but well, dammit, I'm going to say it anyway, because...well, please let me assure you that you don't need Matthew's or my permission to date Jason if you want to. That's your business. But if you did need our permission, you'd have it. Unequivocally. What I'm trying to say is...your feelings for Jason, that's between you and him and no one else.

And, and when you're ready to talk, know that I'm here. I'll always be here.

There was another slight break and then a sigh. Christina clenched her teeth together, her lips silently mouthing the words she knew by heart now.

Okay. I love you.

This was followed by the soft click of the phone as Mary hung up. Within seconds, the call was quickly replaced by the automated sound of her voicemail system prompting her to select an option from the menu.

Blindly reaching over to where her phone rested on the nightstand, Christina's fingers moved on memory, navigating the keypad with ease as they located a particular number on the screen. For a moment, silence filled the room and then, just as it'd done countless times in the half hour since Christina had first listened to it, that voice returned, replaying again...

Christina, it's Mary—

Squeezing her eyes shut, clamping her jaw, Christina forced herself to breathe evenly. Only it wasn't Mary's face which swam against the black canvas of her eyelids with the action. It was her mother's.

Chapter Sixteen

Christina didn't call Mary back. She tried. She got as far as dialing her number a couple of times the night before but always, she'd freeze just at the last, the call remaining unfailingly unsent. She wanted to call her. Desperately. She wanted to see her, to hug her, to plead for forgiveness, to promise to never fail that woman so miserably again. But fear stuck in her throat, cutting off her air supply. She wasn't sure how to do those things—how to talk to her anymore, she wasn't sure who to be with her. Christina wasn't sure she could handle the very real possibility that she'd ruin even that. It felt safer somehow to know it from a distance, propped up by the words in that voicemail, that they would be okay. It felt safer to let matters rest, to keep from expecting too much, wanting too much. At least, until she found her voice.

Pushing her phone deep in her purse, Christina recused herself from the temptation as she entered her office the following morning.

She was just sitting down in her chair when Mr. Gordman arrived. Smiling up at him in greeting, she forced a nonchalance she was far from feeling. "Good morning, sir."

Yawning as he entered her office, Mr. Gordman offered her a smile. "'Morning, Christina."

"Tired?"

"Oh, God," he groaned, setting his briefcase down to unburden himself of his coat. "Yes. Jas"— pausing, Mr. Gordman coughed— "that is, I stayed up late last night watching soccer. Too late."

Christina pretended not to notice the stumble, the deliberate revision of his words. Ironically, it was all the more conspicuous in its absence. Still, she went on as though nothing were amiss. "I've heard that one before."

"Someday I'll learn," he replied laughingly, reaching down for his briefcase and heading toward his office door.

Alone again, Christina tried not to flinch. That morning would probably prove the future of their conversations, she knew. Gone would be the days when Jason's name was thrown casually into talk of Mr. Gordman's personal life. Gone would be the days when she could live vicariously off those crumbs of information that kept her, in a weird sort of way, close to him.

"It was one conversation," she muttered to herself, her eyes skipping over to her computer screen as she reviewed Mr. Gordman's schedule for that afternoon. "Don't exaggerate."

Exaggeration or otherwise, she felt a knot forming in her stomach. First Mary and now Matthew? And it was all to do with someone else. With Jason.

"No," she whispered. It was unacceptable. Shifting, she looked over at her filing cabinet, her eyes unconsciously seeking out her phone from inside its metal depths. Just as quickly, her gaze slid over to stare guardedly at Mr. Gordman's closed door. But she didn't reach for her purse nor did she attempt to knock on her boss's door.

Damn Jason. Why'd he have to press her resistance?

And damn Mary. Why'd she have to press for her secrets?

A rush of resentment settled in the base of her stomach, heating her skin as her brain whirled, clicking and shifting for a way out of this mess. Her body buzzed, vibrated with a sudden need to move, to react, to do something, anything! To repair, to outrun, to squelch the ache consuming her.

At the thought, her eyes zoomed back to her filing cabinet as she mentally canvassed the items inside her purse, only this time it wasn't her phone she envisioned, but something hidden at the bottom of her bag, it's coiled shape bulky and weighted.

Later, she'd tell herself she wasn't sure what had prompted her decision, she'd swear it had been an act of rash impulsiveness that had been born of desperation, something she couldn't explain even to herself. She'd tell herself she hadn't known what had provoked her, what had compelled her. She'd swear she'd had no known intention behind her actions—

These excuses already brewing in the back of her mind, before she had time to think, Christina pressed her finger down on the intercom. "Mr. Gordman," she said, her voice coming out breathlessly. Without waiting for a response, she continued: "I forgot to mention, but I'll need to leave work a few hours early today if that's all right with you?"

She didn't bother to offer him a reason and, true to his nature, Mr. Gordman didn't ask, his voice neutral as he assured her that wouldn't be a problem. "Sounds good. I've got that meeting at three o'clock but as long as that's all prepared, I don't see any issues with that."

As the afternoon wore on, she'd almost wish he *had* questioned her insistence on leaving. If he had, she would have probably buckled, fobbed off his curiosity; she'd have further lied, back-pedaled more than likely with some lame excuse, 'Where am I going? Oh, actually…wait, what's today's date?' she'd have improvised, laughing nervously as her eyes darted blankly at the calendar on her desk. Her courage would have undoubtedly flagged in that instance. 'Never mind. That's not until next week…. My mistake. Disregard.' She'd have stayed at the office and carried on as usual.

Only, he hadn't asked and as two o'clock slowly passed, Christina's stomach boiled. Hunched over her computer, her fingers and mind bent to work in a flurried, harassed kind of concentration, anything to beat back the impending time, she found herself ready to leave long before two-thirty that afternoon.

Glancing pointedly at her inbox, she gave it a surprised look. It was empty. That was one good thing about her emotional state of being—there was nothing she wanted to do more than avoid it. Wiping her hands together, Christina reluctantly shut down her computer. She'd probably never been so productive in her life, and for her, that was saying something. Quickly organizing a last batch of papers into a folder for Mr. Gordman's three o'clock appointment, she'd no sooner closed the portfolio than she was pushing back her chair and gaining her feet. Absently, she reached behind her for her spring jacket.

"Going somewhere?"

Spinning furiously at the unexpected sound of a voice behind her, Christina glared across her desk at Jackie. One hand clutched at her heart. "Jesus, Jackie! You scared me."

"Sneaking away?"

Christina rolled her eyes. With a pointed movement, she threw first one arm and then another into the sleeves of her coral trench coat. "No. Don't be ridicu—and what are you doing here?" she asked, her words tripping unevenly out of her mouth.

"Stalking me again?"

Christina would have been mortified to know that she looked both distracted and harried as she stared at her friend. Luckily for her, Jackie *was* her friend, so she kept her mouth shut. Instead, she smiled: "You know as well as I do that I have a meeting scheduled with Mr. Gordman in twenty minutes."

Christina's face stiffened. Of course. His three o'clock appointment with a new client to talk branding opportunities.

Jackie clicked her teeth. "Got a dentist appointment?"

"Huh? Me? No." Turning to the filing cabinet, Christina retrieved her purse from its designated drawer.

"Doctor then?"

"What?" At the question, Christina frowned. She shot Jackie a look. "No."

"Car work?"

"Jesus, what is this?"

Jackie grinned, one finger pointing to the side of Christina's lip. "You've got a smudge of lipstick here."

With an impatient finger, Christina wiped it away, but not before unconsciously turning toward the small mirror she had hanging up on the wall beside the filing cabinet, just to double-check her appearance.

"Off to see Jason then." It was a shot in the dark.

Christina's eyes darted frantically toward Mr. Gordman's closed door. "Enough," she hissed.

Jackie gasped, one hand going up to her mouth. "You are!"

Christina rolled her eyes.

"I mean, it makes sense," Jackie said, glancing down at her wristwatch. "School's almost out for the day."

"Shut up, will you?" Christina grumbled. "Just shut up."

"Finally surrendering, huh?"

"Oh, Jacks," Christina insisted one foot stomping down emphatically with the words. Digging through her purse, she produced the roll of raffle tickets she'd accidentally stolen from the ball game last weekend. She held it out like a weapon. "No. I need to return this. It belongs to the school's baseball team."

Christina had looked smug for all of five seconds after delivering this but then Jackie started to laugh; soon enough, she was guffawing so hard she was bent over double, her hands slapping against her knees.

Christina's eyes narrowed, that foot now tap-tapping an angry tattoo on the carpet. "Are you finished?"

"Seriously? That's the most preposterous thing," Jackie cried, sputtering amusedly over her words, "that I've ever…heard!"

"Excuse me?"

"Come on," Jackie said, jerking her thumb back over her shoulder, indicating Mr. Gordman's door. "You think he couldn't have done that for you?"

Christina hefted up her chin. She could feel her face reacting to the embarrassment inherent in that question. "It's not his responsibility. It's mine."

Jackie shook her head meaningfully, a wry grin replacing her laughter. "It's so telling sometimes... the flimsy excuses people will try to morph into the most logical of reasons."

"Give it a rest," Christina grumbled, but she knew she'd lost so, instead of denying it, she patted the side of her hair. "How do I look?"

Jackie's mirth subsided almost instantly. She gave Christina a considering glance. Then she smiled. "You look beautiful. You always do."

And she did. Her blonde hair, with almost white-blonde highlights, shone from her expertly styled French twist, and her makeup was flawless in a face of classical lines and large, almond-shaped eyes.

Christina nodded once, sharply. Grabbing her purse, she slung it over the crook of her elbow. "Okay," she said, her eyes taking in the big clock, "I'd better get going."

"Good luck."

~ ✩✩✩ ~

Ten long minutes later, Christina's fingers curled violently over her steering wheel as she pulled into the parking lot of the large brick high school. Her eyes flickered naturally to the ballfields sitting a little to one side of the mammoth building. The sight was oddly comforting, familiar. Stabilizing.

Alighting hesitantly from her vehicle, she stopped to gaze at the front entrance—all four glass doors shimmering open and closed with the swell of exiting students. Allowing herself to be swallowed by the mob, Christina moved against the current of feet until she found herself standing inside a lofty commons area, the gray-and-maroon flooring trampled underneath the hurry and scurry of teenagers hustling to their cars or various sporting fields or drama departments. The air was alive with relief and procrastination and indifference.

Not a single student stopped to stare at Christina as she floated past the packs of girls giggling together or the boys lounging in the random array of chairs plastered about—nor did the group of students bent over a large poster stop to glance up at her as she slowed her steps, her head swinging from left to right, her eyes searching.

No one paid Christina the least bit of attention. Still, she swore she felt the weight of all eyes on her anyway. The very rhythm of her walk changed. Circumventing the throng of bodies, Christina felt her skin tingling. What if he'd already left? What if he was already heading for the parking lot, getting into his car? What if he had students staying after, waiting to ask him questions about a recent test? What if…

Christina knew then she'd probably made a mistake, meeting him on his home turf. No, not meeting him, surprising him. Ambushing him. She didn't belong here. It was conspicuous. Obvious. Dammit, Jackie had been right. It was too late to turn back now. Carrying her head a little higher, Christina forced her legs to pump faster when her gaze latched onto a sign held above a door just past the main commons.

The Office.

Coming up to it, Christina was grateful to see the door was open. Gaining the entrance, she saw what must have been a teacher leaning against the copier while another busily tacked something onto a bulletin board against one wall. Smiling brightly, Christina was determined not to quail under the steady gaze of the only other occupant in the room, a thirty-something woman sitting rather primly behind a high, white built-in desk that clearly denounced her as the school receptionist.

"Hello?" The woman asked politely, raising her eyebrows expectantly as Christina approached. "May I help you?"

"Hi," Christina said, her voice a little breathy. "I'm looking for a…ah, a Mr. Gordman? Jason Gordman?" Christina smiled when the receptionist frowned at the words. "Could you tell me where I can find him?"

"Is he expecting you?"

"Uh, no, I don't think…."

"Do you have a visitor's pass?"

"A what? No—that is, I'm dropping something off for the baseball team." Christina's nerves got the better of her. "I helped out here last weekend. For the tournament?" This rambling tidbit of information was met with tight silence. "I didn't know I'd be in the area this afternoon, so I didn't think to call…"

The woman's lips folded together. "Hmm. Well, the best I can do is try to call him for you. Though I have no idea if he's still here." Her pointed glance at the wall clock overhead was hardly necessary. Christina was well aware of the time.

"Right, okay."

The woman's eyes narrowed. "Hold on." She brought the phone to her ear and punched in his extension. "And your name?"

"Christina DeLuca."

Nodding distractedly, the receptionist said no more. The silence was lifted only by the soft ringing echoing out from her earpiece. The phone rang, another beat of silence and then: "Hmm…" Putting the phone back down on the cradle, that woman's face showed no expression. "He isn't answering."

"Oh. Okay, well…" Christina took a deep breath, "that's all right then. Thanks." Patting the desk in goodbye, she made to turn and leave. "I'll just, I'll try some other time, I guess."

The receptionist sighed, and Christina thought she heard her mumbling something about the school being officially over for the day, anyway…and then that lady's voice rose, addressing Christina once more: "You're just dropping something off, you said?"

Christina paused. She turned back to encounter that hawkish look. "Yes."

"I'll be here for another half an hour. I expect you to pop back in and tell me once you're leaving. And I'll need Jason to come and confirm your visit, too."

Christina's eyes widened. "Y-yes, ma'am," she stuttered, hardly believing the words.

"All right. He's just down that hallway," the woman said, pointing out the door. "Fourth door on the right. And next time, request a visitor's pass in advance."

"I will, I promise!"

Christina didn't wait for the receptionist to change her mind. The sentiment of her softly worded thank-you hanging between them, Christina scuttled out of the office, her feet taking her determinedly in the direction indicated. By now, the hallways dissecting the school were mostly empty, the floors scuffed and dull under the fluorescent lights overhead. Heartbeat shaking her, Christina found her breath wheeling noisily out of her nose as she reached her destination—room 135. Taking a moment to compose herself, she blew a wisp of hair off her forehead, her hands running down the length of her shirt before reaching forward to let her fingers settle over the doorknob.

Knocking on the door with one hand, she simultaneously pushed it open with the other. "Hello?" Christina called out blindly. Tucking her head around the corner, her gaze met an empty classroom. Thirty or so unoccupied desks stood between her and a large whiteboard against the far wall, replete with a single bookcase, crammed to overflowing, nestled in one corner. Directly across from her stood a large teacher's desk. Jason was not seated behind it.

Feeling all of the energy ooze out of her body, Christina sighed. "Dammit."

"Swearing is usually prohibited on school grounds."

At the sound of Jason's quietly amused voice, coming from close behind her, Christina whirled around on a startled cry. There, just inside the door she'd abandoned only moments before, he stood, a cup of coffee in one hand. He raised it up as though by explanation.

"Just got myself a little pick-me-up," he said easily. "I've got papers to grade tonight."

"Oh." She wasn't altogether sure what to do with her face. Or her hands, which were clasping each other tightly across her waist.

He, in contrast, didn't seem the least agitated by her appearance. "This is a surprise."

"You don't look surprised."

"Don't I?" he asked amusedly. "Then I'm hiding it well."

"Oh."

His grin lengthened. Leaning up against the doorjamb, he seemed in no real rush to find out the reason for her visit. "What can I do for you, Christina?"

Under that mocking, mischievous grin, she felt her lips flattening, pulling tight. Scrambling, Christina shouldered her purse free and produced the roll of raffle tickets with a touch of flair.

Jason's eyebrows rose. "The mystery deepens."

Brandishing it defensively, she ignored his comment. "I came to return this."

Jason being Jason, he didn't immediately reach for it, even when her hands shot out, holding it firmly within his grasp. Instead, he brought the cup of coffee to his mouth, taking a long sip. "Okay. I'll bite," he finally said. "What is that?"

Christina all but sputtered, "It's from the baseball tournament!" Her voice was too high, too loud. Straining for control, she lowered it. "It's for, I don't know, raffles or something. I, uh, I took it home by accident."

Jason hardly smothered his laughter. "I see."

Christina glowered. From her peripheral vision, she could see the last straggling teenagers empty out onto the school grounds. Well, at least no one would be around to watch her make an ass out of herself. That had to be worth something. Notching her chin up, she seethed: "I thought you'd want it back, that's all."

Pushing off the jamb, the heavy door shutting quietly behind him, Jason advanced inside the room. He set his cup down on an empty desk. "Yeah?" he drawled.

She raised a cool eyebrow. "Yeah."

He laughed. "Well, thanks for rushing down here to get that back to us." Finally, he reached to take the roll out of her waiting hands. Gripping it loosely in his fist, he smiled. "'Course we have about a hundred spare boxes or so of these…"

Christina felt her teeth gnash together.

"But I suppose it was as good an excuse as any," he continued.

"Excuse me?" With a sort of strength he couldn't be capable of knowing, she brought her eyes level to his.

"You could have dropped these off with the school secretary, Christina," he said meaningfully.

She felt her lips twist at the accusation. She should have known he wouldn't miss an opportunity to poke at her, try to expose her. After all, even Jackie hadn't been able to resist.

"Hell, you could have pitched them into a garbage bin for all they'd be missed."

"How should I have known that?" Her voice rose aggressively, her arms crossing under her breasts.

Casually, he dropped the raffle roll down beside his half-forgotten cup of coffee. Then, with a smirk, he took a step toward her. In response, Christina caught a hurried step backward.

He paused, his head tilting a little at the telling move. "Retreating, Christina? That hardly seems your style."

"I think I've earned that right," she returned.

Jason's lips parted in a humorless smile. Then he took another step closer. "Do you? But I'm not the one playing hot-and-cold."

Chapter Seventeen

Christina balked—not so much by the words but the intensity with which they were delivered. Up to this moment, she'd thought Jason felt little more than mild amusement at her unexpected presence in his classroom. With a quick swallow, she parried his movement, her feet taking her farther and farther inside the room.

"I'm, I'm not playing anything," she insisted, but her gaze dropped away from his nonetheless.

"No? Then why are you really here? And what the hell was that the other night at your apartment?" Yup, he was definitely not amused anymore.

Christina cleared her throat, humility overtaking her. "Look, I probably owe you an apology for the way I acted—"

"I'm not looking for an apology," Jason assured her, his hands coming to rest lightly on his hips. His features contracted in consternation. Probably it was a look he'd perfected all these years with his young pupils. "I'm looking for an explanation."

Christina's eyes skimmed over the classroom helplessly. She was halfway to the whiteboard by now, her back pressing her ever nearer toward it. "An explanation?" She felt her defenses rising. "It was just a few kisses."

"It was more than that."

"Okay, fine. Whatever," she relented.

"That's just it," he argued, and to her sensitive ears, he sounded half-exasperated. "There was nothing *whatever* about it. You threw me for one hell of a loop."

"Because I wanted to sleep with you?"

"Because you wanted me at all."

"Wait." Christina goggled at him. "You can't honestly be telling me that right now."

"Of course, I can," he sputtered, running a hand through his hair. Streaks of the blond-white, brown strands stood up in response to the agitated movement.

Christina's face was pinched. "Remember Easter?"

He shook his head. "That was different."

"Why, because you started it?"

"Yeah, and you ended it," he reminded her. He swore softly, half under his breath. "But before that…" He gestured emptily, shaking his head.

"Before that, there was the employee Christmas party," Christina offered pointedly. "As you well know." Her voice couldn't have been drier. Somewhere in the back of her mind, she recognized that she should be embarrassed by the admission. Instead, she felt a sort of energy steal through her senses when his mask slipped, the vulnerable man peeking through his usual conceit. There was something intoxicating about sharing the burden of open honesty; there was something freeing about staring someone down and finally speaking, finally saying the real things. And knowing that they were responding in kind.

So yes, Christina knew she'd bemoan the memory of this conversation later. She'd review and analyze it until she fell into an exhausted, headachy sleep. But right now, she reveled in the atmosphere wrapping itself around her and Jason, the atmosphere binding them together.

Jason sighed. "I should never have brought that up. I'm sorry."

"No," she assured him, shaking her head, "it doesn't matter. The point is, you wondered then. That night."

"I hoped."

They'd never actually spoken about what had happened after the Christmas party, not really. She'd always appreciated his show of discretion and grace. But it was there, between them, all the same. That night had altered Jason's perception of her. It was what had led to his postulating, what had implanted the tiniest seed of doubt in his mind. It was what had led to those brief, unguarded moments on Easter.

When he'd demanded to drive her home that ill-fated December evening, determined to shield her from the embarrassment of becoming a stumbling, bumbling reality of the woman who never lost control, she should have fought him harder. She should have called for a cab. She should have walked herself to the bus station. Hell, she should have crawled the twenty-odd miles that separated the Gordmans' house from her apartment. Instead, she'd capitulated.

She'd been too vulnerable to refuse him. The temptation had been too accessible and her wits too addled to recognize the potential for danger.

As it was, the ride back to her duplex had been relatively uneventful. She could still remember sitting in that passenger seat, the length of her cocktail dress riding unnervingly high on her thighs, her fingers almost obsessively trying to tug the hemline back down to a more modest spot. Not that it would have mattered much. It had been dark by the time they'd left and the inside of Jason's car, excepting for the pale yellow and blue lights on the dashboard and instrument panel, had been illuminated only by the soft glow of passing streetlights. And besides, his eyes had been focused straight ahead.

Oh, but his aftershave. She remembered sinking into the plush seat and drowning in the scent. Being so compactly enclosed, it had infused the car with a sophisticated manliness— it had been heady and romantic and she'd almost burned her nostrils trying to memorize the fragrance.

That had been fine. Her idolization had been under the guise of darkness. It was when he'd pulled up to her house that things had become…complicated.

With a sudden movement, shaking back her hair as violently as she shook away the offending images clouding her mind, Christina sneered: "You hoped?" A hollow laugh erupted from her raw throat. "Oh, blow it out your ear. You knew exactly how I felt that night."

Jason's countenance flickered with irritation. "You were drunk, Christina. Lousy with it."

When he'd walked her to her apartment, one hand carelessly holding her elbow as she'd struggled to find purchase on the ground, she'd lost control. Staring up at him in the shrouded darkness of her front porch, she'd pouted as he'd taken the house keys from her nerveless hands.

"I hate these parties. Everyone gets a bit tipsy and soon I find myself on the receiving end of a bunch of horny men who want to ravish me."

Suppressing a shudder at the reminder of those damning words, Christina felt the pulsing throb of recollection beating against her flushed complexion, the ensuing memories wedging themselves hatefully between her and Jason. She could still hear the sound of the key jerking in the lock when Jason had turned back to look at her…

"What?"

"Although, actually, maybe I get it," she'd said, grinning up at him. "I'm a bit tipsy now and I think I wouldn't mind being ravished."

The echoed slur of her voice, the sloppy lift of her shoulder, the beguiling invitation which had made itself known in the flush of her cheeks…. All of it forbidden territory, all of it returning to the present with a vengeance, washing over her, over them both.

"Don't," Jason pleaded with her now, one hand reaching forward, reaching toward her. "Please don't do this."

With another backward movement, Christina avoided his touch, shaking her head as she sidestepped his advance. "No," she insisted, her chin notching up a little on the words, "it's the not talking that got us into this mess in the first place. Too many unsaid things, too many unresolved moments. But they're there, all the same. Between us." And now, they were encroaching on her relationships with Matthew and Mary as well.

Jason's arms swung out to his sides impotently. "That night, you were in a vulnerable place. I knew that." His eyes implored hers, begged her forgiveness.

"Maybe," she conceded, "but I made myself clear all the same."

"Maybe," Jason parroted with maddening inflection, "but that's hardly the point. What you were saying, it wasn't...you know, about me or you. Not really."

Christina's lips twitched. "I may have been drunk, Jason, but I remember what happened."

Standing under her porch light, her body leaning against the side of the house for support, she'd hazarded a look at his face. "I bet no one's ever rebuffed your attempt to—"

"To ravish someone?" There had been just the slightest hint of humor threading his words.

"Yeah. I bet not."

If only she'd stopped there. But she hadn't. She'd even gone so far as to ask him... No. Mentally retreating, Christina cringed with newfound humiliation, her mind forcefully blocking the recall.

Perhaps Jason had never been rebuffed, but he'd certainly rejected her that cool December night. He'd been kind about it, gentle even when he'd sighed softly, swinging the door open. "It's late, Christina," he'd informed her quietly. "And you've had too much to drink."

"Brilliant deduction."

His voice had roughened just a bit at her playful rejoinder. "You don't know what you're saying."

"Sure, I do. I'm asking for a little assistance."

But he'd only assisted her inside. And then he'd left her there, alone.

Reliving it all over again, the humiliation and contempt from that evening, Christina sucked in a slow breath. Pushing her gaze back up to Jason's tight features, she tilted her head. "Seems to be a pattern with us, huh? I throw myself at you and you, you…" With a flip of her wrist, she pursed her lips meaningfully.

"That's hardly fair," Jason returned, the edge in his voice thrusting her out of that painful reverie. There was a heatedness to his tone, a tautness in his jawline. "I would never take advantage of you that way. Not ever."

"God save me from decent men," she joked, just as she had that night, when her only solace left had been found in humor.

Jason's lips twitched. "Save yourself from lecherous tools who'd actually take you up on that incredibly tempting offer," he returned, just the same as he had that evening on her doorstep.

Christina nodded grimly at the words, at the perfect recitation—souvenirs of a well-remembered line. The morning after the party, she'd fought for breath, throwing up regrets and remorse and disgust, but it had all been for naught. The next time she'd seen Jason, he'd acted as though nothing out of the ordinary had transpired on her front porch. He'd teased her out of a stonily stiff silence and…poof, they'd gone on as normal.

But it had just been another sham.

"Ah, there it is," she chided mockingly. "That good old Gordman charm. Should I be flattered? I never have been quite sure?"

Jason's eyebrows furrowed. "What, you'd rather I had slept with you that night, when you were so drunk you needed help up to your door? You wish I would have been low enough to have done that to you? That would have made things better?"

"Obviously not," she returned. "But don't stand here and tell me you didn't know. I may have been drunk, but I was far from incoherent."

"Drunk people aren't usually the most reliable."

"No?" she scoffed.

"No."

"Then I guess that explains it."

"Huh?"

"The need for your little theory? On Easter?"

He cocked his head a little to one side. "Wait. Is that why you think I kissed you? To see if I could ravish you, as you'd once implied? To boost my ego? To what? Amuse myself?"

"Well, why else?"

He flinched. "You've got a bad image of men, don't you? Who did that to you?"

A stark, angry silence swarmed around them in the wake of that soft charge. Gaping at Jason, Christina couldn't find the words to speak.

He seemed to be processing them too, his eyes narrowing steadily as he looked down at her. The longer she remained silent, the louder his question rang throughout the white block walls of his classroom.

"You think I was trying to manipulate you in some way?" He clicked his tongue against the back of his teeth. "Or that I was bored and figured you'd be an easy target?"

She felt her face twitch at the words, at their meanness.

He whistled, his face creasing with disappointment at her damning silence. "I see." With a breath of air, he ran a hand through his hair again, only this time his fingers were weary with fatigue. "Wow. I thought you knew me better than that. I thought even you liked me more than that assessment would imply."

"I threw myself at you. Shamelessly," she muttered, her cheeks betraying her discomfort. She felt the toe of her shoe twisting itself against the polished floor.

Jason nodded again knowingly. "Me…and someone from your past, right? And they threw that back in your face, didn't they?"

She didn't answer him.

"I'm surprised at you," Jason confessed.

"At me?" She notched her chin up defensively. There was no way whatever he had to say next would be a good thing.

"A cool, confident woman such as you are—"

"A defense mechanism, surely," she returned.

Jason laughed at her ready response.

"On Easter, you said you'd always thought I hated you," Christina reminded him. Those words, and the kiss they'd shared, slithered across her mind with near perfect detail.

"But you don't hate me."

She nodded. "Exactly."

Jason's forehead crinkled, but damn the man, he still looked mildly amused. "I'm confused."

Feeling flustered, because she wasn't accustomed to talking about her feelings, especially to the one man she'd sworn to keep in the dark, Christina made an impatient gesture. "I wanted you to think I hated you."

"So I couldn't use you."

She reared her head back. "I didn't say that."

"But that's why," Jason confirmed, taking another, almost victorious step toward her. In response, Christina stumbled back in withdrawal, keeping the space carefully between them. "Because you think your only attraction is being, what was that word you used the other night?" Jason asked, but it was obvious he wasn't actually expecting an answer. "Convenient?"

Christina's shoulders drew back, her ears burning against the ugly accusation. "Stop it." She held up a hand. "Just. I've had enough. You don't know me so don't you dare stand—"

"And whose fault is that?" he taunted her and, perhaps in spite of that raised hand warning him off, took an additional step in her direction.

Christina's eyes flickered quickly toward the door, but it was firmly shut and the lights in the hallway, just visible through the thin panel of glass on one side, cast a darkening shadow upon the lockers. No one would be coming in; no distraction would save her. Not this time.

"You want to know why I kissed you?" Jason asked, his question bringing him steadily nearer. At the words, Christina's eyes jerked nervously back to his face. His hazel gaze was watchful, his lips pulling into a smug sort of smile.

It was at that moment that Christina felt the whiteboard meet up against her back. In reaction, her hands pressed against the melamine surface behind her, the glass tray holding the markers biting against her lower back. Still, he didn't stop walking, not until—

"What?" she managed weakly.

"You weren't the only one, you know," he whispered, his steps catching up to her at last. Leaning slightly forward, his body was close enough to promise contact without actually touching. His hands, however, he kept down at his sides, safely out of reach. "You weren't the only one that first afternoon on my parents' doorstep"—his lips twitched humorously—"those documents of Dad's clutched in your arms."

"What?" she whispered again, her body humming so loudly she could hardly take in his words. His cologne filled her nostrils.

"I thought you might have been the most gorgeous woman I'd ever seen," he told her, his head dipping lower. "I still do."

Her intake of breath was a rush of sound as his lips hung, slanted just above hers, so tantalizingly close. "And since we're being honest, let me confess one other thing. I want to kiss you again."

She made a whimpering sound low in her throat, her body stilling, imploring.

"But I'm not going to."

Her gaze colliding with his, Christina's eyes widened. A beat of stark, dissonant static resonated in her head. "Wha—?"

"Not yet," he continued, his nose brushing down to tickle against her own, the action softening the words.

Christina felt her mouth forming a silent question, her senses reeling.

"Not until you trust me," he answered, breathing against her softly parted lips. "Not until you trust the reasons behind the action."

Disappointment and frustration waged equally inside Christina. But when she would have broken free of his proximity, Jason only pressed closer, anticipating the move.

"When I do finally kiss you," he assured her, one finger coming up to trace the edges of her mouth, "I promise you that you'll think about it later, relive it when you're alone."

Against her will, Christina moaned at the contact, the words, the mesmerizing tease. Against her will, her body reacted, softened at the prompting.

"Only that time, you won't be wondering about the motives."

Disoriented, Christina felt the unwelcome rush of air as Jason slowly pulled away from her body, giving her space at last. Her eyes clouded, her head slowly shaking with confusion. "I don't…"

"I won't make the same mistakes that he did."

"He?"

Jason shrugged. "The man from your past. The one you sometimes mistake for me."

She frowned, her teeth gnawing together. "I told you—"

"Nothing left unsaid?" Jason reminded her.

Folding her arms across her chest, Christina stood guardedly. "That part of my life is over. It has nothing to do with, with us."

"Now that, I'm seriously starting to doubt."

"Jason…"

But he only chuckled. "It's fine. I'll wait until you're ready to talk. I can be patient."

"There's nothing—"

"And until then, I'm determined to change your impression of me."

Christina felt her lips parting on an escaped, exasperated laugh. "Confident, aren't we?"

"What are you doing Friday evening?"

The words, unexpected and abrupt, brought her still once more. "What?"

Hazel eyes stared into brown ones. "Go on a date with me, Christina?"

"A what?"

Jason grinned. "A date." His eyes narrowed on her face. "Panicking on me, DeLuca?"

"No." Yes. Absolutely. Her stomach flopped, her hands clenching the material of her coat, her heart thudding with startling intensity. Her eyes lifted to his, and her nerves ran away with her. He was so stunningly handsome.

When I do finally kiss you, I promise…

You don't need Matthew or my permission to date Jason. That's your business. But if you did *need our permission, you'd have it. Unequivocally.*

This is not your past. They are not your past.

Her body rippled, convulsed with the remembered words—Jason's low timbre and Mary's soft pleas drifting past her defenses—followed by the thin thread of her own silent voice begging to believe things were different this time. She wanted that. To be kissed. To be free. She wanted him. And he was standing right there, saying he wanted her, too.

"Do you like lacrosse?"

At the question, she felt her focus pulling, fraying. "Huh?"

Jason chuckled. "The lacrosse game on Friday? For our date?"

Christina swallowed. "I don't remember agreeing to go with you."

Without warning, Jason moved. One hand catching either side of the whiteboard at the back of Christina's head, his body suddenly enveloped hers again. Shocked, Christina sucked in an audible breath at his quick nearness, the heady smell of his earthy, spicy cologne.

"Please, Christina?"

"Yes." It was a whisper of sound, an almost involuntary reaction. Certainly, she hadn't planned to say that.

He winked. "That's my girl." Then, pushing back against the wall, he straightened up once more.

At the flash of solitary air, Christina felt her shoulders relax. "Tease."

He grinned. "All's fair."

"Wait," she said as a new thought occurred to her. He had her so jumbled up inside that she'd hardly noticed before but…. "You're taking me to a high school lacrosse game?" She blinked in consideration. "For our first date?"

He nodded.

"How exotic." She smirked.

"That's actually the whole point," Jason returned easily, but not before a devilish gleam entered those cunning eyes. "I'll be Mr. Gordman there, surrounded by students and faculty members."

"I see."

"No chance for things to get out of hand."

For perhaps the first time since she'd entered his classroom, Christina felt as though she had the upper hand. "Too bad."

His eyes danced with mischief. "Care to change my mind?"

"And ruin the suspense?" Christina taunted. "I think not." Pulling herself clear of the wall, she took her leave then, her body swaying with pure feminine conceit as she headed for the door, her smile an echo to Jason's ringing assurance that he'd pick her up at six-thirty on Friday. It was only at the last minute that she thought to remind him to stop by the receptionist's desk on the way out.

"Please assure her that I was, indeed, an approved visitor."

His wolfish smile followed her out to the parking lot.

As her steps reverberated across the school parking lot, Christina staunchly blanked down the rushing onslaught of doubts stabbing at her stomach, the debilitating swell of a learned flight response: What the hell was she thinking? What was wrong with her? Did she want another emotional fracture? Just another mistake to add to the list?

Her cheeks creased into a frown, her steps slowing as her throat bobbed to the time of the well-rehearsed mantra.

No.

Mary had been right.

This was not her past. Jason was not Bill and Mary was not her mother.

And dammit, she really wanted this. Unconsciously, Christina looked over her shoulder, her eyes scanning the building's exterior windows until she located Jason's classroom. Her lips pulled into a smile.

Picking up her pace once more, Christina repeated a new missive as she gained her car.

She could date him. Openly, honestly. Without guilt or shame. She only had to combat the fear.

"And besides," she scolded herself, but her tone was light as she unlocked her door and swung into her seat. She didn't have the resources to be both thrilled and upset at the same time. "You wanted this to happen. Hell, even Jackie knew it."

Mary had given her blessing just in case Christina needed it. She'd promised that nothing would change between them.

Jason had been right too. Sometimes she confused the Gordmans for the people in her past.

"Well, not anymore," she promised, working diligently to stifle the silent, challenging rejoinder: *This was their chance to prove themselves different. To prove her preconceived notions wrong.*

Chapter Eighteen

Walking into the darkened office the following morning, Christina couldn't fight back the quiet hum murmuring off her lips. It was one of those spring washes—the damp of the early dawn had the smell of approaching summer, of promise. Arriving early, the usually chaotic building offered a half an hour's respite from the upcoming day. She felt energized, rejuvenated as she shucked off her dewy jacket and sat down at her desk.

Flexing her fingers, she leaned close to her computer as she started it up and logged-in. Smiling as the screen flickered to life, her eyes slid thoughtlessly toward her desk calendar. Two more days. Two more days until Friday. Until—

Her thoughts were interrupted by the sudden boom of her intercom sounding off in the silent room. Startled by the unexpected noise, Christina let out a muffled yelp, her fingers curling around the edge of her desk to keep from upending her chair.

"Christina? Christina, when you have a minute, would you come into my office?"

"Mr. Gordman?" she asked tentatively, but she needn't have bothered. She knew it was him. It was just, in all these years, he'd never once beaten her to the office. Spying over her computer, her lips pulled down. No light emitted from underneath his door. But he was obviously in there. "Yes, of course," she rushed to say, pushing her chair back even as she spoke. "I'll be right in."

Something was wrong. Something had to be wrong. He'd lost a big client. They were closing down a department. He had to lay someone off. Maybe her...

Reaching for the door, she paused to collect herself. Deep breath in, deep breath out. With deliberation, she turned the knob in her damp palm, but none of that consternation showed on her face as she poked it into his office with a determined smile. Darkness swelled against the windows, and the only orb of light came from the frosted-glass of his desk lamp.

Christina's eyes narrowed suspiciously.

Still, the quiet alto of her voice betrayed nothing. "Morning," she called, the rest of her body quickly following after as she slipped inside. Closing the door, she lost no time heading for one of the two chairs sitting before his desk. She lifted one eyebrow with forced humor. "You're here awfully early."

Mr. Gordman didn't look good. Sitting in his leather chair, his fingers steepled together on his desk, deep gashes of exhaustion cutting through the lines of his cheeks, he looked grim, stern.

Christina wiggled uneasily in her chair. "Watch stop working?"

It was a lame joke that received little more than a staid smile in return. "I needed a quiet place to think," Mr. Gordman told her. He sighed. "It didn't work."

Christina inclined her head, crossing her legs demurely in what she hoped was the picture of cool composure. "What's going on?"

"We've got a problem here."

"The company?" she asked, but she had a sudden feeling...

"No, not the company," he growled. "You and me."

Christina feigned surprise. "You and me?"

"And Mary."

"Oh."

"You won't talk to her."

Christina opened her mouth to speak, but really, what could she say? He was right. Even last night, snuggled on her couch, she'd managed to avoid that waiting phone call. It didn't make sense. She realized that. After all, Mary's words—that memorized voicemail—had been a big part of Christina's decision to see Jason, to take a chance on her feelings. Only, ironically, Christina hadn't been ready to take a chance on that woman, herself. What if Mary hadn't meant what she said? What if she'd lied—not to Christina, but to herself? What if the reality of Christina actually dating Jason somehow changed Mary's opinion on the matter? It was one thing to say it and another to accept it. It'd seemed easier somehow to push it off. Yesterday had been so good. So magical. It'd been a long time since Christina had allowed herself to believe in magic. So, she'd put her phone away.

Mr. Gordman spread his hands wide, bringing her attention back to the present. "You certainly won't talk to me. Not unless it's business related."

"Mr. Gordman."

"Hell, this is a personal conversation," he said impatiently. "Might as well call me Matthew."

Christina took a deep breath. Her hands trembled in her lap. She felt trapped under that gaze, unprepared. "Fine. *Matthew*," she stressed, her voice cracking, "I really don't think this is the time or place to be discussing such matters…"

"Hell," he said, cursing for the second time. Christina couldn't deny the surprise at this show of irritation. Matthew was a contained man who didn't wear his feelings publicly. For him, swearing was telling. "You're right."

Christina nodded eagerly, gathering her equilibrium. She needed time to think, to sort out her thoughts.

"Have dinner with us instead," Matthew invited, and without giving her time to comment, added: "How about Friday night?"

"Friday?" Christina repeated dimly.

Matthew saw the conflict cross her features. "Please," he added, "Mary misses you." Before Christina could respond, he shook his head. "Dammit, I miss you too."

She gulped and a sheen of tears flooded her eyes momentarily. "Yeah?"

"I shouldn't have poked my nose into your private affairs. I'm sorry."

"It's, it's fine…" Christina blustered, her hands coming up quickly to ward off his words.

"I don't want you to get the wrong impression," Matthew continued, talking steadily over her wild embarrassment. "It had been only too obvious that Jason had upset you over Easter. I'd only meant to get to the bottom of it, make sure it didn't happen again." His cheeks pinkened slightly. "That's why I took him out to lunch last Friday. It's why I excluded you." Christina knew all of this already, but it was nice to hear it from the source. "I'd wanted to talk to him, yell if necessary."

"Really, you don't need to explain."

Matthew smiled at her squeamishness. "I'll only stop on one condition."

"Anything."

"Dinner. On Friday."

Christina sighed. "I'd love to," she confessed, her earlier feelings eased by the earnestness in his face, the desperation of his defense. She was oddly comforted by his interference. Worry. Protection. Love. "Really, I would," she insisted. "But I-I can't."

Disappointed silence met her words, followed by, "I see."

"Because I'm actually going out with Jason on Friday." Christina wasn't sure she'd meant to tell him that. She knew she hadn't *planned* to tell him that. Only, this time, she was determined to keep no secrets.

No shame, no regret.

Just a little fear.

Matthew's body rocked backward a little at the words. "You are?"

"I mean, I hope that won't be an issue for you, as my boss?"

"Nonsense," Matthew assured her, waving the words away. "I'm pleased to hear it, in fact." He smiled to himself. "So, perhaps not quite as upset as I'd thought."

Christina bit the side of her lip primly. "Perhaps not."

He grinned. "Mary will gloat, of course." At her look, he shrugged. "What mother wouldn't?"

Christina lowered her eyes demurely, deciding it was safer to say nothing in response. Still, the admission steadied her nerves. Peeking up at him, she changed tracts, "What about Saturday? Could we do dinner then?"

He smiled slowly. "Actually, Saturday's better for us."

Staring pointedly at her reflection in her bathroom mirror, Christina carefully applied a nude shade of lipstick to her pouting mouth. Standing back, she surveyed the finished product. Her nerves jumped uncomfortably in her neck as she squinted at herself.

She looked fine.

Casual, but not too casual.

"God, get a grip," she muttered, popping the lid back on her lipstick with a decided snap. She'd changed three times, spent over half an hour scouring her wardrobe—the pantsuit had been far too professional and the sundress was choking on its own femininity—until she'd finally settled on a milky white sweatshirt with Jason's high school mascot splashed across its front, which she'd purchased from Mary last year for some fundraiser or another, and a pair of tight, slimming designer jeans.

That was it, jeans and a sweatshirt. Rocket science, really.

She was more than a little disgusted with herself. Especially the way her eyes kept traveling back to the mirror, seeking reassurances. Pathetic.

Her hair was up in a deliberately messy ponytail, with soft tendrils falling against her temples and whispering across her cheekbones. To complete the ensemble, she'd rubbed on a tiny bit of blusher and just a hint of eyeliner.

And the lipstick.

Taking a deep, uneven breath, she exited the bathroom and, checking her watch, took herself stiffly into the living room. With a huff, she leaned against one of the armrests on her couch, her fingers drumming against the leather backrest. The game started at seven o'clock that evening. Jason had said he'd pick her up at six-thirty, and if she were being completely honest with herself, Christina had been slightly let down that he hadn't offered to take her to dinner first. Frowning, she resisted the urge to check her watch again and failed. It was six twenty-five.

One of Christina's booted feet tapped erratically against the floor, her knee jerking with the frantic rhythm. She was tense. Excited and...dammit! Where the hell was Jason?

As if on cue, a knock sounded at the front door, interrupting her thoughts. Pulling herself upright, for an instant, Christina gaped at it dumbly.

"Jason," she whispered inanely, her cheeks taking on a dusty glow as she stumbled into the entryway. She'd barely crossed the space separating her from the door when she was jerking it open.

And there he was, standing on the other side of her threshold. At the sight of him, Christina knew she'd made the right choice in her outfit. He was wearing a pair of faded blue jeans and a red and white plaid button-down shirt, the latter of which emphasized his wide-shoulders and lean waist.

For a split-second, no one spoke. Christina felt tongue-tied, gauche. Feelings she was entirely unaccustomed to experiencing. Then again, she'd also never changed three times for a date before.

"Uh, hi," she finally breathed, leaning self-consciously against the doorframe.

"Hey, yourself," Jason offered with a lightning glance at her that ended with a slow, endearing smile.

Christina felt her teeth push up against the inside of her mouth at that look. Her toes curled inside her low-heeled boots.

"Ready to go?"

With a small nod, Christina moved. Reaching for her purse, which was hanging expectantly on the coat rack just inside the door, she joined him on the porch. Locking up, she soon found herself walking quietly beside him the few yards to his waiting truck.

It was a still evening, and warm for Minnesota temperatures at that time of year. Pushing her sleeves up her arms, Christina sent a half-glance at Jason as they neared the sidewalk. If she felt a titch nervy and conspicuous, like her skin was too tight and her limbs uneven as she trudged toward his vehicle, Jason's parting shot as she scrambled inside did not help matters any.

"I hope you're ready for this."

"Ready for what?" Christina asked suspiciously once he'd rounded the SUV, his body swinging easily into the driver's seat.

"You'll see" was all he said, turning the key over in the ignition. With a quick check in his side-mirror, he pulled onto the street. His eyes were focused on the road before them. "By the way, in case I don't get the chance to say it later, you look beautiful tonight, Christina."

Pressing her lips together primly, Christina simpered under the glow of his compliment. "Thank you."

"But then, you always do."

"Oh, that's not…I mean, it's just a sweatshirt." But she was pleased, beyond pleased, to downplay her attractions.

He chuckled, his eyes still looking straight ahead. "Yeah? And doesn't that say it all."

Christina ducked her head. "Well, you don't look too shabby yourself."

In response, Jason merely nodded, his fingers drumming loosely against the steering wheel as he entered the evening traffic. Silence descended. Shifting a little in her seat, Christina searched for something to say.

"Are you a big lacrosse fan?"

"Hmm? Yeah, I guess."

"I've never been to a game before."

"You'll like it."

"Yeah?" There was nowhere else to go with that line of dialogue. "Only, you'll probably have to explain everything to me." She shrugged. "I'm a rank beginner. I'm not even sure what they call the field—a pitch or a stadium or a track?"

With a glance, Jason looked over at her, a small smile lifting the edges of his mouth. "You're not going to be quizzed on your knowledge of the sport, you realize that?"

"Don't be ridiculous."

"Because you seem awfully preoccupied with it."

Christina huffed. "That's only because—"

"Because you don't know what else to say?"

She hissed in a breath.

Jason chuckled. "You don't have to try so hard, you know, to make conversation."

"Excuse me?"

"I've always thought I was a pretty easy guy to talk to. Certainly, you never seemed so strained around me before."

She shot him a glowering look.

He laughed again, damn him.

"You're insufferable sometimes."

"Flattery, Ms. DeLuca?"

"Don't get conceited," she returned, working hard to keep a smile from gracing her face.

"No ma'am, not me," Jason assured her, braking at a four-way stop before turning left. Staring out at the scenery, Christina felt her legs, pressed close together, tremble with a kind of untold anticipation. Even slightly annoyed with him, she felt a certain thrill at being there, in that car, alone with Jason.

"Why did you think my parents wouldn't approve of the two of us?" The question was as starkly put as it was abruptly spoken.

"What?"

"Because they were behind it, right? That whole charade of pretending to hate me."

Christina's cheeks exploded with repressed words.

"Hey, you're the one who wanted to talk. I figure this is at least interesting."

Christina's fingers fidgeted with the hem of her sweatshirt, her eyes staring resolutely out the passenger window. "I told you already—"

"You told me a bunch of silly excuses," Jason informed her. "My parents aren't snobs. I'm not an employee of my father's, nor an employer of yours, and clichéd or otherwise, no one would have thought much of a romance between us."

"Your family is rich," Christina blurted out.

Jason's eyes widened so much that Christina was oddly comforted by his sheer incredulity. "And you were afraid people would peg you as what, a gold digger?"

She shrugged. Truthfully, she'd only just then stumbled upon the inferred suggestion. She'd never once entertained the notion beforehand. But sometimes subterfuge was a necessary evil. "Well…"

"God, am I so ugly, so utterly repellent that my own charms wouldn't even come into play?" Jason teased her.

"Shut up."

"You may want to take your own counsel on that," Jason retorted.

In agreement to this, Christina clamped her lips together tightly. A row of houses lined the suburban street Jason was driving down. They were only a few minutes away from the sporting complex now. "What does it matter, Jason? I'm here now."

"Yeah, and I guess that's what I'm really asking. What changed?"

"You'd rather I said no to our date?"

Jason gave her a dry glance "Obviously not. But..." Shrugging, he didn't speak for a moment. With a quick glance, he took in her schooled, tight features. A pointed silence enveloped them.

"You know," he said finally, his tone conversational now, just as though the tension from moments ago had never been, "maybe this is why I wanted to pick you up and drive us to the game."

Slowly, suspicion written in the lines marring her features, Christina turned toward him in question.

She saw his lips tug upward, but he kept his eyes fixed on the windshield. "You have a way of bolting when things get a little too, ah, real."

Despite herself, Christina felt her lips pulling open on a scrap of a laugh. "Yeah? Well," she made a point of looking out her passenger door window where tall grass could be seen springing up out of the ditches, "don't be too sure I won't pull a tuck and roll."

Jason chuckled at the words. She loved that sound. A rich, low, almost lazy kind of rumble. She always thought it suited him rather well.

"Okay, okay. Point made. Cross-examination over."

She nodded.

"For now."

Christina was opening her mouth in rebuttal to this when she spied the telltale stadium lights shining ahead, followed shortly by the sight of a packed parking lot. His attention diverted, Jason nosed his vehicle behind the line-up of drivers, his hands steady as he edged into a tight spot at the end of a long row of cars.

Shutting off the vehicle, he turned to Christina. "Ready?"

"You keep asking me that..."

But Jason had already exited, his steps quickly skirting the front of the truck. Christina had no sooner opened her door than he was there, reaching for her hand.

Her stomach coiled at the contact, at his fingers entwining with her own. Pure feminine conceit stole through her body. Pure feminine conceit and…and happiness. Joy. Purchasing their tickets, Christina was aware of the families milled in a semi-circle behind them, watching them.

Chapter Nineteen

It wasn't until they'd entered the sports ground that Christina really became aware of it—the eyes. Staring at them, following them. She and Jason were catching a good deal of attention. By damn near everyone in attendance.

"Hey, Mr. Gordman" packs of girls would throw out, giggling behind their hands as they skittered past.

"Looking good, Mr. G!" young teenaged boys, very cocky in their team jerseys and free from the hallways of the school, would shout at them from across the field.

There were even a couple not-so-subtle winks tossed his way.

"I take it this is what you meant in the truck," Christina stated, nodding after a group of kids who'd been wondering loudly—almost too loudly to be strictly innocent—amongst themselves who the 'lady' was with Mr. Gordman.

Jason gave her a side glance. "Yeah. Sorry. It's always weird for kids, seeing their teachers outside of the classroom, being regular human beings. Sometimes it makes them act a little awkward."

"Hmmm." Christina's eyes narrowed as they walked farther out. "Then what's your excuse for the adults?"

"Huh?"

Christina nodded toward a gang of forty-something grownups, all huddled together with questioning smiles on their faces and arched eyebrows leveled their way, their necks craning as Christina and Jason meandered past, their steps taking them to the stands. "They seem rather intrigued by your human status, too."

Jason laughed. "Colleagues," he offered by way of explanation.

"Yes, thank you. I sort of gathered that on my own," Christina replied smartly.

"They're just curious."

"You don't bring women to the games often then?"

He looked down at her. She couldn't quite describe the look on his face. "You're the first."

"That explains it then."

"Explains what?"

"Why I'm feeling decidedly like a mid-term report right about now," Christina said, peeking up at him mischievously. "Meticulously scrutinized, analyzed."

He laughed again. "Believe me, you've got nothing to worry about on that score."

"Except for her," Christina said, nodding at one particular woman, who was standing a little to one side of the crowd. She was younger than the rest of the staff, her age appearing nearer to Christina's own. She was wearing a beige fisherman's sweater and black slacks, and her straight black hair was falling limply to the tips of her shoulders.

Unlike everyone else, she wasn't smiling.

Her eyes were narrowed on Christina's person.

"*She* doesn't look impressed," Christina stressed.

Jason made a funny face, shrugging a little stiffly. "Yeah, well..." His free hand went up to rub the back of his neck.

And that's when Christina knew.

"You two dated."

He frowned, his steps leading them more quickly to the stands. "Briefly."

"And *you* ended it," Christina continued as they walked on. Was it her imagination, or were the woman's eyes following after them still?

He sighed. "Yeah. I guess." His short answers told her quite clearly that he didn't want to talk about it.

Christina pushed anyway. It was stupid really, but she found herself oddly jealous. Jealous of another woman wanting Jason. Jealous at the notion that she could so easily lose him too, and terrified to swap positions with that poor sour-faced female standing there, her eyes pitifully shadowing after them.

And that's when it occurred to her. "When?"

"Huh?"

"When did you break things off with her?" Christina had a sinking feeling she knew what his answer would be.

"Ah." His left hand was back again, rubbing the side of his neck. His right one tightened reflexively against hers before letting it go as they reached the bleachers.

"When, Jason?" Christina hissed from behind him as they dutifully mounted the stairs, their feet taking them higher and higher into the stands.

Sliding into a row, he paused, his eyes meeting her question hesitantly. "About two weeks ago."

She nodded robotically. It was, after all, the response she'd been expecting. That black-haired waif down on the sidelines looked too freshly hurt to be an old lover. "So, right after Easter?"

"Come on," he said in response, tugging her forward to an opening in the seats. It wasn't until they'd both sat down on the cool metal bench that he spoke again. "Don't back away from me."

She felt her shoulders tense. "I'm not."

"Maybe not physically."

With unseeing eyes, Christina stared out over the lacrosse field. Absently, she felt her hands rubbing against the denim of her jeans. Jason was wrong. She wasn't backing away. She felt…flattered, desired. Utterly afraid. Of what it meant. Of the responsibility. Acutely aware of how easily she could get hurt if she wasn't careful.

She felt both powerful and vulnerable. He'd chosen her but, now that he had, she didn't want him to change his mind.

"It was only partly because of you, so get out of your own headspace," Jason grumbled. He wasn't looking at her, but the grim set of his lips told her he wasn't really watching the people tromping up and down the bleachers, either.

At the challenge, Christina felt a contrary sort of disappointment swell inside her. "Yeah?" She was vaguely aware of the lacrosse teams taking the field, of an announcer talking over the crowds, introducing the players and the upcoming start of the game.

"Yeah," he assured her, and this time his head did turn in her direction. The slightest smile tugged up at the corners of his mouth. "We went on a couple of dates but that was it. There was no chemistry. I would have ended it regardless."

Christina nodded silently, chewing on that thought.

Jason nudged her with his shoulder. "What can I say, I like women who glare at me."

She felt her lips twitch a little. "She was too nice?"

"Way too nice. Hell, she even laughed at all my jokes."

"You tell terrible jokes."

He winked. "Now that's what a man likes to hear."

"Oh, shut it."

In reply, he only grinned, but then his hand reached out, taking hold of hers again. Christina felt her whole body react at the contact. Her breath shook in her throat, and a sort of electric buzz set off along her nerves, a crazy sort of unraveling of desire and anticipation, of wanting even more.

Without thinking, she pressed her palm more closely against his.

"If that's all it takes, I'll never smile at you again." Almost as soon as the words left her mouth, Christina regretted them. She'd sort of given the show away there, hadn't she?

"Well now, hey," Jason said, and those green-flecked golden eyes were staring down at hers. "Let's not get ahead of ourselves. Making you laugh when you absolutely do not want to," he added roguishly, "that's what I live for when you're around."

She snorted. "Yeah? You do it well."

"I know. I've had years of practice."

"Anything to provoke me," she teased.

"Anything to steal your attention," he countered.

Ducking her head, Christina blushed. A surge of pleasure exploded inside her. Threaded itself throughout the whole of her body. A small sound—a whispered sigh of consideration, of recognition—escaped her lips. A smile blossomed across her face. The kind of smile that positively shimmers.

It was all the response Jason needed. Leaning toward her, he whispered close to her ear, "Took you long enough to figure it out."

"But then, you never really needed to."

He sighed. "Not in some ways, maybe."

She let that statement go. "And now?"

"Now?"

"That I'm here."

He shot her a sidelong glance, his lips pulling up gently at the corners. "Now, I'm determined to keep it that way."

Biting off a grin, Christina had no quick comeback to that. And really, she wasn't sure she wanted to say anything anyway. Turning her attention back to the game, she was content to let those last words settle in the air between them.

And so, for the next hour, they watched the game, and the better part of any sort of conversation was directed entirely to lacrosse as Jason pointed out various players and positions and strategies and as Christina joined the throng of bodies to yell and whoop with cheers of support or grumble and moans over bad calls or missed plays. The minutes spun past and soon enough, the game was over.

Jason's school won. The spectators howled in glory, the bleachers a stomp of excitement and friendly good spirits. But when Christina got to her feet, intending to follow the mob heading out to the parking lot, Jason's hand pulled her back down to her seat.

With questioning eyes, she turned toward him.

"It'll be a mad rush out there," he informed her. "Might as well wait here as in the line-up of cars."

"Good point." She was hardly in a hurry to get back home.

"Give it ten minutes and it'll clear out."

"You know," Christina said, her hands folded primly in her lap as her gaze met Jason's, "I wasn't sure if I'd like lacrosse—"

"I know."

She arched an eyebrow.

"You have an expressive face sometimes."

"Sometimes?"

"When you're not on guard."

She rolled her eyes. "Okay."

"You know what it's telling me right now?" They were alone in the stands by this time, with only the game lights casting a shadowing glow down on them.

"What's that?"

"That to your surprise, you had a great time."

"Fact." She tilted her head a little to one side. "And? Is it saying anything else?"

"Oh, most definitely."

"Such as?"

His voice was deep, even. "That you trust me."

She nodded her head. "I think I always have if you want to know."

"In that case, it's also telling me this," he breathed and, bending forward, brushed his lips against hers. It was a light, barely-there touch. At the contact, he growled under his throat. "And this," he added, his teeth nipping and pulling gently at her lower lip.

Sinking into the feel of his mouth, his stubble, his hands against her lower back, Christina didn't offer up a single protest. Whimpering, melting bonelessly against him, Christina opened her mouth in response, contouring it to the demands of his. When his tongue swept inside, she moaned. Her stomach muscles tightened and then relaxed in a shiver of need.

Without thought, her hands moved up his shoulders until they were locked behind his neck. "God," he whispered, leaning back just far enough to breathe. "I've been wanting to do this all night."

"I know," she murmured, her lips unconsciously following his. "I thought those people would never leave."

With a rough bark of sound, Jason laughed. "You're something else, you know that?"

Feeling some of the tension slide out of his body, Christina grinned. "So I've been told. Of course, the context changes from time to time—the adjective too, but…"

"Dangerous. That's the adjective I'm talking about. You're dangerous. A heady cocktail." Jason lifted his head, his eyes glancing around them. With a deliberate move, he slid his body a few inches farther down the bleachers, a few inches farther away from her. "But here, I'm Mr. Gordman, high school PolySci teacher."

"Right." Christina curled her fingers against the underside of the metal seat. "No reason to tarnish your image."

"Honestly, you'd probably increase my popularity with the students."

Christina giggled. "Thank you. I think."

"It was a compliment."

She smiled vaguely, her eyes roaming over the abandoned playing field, the cool smell of night blanketing the air. The parking lot was less than half-full by now. In minutes, she and Jason would have the place to themselves. Caught up in the fantasy of it all, she admitted softly, "I've always wondered what this would be like."

"A high school lacrosse game?"

She elbowed him playfully. "No," she said. "Being on a date with you."

At his look of bemusement, Christina asked, "What?"

Jason shrugged. "Nothing. It's just, you're such a conundrum." He scratched the underside of his chin. "One minute you're the most confident woman I've ever met. Stunningly so. And in the next, you say something like that." He shrugged again.

She averted her eyes. "Yeah, well. I don't date much."

"I got that."

"I see."

"I'm not making fun of you," he insisted, reading her tone of voice accurately. Reaching forward, Jason guided her face back to his.

Christina bit the insides of her cheeks. "Okay."

"And?" he asked, his face taking on a mischievous look, "how was it?"

"The date?"

"Obviously."

She blushed. "It was…nice."

"Nice?" He sounded pained.

"*Very* nice."

"Nice enough to do it again?"

Peeking up at him through the dark fringe of her eyelashes, Christina felt her teeth pulling at her bottom lip. "Yes."

Chapter Twenty

The next afternoon, on her hands and knees in the kitchen, a soapy sponge held tightly in her grip, Christina scrubbed the tiling of her floor. She'd already emptied out and reorganized every drawer and cupboard in her kitchen. She'd polished the dining room table, as well, and even washed the blinds from the two large windows in her living room, both of which offered an utterly unremarkable view of the neighbor's peeling siding.

It had been grueling, exhausting work but it hadn't made one bit of difference. Even now, hours later, sweat dripping into the bandanna she'd wrapped across her forehead, arms aching from the pressure, Christina's stomach flopped and seized.

Anxiety swelled in her person as she relived again the evening before with Jason—sitting with her knees drawn up on those cold bleachers as the night had closed in upon them. She doubted she'd ever forget the look in his eyes when she'd told him she'd go out with him again.

His smile had melted her.

"Only…"

At her one hesitant addendum, he'd waited, one eyebrow raising warily. "Only?"

"Next time, I'd prefer to ditch the chaperones."

"The what?" He'd looked genuinely bewildered for a second until Christina had waved her arm around the stands pointedly.

"Isn't that why you chose this place? So we couldn't get into trouble?"

He'd pursed his lips, his eyes following the direction of her sweeping motion. "Hmm."

"Don't get me wrong," she'd assured him cutely. "I really enjoyed the game but—"

"Seducing me again, Ms. DeLuca?"

"When did I stop?"

"Where do you want to go then?"

"Huh?"

"On our next date?" He'd flashed her a shameless grin. "I'm not leaving anything to chance."

Biting her lip, Christina had faltered. She'd rarely felt as painfully shy around a man as she did with Jason. "I'm not going to say no."

"On Tuesdays, the university offers public admittance into the planetarium."

Christina hadn't quite been able to contain her surprise at this statement, and its rather abrupt inclusion into the conversation. As far as she knew, Jason wasn't into astronomy. Certainly, she wasn't.

But before she could respond, he'd shrugged casually. "I know, I know, but I don't want to wait until the weekend to see you again."

And really, what girl didn't want to hear that?

"And besides," he'd added, reaching up to bop her gently on the nose with his finger, "it's dark in there."

A throaty laugh had filtered out of her mouth at the words, at the teasing glint in his eyes when he'd looked down at her, a look of something more to come.

"Okay."

"Okay?"

She'd smiled, her teeth razing over her bottom lip. "Yeah."

Smiling even now at the memory, Christina felt her stomach pinch all over again with eagerness. Only a few days and she'd see him again. Her fingers squeezed the sponge. And who knew, maybe this time she'd be able to coax him inside her apartment at the close of the evening.

She hadn't even been given the chance last night. Leaving the lacrosse field soon afterward, Jason had driven her home. It had been going on almost nine o'clock by then—hardly late, but he hadn't so much as suggested a post-game drink or dessert. Nothing. He'd just turned down the road, heading back the way they'd come. Later, lying in bed, she'd tried not to worry the issue. After all, when he'd pulled up outside her house, his words had been quietly encouraging.

She'd just unclicked her seat belt when she'd turned to him, her mouth already forming the invitation when he'd shaken his head. Holding up a hand, the action causing the words on her lips to tumble to a halt, Jason had clearly known what she'd been about to say. "Don't ask me to come inside." At her look of consternation, he'd elaborated, "It's hard enough as it is. Don't make it worse."

"Worse?"

He'd pulled a grim face. "I like to think, maybe because I'm a teacher, that I read people pretty well."

Christina had only stared at him. "What?"

"Listen, I'm not going to make the same mistakes as the last guy."

Her eyes had grown wide, wary.

"You don't have to tell me about it. I don't have to know. But whoever he was, he hurt you and I think"—he'd sighed then, and it had sounded almost painful—"I think it would be a mistake if we moved too quickly."

Hearing those words, she hadn't known if she'd wanted to laugh or cry. Jason couldn't possibly know just how far off the mark he was. He was absolutely nothing like Bill. He could never be. And yet…moving too quickly, being reckless, being thoughtless…it *was* what had hurt her last time. It was what had broken her life apart.

So now, there she sat, or rather kneeled, on the floor of her apartment cleaning out her frustration and excitement and anxiety.

If that wasn't enough, there was Mary. Christina was supposed to have dinner at the Gordmans' in less than two hours and she was fraught with, hell, she wasn't even sure anymore. Her stomach rolled at the mere idea. Her fingers clenching around the poor, strangled sponge, she scrubbed all the harder. She still hadn't spoken to Mary, not since that afternoon at the baseball tournament. In the years she'd known the Gordmans, it was officially the longest she'd gone without speaking to the matriarch of the family. At the thought, her throat constricted.

She'd thought about calling her Thursday evening and again, on Friday after work, before the lacrosse game. But, just as before, her fingers had stuck. Paralyzing doubts had plagued her, nettled her. What if, what if it was too little, too late? So much time had passed since Mary's voicemail. What if the conversation flagged, became stilted as both women came to confront the stranger on the line, one of them grappling with the undisguised image of a woman she only thought she knew, the other waging war against the naked truth of her deception? Just the idea left Christina dry in the mouth, her thoughts sluggish. There's no way that wouldn't transcend over the phone waves. No, much better to hold on to the promise of dinner on Saturday, to the harbored hopes she wasn't ready yet to label—better to hold off on the chance of meeting an unwanted alternative.

If her reasoning was faulty, Christina chose to ignore it.

Mary had given Christina her blessing to date Jason. Had been adamant that he wasn't her past. But what if after a little time to really think, to realize the enormity of Christina's transgressions, and the personal, potentially disastrous consequences for her beloved son—what if, by doing exactly what Mary had suggested, Christina was currently in the process of tearing apart the only other family she'd ever allowed herself to love?

If she lost them…

The sudden clang of her alarm clock—indicating it was time she got ready to go—had never produced a sweeter, more well-timed sound. With a relieved plop, Christina tossed her sponge up onto the kitchen counter. Scrambling to her feet, she brushed her hands together in finality. The kitchen, painted a light dove gray, practically winked back at her in cleanliness. "Stop fussing," she scolded herself. "These are the kinds of thoughts that will get you into trouble." Turning on her heel, she stalked into the dining room, past the living room, and into her bedroom.

"In fact," she reminded herself as she threw open her wardrobe, "these are the exact thoughts which had led you to start cleaning in the first place." Nothing like good old-fashioned exhaustion to keep the mind at bay.

Pulling out a white sundress with daisy prints and thin straps from within the oak frame of her armoire, Christina quickly tossed the garment over one shoulder before moving on to the next drawer. Within moments, she was headed for the bathroom, her arms loaded down with clothes. When she re-emerged, she was showered, dressed, and faultlessly made-up. Pushing her hair out of her eyes, she spied the time. Her stomach jolted, rocked when she realized…

The only thing left for her to do was leave.

Pulling up to the Gordmans' house some thirty minutes later, she took a deep, slightly steadying breath before getting out of the car. She tried to compose her features into that of polite interest as she walked up to the front of the house. Hesitantly, she pressed her finger against the buzzer.

She didn't have to wait long before one of the large doors was being flung open wide. Blinking in surprise, Christina saw none other than Mary standing before her. Christina had never known the small woman to answer the door. That had always been Matthew's job.

Christina took a deep breath. "Mary." The word came out even, though a little unnatural.

Mary's hand gripped the side of the door. She opened her mouth as if to speak, but instead, her lips only managed a tentative smile. Then, suddenly, almost before Christina realized it, Mary let go of her grip on the door; arms spreading wide, she charged forward, practically throwing herself on the younger woman.

Shocked into the hug, Christina felt only the thin weight of Mary's arms twining themselves forcefully around her person, heard only the gentle whoosh of Mary's breath at the impact.

"Oh!" Mary cried, and her arms squeezed even tighter. "I've missed you," she whispered into Christina's ear, the words choked and wet.

At the sound, Christina let herself go. Falling into the embrace, she felt her hands pressing tightly to Mary's back, her chin jutting into the crook above her shoulder. "I've missed you too," she returned fiercely. One of her fingers stretched up to wipe away an unexpected tear across her cheek. Light seemed to splinter behind her tightly closed eyes at the wash of love and home Mary's hold offered.

"I'm sorry."

"Shh," Mary soothed, her hands sweeping up and across Christina's back. "It's fine. We're fine." Breaking away to dab at her own eyes, Mary glared at her lovingly. "At least, we'd damn sure better be fine."

Christina's smile wobbled. "We are."

"Good."

"I meant to call you back, only…well, I didn't. I didn't know what to say."

"And that'll be the end of that," Mary insisted, shooing away Christina's words with an impatient flap of her hand. "We talk. That's what we do. Don't you go quiet on me, DeLuca."

Christina's chin trembled. "I'm ashamed of the person I told you about."

"Oh, baby." Reaching forward, Mary laid her palm against the side of Christina's face. "Let her go."

Christina sucked in her lips.

"Let me in."

"It's hard for me." But she pressed her face more fully into Mary's hand.

"Don't you know that you're family? That's forever."

"Yeah?" Christina smiled hollowly, her eyes skipping away to the large staircase over Mary's shoulder. "Well, I'm living proof that that's not always true."

"It's true in *this* family," Mary insisted, her brow line creasing with the words. "And you are as much a Gordman as anyone else here."

That's when Christina did something completely out of character. In a rush of gratitude, she plucked the small woman close to her chest for a second embrace. Bending her head over Mary's dark hair, she breathed deeply. "I love you, Mar."

Mary patted her back. "I know, baby. I know."

"Ah, my girls are back together again." At the sound of Matthew's voice, coming from the doorway leading to the dining room, Christina slowly let Mary go. Sauntering into the room, he raised an eyebrow. "I think this calls for a celebratory drink, don't you agree?"

Christina rolled her eyes.

Mary swatted at his arm. "Way to ruin a moment."

He grinned, unrepentant as ever. "Thought I'd spare both of you another application of mascara."

"Generous of you," Christina muttered even as she ran a finger under her eyes, brushing away any telltale black smudges.

"Drinks?"

Mary smiled. "Yes."

"Scotch?" Christina asked.

"Of course, of course," Matthew said, picking his way toward the living room. "Follow me."

"And I don't want to hear any nonsense about us weeping women, either," Mary started, following right behind him. She shot a wink at Christina. "He's been as mopey without you as I have."

Matthew glowered back at his wife.

"Well, you have." She made a face at Christina. "He has. He kept going on about how he missed you at work, which was ludicrous because you were right outside his do—"

"I'll open the most expensive bottle of wine we've got if you'll shut your yapper, what about it?" Matthew said, his voice at its most pleasant when he turned to his wife.

Christina smothered a chuckle.

Mary only smiled wider. "Deal."

His look of relief was so utterly genuine Christina could do nothing but laugh, and with it, she felt the last of her tension and nerves leave her.

Of course, she knew the topic would get brought up at some point. Sure enough, as they sat down to the meatloaf and mashed potatoes that Mary set lovingly on the table, Christina was proven correct.

Pushing her chair in tight to the table, she'd only just reached for her fork when Mary asked oh-so-casually, "And...? How are things with you and Jason?"

"Mary." There was no mistaking the warning note in Matthew's voice, his eyes flicking worriedly over to Christina's face, gauging her reaction.

"If you didn't want me to ask, then why'd you bother to tell me about their date?"

"Because you'd have murdered me if I hadn't."

She pursed her lips, her eyes sweeping back toward Christina. "True enough. Though next time, I expect that information to come from you."

"Yes ma'am," Christina was quick to reassure.

"So? How was it?"

There was no denying the delight on Mary's countenance, her hopeful expectation. Seeing it, Christina found herself smiling shyly in response. Her fork skimmed over the creamy mashed potatoes, her eyes watching the action intently.

"Good," she offered lamely. Good didn't even almost cover it, but she figured it was the safest description at her disposal. "We had a good time."

"Yeah?" Leaning forward, Mary all but chirped across the table at her. Reaching out, her hand patted Christina's wrist. "I'm glad."

Christina's mouth quivered into an even bigger smile.

"And?" Mary asked conversationally as she spread butter on her roll. "What did you do?"

"Mary."

"What?" she asked artlessly, turning toward her husband and raising one plucky eyebrow.

"Perhaps Christina doesn't want to talk about that?" he said pointedly.

"Pooh," she insisted. "Just look at her face. She's dying to tell someone about it."

"His parents may not be her first choice."

Mary chewed on that for a second, but then she was shaking her head again. "Then she's going to have to get over it. I won't be shut out of her life again. Period. And she promised me—"

Unable to take it anymore, Christina heard herself talking: "We went to a lacrosse game." At the words, all conversation died. Shifting eagerly back in her direction, Mary pressed her fingers together in anticipation.

Christina felt her face heating up. It was unnerving, being watched that way. "It's a very interesting sport."

"Uh-huh," Mary said with patent disinterest. "He was a gentleman?"

"Oh, Mary!" Christina laughed. "Of course, he was."

"And?"

"And what?"

Mary narrowed her eyes. "Don't hold out on me, girl!"

In answer, Christina speared her fork into the meatloaf. Bringing a bite up to her mouth, she took her time chewing it.

"Pert little thing, isn't she?" Mary asked her husband.

"Don't tell me you've never noticed before?"

"Fine, whatever," Mary said then. "Have your privacy."

"Thank you." Christina's voice could have hardly been drier.

"But at least tell me this—"

Matthew made a face.

Christina shook her head in resignation.

"Are there future plans in the works?"

Biting down on her lip did absolutely nothing to stem the smile blossoming across Christina's features. Which, really, was all the answer that anyone needed anyway.

Leaning back in her chair, Mary sighed, a look of utter content on her face. Reaching for her glass of wine, she smirked. "I take it that's a yes?"

"Geez, Mary!"

"Yes," Christina said with exaggerated patience, "that's a yes."

"I told you," Mary said to her husband with smug satisfaction.

He raised his hands. "I never disagreed with you."

"You told him what?" Christina asked, her eyes narrowed suspiciously.

Mary was all innocence. "What? Oh, nothing…"

Matthew hitched a thumb toward his wife. "Don't pay her any attention. That's been my motto sinc—"

"And that'll be enough out of you," Mary assured him.

"You told Matthew what?" Christina insisted.

Mary avoided that stark gaze. "Just that I had a feeling. You know, about the two of you."

Christina felt the first stirrings of unease roll through her person. "It was just a date, Mary."

Mary nodded quickly, her mouth thinning out. "No, I know."

"Anything could happen. Or not happen." Christina wasn't entirely sure who she was trying to convince, herself or Mary. Don't get your hopes up. Don't read into anything. The fantasy was all good, but the reality could hurt.

Chapter Twenty-One

Christina was just closing down her email when her phone, tucked in its habitual spot beside her keyboard, buzzed quietly on her desk. Glancing down at it, she bit back a smile.

FROM: Jacks
4:57 p.m.
> *MESSAGE: Girl, get your butt down here after work.*
> *Be ready to dish.*

Rolling her eyes, Christina nevertheless set her phone back down on her desk with a giddiness of movement that was telling. Scrolling over her computer screen with her mouse, she exited all her programs for the day before pushing back from the desk. Sparing only enough time to pocket her phone, she rose from her chair and, reaching inside the bottom file drawer, relinquished her purse while her other hand quickly nabbed up her jacket.

It wasn't quite five o'clock yet, but Christina was officially done for the day.

"Be ready to dish," she muttered laughingly to herself. "Whatever." But she wasn't headed for the parking ramp. Not just yet.

Minutes later, reclining back in the swivel chair she'd quickly commandeered upon entering Jackie's basement office, she rested her legs on top of the large architect's desk in front of her, deliberately taking her time. She hadn't said a word when she'd strolled inside the room only moments earlier—she'd merely smiled and plunked herself down on the seat, her eyebrows arched coyly. Jackie, sitting on top of the other desk in her cluttered office, scowled darkly.

"Well? Come *on*."

Christina only shook her head innocently. "Come on, what?"

"What happened on your date last night?"

A small, sly smile spread across her lips. "We had a good time."

Jackie reached for the first thing within her grasp—a paperclip—and without a thought, she chucked it at Christina. Ducking, the older woman dodged the hit. Throwing up her arms, she laughed. "Okay, okay. But honestly, there isn't much to tell."

"Did you kiss under the stars?"

"God," Christina muttered with mock disgust.

"Either start talking, or I start filling in the blanks for myself," Jackie purred maliciously. "And believe me, I have a dirty mind when I set myself up for it."

"I promise, the reality won't live up to your imagination."

"Christina!"

"Okay. Well, the date started at this place called Pete's Bar."

"Do tell?"

Jason had called Christina earlier that afternoon with the idea of stopping in there for a quick cocktail before heading to the planetarium. He'd pick her up at five-thirty if she was agreeable to that.

She'd never been to Pete's Bar before. Walking inside the joint hours later, she'd been mildly surprised by the décor: scuffed but clean wooden floors, an alcove hosting a gathering of tattered club chairs that had seen better days (better decades, really), and a large, oddly-shaped bar squatted directly in the middle of a grouping of tables. Covered with navy panels and a silver-speckled Formica countertop, it wasn't exactly boasting the height of fashion.

Nabbing a seat at one of the octagonal tables clustered around the bar, Christina smiled demurely at the harried server who came up to grab their drinks. Her eyes traveled leisurely around the building as Jason took the seat opposite of her.

"I know," he said, as if reading her thoughts, "it's not exactly high class but…"

"It's comfortable."

"Yes."

Shrugging at Jackie as the memory washed over her consciousness, Christina made a face. "I mean, mostly we just talked."

"About what?"

Christina scrunched up her nose. She was hesitant to admit that part. "Just stuff."

Jackie pursed her lips. "Really?"

"Nothing interesting."

"I sincerely doubt that."

"Why?"

"Your prevarication, for one thing."

"It's stupid."

Leaning back against the wall, her legs crossed over her paper-strewn desk, Jackie would not be deterred. "I'll be the judge of that."

"Don't laugh."

"Now I'm really intrigued."

Giving up the cause, because there was no way Jackie wasn't getting it out of her now, Christina sighed. "The conversation came up—what if, what if we'd met in like an alternate universe."

"Okay, you lost me."

Christina felt her cheeks pinkening. "I don't remember how the conversation got started exactly…"

Oh. Wait. That was it. She'd just taken a swig of her beer when he'd lifted his gaze. An ease of expression had settled across his face when he'd opened his mouth to speak. Her mind flashing in reverse, Christina's memories seized, took hold as they transported her back in time…

Cupping the pint glass in his hand, Jason lifted it to his mouth. "How was work?"

Shaking her head roughly, Christina held up a hand: "No. No shop talk."

Leaning back in his chair, Jason surveyed her reaction. "Right. I bet it's awkward to complain about the boss to his son."

"Sometimes I wish you weren't his son."

Coughing, Jason hurriedly swallowed the drink of beer he'd just taken. "What?"

"No, no," Christina said, her hands flapping anxiously at the look on his face. "I didn't mean it like that. I meant, what if—"

"I know what you meant," Jason assured her, setting his glass carefully back on the table. "What if I wasn't a conflict of interest, as I believe you once called it."

"Or, or what if I'd gone to work for a different company instead."

Jason inclined his head. "In both scenarios, then I guess we wouldn't have met."

"Or maybe we'd have met in a different setting."

"Ah." He nodded as understanding fully dawned.

"Without the forced familiarity and proximity of my working relationship with your father."

"And how exactly would that version of things take place."

Christina stopped to consider the challenge of his words. Peeking up at him, she saw only entertainment and mild amusement. Feeling her shoulders loosen, Christina looked around the bar.

"Well," she shrugged, "what if, one afternoon after work I stopped in here for a beer."

"Pete's?"

"Yeah."

"But you'd never been here before today. What would be different in this alternate universe?"

She chewed on one side of her lip. "Maybe I never applied to your dad's firm. Instead, I took a job near here." She pointed out one of the windows absently.

Jason nodded, playing along. "Okay. So, one afternoon, after finishing up for the day at your new job, you come in here. What happens next."

Swiveling her head around the room, Christina took her time in answering. "I suppose, I order a beer."

"Obviously."

"And then I grab a seat at one of those club lounge chairs. I take out a book but, before I start reading, I find myself staring out the large storefront windows, just daydreaming."

"This is starting to sound like the beginnings of a musical."

"And then you walk in."

"Okay."

Christina raised an eloquent eyebrow. "And then what?"

"Huh?"

"What do you do?"

"When I'm here? I usually order the ploughman's lunch and a stout."

"Okay. But how do we meet?"

Jason grinned, leaning on the table with his forearms. He turned his head as if picturing Christina sitting in the currently empty lounge chair. "I see you sitting there, across the way."

"Yeah?"

"I think you're beautiful."

Christina tucked her chin a little at the words.

"At first, I wonder if you're waiting for someone."

"But I'm not."

"Right. And that's when I see the novel in your hands."

"And?"

"Well, that gives me pause. A fellow reader, I don't want to interrupt. Only."

Christina raised an eyebrow.

"Only, as I'm looking at you, you suddenly glance over in my direction."

"And I see you."

"Do you smile at me?"

Christina laughed lowly. "I mean, it's only the polite thing to do."

"I smile back." He wiggled his eyebrows. "Slowly."

"God."

"Suddenly, the waitress appears before you."

"What?"

"Exactly." Jason winked. "You are so startled by the unexpected sight of her, asking if you'd like to order anything to eat, that you knock over your beer."

Christina giggled. "Poor server. "

"Don't worry, she jumps out of the way before she can get splattered."

"Thank goodness."

"And I, gentlemen that I am, am on my feet within seconds, grabbing for the stack of napkins readily available on my table to come help."

"The sucker for a lost cause," Christina said drolly.

"No. But I see my chance. To talk to the beautiful stranger sitting in a locals bar."

"Poetic."

"I try."

"But alas," Christina interrupted, "I'm a self-sufficient creature and before you can get to my table, I'm already on my hands and knees, with my own napkins, mopping up the mess."

"But I offer to help anyway."

"And then, both of us ducked low under the table, we look up at one another—"

"And we both start to laugh."

Christina made a face. "How romantic."

"Oh, I'm only getting warmed up," Jason assured her. Grabbing for his beer, he took another long drink. "Once we've cleaned everything up, I give you my hand and help you to your feet."

"It does a funny thing to my stomach. When you touch me."

"Isn't that a bit cheesy?" he teased.

Christina tilted her head in consideration. "No," she admitted softly. "Not if it's true."

Jason smirked but all he said was, "Looking at the wreckage, I realize that your chair is wet, and the table is now sticky."

"And my drink is gone."

"I do the only thing proper."

"You invite me to sit at your table."

"You're sort of stealing my thunder here."

Christina laughed guiltily. "Sorry."

"And you accept my invitation."

"Of course. Who could resist those charms?"

"I don't know. There was this woman I knew…held out for over four years."

"Don't get distracted," Christina said, batting at his wrist. "What next?"

"I order you another beer."

"Okay." Christina pursed her lips. "What do we talk about while we wait?"

Jason considered this for a moment. Then a smile appeared, crinkling the corners of his eyes. Christina had never quite trusted that smile. "I ask you your name."

She rolled her eyes. "Boring conversation."

"Fine. I ask you what brings you here."

"To Pete's or to Minnesota?"

"Definitely the latter."

"And how did you know I wasn't from the area?"

"You came into Pete's Bar in an outfit like that," Jason said, his eyes taking stock of her satin blouse and pencil skirt. "That says it all."

She laughed throatily. "I tell you that I saw a picture of Minneapolis on a postcard."

"Hey now," Jason admonished her, "that line didn't work in *this* universe."

She shrugged. "Fine, you don't believe me," she considered. "It only adds to the mystery surrounding me."

"Touché."

Christina leaned forward then, her hands resting beside his on the table. "Glancing around the bar, I think to myself that nothing actually brought me here, but I'm suddenly aware that I could be made to love this city. I think I could stay forever."

Jason was silent for a moment. "That's an awfully big thought."

Christina wiggled in her chair. "Yeah."

With a sweeping move, he laid one hand atop hers. "I'm not complaining."

"Okay," she said, blowing out an unsteady breath. "What happens next?"

"We share my lunch."

"Generous of you."

"I thought so."

Christina made a comedic face. "But…the waitress has been sending speaking glances our way."

"She wants us to pay."

"Yeah."

Jason nodded slowly. The game was winding to a close. They could both feel it.

"I'm afraid."

"Afraid?"

"That I'll never see you again."

"Ah." Jason took a drink of beer. "I guess, maybe there are some good points to being the boss's kid, huh?"

In response, she'd merely tipped her head in agreement and he'd changed the subject. To something innocuous and casual. Playing her part, Christina hadn't thought beyond the impulse to be happy—to smile and laugh, to lean forward and let her fingers run along the back of his hand as they'd finished their drinks…

Shaking her head clear of the picture of them, huddled across the small table of that dinky little bar, Christina slowly became aware of her surroundings—namely, she became aware of Jackie sitting on her cluttered desk, eyes studying Christina intently as she waited. Waited for an explanation, waited to hear about that silly, stupid conversation.

"So?"

Christina let her legs swing down to the floor. But she shook her head, her face slightly flushed when she muttered, "Oh, it was nothing. Just dumb conversation."

Jackie's head tilted a little to one side, her mouth curling upward. "Okay. Well, how was the planetarium then?"

"I don't know, dark?"

Jackie gave her a look.

"No, it was good," Christina assured her. "It was cool."

"And?"

"And what?"

"What happened?"

"Besides a neckache?"

"Christina," Jackie grumbled.

"Okay, okay. I'm sorry," Christina said, holding up both hands. "Honestly though, not much happened. We didn't really talk. We just sat there, looking up."

"Holding hands?"

Christina took a deep breath. "Yes," she admitted, "holding hands."

"Magic."

Christina rolled her eyes. With a plop, she brought her chair fully upright. "I don't know I'd go that far, but it was nice."

"Nice?"

"Yeah. It was nice."

"That sounds a bit…watered-down."

Christina got to her feet. "No."

"So you won't be going out with him again?"

"What? No, I didn't say that."

"But you're not excited about it?" Jackie guessed shrewdly.

"No! That's not—"

"Ugh. That's unfortunate."

"Jackie!" Christina stomped her foot, her lips twisting in a frown. "Stop it."

In response, Jackie scooted off her own desk. Wiping her hands on her jeans, she shrugged. "You first."

"Excuse me?"

"It's okay to hope, you know," Jackie said softly.

Christina scoffed. With a flippant look, she strode forward, intending to leave Jackie's office.

"No, really. It's not a mockery of the human experience to dream a little."

"Oh, geez."

"And besides," Jackie continued as though Christina hadn't spoken, "this act of casual indifference isn't fooling anybody."

At the door, Christina paused. Placing one hand on the wall beside her, she looked back at her friend. "You're really enjoying this, aren't you?"

Jackie raised two innocent eyebrows. "What?"

"'Night, Jacks."

"Night, daydreamer."

"Shut up," Christina called down the hallway, but the laughter in her voice was no threat at all.

After all, Jackie wasn't entirely wrong. Christina frowned at the thought. She'd had a marvelous time with Jason at the planetarium. She'd held his hand and stared up at the stars and realized that he could have taken her to view a lineup of dumpsters at the back of an alley and she'd have enjoyed the experience. It was a liberating and frightening realization.

She'd had no idea until then, no idea until he'd turned to look at her in the dim lighting of the building, winking at the moderator's dry mythological description of Orion the Hunter, just how much she loved him. It was sobering and overwhelming. She'd thought she'd done a better job of protecting her heart. She could only pray that giving it to him was all the more safety she needed. It was that or she'd set herself up for the biggest fall yet.

Chapter Twenty-Two

Closing her eyes, Christina forced herself to take a deep breath in. After all, she supposed he had a right to ask, it was just.... Christina mentally counted to ten. She didn't want to argue with Jason. Not tonight. Not when everything had been going so well between them. Clenching the phone tight to her ear, she slowly eased another deep breath out.

Jackie's words that fateful night in her office had stuck with Christina. Whether or not she showed her vulnerabilities to the world didn't make them any less real. She was done pretending otherwise. She was done pushing Jason away, acting as though she didn't desperately want him in her life. And so, when her and Jason's third date had led them right back into the halls of Jason's high school, Christina hadn't bothered with pouting artifice. Instead, she'd simply said yes when asked to accompany him as a chaperone for the prom.

Meeting him at her door, Christina had sucked in a breath as her eyes caught his appearance—a dark, expertly tailored suit with a white, stiff-collared shirt and black tie. The outfit had contrasted his blond-streaked brown hair, the lines emphasizing his broad-shouldered, trim physique.

"You're a knockout," he breathed, stealing her words when his eyes came to rest on her face.

Christina smiled tremulously, her hands slimming down the sleek plum-colored dress. Modestly cut, the length came down to the tips of her pearly-pink painted toenails.

"Thank you. You're quite something yourself," she replied, taking his arm as he led her out to his waiting vehicle.

"Thanks for this," he added as he opened her door. He gave her a devilish wink. "I know going to a high school dance isn't exactly what you had in mind, but it's part of the job description."

Flashing him a quick grin, she forced herself to admit the honest truth. "I've never looked forward to prom more."

Leaning forward, he answered her with a light, brushing kiss. "Me neither" came the growling reply before he moved back, quickly shutting her door.

Walking inside the garish lights of the auditorium, Christina had allowed herself to lean just slightly against Jason's strength as the grand march started, nervous students walking arm-in-arm through the throng of parents when their names were announced, marking the start of the evening. If Christina had supposed she and Jason would spend the night strolling along the four walls, their eyes watching for any supposed mischief, she was delighted to be mistaken.

No sooner had the strains of the first song swept out across the speakers than Jason was guiding her gently into his arms.

"Aren't we supposed to be...you know, chaperoning?" Christina protested weakly, her arms already reaching up to twine around the back of Jason's neck.

"What better way than this?" he teased her, his breath warm at her temple. Glancing up, she saw the mischievous glint of his eyes. "Right in the thick of things."

"You're impossible," she told him, but her body melted rather tellingly against the hard, close brush of his thighs, the sturdy wall of his chest.

"As I recall," he murmured, his lips brushing deliciously against her ear, "we dance rather well together." And they had, his arms pressing her ever-nearer, Christina's eyes coquettish, her nails possessive as they stroked the hair at the nape of his neck while they'd twirled around the floor.

That night, when Jason had dropped Christina off at her door, he'd finally accepted her invitation to come inside. Stepping into her apartment, Christina had barely had enough time to slip off her shoes when she found herself being swept back into Jason's arms.

"Oh," she sighed when she felt his arms slink around her back, the warmth of his palms resting against her shoulder blades, drawing her closer. With a low laugh, she tilted her head backward, glancing up at him in the dim light of her entryway. "Missed me in your arms already?"

"You have no idea," he growled, his lips nibbling against her ear.

She felt her neck dip a little, granting him greater access to the sensitive skin. "Thank God. I thought I was the only one."

He chuckled, his lips abandoning her ear to crest across her jaw toward her mouth. "I've been waiting for this all night."

Christina moaned, her lips an open invocation.

"Hell, Christina—" The rest of his words were lost, swallowed as Jason's lips fitted themselves to her own, his tongue thrusting inside her mouth, his fingers pushing themselves deeper into her hair.

When, moments later, Christina took a step backward, Jason allowed their lips to break apart. Her cheeks were delightfully pink, her breath coming as hard and heavy as his. The mingled sound swirled around them. Her hand grasping his, her fingers tangling with his own, she smiled in reply to his questioning look.

"Come on," she whispered, tugging him forward.

Silently, he followed her into the living room. Other than the light from a lamp on one of the end tables, which she'd deliberately left on, the apartment was cast in darkness. "Christina?" His voice was hoarse but searching, his eyes pinned unerringly to her face.

Tilting her head a little to the side, she paused, looking up at him. "Stay."

In answer, Jason groaned before capturing her mouth with his again....

The next morning, her eyes sweeping open leisurely, Christina hadn't bothered to fight back the stupid, silly smile that marked her lips. Only, one hand sliding across her bed, she'd found the other half empty. Momentarily confused, she'd hauled herself into a sitting position—and that's when she heard it. The muffled sound of movement coming from the kitchen. Hard on the heels of this discovery was the hickory scent of sizzling bacon and something else frying on the stove. Her nose twitched hungrily.

Shuffling into a thin cotton bathrobe, Christina entered the kitchen. Jason was standing barefoot in front of the oven, wielding a spatula with easy finesse, wearing only his dark slacks. It was incredibly sexy.

"Mmm," she mumbled, stepping behind him to peer over his shoulder. "Something smells good."

Turning his head, Christina was rewarded with a quick kiss on the nose for her praise. "Eggs, bacon, and hash browns. I hope you're hungry."

"When I'm not cooking," Christina informed him pertly, her feet taking her quickly to a cupboard to bring down some plates, "I'm always famished."

Taking their food to her rarely used dining room table, Christina had a forkful of eggs in her mouth when Jason leaned back in his chair. "Have you got anything planned next Friday?"

Swallowing, Christina hadn't stopped to consider her words. "I don't know, do I?"

Across the expanse of the table, she'd watched the slow, sexy smile settle over his features, and her toes had curled. "That's just what I was hoping you'd say."

Yes, Jackie's words had stuck with Christina. Gone was the guarded reserve, the duplicity of self-preservation, the charade. She was in love with Jason, falling harder with every passing day. The time had come for her to accept that. The time had come for her to show it.

Her soft acquiescence at the breakfast table that morning had been testament to that. The easy, quick surrender to spending time with him. Maybe she hadn't laid her feelings bare, but they'd been there, all the same. It had been the first step. The next came when she and Mary surprised Jason by showing up to watch one of his baseball games. Cheering loudly from the bleachers, Christina had offered him a tiny wave when his hazel eyes had widened at the sight of her alongside his mother.

After the game, he'd walked her to her car—to the patent amusement of the team manager. Reaching for her hand, he slowed his steps as they gained the parking lot, his fingers squeezing hers comfortingly. "That was a nice surprise."

Tilting her head back, she grinned up at him from the glare of the overhead lights. "To my surprise, I find I'm becoming rather fond of baseball."

He chuckled. "Yeah?"

She nodded slowly. "Yeah."

"You're awfully brave when there are busloads of teenagers milling about," he murmured wickedly.

Snaking forward, her hand tugged the ballcap off his head. Settling it over her hair, she smiled saucily. "Come over later, I'm only getting warmed up."

As the snowy spring faded into a burgeoning flush of impending summer, Christina had conceded to Jackie's words. She'd made herself available to him, made herself as transparent as she knew how to be. The resulting weeks had been almost perfect…a vision of everything she'd always been too afraid to hope for, too afraid to want, everything she'd never allowed herself to imagine.

Except. Now, pressing the phone closer to her ear, Christina sighed. Except for that one small point of contention.

Jason's absolute, stubborn resolve to gain insight into every damn nook-and-cranny of her life.

Namely, her past.

Christina's lips thinning at the thought, her fingers curled into the palm of her left hand. They were adults, for God's sake. They didn't need to share every secret between them. They weren't codependent children. They didn't need to divulge every sweep and purview, confess to every scrap of gossip or minute detail to one another.

Closing her eyes, Christina shook her head, her face contorting with the motion. It was hardly Jason's fault that his curiosity only seemed to grow with every passing attempt on her part at evasion, with every nuanced avoidance of any time in her life before moving to Minnesota. And yes, okay, so maybe that was hardly a small area of hedging. They were, after all, talking about twenty-three years of her life. But she wasn't interested in discussing those times. They were no longer relevant. She'd seen to it, sworn herself to that fact.

That part of her life was over, better left behind her. She had no intention of bringing it into her future, so she saw no purpose in talking about it now.

Jason, however, didn't seem to get that.

Seeking the right words, Christina stalled. The call had started out so well. She'd just finished dinner, her fingers, submerged in the warm dishwater of her sink, busily scrubbing a plate when she'd heard her phone ringing. Like a shot, she'd abandoned the cleaning, rubbing soaking hands furiously against her jeans as she'd skittered into the living room where her phone sat on the end table.

She'd known who was calling her.

"Hi, Chrissy."

At the sound of his voice, she experienced that now-familiar shiver of sensation race across the band of her stomach. "Hey, yourself."

It had all started out so well. Plunking down on the couch, one stockinged foot circling the thin carpeting, she'd casually asked about the baseball clinic his school was hosting that weekend. Jason had spent the majority of the evening arranging everything for the visiting players.

"Almost finished with the set-up," he said, and she could almost picture him sprawled out on his large suede couch, his socked feet crossed at the ankle over his ottoman coffee table. "Bob and I'll have to finish up a couple items for registration"— he yawned—"but there'll be plenty of time after school tomorrow." Though classes had officially let out for the year the week prior, she knew he was still busy each day with end-of-year conferences and seminars.

"You're tired," she noted.

"Not too tired to talk to you."

She smiled. "What do you want to talk about?" Later, she'd identify this question as her first mistake.

"What have you got planned for the weekend?"

"You mean other than spending both days weeping for missing you?"

"Other than that, obviously."

Christina smirked. "Then I've penciled in time for some pensive pining."

"Good idea."

"Oh. And after that, I thought I'd break into a wild rush of sentiment and spend the remaining hours idolizing you from afar."

He laughed. The low sound rushed seductively down the line. "Sounds like a full weekend."

"Not nearly as full as yours," she returned cheekily.

"Yeah," he agreed quietly, the humor seeping out of his voice with the one word. He sighed.

Hearing the telling sound, Christina changed tacks, her voice taking on an impish edge when she said, "And you'd be lost without baseball, so you might as well quit trying to solicit my sympathies."

Jason snorted as he was meant to do. "Yeah." The word held more promise than before.

"What do you love most about it?"

"Baseball?"

"Yes."

"Whew."

Christina smiled at the sound.

"I don't know...there's so many things."

Snuggling into the couch cushions, Christina pursed her lips. "Take your time then. I'm in no hurry."

At that, he'd started talking to her—about the joys of watching the kids grow into the sport, seeing their pride and commitment to the game, to the team. He talked about the mathematics behind the strategy, the camaraderie between the players, between the community, and the memories from his own youth that went along with all of it.

"You played shortstop in high school?" she asked.

"And college."

Christina nodded. "And were probably tossing the ball with your dad before you were fully walking yet."

"Pretty much."

With a flick of her eyes, Christina caught a flash of the time displayed on the wall clock in her living room. Battling back a surge of guilt, she felt her lips twisting. It was getting late. Though she had to work in the morning too, she knew Jason had an even longer day ahead of him. She knew she should get off the phone. Instead, she let images of Jason as a small boy flood her head, distract her. Of course, she hadn't known him then, but she'd seen enough pictures to conjure up a general likeness.

Humming softly at the image, she felt her lips tremble with affection.

"You sound like you're smiling."

"Just picturing it."

"My glory years?"

"Your chubby arms flinging balls any which way, making Matthew run hither and dither chasing them around the yard."

"Please," he said, sounding disgusted, "it wasn't that bad."

Christina laughed.

"What about you?"

"Me?"

"What did your childhood look like?"

The question produced an echo of sound in Christina's mind—her laughter as she skipped freely beside her mother on their way home from church on Sundays, her hand enveloped carefully in Natalie's sure grasp; the quiet, piercing strain of piano keys as Christina played alongside her college orchestra—the sharp applause, the crinkle of professionally-wrapped bouquets her mother had brought to each and every recital and concert; the quiet melodious sound of her father's voice as she'd lay in bed at night listening to bedtime stories, the whisper of her mother's silver-handled brush as she combed and braided Christina's hair before the bathroom mirror....

The memories were overwhelming, astounding, blinding in their intensity. Swallowing with difficulty, Christina felt her shoulders tightening, her stomach clenching as she fought back the emotional reminders.

She knew it wasn't reasonable, the sweep of irritation that his words inspired in her. Nor was it unexpected, his continued, persistent interest. In fact, she should have seen it coming. Just lately, Jason seemed determined to find ways to incorporate such topics, to lead their conversations in that direction. As such, she now knew that he'd broken his arm when he was eight climbing an apple tree on his grandparent's farm. She knew that he'd landed the starring role in his junior high school theater play and that one production had forever cured any desire on his part to act. She knew he'd also played quarterback in football and he'd run track in college. Her head relatively spun with the information he'd supplied and, in reaction, his consternation had only become more pronounced at her lacking response. No, she'd never broken a bone. Her acting performances didn't warrant mention, and she'd rather hummed along noncommittally to stories of his athleticism.

And yet, wasn't she guilty of the same thing she found herself so incensed at with him? Hadn't she just been caught greedily slurping up visuals of Jason as a small boy, as a baseball player, the Jason he'd been before she'd met him?

Wasn't she equally desperate for each scrap of information that had any connection to this man?

So, okay, she wasn't being fair. She knew that. She didn't want to argue with him, she didn't want to alienate him. But unlike him, her past was better left where it was, far behind her. Unlike him, the only connection between her past and her present was ugly, scarring. Unlike him, she'd spent years keeping everything about her life from before from seeping into anything about her life afterward.

It was too painful to talk about. It was too painful to think about. That's what hurt the most, the memories that had stopped, abruptly, when she was twenty-three years old. She'd thought those would be infinite, growing with her throughout her life. How wrong she'd been.

"Christina?" The soft command in his voice nearly undid her, thrusting her back into the present. Closing her eyes, Christina forced herself to take a deep breath in. Her knuckles grew white around the phone in her hand. She didn't want to fight with him, but she didn't want to talk about this.

She sighed roughly. "My childhood? I mean, I don't know…"

"No?" There was no disguising the mockery in the question.

"It was unremarkable."

"What did you look like?"

"Blonde, skinny, freckles across my nose."

"That could describe you now."

"I was shorter then."

"And?"

"And?" she wailed softly. "Jason, what could it possibly matter?"

"Says the woman with the huge advantage."

"Excuse me?"

"My parents."

Christina felt her breath freezing in her throat.

"You don't have to wonder. You already know all there is to know about me, replete with the embarrassing confirmation photos that Mom insists on throwing out at any imagined gathering."

She stiffened. She had a terrible idea she knew where this was going. It turned out she was correct.

"But I've never met your parents. I've never been given the pleasure of seeing you squirm when they reminisce over your adolescence while someone sits on the other side of the table, eating it all up."

"No." The word was so soft she doubted he'd heard her.

"Christina?"

"What?"

"Are they, are they still alive?"

Her stomach revolted. "What?" The explosion of her voice surprised even Christina, her body hurtling forward on the couch in ready attack. "Of course, they're still alive!" Yet even as the words left her mouth, Christina couldn't suppress a chill. It'd been years since she'd so much as heard from them. Still....

"I'm sorry," Jason said, his words contrite, soothing now. "I didn't mean to upset you."

"You didn't."

"Obviously, that's not true."

Christina's eyebrows puckered, her face tightening.

"It's just, you never talk about them," he insisted, sucking in a breath of air.

"So you figured they were dead?"

"You spend every holiday with my family. Even your birthdays. I don't recall you ever going to visit them."

Holding onto her temper, Christina conceded his point. "I suppose it's hard to understand that some families aren't close."

"That's not what I meant—"

"My father's a lawyer. My mother is a housewife." The words were as flat and unemotional as they were sudden. "She loves to garden and he reads political thrillers."

At one end, a beat of silence, of hesitation…

At the other, a haggard breath—almost a growl.

"Anything else you'd like to know?" The hardness in Christina's voice, the cutting quality was etched into the very lines of her face.

Another pause, shorter this time. A sigh. "It would appear not."

The line seemed to be strangling in silence, in resentment.

"Look, it's getting late," Jason muttered. Christina closed her eyes on the weary tone. "I should probably let you go."

"I'm sorry," she said softly, gentle now.

He didn't need her to explain. "It's fine," he uttered quietly. "I'll call you tomorrow—"

"No, wait," Christina cried. "Not...not like this. Don't hang up like this." She hated the weakness in her plea, but she meant it all the same.

"Christina."

"Not when you're mad at me," she pressed.

There was another lengthy sigh. She didn't dare remember how many he'd issued throughout the conversation. "I'm not mad."

"Did I tell you how much I'm going to miss you this weekend?"

What followed was a weak laugh. "Probably not enough."

"Then let me enlarge upon that."

"If you insist." Chuckling, Jason let it go. Christina loved him even more for that.

It had been a rough conversation and the weekend that followed it was particularly long for Christina, who'd wanted to do nothing more than reassure herself that she and Jason were fine, that whatever awkwardness had lingered by the end of their phone call was well and truly over.

By Monday, she had her answer. He asked her over to watch a movie that night. Snuggled up beside him on the couch, she waited for it all night—that one searching question, that subtle prompt to bring up the subject of her past. It never came. Falling asleep that night, her head cradled against his bare chest, Christina curled her body possessively against his. The action caused his arm to tighten across her shoulders.

"Goodnight," she murmured.

"'Night, babe."

Lying there, Christina's eyes fluttered slowly shut. Yes, okay, that last conversation had been rough, but perhaps it'd also been necessary. Perhaps now they could move beyond it, as she'd learned to do years ago. The past held nothing but a locked door. Natalie had seen to that and Christina, ever the faithful daughter, was doing her best to adhere to that rule.

Chapter Twenty-Three

She'd been a fool. Standing, half-hidden in the doorway of Matthew's office, Christina only completely understood it then. Her hands tightened automatically on the doorknob, her mind screaming at her to retreat, retreat! Or, at the very least, to speak, to announce her presence. Instead, she stayed silent, listening, intent.

It must be said that Christina was not an eavesdropper by nature. Indeed, she'd never have entertained the notion of something so underhanded or sneaky, but then she'd never heard the sound of her whispered name being discussed behind her back before, either. Almost before she knew it, she was leaning closer, her ears pitched to hear the hushed conversation taking place about her, without her.

She hadn't meant to listen in on their private conversation; they hadn't meant for her to overhear them. No. It had all started by accident and if it hadn't been for her damned phone…

Carefully getting the last of a contract printed before the end of the day, Christina's eyes had twinkled in expectation when her phone buzzed with the telltale sound of an incoming text message. Snapping the freshly printed contract off the printer tray, she'd been on the verge of entering Mr. Gordman's office with the necessary paperwork when it had buzzed again.

Grabbing it from beside her keyboard, Christina grinned at the notification that splashed across her screen. With an expert scroll of her finger, she read the missive:

FROM: Jason
4:59 p.m.
       MESSAGE: Dinner tonight? My place.

FROM: Jason
5:00 p.m.
       MESSAGE: I have wine… :)

In response, her fingers flew across the screen.

FROM: Christina
5:00 p.m.
       MESSAGE: Think it's that easy?

FROM: Jason
5:01 p.m.
       *MESSAGE: For dessert I'll give you free license
           over my body.*

Laughing richly, Christina shook her head as she read that last comment. Biting down on her lip, she let her fingers roam over her keyboard.

FROM: Christina
5:02 p.m.
       MESSAGE: You were right. It is that easy.

Without waiting for his response, Christina set her phone down, replacing it with the contract now resting on the edge of her desk. Banishing the girlish grin from her face, she turned back toward Mr. Gordman's office, knocking perfunctorily on his door.

"Got the contract?" he asked, not bothering to lift his head at her entrance.

"Right here, boss."

He held out a hand. "Thanks."

"No problem." Christina shot a fleeting glance to the clock hanging on the wall. "If there's nothing else…?" she continued pointedly, hoping to keep the eagerness out of her voice.

"No, no. Get out of here," he replied, finally offering to flick his gaze up to hers with a smile. "I'm right behind you."

Edging back for the door, Christina smiled. "See you tomorrow."

"Indeed."

Without loss of time, she moved to the filing cabinet, flinging the bottom drawer open to haul out her purse. Throwing it over her shoulder, a low hum murmuring off her lips, she paused only long enough to shut out the set of overhead lights directly above her desk before walking briskly onto the main floor, her steps taking her unerringly toward the exterior doors. A smile tugged at the corners of her mouth as her shoes, beating a harsh tattoo on the concrete stairs of the parking ramp, took her toward her car.

Slipping into the driver's seat of her car, one hand went to insert her key in the ignition while the other rummaged blindly through her purse; she hadn't had time before to see if Jason had responded to her text before she'd left. With a twist of her wrist, she brought her vehicle to life, but Christina hardly spared that notice.

"Where in the world…?" Exasperation lined her words as Christina tugged her purse more securely on her lap. Yanking it open wide, her head bending over it in inspection, her hands shuffled, her eyes roaming past miscellaneous tubes of lipstick, her wallet, a small compact brush…. Groaning, that's when Christina realized her mistake.

She'd left her phone on her desk.

Dammit.

Gritting her teeth, Christina contemplated leaving it there overnight but rejected the idea almost as quickly as she'd considered it. With a huff, she scooted back out of her car, her feet pumping hurriedly in her rush. The office was silent, the walls casting shadows on the empty furniture scattered about the main floor, but when Christina reentered her office, she saw through Mr. Gordman's partially-opened door the low light from his desk lamp still shining limply in the approaching gloom of evening. Shaking her head slightly, Christina skirted around her desk, her fingers reaching, grasping for her phone when she heard it.

That whispered name.

Her name.

Only it wasn't Mr. Gordman speaking.

It was said in the quiet tones of a small woman with short brown hair threaded with hints of silver, in a voice both immediately familiar and startling. It was said by a woman who'd clearly snuck into the room minutes after Christina had exited it, a woman who'd deliberately wanted to wait until the topic of her conversation was out of the building.

"It's Christina."

Freezing, leaning across her desk, Christina's eyes rounded, her fingers stilling as she strained to hear what Mary said. She wasn't sure why, but she knew, from the tiniest tremor in that beloved voice that Mary wasn't saying something pleasant.

"Christina?"

"It's just, I'm a bit worried," Mary admitted quietly. "Especially after having lunch with Jason today."

"About what?"

Sucking in a breath, Christina heard Matthew's voice float across the room. She knew she should grab her phone and silently slip out, back the way she'd come, leave them alone. To her credit, she did seize her phone and ease away from her desk, only her feet took her stealthily closer to Matthew's door, not away from it.

This was obviously meant to be a private conversation, she assured herself, a privileged—

"You don't know but…" Mary paused miserably, "something happened to Christina. Something in her past. It's why she left home all those years ago. It's why she's never gone back."

Inching a little closer, Christina just peered into the shadowed room. She saw Matthew's accompanying frown. Mary had her back turned to Christina, but her voice betrayed her emotional turmoil.

The atmosphere of the room changed, electrified at the words, at Matthew's low, hesitant response: "Okay?"

"And it's, it's dark and ugly. Painful. So painful that, even after all this time, she can't let it go, hasn't even begun to heal—"

Matthew stilled. "What the hell are you talking about?"

"Don't tell me you've never wondered…?"

"Well, sure," he conceded gruffly, "but Christina's a private person."

"It's bigger than that."

"Jason told you this?"

"No." The word, wrenched from her small body, swelled around the room meaningfully. "And that's the whole problem. He doesn't know, either. Fact is, I don't think she intends to tell him."

Matthew leaned back in his seat. With his elbows on the armrests, he brought his steepled fingers up against his chin. "Well," he said slowly, expelling a soft breath, "that's her business."

"That's just it, I think he *needs* to know. I think *she* needs him to know."

Matthew narrowed his eyes. "Okay, out with it," he ordered. "You've sufficiently built up the drama of the moment."

"This thing, it shattered her, morphed her entire world, colored everything she ever knew." Christina, pressing closer to the doorway, could just make out the shape of Mary's animated movements by the glow of the sole desk lamp. "It's consumed her until it's become so much a part of her that…" With an impotent lift of her hand, Mary left the sentence unfinished.

From her slim view, Christina watched Matthew rub a hand against the side of his face. Her breath rattled loosely in her mouth, bile rising in her throat as she waited.

"You think it'll come between them."

"It already has." Mary's voice was high and taut. "Jason's noticed that there's something she's keeping from him, that she's shutting him out. At lunch today, he said that she won't…that she won't talk about anything to do with her life before she moved here. Nothing. When he asks, she just closes up, changes the subject, acts as though it never happened." Mary's shoulders drooped. "She won't say anything at all—"

"Except to you," Matthew murmured perceptively. "She obviously spoke to you."

"Yes," Mary confessed, shifting in the leather seat. "Yes, she told me. I-I don't think she meant to but…"

Matthew ran a hand across one side of his jaw. "I don't suppose you can tell me what happened to her?"

Christina held her breath, her heart beating like a demented thing in her chest.

"No. Only to say we are a product of our past. Even if people *do* change"—Christina cringed at the incredulity she was sure she'd picked up in Mary's tone—"we take our baggage with us, whether we want to admit it or not."

A shrill silence accompanied the words, weighted the room…

"That's why I came here today, I suppose," Mary continued, sighing wearily. "Part of me was hoping she'd still be here. That I'd be able to catch her alone…"

"And the other part?"

"The other part is glad to be sitting here with you."

"Afraid, Mar?"

Mary squirmed in her seat. "Only that I'll make a liar of myself. I promised her that nothing would change between us once I found out. If I speak to her now…" Mary shook her head. "I can hardly tell Christina what to do or how to be, but"—with a flourish, Mary's arms swung out to her sides—"dammit, I don't want him to get hurt! I don't want either of them to get hurt."

Matthew inclined his head. "It's that bad?"

"People have a tendency to recreate their history. Especially when it's left unresolved."

"And you think she'll do that."

"I think she already has, a little. It's why she was so terrified to admit her feelings for him in the first place. It's why she's keeping secrets from him, hiding a part of herself away, keeping him in the dark. It's become a habit for her."

"I see," Matthew said.

"Knowing what I know, I'm concerned that—"

"That once a cheater, always a cheater?"

The hard, brittle question, coming from within the shadows of the doorway, sent Mary spinning around, her hand coming to slap against her racing heart. Echoing her movements, Matthew's head turned sharply toward the sound as well.

"Christina! No!"

It must be repeated that Christina DeLuca was not a woman known for listening in on other people's conversations. She hadn't even known Mary was in the building when she'd heard her talking. Nor was Christina particularly proud of what she'd done. None of these objections were enough to keep her silent for one more tormenting moment of Mary's analysis.

It shattered her….

We are a product of our past.

I can hardly tell Christina what to do or how to be…

People have a tendency to recreate their history. Especially when it's left unresolved.

Mary couldn't have put it any plainer. She was troubled about Jason. No. Correction: she was troubled about Jason dating Christina.

Standing there, shaking under the force of her feelings—the agony of realizing she'd been right all along, that she had lost the Gordmans' as surely as she'd lost her parents once the truth had come out, the raging anger that she'd done this to herself, the shooting pain that Mary had betrayed her, just like her own mother had, and the paralyzing knowledge that despite it all, history *was* repeating itself—Christina felt something snap inside her.

Thinking it over later, she figured it was this maelstrom of emotions which had spurred her on. At that point, she'd known that there was no going back. Things would never be the same. She'd lost the second family she'd ever known. Only this time, perhaps because she knew firsthand what would follow this separation, the hurt went deeper, spread wider throughout the fibers and nerves of her body, pushing and pinching at her breath, her heart.

There was no possible recourse of repair. Even if she ended things with Jason, her relationship with Mary and Matthew would never again resume its old footing. It would be forever marked by the impact of this telling moment. And if she didn't end things with Jason, what possible chance did they have anyway, especially if this was the kind of reception they could expect? No, she wouldn't come between a child and their parents. She wouldn't be Bill. No matter how much it broke her heart.

It was just like four years ago. She knew it now as surely as she had known it when her mother had left the sharp sting of her handprint against Christina's cheek. Everything was gone, with no hope of a misunderstanding or exaggeration. Only this time, despite the knocking of her knees, the churning acid spewing in her stomach, the goodbye lodging itself in her chest—of never seeing them again, never sharing in their jokes, their dinners, those stupid card games—despite the loss stealing her warmth, Christina found a strength she hadn't possessed with her parents. This time, she wasn't going to run off into the night without defending herself, this time she wasn't leaving quietly.

This time, she would have her say.

Pushing herself forward, though her legs threatened to collapse under her weight, that's when Christina had heard her voice carrying out into the dim room with a surprising coolness: *That once a cheater, always a cheater?*

She barely processed Mary's instinctive denial. Laughing roughly, Christina only shook her head. "As you said, we *are* a product of our past."

Mary's lips trembled. Christina could see them quivering from clear across the room. "Christina, I'm not sure what you *think* you heard..."

"Only the things you just said yourself," Christina assured her, nodding grimly.

"But...no, I didn't—!" Mary sputtered incoherently, her large eyes widening. Half-turned in her seat, she brought her hands up to the armrests, clumsily gaining her feet. "Christina, wait, let me explain."

"I don't think that'll be necessary," Christina insisted, her face contorting on a hideous laugh. "I do believe I got the gist of it."

"Watch your tone," Matthew interrupted, his hands spreading wide on his desk as he half-rose himself. "I won't have you talk to my wife in that way."

Christina felt her body start, recoiling at the dark command.

"Don't you dare bark at her, Matthew," Mary said, rounding on her husband. "She has every right to speak to me however she wishes! I deserve it anyway." Turning back to Christina, her eyes stared pleadingly. "Christina, I didn't mean it that way—!"

"You mean I misunderstood you when you said you feared I'd recreate my past?"

There was the slightest pause. "No," Mary admitted, and then: "Yes. I mean..."

Christina raised her eyebrows incredulously.

Mary faltered: "Yes, I said that but, I think you misunderstood the reason *why* I'm concerned. Christina, you've bottled this up inside of you for so long, and I'm afraid that if you don't let it out now, if you don't *really* talk about it and let others in, you'll never truly get over what happened."

"Talk about it?" Christina's voice was bitter, hard.

"To Jason," Mary clarified. "If you keep pushing this hurt down inside of you, hiding it away from the people in your life, it'll fester and infect everything around you."

Christina nodded woodenly. "I see."

"Sweetheart, your heartbreak is as real today as I can only assume it was all those years ago. What you've been doing— shutting everything up inside of you, pretending it didn't happen, pretending that your life only started once you left Illinois—it's not working. If you can't learn how to accept what happened and move on, well how can you and Jason truly make something of your feelings? It'll always be there between you—"

"My affair, you mean?" Christina scoffed, her hands balling into fists. She did her best to avoid looking at Matthew, but it would have been impossible to miss the high lift of his eyebrows as he lowered himself back into his chair.

"No. I mean everything that transpired because of it. The losses, Christina. They're what's standing between you two, only if Jason doesn't know about it, he won't be able to help you confront them. And you won't ever be free of them."

"So talking about it, that's what'll help?" Christina almost spat out the words. "That's rich, Mary, since you're the only person I've ever spoken to about it, and here *you* are throwing it between us."

"No. Honey, no, that's not what I'm doing."

"No? That's what it sounds like to me. Now that you know what happened, you don't want Jason involved with me."

Mary gasped. "Christina! How could you think that!"

Christina shrugged fatalistically, but all the same, she took a deep, steadying breath. "I can hardly say I blame you. Only, I wish you'd been honest from the start."

"No!"

"Oh, I know you tried to believe otherwise, but I changed in your eyes. Once you knew. Especially now that Jason's involved." Unbidden tears clogged in her throat, half-drowning the last of her words.

"That's simply not true. I'm sorry if you think that, but it's—"

"Maybe, maybe not," Christina consented. "But with my checkered past…"

"You're upset," Mary said, her voice changing on the wings of a new tact. "I understand that. I shouldn't have talked about you like that. It was unpardonable of me."

"You want to know why I, what's the wording you used, shut everything up inside me?" Christina asked, her voice almost conversational now. She even smiled. "Because this is always going to be the last conversation I'll have."

"The last?"

"The goodbye scene."

"Ah, the self-fulfilling prophecy then?" Matthew asked quietly, but neither woman gave him much notice.

"We," Mary insisted, her arm waving between herself and Christina, "we will never say goodbye. I've told you that before but if you need, I'll say it as often as you'd like."

Christina smiled in disbelief.

Mary didn't miss a beat. "I mean it. Goodbye is the last thing I will ever accept from you. In fact, that's my entire point. That's the entire reason that I came here. It's why I spoke to Matthew. Because I want so much for things to work out with you and Jason. I'm rooting for the two of you. I always have been. That's why I said what I did just now. Because I'm afraid—"

"There's that word again," Christina intoned.

"If you can't let go of what they did, if you can't believe that Jason would react differently, if you can't believe that I still love you…" She took another step toward Christina. "That's what breaks my heart. Not what happened. I told you, I don't care about what happened. I only care about how you handle it now."

"And with whom."

Mary's head hung in defeat. "Yes. And with whom."

"I guess you were wrong, after all."

"Excuse me?" Mary asked, but she sounded exhausted.

"I did need your permission to date Jason. And by the looks of it, I don't have it." On that note, she turned around. An ominous, damning sort of silence greeted her words as she stalked toward Matthew's office door. It was only as she crossed the threshold that she muttered, "Of course, you're probably right. Haven't I known that all along?"

Chapter Twenty-Four

Christina could hardly see through the tears obstructing her vision, could hardly focus for the shuddering sobs wracking her shoulders as she pulled jerkily out of the parking garage. Perhaps it had been the shock of her sudden appearance and then disappearance, or maybe it had been the last remaining remnants of respect—then again, it could have been due to a simple lack of wanting to do so, but that was a consideration she wasn't yet able to entertain—but neither Mary nor Matthew had attempted to follow after Christina when she'd wrenched herself out of the office, her shoes loud on the flooring as she'd raced past and around the maze of desks on her way to the front entrance.

She hadn't been quite quick enough to outrun that last image though—of Mary slipping out from around her chair, her arms gesturing wildly, face contorted as her voice pleaded after Christina's hasty retreat, imploring her to come back, to stop…!

But Christina hadn't stopped, hadn't allowed herself to be stopped. What more was there to say, anyway? Turning onto the street, she pressed her foot down too hard on the accelerator, her small car jumping a little in response.

She wasn't entirely sure how she managed the drive. Shivering a little as she stared down the block of houses, a view which had only recently become somewhat familiar to her, she felt her hands grip the steering wheel. She didn't remember turning down the streets, stopping at the lights, exiting the city and entering the surrounding suburb. Staring out her windshield, Christina let her eyes roam the vague scenery before her. Her nerves were raw, shredded past the point of reason or logic. She knew she should have gone home, but she hadn't.

No, instead she was bent on recreating her past.

"Well hell, who said Mary was wrong?" Christina muttered as she stared out the window. Parked somewhat crookedly on the side of the street, she slowly peeled her hands from the steering wheel, carefully cut the engine. For a moment, she just looked at it. Jason's home. Two-story, white vinyl siding, attached garage, small yard. The lights were on in one of the downstairs windows. He was home already.

She was hours early for a dinner that would never happen.

With a jerk, Christina thrust the thought from her mind. Yanking down the visor, she glanced at her reflection in the small compact mirror attached there. With a frenzied sort of motion that stung the sensitive skin, her fingers wiped at the smudges of mascara underneath her eyes, the dried tracks of tears against her cheeks, the lipstick lost to the worrying of her teeth. Studying herself, Christina grimaced. Her nose was blotchy from tears, her eyes stained red. With a snap, she closed the visor, wrenched out of her seat belt, and felt her hand reach for the door handle.

It was the longest walk she'd ever made, longer even than that night when Bill had turned his back to her. Her feet stomped unsteadily across the empty street, her breath straining as she advanced upon the three short steps which would take her up to his small porch.

She had one foot on the bottom-most tread when the door opened ahead of her. Pausing at the unexpectedness of it, she'd sort of been counting on the element of surprise, Christina felt the impact of Jason's gaze like a live thing. Tensing, for a moment, she didn't move.

Half-shadowed by the light spilling out from the room behind him, nonetheless, she could still see the look of mingled concern and confusion crossing his face as he watched her.

"Christina?" Jason was holding his cellphone in his right hand. "What's going on?"

At the words, she reacted. Like a shot, her feet tripped the rest of the way up the porch steps. He knew. There was no preamble in his voice, no shock at her sudden, unannounced entrance.

His next words confirmed it. Half-lifting the cell phone in his hands he said, "I just got a call from my mom and she—"

Before he could finish, Christina fetched up beside him. Shaking her head fiercely, she placed her hands on his shoulders. "Shh," she whispered unsteadily, pushing him gently back inside the house.

Blindly, he followed her lead until they were both standing inside the open hallway leading off from the front doorway. "Christina?"

She was still shaking her head. "I just want one last moment," she whispered, and then her hands were reaching up around his neck. Pressing her body tight to his, reveling in the answering flash of need she saw flickering in his gaze, Christina's fingers curled around the back of Jason's head before she guided it closer to her own. "Just one last…please—" and then her lips were on his, her mouth twisting against his in a frenzied motion.

He didn't resist. His hands cupped the sides of her hips, holding her steady as their tongues met under the heated exchange. Moaning at the instant pitch of her stomach, at that feeling she got whenever he got this close, like gravity had given away, Christina felt her legs brush up against his, her whole body tingling as his teeth pulled at her lower lip, his thumb brushing away the stray tears which had leaked out of her tightly closed eyes.

All too soon, however, Jason was pulling away, his brows furrowing with disquiet as he stared down at her. "What's going on?" he asked again, but this time there was no mistaking the authority in his voice, the demand for an answer.

Her lips wobbled. Closing them tightly, Christina untangled herself from his arms. Shakily, she ran her fingers through her hair. "Jason."

"One last what?"

Her lips pursed to keep the sobs from filtering out of her mouth. Taking a deep breath, Christina edged closer to the door, farther from Jason, her eyes not quite looking back at his. "This thing between us," she muttered, her hand fluttering wildly, "it's not going to work. I can't, I can't do this."

Jason's eyes closed. A small crease worked its way between his brow line. But when he reopened them, Christina was taken aback by the anger radiating there.

"You know, Christina," he said, his voice low, "this on-again, off-again thing that you do, it's getting pretty irritating."

She sucked in a breath. "I'm not—"

"Yes. You are. You do it a lot. All the damn time, actually. Only I'm not interested in it anymore. I mean, what is it? The drama? Do you thrive off it? I don't get it."

Christina didn't bother to fight back. She deserved his anger. She knew it. Instead, she smiled sadly. "No. It's not the drama."

"Then what?"

She shrugged fatalistically. "It's the inevitable conclusion, that's all."

"What?"

"Your mom agrees," Christina assured him, a humorless laugh bouncing past her tight lips.

Jason rolled his eyes. "You know what, I'm over that too."

"Excuse me?"

"This little game you seem to like playing, where you answer my questions with cryptic remarks but don't actually tell me anything." He took a slow, deep breath. "Talk to me."

"You don't want to know."

"Goddammit, Christina!"

At the growl in his voice, she felt her eyes round. In all the years she'd known him, Christina wasn't aware of ever hearing Jason raise his voice. Not to her. Not once.

"I'm not doing this with you anymore. Either talk or go." With a thrust of his hand, Jason gestured toward the door behind her. But despite the exasperation in his voice, she could see the hurt in his face, the uncertainty and bewilderment.

Christina made a quick choice. After all, she probably owed him at least that much. "Fine," she conceded with a self-deprecating motion. If he thought he wanted to know, well then, she'd tell him. His distaste would actually make this easier. "If that's the way you want it."

With that, Christina started speaking, her words at first jumbled and out-of-sequence, but slowly the story emerged. Standing under the bright overhead lighting in the squat hallway, Christina heard her voice, hoarse with unshed tears, tight with the knowledge of what would come next, telling Jason everything she knew would effectively end things between them.

"I was young and stupid, and he said everything I wanted to hear. Not that I didn't know perfectly well what I was doing. I did. He had a wife, children...."

Her mouth shook so hard over the words Christina had to stop frequently and repeat herself. For his part, Jason didn't interrupt her, but his eyes showed his shock and discomfort as she continued.

"It went on for a while. Too long. Right there under everyone's noses. Until, until one night at my parents' home..."

Her hands fluttered around her body, their movements growing more and more agitated as the tale spilled out into the open, her sobs growing sporadic as she reached for the end.

"My parents kicked me out. They, they told me I was no daughter of theirs and...and you know what, that's not even the worst part. I was okay with that. At first. I thought they'd come around once Bill and I showed them how serious we were..."

And on and on Christina talked, the narrative bubbling, rambling out of her at odds and ends until she'd finally run out of story to share.

"That's when I moved here. I got a job with your dad's company and," she shrugged, "and, you know everything else." With a bravado she was far from feeling, Christina brought her eyes back up to Jason's face as she waited, her knees trembling, for him to speak.

The end of her saga was met with an eerie calm, a growing quiet settling on the room around them. Jason's nostrils were flaring as though he were slightly out of breath. His forehead was crinkled in thought. And then, finally, he held up a hand. "Are you still in love with this guy, this Bill?"

It was the absolute last thing she'd expected to come out of his mouth.

"What?" Christina screeched. "No! What? How could you even possibly think that?"

Jason frowned. "Well, I'm not really sure what to think. Are you afraid that I have a secret wife in the background?"

"Don't be ridiculous," Christina snapped, brushing away at the tears trickling down into the sides of her lips.

"Then what does that story have to do with *us*? And more specifically, why is it inevitable we'll break up?"

Her eyebrows arched. "Were you listening to me?"

"Yes," Jason said, and his tone gentled. "And I'm sorry for what happened to you—"

"Don't. Don't be sorry on my account. I was no victim."

"It doesn't sound like it from here," Jason assured her.

Slicing her hand through the air, Christina's voice sharpened. "I'm not sure if you're deliberately missing the point or what."

Jason shook his head. "No, but maybe I am missing something. You did a terrible thing. Terrible things happened to you as a consequence. And I *am* sorry about the way it all transpired. But that has nothing to do with *you and me*."

"Your mother is afraid that I'm going to recreate my past." Christina's words fell hotly between them. And then, a small bubble of laughter rose in her throat. "And really, she's probably right."

Jason rubbed a hand against one side of his face. "Yeah?"

"I should have never let anything happen between us. It is history repeating itself. My boss's son? I mean, it's a pretty similar line to my father's business partner, don't you think?"

Jason's lips twitched. "No. In fact, I think that seems a bit melodramatic."

"Not at all," she sneered.

Jason opened his mouth to respond but Christina cut him off with a brutal wave of her hand.

"Don't you get it? I lost my parents' respect. I lost them entirely. I promised I would never do that with Mary and Matthew. I swore it."

"Christ," Jason said softly, "so that was it."

"But you wouldn't take no for a damn answer." Though it was a strong accusation, Christina couldn't hold back the soft affection in her voice.

"And my parents didn't seem to be anything but thrilled," he returned. "Not seeing much of a pattern there."

"That wasn't the impression I got this evening."

Jason sobered a little at the words. "Yeah, what happened tonight?"

"Your mother's worried about you. She, um, she already knew about, about me and Bill. She told me it didn't matter." Christina lowered her eyes, but Jason wasn't fooled by her seemingly casual shrug. "Only, now that we're together she's, she's worried about you dating me."

Jason's eyes narrowed. "That wasn't the impression I got when she called me a little while ago," he said, throwing Christina's words back at her. "She seemed worried about *you*."

Christina sighed. "You honestly think, after everything I just told you, that nothing would change between us? That your image of me would be the same as it was last night?"

Jason's arms swung out impotently at his sides. "Yes. I do." Pausing, he considered, "Except, I guess now I know a little more about why you're so guarded about your past. I understand why it's hard for you to bring it up, talk about it—a place you were told to never return."

But Christina only shook her head. The action was so violent, so aggressive, her neck pinched tight. "Yeah, your mom thought nothing would change between us, either. But tonight, we both found out that wasn't true." She sucked in her lower lip. "You wouldn't be able to help it, seeing me differently, checking up on me when I tell you I have to work late, or worrying when I say I'm going out for drinks with the girls...."

"Ah," Jason said knowingly, "I'll start to worry that you're cheating on me, is that it?"

She smiled. It ached with sadness. "Maybe."

"Because you've frequently cheated on your boyfriends?"

Christina squirmed under his gaze. "No, technically, I've never cheated on *my* boyfriends. But I was a cheater."

Jason nodded slowly. "And that's a life sentence?"

She laughed. It had a wateriness to it. "You really think you could trust me now?"

A stillness, a brief but telling silence exploded at the question. Jason's eyes were shadowed with emotion, his lips thinned and his cheeks taut with feeling. Somewhere in the back of her mind, Christina noted that he hadn't tried to reach for her. Not once. Not once he knew.

She nodded, resigned. "Yeah, I didn't think—"

"No."

At the hard word, Christina froze. "Excuse me?"

"This isn't really about my parents—or how they feel about us dating. Just like it's not really about an affair you had when you were barely out of your teens."

"No?" Christina felt some of her composure slip. Her chin lifted a little. "Then what is it about?"

"You're afraid," Jason assured her coolly. "You're so afraid to trust, to love, that you'd rather throw up any excuse to remind yourself, to remind everyone around you, why it's a terrible idea than to actually take a risk."

She blinked.

"You don't believe you'll ever recreate your past, at least, not in the way you're trying so hard to convince me. You won't cheat again. You can barely speak the words, they disgust you so much," Jason informed her.

"As for my parents approving of us? Please, that's so flimsy it falls apart every time you bring it up, so I won't bother dignifying it with any further response. It only offers to insult everyone involved."

"Got me all figured out?" Christina's voice dripped with ice, with disdain.

"Yeah, I think so," Jason said. He waved toward her general person. "I even know what you're doing now—putting on that hard, cool persona to hide behind. But it doesn't fool me. I'm not sure it ever did. You wear that prissy attitude like armor."

Her eyes narrowed, her back stiffening.

Jason took a step toward her. "It all boils down to the fact that you're still hurt. Deeply hurt. Everyone in your life, everyone who was supposed to protect and love you, they left. The moment you made a mistake, the moment you showed yourself to be a human who'd done something wrong—with a man, by the way, who took advantage of you—the moment you made a mess, they turned their backs on you. Forever."

Her lips quivered a little, but she didn't give him the pleasure of an answer.

"The only love you've ever known taught you about conditions, about terms and contracts. That's why you swore you'd never let what happened with your parents happen with mine, because you honestly think it could. And that's why you hide behind your status as an adulterer, because it reminds you how fickle love can be, and it keeps you in check, doesn't it? Never letting it go means you can never make another false move. You cling tight to your past, to those relationships, so you can never forget the pain, so you can stay safe from getting hurt again."

Jason sighed. "I understand why you wouldn't want to live through that again, I do, but that's just it. What your parents showed you, what Bill did to you, that wasn't love, Christina."

She felt her stomach constrict, her heart beating too quickly, erratically at the words, at how much she wanted to believe them. At how much she wanted to lean in and rest her head against his shoulder, let him take some of the weight hanging off her bones.

But old lessons died hard. Christina knew that she could survive walking away from Jason. She could go on, walking away from his family. As long as it was her choice. The alternative, if she stayed and *they* left, and ultimately, they would…Christina couldn't live through that. Not again.

Jason's voice drifted over her thoughts: "At least, that's not the kind of love you'd know from me or my family. I think you know tha—"

"No." Holding up a hand, Christina shook her head. "Please, just stop."

Jason's chin dropped just the slightest bit.

"I can't, I can't *do* this," she pleaded, her eyes ravaged as they glanced up at him.

Jason's hands clenched into fists at his sides, his jaw twitching slightly. "I'm not Bill."

Instinctively, Christina reached for him, but halfway there, she let her hand drop back down limply to her side. "No. Never that."

"I'm not sending you away."

"No," she agreed again, her mouth smiling tremulously. "Instead, I'm doing that for you."

"Don't."

"I could say the same to you," Christina whispered, her feet taking her backward until she felt the door come up behind her. Her hands reached blindly, grabbing for the doorknob. "Don't watch me leave. Don't call me. Just don't." With a twist of her wrist, Christina opened the door and, gentleman that he was, though his face contorted with pain, Jason turned his head away as she slipped out the door.

Staring blankly at her computer, Christina felt her right cheek twitch a little with feeling. Her eyes scanned over the information displayed across the blue-white glare of the screen, her finger hovering over the print button—there it was, in black and white, a plane ticket to Illinois.

A plane ticket back home.

"This is stupid," she muttered to herself, her words slurring together a little. Beside her, on the kitchen table, was the same bottle of whiskey she'd been drinking that fateful night when Jason had shown up outside her door after his lunch with Matthew. It seemed she was doomed to drink it in his honor. "You've already purchased the ticket. Just print the damn thing." Her finger did as commanded.

Tipping back another long swig of alcohol, she listened as her printer sputtered and coughed into life, the zip-zip of it as it slowly stained the paper with the airline company's logo. The departure date jeered at her.

"Tomorrow," Christina mumbled, her laugh a gurgle of drunkenness.

Technically, she was wrong. It was currently 12:42 a.m., which meant Christina would be boarding a plane to go back to a place she'd always sworn never to set foot in again, in less than twenty-four hours.

She giggled. Actually, she'd be leaving in less than fifteen hours. Thirteen hours and eight minutes.

"Christ," she swore, rubbing her wrist over her mouth. "I should probably get some sleep." But she didn't move. Her thoughts just kept playing on repeat—echoing again with Mary's concerns, shifting to consider Jason's vehement defense. Her eyes flickered unerringly toward her phone. Mary had tried to call her no less than five times that evening, but when Christina had abruptly ended the last attempt, the older woman seemed to have finally conceded defeat. The phone remained silent now, the screen dark. Unmoving.

Then her eyes returned to the printer. She hadn't meant to buy the ticket. At least, not really. Thing was, she'd just sort of done it. She hadn't planned it exactly, but she'd certainly known what she was doing when she'd walked inside her apartment and, nabbing up the whiskey, had brought herself to her laptop. She hadn't stopped to consider the reasons, to analyze her abrupt decision—they were too obvious and far too painful.

Snatching the ticket off the printer tray, Christina folded it carefully before placing the piece of paper inside her purse. She wasn't interested in the introspection now, either. She'd done it. There was no going back.

She'd promised herself she'd never allow her mother the pleasure of kicking her off the premises again, of dismissing her daughter as though she didn't exist, as though she wasn't a scared kid who'd desperately needed a little mercy. She'd promised she'd never again put herself in a position to watch the triumph glint off those cold eyes as Natalie DeLuca watched her only child slink away, out of sight and into the mists.

"You must really love him," she whispered to herself, her eyes half-closed in her stupor, her hand reaching lazily for the bottle. "Or you're an undiagnosed masochist."

Chapter Twenty-Five

The next morning, her head buzzing somewhere between a hangover and a jangle of tense nerves, Christina carefully packed her suitcase. She made more than most receptionists due to her high qualifications and Mr. Gordman's overt generosity regarding raises over the years, and her wardrobe was testament to this fact. If there was one thing Christina never skimped on it was personal appearance. Her makeup was top of the line, her clothes boasting designer labels. Now, spreading them out across her bed, she deliberated what to bring. She wouldn't be showing up on her mother's porch in anything less than couture.

Finishing that daunting task, she then sat down at her computer, still set up on the dining room table from the night before, and opened up a blank document. Her fingers trembled, but then what was that saying, in for a penny, in for a pound? Sitting there, her back ramrod straight, she wrote one of the most difficult letters she'd ever forced her mind to conjure. That done, she called Jackie.

It was on the third ring that the other girl answered the phone. "Hello?"

"Hey, Jacks," Christina said, using the nickname with a forced casualness that wasn't lost on the younger woman.

"Hey."

"I hope I didn't catch you in the middle of something?"

"No. I was just sitting here…" Which was exactly what Christina had been hoping to hear.

"Good. Actually, I've got a favor to ask of you."

"Yeah?" Christina could practically see Jackie wagging her eyebrows. "Another hot date with Ja—"

"Can you come over here?" Christina asked the boom of her voice cutting Jackie off ruthlessly. She glanced at the oven clock in her kitchen. Her fingers curled around her phone. "Like right now?"

"Uh, yeah," Jackie said, her tone betraying confusion and more than a hint of hesitation. "Hey, is everything okay?"

"Five minutes?"

"Five? Jesus, you know I'm almost on the other side of the cities from you?"

"Ten then?"

A long sigh. "Ten it is." And somehow, in between the Saturday morning traffic, Jackie managed to slip her car into park outside Christina's home in just shy of twelve. Christina had left the front door unlocked and slightly ajar. "Just come inside," she'd called out as that girl had been making her way gingerly up the walkway.

"All right. That's it." Stomping inside the long, narrow hallway at the entrance to Christina's apartment, Jackie slipped off her shoes. Talking as she walked, she placed her hands on her hips as she cried out, "What the hell's going on?"

But when she advanced into the living room and saw the stuffed suitcase sitting tidily off to one side, the humor lacing those words died instantly. Her eyes darted to where Christina could just be seen through the open doorway of her bedroom, now carefully re-hanging the discarded clothing still littering the area.

Without bothering to ask, Jackie walked inside the room. "Christina?"

At the warning note in Jackie's voice, Christina dropped a now impossibly wrinkled shirt back onto her unmade bed. Her eyes were bloodshot, her usually groomed hair sticking up in static patches, her skin almost translucent.

"I need you to do me a favor."

"You already said that," Jackie reminded her. Her eyes skipped over the bed. Shirts and skirts and whatnot swirled dizzyingly before her. It was so unlike the Christina she knew— so ordered and precise—she could hardly take her eyes off the mess.

"I'm taking a trip."

The left side of Jackie's lip twitched. "Uh, yeah. I can see that."

Christina moved restlessly. "Unfortunately, it came sort of, um, unexpectedly."

"Is everything okay, Christina?" It was the second time she'd asked that question but the first time a thread of sympathy coursed through the words, highlighting a note of disquiet.

"Yes. Yeah." No, absolutely not. "Everything's fine."

"Okay?"

"It's just, I didn't have time to tell Mr. Gordman about it."

Jackie's eyes narrowed. "What do you mean you didn't have time?"

"Typically, Mr. Gordman requires time-off requests in advance," Christina mumbled inanely, her hands picking up accessories only to drop them back on the bed. Her eyes stared somewhere above a sparkly belt and a corduroy hat.

Jackie nodded slowly. That was pretty common practice in every department at the company. "Okay," she repeated.

"But as I said, there's not been time."

Jackie's consternation grew. "You can't just tell him?" Like she'd done with her? The second part of the question, though unsaid, stretched meaningfully between the two women. Though Jackie and Christina were friends, they hardly shared the level of familiarity that Christina did with their boss. Both women knew it.

Christina absolutely would not meet that probing gaze. She flapped a hand dismissively. "Oh, you know how he is. I'd be grilled all day and night—" she laughed woodenly. "Forced to check in every couple of minutes. I don't have time for that." Without meaning to, her gaze went to her phone. Mary had tried to call again that morning but only once. Much like the night before, she hadn't left a message. Nothing.

Jackie cocked her head disbelievingly. "Right."

"Look, I wouldn't normally ask you to do this, but it's kind of an emergency."

Jackie frowned, her arms coming up to cross over her chest. "But you just said—?"

"Not that kind of emergency."

Taking a step forward, Jackie's eyebrows smashed together. "You're not making any sense."

In response, Christina's lips trembled. "I know." Thrusting forward a slip of paper, she pushed it on Jackie, forcing that woman to uncross her arms, take it in one hand.

"What's this?"

"My time-off request. I need you to give it to Mr. Gordman on Monday. Please apologize on my behalf. Explain the situation."

"I don't know the situation."

"It doesn't matter," Christina said enigmatically. "He won't ask."

Jackie nodded. This was getting weirder and weirder. Christina could have easily emailed this to him. She could have just as easily called him as she had Jackie. She could have…. Still, they both knew that Jackie would do as asked.

"And if he won't accept that," Christina said, her voice interrupting Jackie's private thoughts, "then please hand him this." From her back pocket, Christina brought out a sealed envelope. She pressed it into Jackie's other hand, compelling the younger woman to grab hold of it.

"Christina?" Jackie's voice was high, searching. "What is that?" But she knew.

Christina shrugged. "My resignation."

"Jesus!" Jackie cried, shaking the letter in her friend's face. "Isn't this a bit much?"

The blonde woman didn't answer though, her hands merely going to fold up another article of clothing.

"Listen, you said this is a, a kind of emergency?" Jackie reminded Christina, her voice coming too quickly. This was definitely strange. Something was wrong. "He's not going to require your—"

Christina's head bobbed up sharply. "Just in case, okay?"

"In case what?" Jackie was practically shouting now, her arms reaching out to the sides. "Christina, what the hell is going on?"

"Nothing. Just—"

"Why didn't you call Matthew?" Jackie asked. "The real answer this time. Why'd you call me?"

Christina blinked down at her bed, her fingers robotically working on another shirt. "I-I can't."

"What?" Jackie's face contorted. "You can't just give me this," she said, waving the envelope between them emphatically, "and then not tell me anything."

"It doesn't matter. Matthew will know."

"So, why even give me your notice?"

"Because he might demand it."

It all looked the same. Parking her rental car safely to one side of the residential street, for a moment Christina hesitated, her hands still curled around the steering wheel, her right foot pressed against the brake pedal. Her eyes focused on the punctilious brick home to her left. The same blossoming bushes adorned either side of the paved walkway leading up to the covered porch. She was pretty sure those were even the same cushions on the patio furniture, only slightly aged by the sun.

The only thing different was the vehicle parked in the driveway. Same manufacturer, newer model.

It was only when she started to feel like an intruder—was that a neighbor's blinds twitching just slightly?—that Christina slowly levered herself out of the car. Her hands clutched the sides of her purse as she looked up and down the empty roadway before crossing the street. Her legs trembled when she reached the short driveway, but her eyes never betrayed her trepidation. Instead, they stared straight ahead.

She hadn't bothered to call and warn them. Truth be told, she hadn't known if they still had the same phone numbers. And honestly, she'd been too afraid to find out they'd changed them—this would have somehow put to bed any half-smothered hope that they still cared, even a little bit. Hell, until she'd arrived, Christina hadn't even been sure they still resided at the same address. Then again, perhaps she'd sort of hoped for that eventuality. If not, she could just drive on, forget this whole sorry business and head back home, no one any the wiser. (But more than that, she had been paralyzed by the fear that, given advanced warning, they'd tell her not to bother coming at all, that there was no need, no point. That, given advanced warning, they'd have made sure to be gone when she arrived.)

With an abruptness that spoke of desperation, Christina shook away the offending thoughts, the resuming fear that she'd made a mistake. Again. Gaining the front door, she was vaguely surprised that she'd made it that far up to the house without being seen. Natalie DeLuca was not one to be taken by surprise; it would have suited that woman fine to have met an unexpected visitor halfway up the drive with the offer of fresh coffee and homemade rolls. But when Christina gained the doorway, she was forced to ring the doorbell.

Oddly, that hurt more than she'd expected. Another locked door where it concerned Christina and her mother, Christina and her childhood.

Standing there, feeling the soft heat of the late afternoon sun, Christina counted slowly in her head, anything to distract her nerves. She got up to seven when she heard the muffled sound of shuffling footsteps. By eleven, the door swung open.

If Christina had hoped to surprise a look of amazement on her mother's face, she was doomed for disappointment. Other than a quickly stifled tremor crossing her harsh features, features that seemed tauter, harder than Christina remembered, that woman didn't so much as blink at the sight of a daughter she hadn't seen in years, a daughter she'd all but given up on ever seeing again.

For a moment, silence reigned as two women stood facing off, facing one another.

"Christina." Natalie said the name primly, her lips spreading into a thin line, her head inclining just the slightest bit.

Registering this lack of greeting, Christina swallowed back the rise of bitterness tasting on her tongue. She really should have known better. What had she expected? That perhaps her mother had missed her as much as she'd been missed? That she'd regretted her daughter's exile all these years—had she expected tears, arms opening wide in reunion?

The thought was so ludicrous Christina had to fight down an answering smile. Instead, she kept her voice composed, soft as she returned, "Mother."

Another stretch of silence followed the terse exchange. Christina's eyes were hidden behind her sunglasses. Nicely disguised, they nonetheless implored Natalie, waiting for a sign, a movement, a flicker of emotion. Anything. But nothing happened.

In the cloying stillness, the unnatural calm surrounding mother and daughter, Natalie's only change of expression came in the rise of one pointed eyebrow. "Is that it, then?"

Christina blinked, taken aback by the words, the boredom stamped upon them. "Excuse me?"

"Well? I assume you came here for a reason…or do you just intend to stand there all day? I've got things to do," she said, waving absently behind her.

Despite herself, Christina heard a gurgled sob escape her tight throat. Clamping down hard, she took a measured breath. "You haven't changed, I see."

Natalie DeLuca crossed her arms over her chest. "I wasn't the one who needed to."

"Of course not." Christina nodded slowly.

Natalie heaved a great sigh. "What are you doing here, Christina?"

"Honestly, I don't know," Christina admitted on a humorless laugh. "I'm not sure why I came here. I thought…" Raising her arms impotently, she sighed before letting them fall back to her sides again.

But Natalie seemed more impatient than interested when she asked, "You thought what?"

"I guess I thought you'd invite me in."

"For goodness' sake." With a long-suffering sigh, Natalie moved. Stepping backward, she begrudgingly beckoned Christina forward. "But I don't have all day. We've got plans tonight."

Pushing her sunglasses up to the top of her head as she walked inside the bright kitchen—same floral curtains at the windows, same oak cupboards with that same hideous ceramic cookie jar shaped like an apple on the counter—the laugh that burst out of Christina was filled with resentment, bitterness. "And Natalie DeLuca doesn't break her commitments."

Her mother's lip thinned. "Jokes, Christina?"

"No, Mom, just a long-lost daughter. Hardly of importance."

Natalie's back straightened. "It was your choice to drop in like this."

A sputtered laugh. "God! Why am I—"

"You will not take the Lord's name in vain in this house!"

But Christina hardly heard her. Avoiding the heat in Natalie's gaze, her arms crossed down at her hips, Christina took in the spotless countertops, the window looking out at the lilac bushes at the edge of the property, the unadorned refrigerator door, anything to keep from staring at her mother.

"You're right. It was my choice to see you. I don't know what I was thinking. I guess, that my presence would actually mean something to you. That it would be enough."

"I see," Natalie said slowly, cruelly. "So now I've disappointed you?"

Christina shook her head. "I should be used to your indifference."

"I was a terrible mother then? Is that it? You threw dirt on our family name, forced your father to work alongside a man he learned to loathe, forced me to invite his wife—Bill's *wife*—into this house for coffee dates and fundraiser parties, all the while pretending that you hadn't, that you hadn't...!" Her voice grew to a terrible shrill. Christina's eyes closed. She hated to think of Bill's wife, Andrea. She hadn't known the woman well but, no matter that, Andrea had never deserved what Christina had done to her. She'd never deserved any of it.

"And you know what," Natalie spat, her voice bringing Christina's eyes open once more, though they still refused to meet the anger, the wrath radiating off her mother's face; they continued to study the refrigerator door. "She *knew*. She knew what you'd done. It was there, in these little comments she used to make. Comments I was made to ignore or misunderstand."

"Did she, did she ever leave him?" The question was a whisper, a plea.

Natalie's lips twisted. "Oh, I think you know the answer to that. What would have happened to her monthly allowance? What would people have said? No, she didn't leave him."

Christina paled.

"All these lives upended and why? Because I didn't hug you enough?"

At the meanness in the accusation, Christina's resolve strengthened. "I made mistakes. I know that. And I'm more sorry than you could possibly know. If I could..." Christina shook her head. "But you, you never even let me apologize. You never gave me the chance to do anything. You just stopped. You stopped caring, stopped being my mother." Her voice growing steadily, the fervor of her words producing an equal emotional response, Christina wiped a hand under her nose, sniffing inelegantly. "You stopped *loving* me."

Shifting fully in Natalie's direction at last, Christina's eyes clashed against the echoing fury of her mother's gaze, the charge spanning between them with the force of four lonely years. "In all this time, I could have been dead for all you knew, but that was hardly a concern. Not to you. After you threw me out, that was it. You never once tried to contact me. You never once reached out." With a self-deprecating huff, Christina snapped her fingers. "Nothing."

The words hung in the air, the resounding indictment stinging Christina's ears, surrounding her in a hollow victory of condemnation. Natalie's lips pulled into a snarl, her fingers flexing down at her sides. But otherwise, she remained unmoved.

"God," Christina cried, shaking her head so hard she almost upended the sunglasses perched precariously atop her head. She laughed bleakly. "Never mind." With a half-turn, her feet took her smartly back toward the front door. "Sorry for wasting your time—"

She was already reaching for the handle when a sharp voice rang out: "You changed your phone number."

Chapter Twenty-Six

At first, Christina wasn't sure she'd heard her mother correctly. But as the seconds ticked past with a sickening sort of certainty, the weight of what Natalie said finally sank through. Pressing one hand against the front door, Christina gathered her equilibrium. Twisting her neck, she stared across the expanse of space, her eyes searching for reassurances as they located her mother.

"What?" she whispered.

But Natalie DeLuca wasn't about to fall apart. Other than a simple shrug of her shoulders, she went on as though nothing explosive had been said. "Your phone. You switched providers or something."

"You called me?"

Natalie made a face. "Well, don't be childish! Of course, I called you."

Pushing off the door, Christina felt first one ankle and then another rotate back around, rotate back toward her mother. "There's no *of course* about it. I waited. For four months, I waited for you t-to say something, do something…anything! You never did."

Natalie's eyes shimmied a little to Christina's left. "It took me some time."

"Time?"

"To come to grips with what you did."

Christina's breathing was harsh, so loud in her ears that she held up a hand impatiently, stemming any more explanations on that front. "When?"

Natalie sighed impatiently. "When what?"

"When did you call me, Mother!" Christina's voice was insistent, her face pinched.

Natalie's shoulders hitched. One hand came down to play with a ring on her right hand. "It must have been sometime near March."

Christina felt her chest constrict. Her heart rate picked up. "Nine months."

"Give or take."

"You waited nine months? Nine months to contact me, to see if I was okay?" At the realization, a little of Christina's strength, her animosity flooded back. Her shoulders straightened. "You waited *nine months* to decide I was worth a *phone call*—a measly phone call! Nine months." The words tripped spasmodically out of her mouth. "Do you have any idea what it was like for me out there all alone, terrified?"

Natalie's hands clenched into fists. "You did that to yourself."

Christina scoffed. "Sure, I did. But still…"

"I *needed* that time, Christina," Natalie said, her voice hardening. "To process what you'd done, to come to terms with the daughter I thought I knew, the daughter who had betrayed everything I believed in."

Christina heard her mother as though through a distance. Surprisingly, her recriminations no longer possessed the strength of that one long ago night. Oddly, they didn't possess the strength of the remembered words from her memories. Instead, a new set of whispered pleas overrode those, made pittance of their worth: *Mothers don't turn their backs on their babies. Not ever. …. Christina, I love you…. Nothing will change that.* Christina's breathing slowed, her feet finding solid ground beneath her. She almost smiled.

Natalie continued, "I wasn't in a frame of mind to, to—" Her hands flapped about the air wildly as she fought to find the right words.

"To care about what happened to me." The anguish of moments ago was lost in Christina's voice now, replaced with only a matter-of-fact answer.

Natalie's eyelids flinched at the words. "Say what you want, but I did try."

Christina nodded. "Only it was too late. I'd already changed my number." Christina waited for a split-second before adding, "You tried. Only, you didn't try that hard."

Natalie stiffened noticeably. Her eyes narrowed into slits, her voice hissing in defense. "I did the best I could with what information I had."

Christina smiled faintly. "Yeah? Well, it wasn't enough. Y-you didn't love me enough."

"I'm not sure what you—"

But Christina wasn't finished. Her voice rose, cutting her mother off. "I know that now." And suddenly, she did know it. There was something about coming back home, staring into the eyes of the mother she'd mourned for years that solidified it all for her. There was something about replacing the memories, coming to grips with an awakened play of emotions, that eased the old ache, that fortified everything Mary had begged her to understand.

She smiled somewhat whimsically. "For years, I thought I didn't deserve to be loved. Because of what I did, because of what you and Dad did to me in response. I cut myself off from the world, drove people away, kept anyone from getting too close." Christina took a deep breath, her words quivering. "But then I met this family."

Absently, she brushed aside a stray tear, her fingers cold against her skin. "I met this family, and they just pushed their way past my defenses. They wouldn't stop. Not until I let them in." Christina smiled softly. "But even then, I only allowed them so far. I never truly believed in their love. I was just so damned afraid of losing them like I'd lost you and Dad. I was so afraid of letting it matter, you see? I refused to let them get close enough, refused to let them mean enough, to hurt me."

Natalie's tan complexion paled a little.

"But little by little, they crept in, and before I knew it, I loved them back." She shook her head. "But I was so terrified to feel again that I refused to acknowledge it. Instead, I pushed them back, pushed them away." Her lips trembled. "But they wouldn't budge. They wouldn't let me go." Everything looked clearer from a distance somehow. Christina could see that now, how much Mary and Matthew loved her. How desperately they'd hurt for her. Her phone, sitting in her pocket—the missed calls, the unanswered text messages, were proof of that. "Despite everything I said and did, no matter how much I fought it, they still only wanted to protect me. *Me*."

Even after the snarling accusations, the way she'd spoken to them, behaved toward them—her lips and words biting, her hands pinned on her hips as she'd spewed her rage and betrayal—they'd only wanted to soothe her pain. Christina felt her heart rock against the walls of her chest. She'd hurt Mary. Deliberately. And what was the first thing that woman had done? She'd called Jason, told him to take care of Christina, to be gentle with her.

And Matthew? According to a message left by Jackie that very afternoon—a phone call that Christina hadn't been able to bring herself to accept, watching frozen as her phone buzzed on the console of the rented car, too afraid of what she'd hear— according to that call, when Jackie had walked into Mr. Gordman's office to deliver news of Christina's absence, he'd only sighed at her bumbling explanation. "Tell her"—he'd apparently wiped a hand wearily over his mouth—"tell her to take all the time she needs. We'll, we'll be here when she gets back."

She had almost missed it. All that love.

Natalie's voice ripped Christina out of her reverie. "I'm the monster, is that it? Because I wouldn't shield you from the consequences of your actions? I'm the monster because I raised you to know better, to be better than an adulterer?" She nodded primly, her eyes narrowing into little more than green scratches of anger. At one time in her life, Christina had been more afraid of that particular countenance than any schoolyard bully. "I see."

"No," Christina countered. "No, I didn't say that."

"Then what are you saying?"

"I'm saying that you were wrong. You and Dad. You were wrong to cast me aside at the first sign of fault, as though I wasn't still your daughter, as though I wasn't hurting and scared. I'm saying you were wrong to wash your hands of me when I failed you—"

"You turned our world upside down!"

"Mine too," Christina admitted. "And I paid for it. I paid for it for so long. Too long. Believing myself unworthy, measuring others' love by the standards that you had set by me." She sniffed. "I don't know, Mom, maybe it's too late for us, maybe the hurt here can never be healed."

Christina took a deep, steadying breath. "Because I look at you and all I see is your disappointment. Still. After all this time. I'm standing here in front of you, a half-forgotten child, and that's all I read on your expression."

Natalie's eyebrows lifted.

"But I hope it's not too late for them. For Mary and Matthew." And Jason. God, she prayed it wasn't too late for Jason. "I hope I didn't ruin my chances with the only real family I've ever known, and all because I couldn't reconcile the differences between them and my past."

Natalie's lips smashed together, the skin crinkling unbecomingly at the corners.

"You asked why I was here, Mother. That's why. *They're* why. I'm doing for them what you never did for me. I'm fighting."

At last, Christina ran out of breath. As it was, she'd hardly planned to say as much as she had, hadn't thought far enough ahead to know the point of it all. She only knew a sense of cathartic release as she heard the words, felt them pass through her lips, and knew the truth in their depth and heaviness. She wanted to keep repeating them.

She wasn't afraid anymore. Mary and Matthew *would* be there when she got back home. They'd be there waiting for her. Despite her words, she knew she wasn't too late. At least, not for them. Now, it only waited on Jason.

Her stomach pinched. Had his patience worn out? Had his interest waned in the midst of her self-imposed drama and theatrics? He'd waited a long time for her, what if the reality of her brokenness had proved to be too—

Mentally throttling the thought, Christina gathered what little composure she had left. Thoughts of Jason would have to wait. She couldn't afford to lose the dignity it would cost her to break down in front of her mother. Not now. Not after all she'd said.

Hefting her chin up to a haughty angle, Christina smiled not unkindly. "I won't keep you any longer, Mom. I know you have things to do yet tonight." With a tremulous smile, she edged back toward the front door yet again. But she was amazed at the strength she felt in her legs, the grace she recognized crawling up her spine. On that knowledge, she pulled herself to a quick halt, and with a tug of her fingers, she zipped opened her purse. Digging through the contents, she pulled out a small business card. Two sidesteps took her to the kitchen table, where she laid it down with a pat of her hand. Pausing as she straightened back up, Christina glanced over her shoulder. Her mother hadn't moved, hadn't spoken. The only outward sign of reaction lay in the creases curving down her cheeks.

"It's got my phone number on it," Christina said, nodding toward the card. And then she was back at the doorway again. "For what it's worth," she added, her voice soft now, "it was nice to see you, Mom."

Pushing open the door, she was over the threshold before she heard it. The soft padding of feet. The accompanying words so quiet, she almost missed them. "You look just like me. I'd almost forgotten how much."

Christina bit her lip, her legs stilling. That was as close to any sort of capitulation as Natalie was likely to get. Glancing over her shoulder, Christina suppressed the urge to cry. Standing at the head of the table now, Natalie was holding the business card in a tight grip. Her right index finger skimmed across the top edge. "You won't change it again?"

Christina didn't have to ask what she meant. "You'll call?"

Natalie didn't lift her eyes from the stylish font on the cardstock. "I'm sure your father would love to hear from you."

There was a short pause.

"I won't change it."

Adjusting the headrest of her seatback, Christina wasn't sure what was biting at her stomach harder—the simple feeling of travel anxiety or the mounting awareness that, after five days in Illinois, she was minutes away from liftoff, which meant she was mere hours away from Minneapolis.

Which meant Matthew and Mary.

Jason.

"You're a damn fool," she muttered, buckling herself snugly into place. To the wide-set man stuck beside her in seat 8B, she probably looked like a total buffoon. Unfortunately for him, Christina wasn't in a frame of mind to care.

As for Mary and Matthew, Christina was almost feverish in her desperation to see them. To apologize, to look into their faces and know that they forgave her and that everything would be all right again...

They weren't like her mother. She knew that. Fingers clenched against the armrests, she nodded her head sharply. They would get past their disappointments, their hurts.

Right?

Except. What if she was wrong all over again? It had been so easy to be positive while sitting across from her mother the last few days, so utterly necessary to believe in the elder Gordmans' love, especially in the wake of that woman's cool reception. Christina's sanity had depended upon the absolute guarantee of their loyalty, their steadfastness, their acceptance and compassion. Which was why she hadn't called them, hadn't reached out to them once since she'd left town. If they'd refused her apologies, well, Christina hadn't been quite able to face that possibility, not while in her mother's care. But now, with the rattle of the plane vibrating her seat, with the stale air wrapping itself inside her lungs, Christina felt a newfound crush of uncertainty fall upon her shoulders. What if she was just deluding herself? What if she was setting herself up for another aching failure?

And then there was Jason.

"I wouldn't blame him if he laughed right in my face," she muttered, her fingers reaching for and furiously flipping through the pages of an in-flight magazine. He'd accused her of playing it hot-and-cold. Going back to him now, well, wasn't she just proving him right? Why would he believe her? God, he'd begged her to trust him and she'd walked away. How could she possibly expect him to do what she'd been unwilling to even try? She'd all but sworn that she couldn't have a relationship with him and all the while, he'd been right. She'd been too scared, too hurt to take a chance, but she'd been wrong. Without him, she was suffering in ways that didn't bear contemplation.

"God, you really are an idiot," she grumbled, tossing the magazine down on her lap in disgust. "Why do you think he'd even care?" Her stomach knotted; her chest ached. She used to wrap her loneliness around her like a shield; now it suffocated her senses.

If only he'd listen. If only she could make him listen.

Mere days spent with Natalie DeLuca had done something miraculous to Christina. It had transformed, or perhaps simply reasserted the family dynamic. Mere days had rewritten what she'd misremembered. Or maybe it hadn't been so miraculous after all. Maybe she'd always known, but this visit had just put it all into a tangible sort of clarity. Sitting at the family dining room table three of the last five evenings had forced her to see what her younger self had been unwilling to recognize.

Natalie DeLuca loved no one as much as she loved herself.

She was a selfish woman. Whereas other parents worked frenziedly for their children to lead better lives, to enjoy the riches and privileges that they, themselves, had been denied, Natalie wouldn't have stomached the notion. Indeed, she would have never considered the idea of it at all. To be fair, it wasn't as if she'd have relished the thought of Christina suffering or struggling, but there was a limit to where her goodwill ended and her jealousy began.

"Which is why she married Dad," Christina reminded herself, but there was no anger in the accusation.

Christina no longer wanted to fight for her mother's affection. She no longer felt like she needed to. In mere days, Christina had come to accept what had for years seemed so elusive. In days, she had come to acknowledge as the truth what she'd spent years trying to bend. Natalie would always be Natalie. It was as simple yet confusingly complex and wholly uncontrollable as that. Christina couldn't morph her into someone she wasn't any more than Natalie had been able to do that with her daughter. It didn't make it hurt any less, but it was oddly comforting nonetheless. Letting go. Forgiving Natalie, forgiving herself. Moving on.

If Natalie would always love Natalie first, Christina's father would do the same. He lived to come home to his wife each night—to lean eagerly across the table as she regaled him with some drawn-out story of her afternoon at the country club or latest fashion trip or whatnot, to find reasons to touch her, his fingers brushing against her shoulder, her hand, his body resting comfortably, closely beside hers as they sat down in the small sitting room to relax in the evenings.

He truly treasured her.

"He was happier to see her each evening than me," Christina surmised, completely ignoring the stranger beside her. He, however, couldn't help but stare jowl-jawed at the woman talking to herself, his expression nonplussed. Any minute now, he'd be flagging down a flight attendant, asking politely to be transferred to another section of the plane. "Four years. Might as well have been a long-lost aunt with whiskers on her chin."

Granted, Edward DeLuca had sounded absolutely bemused, stunned—half-expecting a stranger's voice to answer the phone when he'd called her that first evening, after Natalie had informed him of their daughter's unexpected return home. In fact, he'd been almost pathetically eager to see her.

That had healed quite a bit.

Still, as much as he'd glorified in seeing his daughter—how many times had she found him simply staring at her, his eyes transfixed, wet behind their heavy lashes, his mouth quivering with delight?—Edward had never counted the cost of losing her to Natalie. The pain of that admission rippled with residual resentment but she quickly suppressed it. She'd finally come to accept it.

Those were the terms and conditions.

"It's a strange thing, isn't it?" Christina asked, turning abruptly to blink back at the balding man squirming so blatantly beside her.

"Huh?" His voice squeaked in surprise.

Christina didn't bother to explain. "It's like, I don't know, you hold all of these terrible memories in your mind. These things that happened and you can't get over them until, I don't know, until one day you go back in time, so to speak, and you realize…" She spread her arms out rather majestically. "You realize there's no point in being angry anymore. There's no point replaying all that old hurt. You can't make people change. You can't rewrite history. You can only let go of trying to control it all, of trying to predict everything, and just move on and…" Her voice petered out, her thoughts scrambling to make sense of all the emotions screaming through her body.

"And?"

Christina was vaguely surprised he was even bothering to listen to her. "And you finally understand that you can be worth more and still be willing to take less at the same time."

Because that's how she felt.

The stranger nodded slowly. "But why would you settle for less?"

She inclined her head a little to one side. "You wouldn't, not unless you were getting the rest from someplace else."

Which brought her straight back to Matthew and Mary.

"And Jason," she whispered.

"Who?"

Smiling half-apologetically, Christina waved her hand dismissively. "Oh, nothing. I'm sorry. I'm just babbling." She threw him a long look. "It's been one of those weeks. I'm still trying to process it all."

He smiled encouragingly. "Well, it's a long trip, if you need someone to talk to…"

And that was all it took. Angling her body fully now, eagerly in the direction of her airplane companion, Christina told him everything. Absolutely everything. From her affair with Bill to her anxiety with Jason to her blowup with Mary and Matthew. It was so unlike her usually reserved self that Christina was under no illusions about the compunctions she'd suffer later, remembering her impulsive tell-all. But what was it they said about strangers? It's easy to talk to someone you'll never have to meet again.

And after a week with Natalie DeLuca, after a week without the Gordmans', Christina needed to talk to someone.

Her travel companion—whose name she later learned was Gary—sat patiently while she let the story tremble loose and jumbled from her mouth. Her hands waved abstractly throughout the long tale. But alas, she came to its trailing conclusion.

Shrugging, she said, "That's how I ended up back in Illinois."

Gary nodded thoughtfully. "And it was successful?"

Christina started to speak and then stopped. She took a moment to consider before responding: "Yeah. I guess. I mean, my mom is always going to be who she is but…"

He waited.

"I think I've finally learned to accept that, to accept who she is. And I think, maybe, she's started to forgive me for who I'm not."

"Ah." He leaned back in his chair in a satisfied sort of way. Christina wished she could feel half as contented. "And have you?"

"Have I what?"

"Learned to forgive yourself, or rather, who you once were?"

She tilted her head a little to one side, her eyes darkening on the question. The answer was a long minute in coming. "Yes. Yes, I think I have."

"That's pretty big."

"Yeah." She shrugged uncomfortably. "I mean, I'm never going to be proud of that moment in my life."

"But you can be proud of what you did from that moment on, what you did *because* of that moment, who you became."

"Yeah." Christina let out a weary breath as the beginning of a smile edged around her mouth. "Yeah, I guess I can."

"Depth comes from wisdom and a lot of wisdom comes in the aftermath of mistakes."

She shifted in her seat. There was something comforting about this man with his receding hairline and fleshy face. "Well, I've got one thing accomplished at least. I made peace with my parents."

"And what's next?" But she had a feeling he already knew what she'd say.

"Talk to Mary and Matthew." She smothered a hysterical laugh, her glance exasperated when it met his. "Pray Jason hasn't given up on me."

"You still doubt him?"

Christina's eyes clouded. "No. Yes. I don't know…"

Gary gave her a measured look. "From what you've told me, he's more than deserved a little faith. Give it to him."

"No, I know." Christina looked down at her lap. "But that's just it. He's different than the rest."

Gary inclined his head. "Hmm."

"That is, I want Jason to be different. T-to love me differently than the rest," she confessed, her eyes refusing to leave her lap as the admission tumbled out of her mouth. She shifted in her seat again. "I mean, I know he'd always be there for me if I needed him. But…"

"But you want more than that."

She nodded. "And you know what? I had it once. I just didn't realize it soon enough."

He smiled, but there was something slightly sad about it. With a flick of his wrist, Gary looked down at the watch nestled against the smattering of hair there. "We land in less than twenty minutes." There was something so pointed in that statement, especially when he looked over at her, his eyebrows rising expectantly.

She stared back nervelessly. "Yeah?"

He whistled, not bothering to answer her directly. "You can only delay the inevitable for so long."

"That's what I'm terrified of."

"I assure you, it's scarier not knowing."

She nodded. "I suppose."

With a gentle movement, Gary reached out, settling his palm over the back of her hand, which was resting on the armrest. The contact was light, brief.

With a flick of her eyes, Christina brought her gaze up to his face.

"Don't wait."

"I-I won't." She chewed on her lip. "But…well—"

"It's easy to find an excuse."

"No, I know but…"

Gary leaned forward. "If this family is anything like you've described…"

Christina smiled. "Oh, they are," she assured him. "That and more."

"Then I have a feeling your being there would only make their holiday weekend."

Because the next day was the Fourth of July. Independence Day. Christina nodded once with a jerk. "I've never been allowed to miss a family gathering. Not one. Not since I met them."

"And it's why you're heading home now, isn't it?"

Home. She was going home. Christina smiled tremulously. "Yes." Her mother and father had expected her to stay throughout the weekend. They were having guests at their place. They'd extended the invitation to Christina, but she'd hedged, told them she had other plans. She only prayed she was right.

He smiled softly. "You'll probably find they've been waiting for you."

"I hope so."

"Can I offer one last piece of advice?"

Christina waved a hand in weak consent to this request.

"As a man who's been married almost fifteen years, don't get distracted by pride."

"No, I won't."

"It's your turn. You're ready." He nodded perceptively. "Be daring with it."

Christina laughed softly at his knowing response. "Got some experience in this department then?"

He winked. "You don't stay married for long if you don't pick up a few things along the way."

Just then the pilot's fuzzy, disembodied voice came over the loudspeakers, informing the passengers of the approximate time, temperature, and an estimation of arrival as they approached their destination.

Christina's face cleared. Her fingertips reached forward, just brushing against Gary's shoulder. "I—thank you. I'm sorry you got stuck with me," she said amusedly, "but I'm grateful you had nowhere else to go."

He chuckled. "Nah. I rather enjoyed the company."

She inclined her head. "Thank you for saying that, even if you're lying." She wrinkled her nose. "You know, I never even asked your reason for flying?"

"Work conference."

"God," Christina made a face, "now I feel like a complete jerk."

He raised one eyebrow.

"I didn't even ask what you do for a living." She sent him a rueful smile. "I'm not usually so self-centered, I promise."

Gary laughed. "Not to worry. Tales of my trip would have made for boring conversation anyway."

"So?"

"So?"

"What *do* you do?"

Gary seemed to hesitate for a moment. Then he coughed. "I'm an author."

Her smile slipped. "Please tell me you're joking."

"'Fraid not."

"God." Blowing out a breath, Christina cringed. "At least promise me I'm not going to be written into your next novel."

He really laughed then. "I'll do my level best."

"Well," Christina said, with a sideways grin, "no wonder you're such a good listener."

Chapter Twenty-Seven

It was early evening when Christina's taxi driver braked to a stop outside her destination. Looking out the passenger window, she stared up at the darkened windows of the house before her. Her stomach clenched as she slowly alit from the vehicle. The fingers of her left hand curling tightly around the handle of her suitcase, she breathed in the humid summer air. In the dim shadows of nightfall, she reminded herself of Gary's sage advice.

She wasn't going to get caught up in excuses.

She wasn't going to chicken out.

She wasn't going to get so caught up in good intentions that she let all her resolutions fall apart.

She wasn't.

Reaching the wide steps leading to the front porch, Christina's actions were automatic as she lifted her feet, climbed to the landing above—her right hand slipping inside her purse, her fingers tangling with the silky inner-lining until she found what she needed.

"I'm going to make amends," she promised herself, her throat bobbing harshly as she produced her apartment keys. Shaking her head, she sighed as she spanned the porch, shuffling toward her door; unlocking it, she let herself inside the quiet building.

Gary had been right. She knew that. "Tomorrow," Christina murmured. Her voice sounded pale as it bounced off the entryway walls. And then, *"Tomorrow."* Her stomach twisted. "Which means tonight I'll need to, to—" To what? she silently asked herself. Get a grip? Find the advantage? Rebuild that cool mask of coiffed hair and couture clothing that nicely made-up for her vulnerability?

She'd need whatever protection she could muster if she was going to face them all at once. Mary, Matthew, and Jason. Still, she was almost grateful she'd find them together the next morning. Find them? She scoffed. More like she'd bombard them. But she couldn't, she didn't have the courage to say what she needed to say more than once. She needed them all there and she needed.... God help her, she needed what little element of control she could muster.

Shucking off her shoes, Christina felt a chill of loneliness envelope her. Abandoning her luggage, she moved, rushing into the living room and turning on the lamps situated on either side of her couch. The soft glow was quickly followed by the glare from the overhead light in her dining room, and the fluorescent bulbs of the kitchen, Christina's hands flicking on light switches with each room she entered.

Standing in the sudden flood of stark illumination, however, she frowned; rotating slowly around, Christina took in the empty sink, the dust coating the seldom-used dining table, the quiet staleness of a silent house.

In hindsight, the lights off might have been better. With a sigh of exhaustion, Christina retraced her steps, shutting out the explicit evidence of her solitary existence. Back in the living room, with just a single lamp on now, Christina's feet marched aimlessly across the thin carpeting, pacing back and forth. Keeping time to her frantic, whirling thoughts. Without Gary, without any sort of distraction, Christina found the same doubts returning, the same fears snipping at her sides as when she'd first boarded the plane for Minneapolis.

Relentlessly, her hands kept reaching for her phone, her fingers skipping abstractedly, but determinedly across its screen as she'd type out various versions of the same text message, all a different combination of: 'I'm sorry. I was a jerk. I miss you—' only to have each and every attempt derided and just as quickly deleted. Now that the inevitable confrontation was imminently forthcoming, Christina couldn't seem to curb the anxiety that bit at her, couldn't seem to keep from rushing the wait; she couldn't push thoughts of the Gordmans, and the apologies owed to them, to the back of her mind.

Until now, until Gary had forced her into a time-stamped deadline, Christina had been only too eager to wait, to hold off. She hadn't intended to *avoid* them exactly, it just hadn't been something she could handle from Illinois. She'd been exhausted enough wading through her and Natalie's emotional turmoil to take on another family. Instead, she'd happily sank into the escape of *tomorrows*.

Only now, tomorrow was actually happening tomorrow. Staring down at her phone, Christina wavered. She wanted to prepare them. No, she recanted, that wasn't quite true. She wanted to prepare herself for their reaction. With a sigh, she repocketed her phone. "You can't cheat your way out behind a screen," she insisted, plopping down on her couch.

But there was something else holding her back, something she almost didn't want to admit to herself. Because as much as she knew she needed to be the one who reached out first—after all, hadn't she been the one to leave them, to lash out and run away? Even knowing this, she couldn't help a small flicker of hope that they'd seek her out, wonder what she was doing, ask her over for watermelon and grilled burgers as they'd always done before.

Not once in four years had they forgotten to include her.

What if—she cut off the thought, though it niggled unavoidably at the back of her head. What if they weren't ready to forgive her? What if they hadn't missed her as much as she'd missed them? What if…God, what if she were nothing more to them than a passing hurt, as she'd so obviously been to her parents. Because, though she'd tried to deny it all these years, the Gordmans were much more than that to her.

She knew it was ridiculous. How many times had Mary called her? How many attempts had there been at communication? Five? Six? Still, a low, mean voice murmured in her ears, she hadn't tried to contact Christina once since last Sunday. It hadn't taken long before she'd given up.

No. "On Monday she would have found out about my leaving for home," she argued. Nodding, Christina reminded herself that she'd been thankful for that in Illinois.

"She gave you space, which you wanted. Remember that." She shook her head. "Besides, it's not as if they even know you're back in town. And either way," she maintained, her voice reassuring in the silence, "it's your turn. This time, it's on you." If the words didn't boost her confidence, they at least strengthened her resolve. She knew what she needed to do, even if it meant barging into a family picnic uninvited. Now she only needed to hold onto her nerve.

They didn't know she was back home, she repeated silently to herself. That was all. Christina curled her hands into fists, her fingernails digging into her palms. Otherwise, they *would* have called; that hope was paramount above all, despite her determination to make the first move. After all, how could they know? She certainly hadn't told them when she was returning. She hadn't had the courage. The only information they'd been able to glean about her whereabouts had come from Jackie, and admittedly, Christina hadn't told her much, either.

It was at that reminder that Christina finally found the distraction she craved. Digging out her phone yet again, she felt her fingers scrolling down her contact list, but this time in search of a different name. She needed something to stop her thoughts, to keep her fingers from singularly drafting and redrafting texts—one of which she was afraid she'd finally end up sending—so she called the only person who would understand. And who might unwittingly give her some reassurance.

"I take it you're back." No preamble, no hello; instead, the answering voice on the other end of the line was decidedly dry.

Sitting cross-legged on her couch, Christina settled herself comfortably against her decorative pillow. "Yeah."

"Thank God."

"Miss me?" Christina joked darkly. She looked disjointedly around her living room, her attention caught by the glare of a car's passing headlights shining through her window.

"More like terrified…"

Christina snorted.

"…that you weren't coming back."

"Ever the dramatic one."

"You should have seen your face last Sunday."

Christina swallowed the immediate retort that sprang to mind. Her tongue came out to wet her lips at the accusation, the concern still threading those words. "Yeah, I, uh, sorry about that."

"Everything okay?"

"I hope."

"Prevaricating again?"

Christina laughed at the irritation present in her usually unruffled friend. "No. No, at least, I'll tell you all about it. Just, not now."

Jackie made a noncommittal sound.

"How was work?"

If the question was unusual—and it most certainly was— Jackie didn't make comment of it, at least not directly. She sighed. "Still fighting with Mr. Gordman then?"

"What?" Christina sputtered. "N-no."

"Clearly you are" came the dry response. "Otherwise, you'd already know how work went."

Rubbing one hand against the side of her forehead, Christina wondered if she hadn't made a mistake after all, calling Jackie.

"You should have seen him this week," Jackie went on to say, taking it easy on her friend at last. "He wouldn't even hear of hiring a temp to do your work."

Christina's brows furrowed. "What? Why?" He always used a temp. It was company policy. Hell, it was her own personal policy; without one, she'd find herself buried in a week's worth of work.

"He said that if you weren't there, he'd just do it all himself. He didn't trust anyone to do your job."

"Oh, please."

"I'm serious. He stayed late every night, filling in for you."

Christina made a face, but her stomach was doing funny things in the face of that bald, telling statement. "Great. I can only imagine the mess that's waiting for me! He can do little more than peck at a keyboard."

Jackie laughed. "Poor you." There was the slightest hesitation on the other end of the phone. "What happened, Christina?"

Blowing out a breath, Christina shrugged. "I fell in love with the wrong guy."

"With Jason, you mean?"

"Yes. No, I mean…" Christina sorted through her thoughts. Drawing up one knee, she hugged it close to her chest. "A long time ago, I fell for the wrong guy."

"Yeah," Jackie said, her voice soft, understanding, "I sort of wondered."

"And then I took it out on the wrong guy."

"Jason." This time it wasn't a question.

"Yeah. And Matthew." Christina swallowed hard. "And Mary."

"So now you're hiding."

"Pretty much."

The phone was silent for a minute. "You sound better this week."

"I feel better," Christina said, and she knew it was true. She felt steadier, surer of herself. Except… "I—Jackie, I said some pretty terrible things to them. All of them. Right before I left." Her lips twisted painfully. "I'm not sure that they even want to hear from me."

"I've never pegged you as a coward."

Christina sat up with a jerk. "I'm not! I'm just, I'm trying to figure out what to do, how to make it up to them."

"And what have you come up with?"

Christina stalled. "Well…"

"Are you sorry?"

"Yes."

"Then tell them that. Start there. It's as good as any new beginning."

"Right." Christina looked longingly over at the steamer trunk before her couch. Her fingers itched to lift the lid. Just thinking about going to the Gordmans' tomorrow had her tongue quenching for a taste of whiskey….

"Look, no one likes to be the one who has to apologize."

"It's not that."

"Then what is it?"

Christina wasn't sure how much to share. It wasn't in her nature. "What if it's not enough? My apology? What if—" But she didn't finish. The words were stuck in her throat.

Jackie digested this for a moment. When she spoke next, her voice was challenging. "Then what will you have really lost?"

Christina pulled a face. "I'm not following."

"It seems to me, if you do nothing, you've lost them anyway."

The next morning came with the blink of restless sleep. Groaning, Christina turned blindly toward the twang of her incessant alarm clock. Her eyelids felt thick, her wits addled, but with a muffled groan, she pushed off her blankets. It was hours still until she needed to leave, hours until she knew the Gordmans' would start up the grill—after all this time, she was well aware of their tendency to coordinate a one o'clock lunch. More than that, she was fully prepared to learn that a houseful of family and friends would be in attendance, their individually embossed invitations instructing them to arrive sometime after noon. All of which meant that Mary, Matthew, and Jason—and at one time, Christina—would be at the house, ready and waiting, by no later than eleven that morning. And that's when she meant to arrive. Eleven o'clock on the dot. Leaving no chance for outside witnesses to descend, to observe what she needed to say, what she needed to do.

The dawn heralded hours to prepare. She'd need all that remained to get herself in check, to arrange for the perfect outfit, the perfect hair and makeup. She needed whatever time she had left to bolster the only best defense she had. She needed the guarantee that her physical exterior would in no way reflect the emotional upheaval of her interior.

Laying there, looking up at her ceiling, her thoughts drifted sleepily. The pure whiteness of the overhead space offered a brilliant backdrop for her daydreams.

She'd walk up to the Gordmans' house in that flowing, butter-colored sundress she'd bought in Florida last summer; the thin straps outlined her toned arms and the flowing, thin sweep of the skirt swirled gracefully around her long legs. Before she'd even reach halfway up the driveway of their home, however, the front door would be flung open and Mary, bustling past Matthew, an apron tied loosely around her waist, would cry in greeting. Running forward, that woman wouldn't slow down until her arms were thrown around Christina's shoulders.

Half-strangled, wet laughter would float out of Christina's mouth as her own arms weaved around Mary in a tight embrace. Then she'd feel the weight of Matthew's hand against her back, his voice in her ear as he'd whisper: "Glad to have you here."

And then, over Mary's shoulder, Christina would spy Jason standing there, a little ways back.

"I'm sorry," she'd mouth to him as she slowly released Mary, slowly pulled herself free. And then, in an instant, she'd be swooped in his arms, her mouth crushed under his....

"Yeah right," Christina muttered, rolling out of bed. Shuffling to the bathroom, she put a firm hold on those dreams as she turned on the shower.

By ten-fifteen, Christina was dressed and ready to go. She'd opted for the yellow sundress—a last-ditch hope that her dream would turn out to be prophecy. The thin straps bit softly at her skin as she prowled restlessly, pacing up and down the length of her apartment as the minute hand on the clock slowly inched closer toward the half-hour. Her hair, curling gently down her back, swished anxiously from side to side as nausea scratched greedily at her insides. Her eyes, expertly enhanced by the aid of makeup, were clouded with fear, tension…

10:28 a.m.

"It's time," she finally murmured to herself, the sound of her voice only proving to heighten her nerves. With a start, she reached for her purse, dangling on the back of the dining room chair where she'd slung it the night before. Exiting the house, she tried to steady her breathing, the swirl of the cotton dress playing softly against her skin as she took the steps from the front porch to the sidewalk and then across the street.

The entire ride, she rehearsed what she would say. She had her speech nicely in hand, having spent the majority of her morning memorizing the tone, the inflection, the metered pace of the words. Holding onto them tightly now, she turned onto the Gordmans' street. Butterflies sprang dizzyingly in her stomach as she watched the massive stone structure of their home come into view.

"Just breathe," she cautioned herself as she crawled carefully past the Gordmans' driveway, her eyes vigilant for unsuspecting vehicles. Exhaling softly, she saw only Jason's car parked out front. Mary and Matthew's SUV's could just be seen through the open garage door, both snugly settled inside.

With a hard crank of her hand on the wheel, she turned her car back around, and this time, she didn't drive past their house. This time, she pulled in. Braking behind Jason, she cut the engine. Fumbling slightly, she unclicked her seat belt, her hand reaching for the door handle as she blindly pulled it open.

Scrambling out of the vehicle, Christina had taken little more than a handful of steps when she heard it. Stopping like a shot, she froze at the sound of Mary's laughter wafting over the air, through the trees. The sound echoed from behind the house.

Snapping her shoulders straight, Christina felt her feet ditch their original path. Veering away from the front walkway she left the gravel drive, her shoes sinking delicately into the immaculate grass surrounding her on either side, her stride taking her around the side of the house, toward the backyard.

Marching forward, she counted her steps. It was already hot outside, with a soft breeze carrying a hint of reprieve—of course they wouldn't be sitting inside. With a large gazebo set in the back of the house and more than enough lawn to spare, she should have known this was where they'd congregate. It was where they always spent summer gatherings. Her faltered steps foretold more than words could have expressed her shattered wits. Sucking in her cheeks, Christina prayed for the equanimity this visit would require.

In some ways, the reality of what happened next fully lived up to the dreams she'd been surviving on.

In some ways.

Chapter Twenty-Eight

No one saw her at first. Stepping fully into the backyard, Christina slowed her steps, her feet almost silent as she approached the brick-paved patio courtyard leading off from the back door of the kitchen. She spied Matthew first, his large outline standing a little to one side, in front of the massive built-in grill—a white chef's hat perched jauntily atop his head. Then she saw Jason, or rather, the back of his head. He was sitting in one of the floral garden chairs scattered pleasantly around the outdoor space. Opposite him was Mary. Laughing at something he'd said, her mouth was slightly open, her hair lifting gently in the air. It was in the midst of her merriment that the older woman spied Christina.

Stilling, her eyes widened. In a sudden movement, Mary wrenched herself forward. She was halfway out of her seat before Jason thought to turn around, his eyes following after her, before Matthew had the presence of mind to notice the direction of his wife's rapt stare.

Jason seemed to recoil, his head jerking at the sight of her. Matthew slowly, almost robotically lowered his spatula to the small counter space beside the open grill.

"Christina?" Mary whispered unbelievingly.

Seeing her, Christina's eyes watered. "Hi, Mar." Her legs felt heavy, weighted but she forced herself to take another step forward. Seeing the telling move, Mary seemed to recover herself; springing into motion, her arms were already opening as she advanced on the younger woman, her legs brushing past her husband with a speed that belied her age.

At the sight, Christina's lips trembled into a smile, her own arms sweeping wide, waiting—

"Oh, honey," Mary breathed when she was finally close enough to tug Christina into a tight hug. "Oh!"

"I'm sorry," Christina whimpered, her head bowing over Mary's shoulder, her arms snaking around that woman's waist. This wasn't how she'd planned to start off the conversation. Every word of that pat speech had flown out of her mind the moment she'd rounded the corner of the house, leaving her swimming in a sea of uncorked emotion. The rattle of her breath, the wobble of her knees distracted from the need to make herself understood. Instead, she was stuck with: "I'm so sorry!"

"Hush," Mary insisted, pulling Christina closer.

"I was ghastly to you." With a movement, her eyes flickered until they landed briefly on Matthew, still standing beside the now-forgotten grill, and then, with more difficulty, to Jason. "To all of you," she admitted. Matthew silently nodded his head. Jason, who was also standing now, one hand curled against the back of his patio chair, simply watched her, his face a blank, expressionless canvas. Lowering her gaze again, Christina's eyes returned to Mary. It was safer there, more welcoming. "I didn't mean it! I'm not sure if you can ever forgive—"

"No, baby," Mary said, her words half-smothered. "There's nothing to forgive. You have nothing to apologize for."

"I do," Christina returned, reluctantly breaking her hold on Mary. Taking a short step backward, she gazed out at the landscape, her eyes carefully looking into the middle distance. "I do."

"No." Mary shook her head forcefully. "If anyone needs to be forgiven, it's me. I should never have said what I did."

Shifting, Christina forced herself to see the tears she'd heard only moments before in Mary's voice. "But you were right. Everything you said—I was doing what you feared I would.

Recreating my past, confusing everything, and all because I was so afraid to lose you."

Reaching forward, Mary captured one of Christina's hands. She squeezed it gently. "How many times do I have to tell you, you can't possibly lose us?"

"I know."

"Never again," Mary said, dabbing at her eyes. She glared lovingly at Christina. "Don't you ever run out on us again."

Christina swallowed thickly. "I'm sorry."

"And stop that, too," Mary insisted, shooing at Christina's words with an impatient flap of her hand.

Christina laughed roughly. "Okay."

"You can be mad at me or embarrassed or just plain hurt," Mary continued, her breath coming as fast as the words, "but never stop talking to me."

Christina's chin wobbled. "No."

Mary gave her a pointed look. "It's becoming a bit of a habit with you lately. Knock it off already." The accusation was softened by the concern, the affection threading the words.

Christina looked down at her feet. Her toes peeked back at her from her strappy sandals. "I just, I couldn't bear the thought of having you turn your back to me. So I turned mine on you. I thought, if it was my decision, it wouldn't hurt as much."

"I hope you were wrong," Mary muttered, crossing her arms over her chest.

Christina smiled at the disgruntled note in that woman's voice. "Dead wrong."

"Good," she muttered, one hand brushing at a loose tear. She sniffed. "Because we've been absolutely miserable without *you*. Haven't we, Matthew?"

Half-afraid of what she'd find there in answer, Christina brought her eyes hesitantly around to him. She hadn't realized he'd moved closer. Spanning the lawn, he was less than a foot away from Christina by now. But Matthew didn't even need to speak—it was all written there, clearly on his face. "And worried," he added, but without any reprimand in his voice. "How was your trip?"

Christina felt her chin wobble. "It was…" Her eyes swiveled to Jason. She flinched at the look on his face. "I went home," she whispered, her eyes beseeching, pleading silently with his from across the way.

But it wasn't Jason who answered. "Yes," Matthew replied gently, "that's what Jackie said."

At his voice, Christina snapped back to attention. Turning to him, she winced. "I know. And I'm sorry about that too."

Matthew held up a hand. "It's okay, Christina. Really." His voice was kind but firm. "We understood."

"How, how did it go?" Mary asked nervously.

Christina blew out a harried breath. "Better than I expected. Less than what I deserved." Smiling weakly, she continued, "And I have you to thank for helping me realize that. I have all of you to thank." Her eyes returned helplessly to Jason.

There wasn't so much as a flicker of response.

Digging deep for breath, Christina felt her lips part. "Despite that, we talked—me and my mother. I'm not sure if she'll ever truly be able to forgive me but she's trying anyway. And that's more than I hoped for."

Mary brought a hand to her chest, but Christina wasn't sure if it was in relief or fury.

Her stomach knotting, Christina knew she had to finish. They deserved to hear it all, no matter how desperately she wanted to push the words inside. "She'll never be like…she'll never be what you showed me a family is supposed to be," Christina said, shifting uncomfortably underneath a sentimentality she didn't often express. It was hard, being this open. "But then again, I'll never be what she's always thought a daughter should be." She laughed without humor. "So, there's that."

Mary frowned, but at a small nudge from Matthew, she remained silent.

"It was funny, I didn't even know how much you all had changed me, changed the way I looked at my past, until I went back there."

Jason scowled, the first sign that he was even listening to her. Christina tried to take heart in that small gesture of reaction. It was something.

"Even you," she uttered, nodding at him bravely. "Especially you. Though I doubt you'll believe that. I've given you little enough reason to, after all."

Jason's lips jerked, pulling down at the words. For a moment, it looked like he was about to speak, his mouth parting open just slightly.... But no words came out and, sighing, he only shook his head. That's when Christina broke his gaze.

Swiveling back to Mary, she gathered what remained of her courage, which was admittedly dismal. She refused to focus on the tightening in her chest. There was no response, hardly any reaction from him. She'd never thought to appreciate how painful that would be.

"Going there, seeing her again, I realized a few things." Taking a deep breath, Christina almost wished someone would speak, would interrupt her, but no one did. "Like how much I'd hurt for her and, and how little she'd hurt for me. I'd spent these last years using her as the center for everything I did. But she'd just moved on with a new life, half-forgetting she'd ever had another one."

"I'm so sorry," Mary whispered, tears resting just inside her eyes.

Christina smiled, her gaze lowering away from the stark expression on the other woman's face. "Thank you. It wasn't until I came face-to-face with that knowledge—when she saw me for the first time in years, standing on her front porch." Christina swallowed with difficulty. Breaking down now wasn't an option. "It wasn't a reunion for her." Despite her best intentions, Christina's voice cracked over the last words. With an impatience born of embarrassment, she wiped a hand under her nose. "It wasn't the thing dreams were made of, because those only exist when you've actually dreamt for something to happen."

Reaching forward, Matthew laid a hand on her shoulder. With a hard intake of breath, Christina closed her eyes momentarily at the soft weight.

"It wasn't until I was standing there, looking at her, calling myself ten times a fool because I'd hoped"—Christina pursed her lips, taking comfort in the pressure of Matthew's hand, the pain emanating off his face—"I'd hoped a lot of nonsense. And it hit me, that all this time, despite everything, I'd still been fighting for her, and she'd, she'd called it long ago.

"And suddenly I was terrified to be like her," Christina said. "I didn't want to be so hard, so callous that I could just stop caring like that, stop feeling. An-and, I was. Becoming like her, I mean. I was doing that with you. I was closing off a part of myself so that, so that—"

"No. No, you could never be like that," Mary insisted, wiping at her eyes. "Not even if you tried."

"I don't ever want to be anyway," Christina returned. "It was like, I saw her, and this flip switched or something and everything made sense." Smiling clumsily, Christina bit her lip. "I couldn't help comparing everything with you—" Her gaze swiveled to include Matthew. "As I was standing on her doorstep watching her reactions and hearing her responses to everything I said, I couldn't help comparing it all to this moment, when I knew I'd do the same thing on your doorstep…or, on your lawn anyway."

Matthew's hand tightened on her shoulder.

Christina sniffled, laughing a bit weakly. "And I knew you'd forgive me. I knew you would still love me."

"Well, of course!"

"You've always been on my side," Christina continued doggedly. "Even when you probably didn't agree with what I was saying or doing."

"That's love, baby."

"Not the kind I grew up to know," Christina mumbled.

Mary nodded silently. Matthew's hand squeezed one last time before dropping back down to his side. Jason still hadn't spoken.

"Don't get me wrong, my mother loves me. I think she loves me as much as she can, but there are limits to her love and they're shallow and unrelenting. And really, I think that says it all." Christina heard the words through a haze. The more she spoke, the easier they tumbled off her stiff, unyielding lips. "She doesn't have the capability to love like, well, like you. And I can fight that all I want, but at the end of the day, that's the fact."

"Oh, baby," Mary said again.

Christina waved the sentiment away. "Don't. After all, I-I have you, don't I? That's enough. It's more than enough." Before she could speak, Christina felt herself being hauled back into Mary's arms again. Wrapped up tightly in that hold, Christina let her cheek nestle softly against the crown of that woman's head. "I can't pretend to be someone I'm not. And neither can she." Straightening up, Christina gently extracted herself then. "It's time we learned to accept one another. Past time."

"Yes."

Christina took a deep breath. Her eyes, haunted now, beseeching, forced themselves to see past Mary's shoulder and a few feet behind Matthew to where their son still stood. Looking up at him took great effort because what she would say next mattered most of all. But she did look at him. He scowled slightly, but Christina only pulled her shoulders straight. "I also realized that you were right, Jason." At the words, Matthew and Mary exchanged glances. "You told me I was hiding behind my mistakes not because I couldn't forgive myself, but because I wouldn't."

He inclined his head.

"You said I wouldn't forgive myself because I liked it that way. If I couldn't let go of my past then I couldn't let someone in again, and if I couldn't do that, well then, I couldn't be hurt again by someone who was supposed to love me." Christina's voice gave a little. "I think I knew you were right even when you said the words."

Jason's eyes narrowed, but his expression remained unreadable.

She swallowed back the urge to shout, to scream, to march up to him and shake him. "The thing is, I fell in love with you years ago," she said instead, her face flushing defiantly. "Almost from that first moment."

Mary made a soft sound.

Jason's face contorted, his eyes dropping away.

"But I kept putting the memory of Bill between us. Because I was scared, and I resented what you made me feel. It was an easy excuse, one I didn't have to examine, because it kept me safe."

Out of the corner of her eye, Christina saw Matthew silently motion to Mary.

Offering Jason a wobbly smile, Christina continued, "Except. Except, it didn't work. I wanted to be with you so much that it overrode my fears."

Jason let out a strangled laugh, but there was nothing of humor in the sound. "Never for very long."

She shook her head numbly. Those were the first words he'd spoken. He hadn't unbent an inch. "No, never for long enough," she admitted quietly. Shifting uneasily, she plowed ahead anyway. "But I'm done with that. I'm done letting Bill have any sort of control over me. He doesn't get to be the reason my heart breaks for a second time."

Jason's eyes closed. "Christina…"

But she couldn't stop. "Look, I know I screwed up!" Her eyes widened, pleading with him to stay, to listen. "I pushed you away. I said terrible things. I never gave you a chance."

His hands curled into tight fists down at his sides.

"I never gave *us* a chance." Her eyes remained fixed on him, her concentration totally alerted to every facial nuance. She was so absorbed that she hardly heard the sound of the backdoor opening and closing behind Mary and Matthew, who slipped unobtrusively into the kitchen. Probably, they were too embarrassed for her to linger outside any longer. "If you can't, or don't, want anything more to do with me, then that's okay. But I promised myself I wouldn't do what my mom did. At least, I wouldn't do it any longer."

His brow furrowed.

She lifted one shoulder. "I wouldn't just let the person I love walk away without a fight."

"*I* wasn't the one who walked away," he growled.

"No, you didn't," Christina agreed, lowering her eyes for a moment before raising them once more, searching his again. "But you deserve a fight, either way. So, I'm here. Ready to do that. If you want."

His lips twitched. "You should have gone home years ago."

She snorted. "Don't I know it."

Jason took a short, hesitant step toward her. Christina tried not to notice how her heart contracted at the movement. Then he stopped. Far too soon, he stopped. "I don't know, Christina," he admitted wearily. One hand motioned between them. "After everything, this all feels a little fast to me."

Christina felt her throat constrict. "Fast?"

"Last week..." Jason ran a hand through his hair. "Last week, you didn't trust in your feelings for me, or mine for you. All these years, you've told yourself, convinced yourself, that you only wanted me because you shouldn't, because that's how it'd been with Bill—like it was some psychological defect for destructive behavior or something. And you felt certain that I'd never want you if I knew about your past."

Christina winced at the remembered words.

Jason's voice gentled. "And I get it, that you threw him between us to protect yourself, but it doesn't change the fact that you truly believed those things, that some part of you really believed that you and I were no different. That what we had was nothing more than...nothing more substantial than that. And then"—Jason snapped his fingers together—"just like that, you were telling me goodbye, shutting me out again. It was that easy for you to go."

Christina swallowed an instinctive desire to argue.

"And now, now you're standing here telling me that after one visit with your mother everything has changed? Now, suddenly, you believe *in* us? You want this?"

Christina took a quick breath. "No. That's not.... You're twisting my words."

He took another step toward her. "Then explain it to me, because I don't understand."

"When I saw her, after all these years, all I could think about was how much I'd let myself lose that awful night she threw me out and Bill threw me over."

Jason's eyebrows arched slightly.

"I realized," flinging her shoulders back, Christina plunged forward, "everything I was doing to prevent another heartbreak, all the lies and guilt and fear, it wasn't worth it anymore. Not when it was costing me happiness. It wasn't enough. Not when it cost me you."

Jason's lips thinned, his throat bobbing jerkily.

"And it hadn't worked, anyway," she continued, her eyes imploring his faith. "My heart broke just the same."

Jason sighed. There was a rough, hesitant sound to it. "Christina…"

"I'm not saying that I'm not damaged. I am. I'm damaged." Her voice shook a little. "But I'm healing."

Jason pulled a face. "I'm not sure—"

"Look, I don't know what more I can do to convince you," Christina cried softly, her arms flying out to the sides. "You're right, I can't argue against a single doubt you have. I've earned each one of them. And yet, even knowing that, I'm standing here, my heart shaking in my mouth, telling you that I love you. And any second now you're going to reject me, tell me it's too late." She took a quivering breath "But I'm here anyway. Risking it all. For you."

Jason opened his mouth to speak, but Christina held up a hand, forestalling him. She wasn't ready. She wasn't ready to hear it yet.

"It took me a long time to get here, and I guess after one trip back home, it might seem fast to you, but don't all decisions seem that way once they're finally made? But it wasn't fast, Jason. It was four years. Four years of loneliness and fear and punishment. It took that trip back home for those feelings to finally be realized, exorcised, resolved. And I deserved that catharsis."

"Absolutely, you did," Jason assured her, "and I'm glad you got it. But a week ago you were this sure that we *wouldn't* make it. And now," he shrugged, but there was a look of finality about it, "now I'm supposed to believe you when you say the exact opposite? I'm supposed to trust that?"

Her jaw clenched stubbornly, achingly. "Yes, if you'll just—"

"I'm sorry, Christina," he said, but he wouldn't meet her eyes anymore. "It's too much."

She blinked. "If you'll—"

"And the problem is, from where I'm standing, nothing is different, *nothing's changed*—one minute you're in and the next you're out." Lowering his head, Jason closed his eyes, blind to the tears flowing down her cheeks. "This conversation is déjà vu all over again."

"Jason?"

"I can't do this. Not again."

Christina's voice rose urgently, one hand lifting up as though to touch him. "Please."

But this time, Jason didn't wait around long enough to listen. This time, he was the one who walked away. With a rough shake of his head, he turned abruptly on his feet, his stride quickly disappearing from sight as he rounded the side of the house. A moment later, Christina heard the distant sound of footsteps on gravel, the click of a disarmed car lock. And then the roar of an engine turning over.

Standing there, her arms wrapped around her stomach, Christina watched the lawn, the surrounding semi-circle of trees bordering the edge of the yard, the grill and the patio table...she watched it all blur as his words penetrated.

Her chin slowly dimpled with the weight of her breathing, the weight of his absence. Standing there, her shoulders shuddered, wracking her body in silent convulsions. He hadn't even looked back. The first quiet sob fell from her tight lips then. It was followed by a thick, aching anguish that nicely disguised the whispered sound of the kitchen door opening and closing behind her.

He hadn't even looked back. He'd just...left. Then again, it was nothing more than she'd expected, after all.

Chapter Twenty-Nine

Christina wasn't sure how long she'd stood outside on the Gordmans' lawn before she'd felt the pair of hands come to rest against the backs of her shoulders. But it hadn't been Jason, and when Christina had jerked around with the hope of it shining helplessly in her eyes, Matthew had winced.

"I'm sorry," he said softly. It was one of few times that Christina could remember him bringing her slowly into his arms, rocking her softly as she cried into his shirt. His hands rubbed soothing circles against her back as they stood there.

When she finally caught her breath enough to compose herself, Christina pulled out of his embrace, her face blotchy, mascara smudged under her eyes. "Thanks."

"Give him time."

She nodded with a jerk. "Not that it'll do me much good." Face twitching slightly, she muttered: "He left, didn't he?"

Wordlessly, Matthew nodded.

"I'm sorry. I've, I've ruined your party."

"No, Christina."

With a shaky breath, she tried to smile. It was as watery as her voice. "I should go."

"You don't need to do that."

"I'd be terrible company."

And for once, Matthew submitted to this quietly.

"You'll tell Mary?"

"Yes." Throwing an arm across her shoulders, Matthew steered Christina discreetly back to the front drive, his sturdy strength walking beside her to her car. Helping her inside, he bent down long enough to say, "It took guts, kid. See you at work Monday?"

She assured him that she would.

"Call Mary when you get home."

She'd promised to do that as well. And she had.

~ ☆☆☆ ~

It was later that evening, Mary utterly unconvinced that Christina was okay but nonetheless helpless to do anything about it in the wake of the younger woman's quivering insistence to pretend otherwise, that the first outpouring of tears finally dried on Christina's cheeks.

She supposed she should be grateful for the short reprieve, the upswell of numbness stealing through her bones.

A movie flashed unwatched on the television. Even if she'd had the presence of mind to pay attention to the actors on the screen, the film of unshed tears in her eyes more-or-less blocked her vision. She was still in her sundress, her hair in a tangle down her back, her makeup long since washed away, and there, beside her, almost bewitchingly within reach, was that same bottle of whiskey, currently unopened, on the trunk before her.

Still, as much as she wanted to drink her sorrow away, she knew it would get her nowhere. Plus, when it came to Jason, she had a habit of doing stupid things when she drank. Snorting, she rubbed a palm roughly across her wet cheek. "Probably, I'd end up drunk texting him."

She could hardly pretend to be surprised by his rejection that morning. As it was, she could hardly blame him for his anger. From the word go, she'd done little to elicit his faith in her feelings.

"At least I've still got Mary and Matthew," she consoled herself. No matter what happened, she wouldn't let what transpired between her and Jason get in the way of that. Her fingers curled on her lap. "We'll make it work somehow. And at some point, I'll stop loving him—!" At the words, she broke off, a new sob escaping from her raw throat.

The thought hurt. Profoundly.

Pressing her hand against her mouth, hoping to stem the rise of another onslaught of the grief she'd only just managed to contain, Christina bit down on her lower lip. Her shoulders heaving with the force of her suppressed tears, she closed her eyes...only to snap them back open at the sudden ringing of her doorbell.

The shrill buzz echoed through her walls, momentarily drowning out the subdued roar of her sorrow. Despite herself, despite knowing that it would only be Mary on the other side of the door, coming to check up on her, or a neighbor coming to complain about the noisiness of her grief, Christina felt a fissure of hope envelope her person.

Throwing her legs off the couch and quickly underneath her, she tumbled upright, her body racing to the door. Gaining the front entry, her fingers scratched at the lock in her haste to open the damned thing. Between the blanket of night and the curtain covering the glass panel, she couldn't make out who stood on the other side of the threshold. Plus, she wasn't ready to look. She wasn't ready to have it all dashed away. Swinging the door open at last, she hardly realized she was holding her breath.

It burst out in a rush of emotion. Blinking in disbelief, she swayed slightly when her eyes lighted upon—

"Jason?" His name came out weakly, incredulously as she stared up at his disheveled appearance.

His hair was rumpled, his eyes narrow as they glared down at her. "Just shut up, will you?"

She wasn't given the chance to so much as agree before his mouth came crashing down against hers. In shock, she felt the imprint of his lips on hers. Her body reacting on instinct, reacting to the blinding shot of joy thrumming through the stunned senses of her body, she felt her arms twining around his neck, her back arching as she rose up on tiptoe, her mouth receiving him wantonly, desperately. There was no room in her scattered thoughts to wonder at his intentions.

"Dammit Christina," Jason muttered against her trembling lips. "Do you have any idea how aggravating you are?"

"No," she answered dreamily, breathily, her eyes staring up at him half-open. "I only know that you're here."

"Yeah, well." With a growl, his teeth nipped at her lower lip, "I didn't mean to be."

"Then why?"

His lips trailing up her neck, he breathed into her ear. "Because I'm in love with you."

Christina felt Jason's hands pressing her closer, more firmly against his body, felt the slight brush of his lips against her hair with something like reverence. A fresh wave of tears coursed down her face. "Thank God," she whispered. Tipping her head back, she gazed up at him. Then she smiled. "Oh, thank God."

With the tip of one finger, he scooped away the wetness trailing her cheeks. "I couldn't stay away."

She nudged him playfully. "Now you know how I felt all this time."

One side of his mouth twitched in response. "I only hope I'm not too late."

Christina smiled. "I think that's my line."

"When you walked out of my house last week." Jason's brows furrowed. "I-I…"

With a trembling finger, Christina pressed it against his mouth, curtailing the words. "I know. And I'm sorry."

"No, let me finish," Jason said, gently shaking her hand free from his lips. "I've spent the last week vacillating between missing the hell out of you and cursing your damn name."

Christina smiled. Jason's thumbs were rubbing delicate circles against her jawline. The warmth of the summer night danced across her bare shoulders, but Christina hardly noticed.

She was only aware of those hands, those eyes gazing down at her.

"It had been so easy once, handling my attraction to you. I'd chalked it up to nothing more than idle curiosity, the thrill of a challenge." He grinned ruefully. "I told myself to forget about it, to let it go. But then, after Easter…"

"Everything changed," she finished for him.

"In ways I wasn't prepared for," he admitted ruefully.

"In ways *I* wasn't prepared for," Christina argued.

"Yeah. In ways you weren't prepared for," Jason agreed, his hands falling away from her face then to rest upon her hips, his grip loose but sure. "And then, just when I realized how I felt about you…you left."

Her eyes flinched. "Jas—"

He shook his head. "In a weird way, your leaving, it put what happened between you and Bill into a new perspective for me. I get it better now, because that's how I felt this afternoon when you showed up," he admitted. "Afraid, angry even, that if you came back you'd only leave again. I wasn't sure I could handle that a second time."

"I won't." Her voice broke vehemently into the night.

"No, I know. I know. What I'm trying to say is, I understand a little better now. Why you did what you did, why you pushed me away. It wasn't until I got home this afternoon, it wasn't until I was sitting in my empty house, so self-righteous with indignation," he admitted with a deprecating face, "that I realized, I was doing the very thing with which I'd accused you. I was holding out for an excuse, holding onto my resentment, when what I really wanted to do was take you up in my arms—"

Wriggling inside his hold, her legs brushing against his, her own arms coming to snake around his neck, Christina tilted her head back. "I'm in them now."

Jason grinned. "Yeah, I figured if I was going to take a page from your book, I might as well do it right."

Christina giggled. "Ah. So now you've come to fight for me?"

"How'm I doing?"

She sighed, her nose nuzzling his. "Better than my wildest dreams."

Dipping his head closer to hers, Jason's lips brushed quickly, with tantalizing softness across her own. "And to think, I've barely begun."

"Well, by all means, continue," Christina teased, her eyes twinkling, her breath a pitchy whisper of sound inside the curtain of nightfall. "I'm not going anywhere."

"No," Jason agreed, his lips coming to press fully against hers now, "me neither."

Lifting up against the brush of his mouth, Christina sighed. They weren't finished talking—she knew that. But the conversation could wait. For a little while longer, it could wait.

ACKNOWLEDGMENTS

This is my third published novel but my first attempt at writing an acknowledgment page. For that, I apologize because so many wonderful people, so many generous hearts, were just as necessary (perhaps even more so) in those first works. To those people, please accept my humble and belated, thank you!

This story, as so many of my stories do, started on my blog, www.litliber.com. To those who read it consistently, who shared in the story, and who offered feedback, or even just words of encouragement and excitement, thank you. So much, thank you. Without that, this story may have never reached the stage of completion. Your reactions and interest always compel me, drive my discipline—and they keep the writing process fresh, innovative, and community-centric.

To my most beloved blog supporter, my cheerleader…my mother, Roni Dinwiddie. Oh, mama, how can I ever express what you've given me? How you've impacted not just this book, not just my writing, but the joys and struggles and bravery involved in creative art? From the time I was a very small girl, I knew I wanted to be an author. And immediately, you jumped on board. You listened to my stories. You even listened to the bad ones; of course, you'll never admit to just how terrible and rough they were—in fact, I think I still managed to entertain you, but then again, you are a remarkable mom.

A debt of deep gratitude goes to my best friend, Angie Little. There are no words to describe how much you've meant to my writing life. I don't know if I've ever met anyone who believed in my work the way that you do. Certainly no one else has so deeply inspired me to believe in it too. To believe it the way you do. You humble me. You build me up. I love you.

To my sister, Amanda Dornhecker. You are not only to be praised as the gorgeous model for this book's cover—for which you posed, time and time again, day in and day out, patiently waiting for me to find that perfect shot—but more than that, you are my solid ground, my diary, my True North. You are the woman I can talk to about anything (and let's face it, I do). You are a part of everything I do. The credit is always owed, in part, to you.

I would also like to thank my writing group, the Ink Slingers—and in particular, Alice, Susan, Megan, and Ruth. For months, you all heard snatched bits and pieces of this story slowly come to life. Your exuberance, interest, dimensional critiques and responses helped me in innumerable ways. The way you connected with Christina (each in different ways), your staunch defense of her right to forgiveness, to love, let me know I was on the right track. Your opinions, thoughts, and reactions helped to enrich the characters, my expressions of them, and their unique connections and relations to the plot. You are, each of you, invaluable to me.

And Kasie Paulson (soon to be Kasie Sundeen). My darling, Kasie. Thank you for always asking questions—for being a true, genuine, faithful fan. Always. In everything I've done, but especially with my writing. It's had a tremendous effect. As I stretch and grow in this industry, I'm constantly striving to better know your patience, your gentleness of spirit, your kindness and generosity. Thank you for continually reminding me what those traits look and feel like.

Finally, to all those who read my work, who cheer and cry and mourn and laugh alongside my characters. I do it for you. Thank you for reading.

A Contemporary Women's Fiction Novel, also by

Amber Laura

Planning her sister's wedding will require humor and imagination, a dash of sibling animosity, and a few white lies…but hey, at least there will be cake. Twenty-Seven Tiered Almond Cake is a light-hearted women's fiction story about relationships, self-reflection, and redemption (there's even a little romance…and a whole lot of cake!)

A Contemporary (Western) Romance Novel, also by
Amber Laura

Cassie wasn't supposed to stay. Her move to Pantula, Texas, working as a student veterinarian in a small animal hospital, was only supposed to be temporary. She wasn't supposed to fall in love. Then she met him. Brannt McDowell, owner of the most prosperous ranch in town. Well, some much for supposed to.

Made in the USA
Coppell, TX
26 November 2020